Two Years
Eight Months and
Twenty-Eight
Nights

Two Years
Eight Months and
Twenty-Eight
Nights

A NOVEL

Salman Rushdie

RANDOM HOUSE

NEW YORK

Published in the United States by Random House, an imprint and division of Penguin Random House LLC, New York.

RANDOM HOUSE and the HOUSE colophon are registered trademarks of Penguin Random House LLC.

Library of Congress Cataloging-in-Publication Data

Rushdie, Salman.
Two years eight months and twenty-eight nights : a novel / Salman Rushdie.
pages ; cm
ISBN 978-0-8129-9891-7
eBook ISBN 978-0-8129-8820-8
1. Jinn—Fiction. 2. Magic—Fiction. I. Title.
PR6068.U757T96 2015
823'.914—dc23 2015008158

Printed in the United States of America on acid-free paper

randomhousebooks.com

2 4 6 8 9 7 5 3 1

First Edition

Book design by Caroline Cunningham

For Caroline

El sueño de la razón produce monstruos
The sleep of reason brings forth monsters

(*Los Caprichos, no. 43,* by Francisco de Goya; the full caption in
the Prado etching reads: "Fantasy abandoned by reason
produces impossible monsters: united with her, she is the
mother of the arts and the origin of their marvels.")

One is not a "believer" in fairy tales.
There is no theology, no body of dogma, no ritual, no institution,
no expectation for a form of behavior.
They are about the unexpectedness and mutability of the world.

GEORGE SZIRTES

Instead of making myself write the book I ought to write, the
novel that was expected of me, I conjured up the book I myself
would have liked to read, the sort by an unknown writer,
from another age and another country, discovered in an attic.

ITALO CALVINO

She saw the dawn approach, and fell silent, discreetly.

The Thousand Nights and One Night

The Children
of
Ibn Rushd

Very little is known, though much has been written, about the true nature of the jinn, the creatures made of smokeless fire. Whether they are good or evil, devilish or benign, such questions are hotly disputed. These qualities are broadly accepted: that they are whimsical, capricious, wanton; that they can move at high speed, alter their size and form, and grant many of the wishes of mortal men and women should they so choose, or if by coercion they are obliged to do so; and that their sense of time differs radically from that of human beings. They are not to be confused with angels, even though some of the old stories erroneously state that the Devil himself, the fallen angel Lucifer, son of the morning, was the greatest of the jinn. For a long time their dwelling places were also in dispute. Some ancient stories said, slanderously, that the jinn lived among us here on earth, the so-called "lower world," in ruined buildings and many insalubrious zones—garbage dumps, graveyards, outdoor latrines, sewers, and, wherever possible, in dunghills. According to these defamatory tales we would do well to wash ourselves thoroughly after any contact with a jinni. They are malodorous and carry disease. However, the most eminent commentators long asserted what we now know to be true: that the jinn live in their own world, separated from ours by a veil, and that this upper world, sometimes called Peristan or Fairyland, is very extensive, though its nature is concealed from us.

To say that the jinn are inhuman may seem to be stating the obvious, but human beings share some qualities at least with their fantastical counterparts. In the matter of faith, for example, there are adherents among the jinn of every belief system on earth, and there are jinn who do not believe, for whom the notion of gods and angels is strange in the same way as the jinn themselves are strange to human beings. And though many jinn are amoral, at least some of these powerful beings do know the difference between good and evil, between the right-hand and the left-hand path.

Some of the jinn can fly, but some slither on the ground in the form of snakes, or run about barking and baring their fangs in the shape of giant dogs. In the sea, and sometimes in the air as well, they assume the outward appearance of dragons. Some of the lesser jinn are unable, when on earth, to maintain their form for long periods. These amorphous creatures sometimes slide into human beings through the ears, nose or eyes, and occupy those bodies for a while, discarding them when they tire of them. The occupied human beings, regrettably, do not survive.

The female jinn, the jinnias or jiniri, are even more mysterious, even subtler and harder to grasp, being shadow-women made of fireless smoke. There are savage jiniri, and jiniri of love, but it may also be that these two different kind of jinnia are actually one and the same—that a savage spirit may be soothed by love, or a loving creature roused by maltreatment to a savagery beyond the comprehension of mortal men.

This is the story of a jinnia, a great princess of the jinn, known as the Lightning Princess on account of her mastery over the thunderbolt, who loved a mortal man long ago, in the twelfth century, as we would say, and of her many descendants, and of her return to the world, after a long absence, to fall in love again, at least for a moment, and then to go to war. It is also the tale of many other jinn, male and female, flying and slithering, good, bad, and uninterested in morality; and of the time of crisis, the time-out-of-joint which we call the time of the strangenesses, which lasted for two years, eight months and twenty-eight nights, which is to say, one thousand nights and one night more. And yes, we have lived another thousand years since those days, but we are all forever changed by that time. Whether for better or for worse, that is for our future to decide.

In the year 1195, the great philosopher Ibn Rushd, once the *Qadi,* or judge, of Seville and most recently the personal physician to the Caliph Abu Yusuf Yaqub in his hometown of Córdoba, was formally discredited and disgraced on account of his liberal ideas, which were unacceptable to the increasingly powerful Berber fanatics who were spreading like a pestilence across Arab Spain, and sent to live in internal exile in the small village of Lucena outside his native city, a village full of Jews who could no longer say they were Jews because the previous ruling dynasty of al-Andalus, the Almoravides, had forced them to convert to Islam. Ibn Rushd, a philosopher who was no longer permitted to expound his philosophy, all of whose writing had been banned and his books burned, felt instantly at home among the Jews who could not say they were Jews. He had been the favorite of the Caliph of the present ruling dynasty, the Almohads, but favorites go out of fashion, and Abu Yusuf Yaqub allowed the fanatics to push the great commentator on Aristotle out of town.

The philosopher who could not speak his philosophy lived in a narrow unpaved street in a humble house with small windows and was terribly oppressed by the absence of light. He set up a medical practice in Lucena and his status as the ex-physician of the Caliph himself brought him patients; in addition he used what assets he had to enter modestly into the horse trade, and also financed the making of the large earthenware vessels, *tinajas,* in which the Jews who were no longer Jews stored and sold olive oil and wine. One day soon after the beginning of his exile a girl of perhaps sixteen summers appeared outside his door, smiling gently, not knocking or intruding on his thoughts in any other way, and simply stood there waiting patiently until he became aware of her presence and invited her in. She told him that she was newly orphaned; that she had no source of income, but preferred not to work in the whorehouse; and that her name was

Dunia, which did not sound like a Jewish name because she was not allowed to speak her Jewish name and because she was illiterate she could not write it down. She told him a traveler had suggested the name and said it was from Greek and meant "the world" and she had liked that idea. Ibn Rushd the translator of Aristotle did not quibble with her, knowing that it meant "the world" in enough tongues to make pedantry unnecessary. "Why have you named yourself after the world?" he asked her, and she replied, looking him in the eye as she spoke, "Because a world will flow from me and those who flow from me will spread across the world."

Being a man of reason, he did not guess that she was a supernatural creature, a jinnia, of the tribe of female jinn, the jiniri: a grand princess of that tribe, on an earthly adventure, pursuing her fascination with human men in general and brilliant ones in particular. He took her into his cottage as housekeeper and lover and in the muffled night she whispered her "true"—that is to say, false—Jewish name into his ear and that was their secret. Dunia the jinnia was as spectacularly fertile as her prophecy had implied. In the two years, eight months and twenty-eight days and nights that followed, she was pregnant three times and on each occasion brought forth a multiplicity of children, at least seven on each occasion, it would appear, and on one occasion eleven, or possibly nineteen, though the records are vague and inexact. All the children inherited her most distinctive feature: they had no earlobes.

If Ibn Rushd had been an adept of the occult arcana he would have realized then that his children were the offspring of a nonhuman mother, but he was too wrapped up in himself to work it out. (We sometimes think that it was fortunate for him, and for our entire history, that Dunia loved him for the brilliance of his mind, his nature being perhaps too selfish to inspire love by itself.) The philosopher who could not philosophize feared that his children would inherit, from him, the sad gifts which were his treasure and his curse. "To be thin-skinned, far-sighted, and loose-tongued," he said, "is to feel too sharply, see too clearly, speak too freely. It is to be vulnerable to the world when the world believes itself invulnerable, to understand its mutability when it thinks itself immutable, to sense what's coming before others sense it, to know that the barbarian future is tearing down the gates of the present while others cling to the decadent, hollow past. If our children are fortunate they will only inherit your ears, but regrettably, as they are undeniably mine, they will probably think too much too soon, and hear too much too early, including things that are not permitted to be thought or heard."

"Tell me a story," Dunia often demanded in bed in the early days of their cohabitation. He quickly discovered that in spite of her seeming youth she could be a demanding and opinionated individual, in bed and out of it. He was a big man and she was like a little bird or stick insect but he often felt she was the stronger one. She was the joy of his old age but demanded from him a level of energy that was hard for him to maintain. At his age sometimes all he wanted to do in bed was sleep, but Dunia saw his attempts to nod off as hostile acts. "If you stay up all night making love," she said, "you actually feel better rested than if you snore for hours like an ox. This is well known." At his age it wasn't always easy to enter into the required condition for the sexual act, especially on consecutive nights, but she saw his elderly difficulties with arousal as proofs of his unloving nature. "If you find a woman attractive there is never a problem," she told him. "Doesn't matter how many nights in a row. Me, I'm always horny, I can go on forever, I have no stopping point."

His discovery that her physical ardor could be quelled by narrative had provided some relief. "Tell me a story," she said, curling up under his arm so that his hand rested on her head, and he thought, Good, I'm off the hook tonight; and gave her, little by little, the story of his mind. He used words many of his contemporaries found shocking, including "reason," "logic" and "science," which were the three pillars of his thought, the ideas that had led his books to be burned. Dunia was afraid of these words but her fear excited her and she snuggled in closer and said, "Hold my head when you're filling it with your lies."

There was a deep, sad wound in him, because he was a defeated man, had lost the great battle of his life to a dead Persian, Ghazali of Tus, an adversary who had been dead for eighty-five years. A hundred years ago Ghazali had written a book called *The Incoherence of the Philosophers,* in which he attacked Greeks like Aristotle, the Neoplatonists, and their allies, Ibn Rushd's great precursors Ibn Sina and al-Farabi. At one point Ghazali had suffered a crisis of belief but had returned to become the greatest scourge of philosophy in the history of the world. Philosophy, he jeered, was incapable of proving the existence of God, or even of proving the impossibility of there being two gods. Philosophy believed in the inevitability of causes and effects, which was a diminution of the power of God, who could easily intervene to alter effects and make causes ineffectual if he so chose.

"What happens," Ibn Rushd asked Dunia when the night wrapped them in silence and they could speak of forbidden things, "when a lighted stick is brought into contact with a ball of cotton?"

"The cotton catches fire, of course," she answered.

"And why does it catch fire?"

"Because that is the way of it," she said, "the fire licks the cotton and the cotton becomes part of the fire, it's how things are."

"The law of nature," he said, "causes have their effects," and her head nodded beneath his caressing hand.

"He disagreed," Ibn Rushd said, and she knew he meant the enemy, Ghazali, the one who had defeated him. "He said that the cotton caught fire because God made it do so, because in God's universe the only law is what God wills."

"So if God had wanted the cotton to put out the fire, if he wanted the fire to become part of the cotton, he could have done that?"

"Yes," said Ibn Rushd. "According to Ghazali's book, God could do that."

She thought for a moment. "That's stupid," she said, finally. Even in the dark she could feel the resigned smile, the smile with cynicism in it as well as pain, spread crookedly across his bearded face. "He would say that it was the true faith," he answered her, "and that to disagree with it would be . . . incoherent."

"So anything can happen if God decides it's okay," she said. "A man's feet might no longer touch the ground, for example—he could start walking on air."

"A miracle," said Ibn Rushd, "is just God changing the rules by which he chooses to play, and if we don't comprehend it, it is because God is ultimately ineffable, which is to say, beyond our comprehension."

She was silent again. "Suppose I suppose," she said at length, "that God may not exist. Suppose you make me suppose that 'reason,' 'logic' and 'science' possess a magic that makes God unnecessary. Can one even suppose that it would be possible to suppose such a thing?" She felt his body stiffen. Now *he* was afraid of *her* words, she thought, and it pleased her in an odd way. "No," he said, too harshly. "That really would be a stupid supposition."

He had written his own book, *The Incoherence of the Incoherence,* replying to Ghazali across a hundred years and a thousand miles, but in spite of its snappy title the dead Persian's influence was undiminished and finally it was Ibn Rushd who was disgraced, whose book was set on fire, which consumed the pages because that was what God decided at that moment that the fire should be permitted to do. In all his writing he had tried to reconcile the words "reason," "logic" and "science" with the words "God," "faith" and "Qur'an," and he had not succeeded, even though he used with great subtlety the argument from kindness, demonstrating by Qur'anic quotation that God must exist because of the garden of earthly delights he had provided for mankind, *and do we not send down from the clouds pressing forth rain, water pouring down in abundance, that you may thereby produce corn, and herbs, and gardens planted thick with trees?* He was a keen amateur gardener and the argument from kindness seemed to him to prove both God's existence and his essentially kindly, liberal nature, but the proponents of a harsher God had beaten him. Now he lay, or so he believed, with a converted Jew whom he had saved from the whorehouse and who seemed capable of seeing into his dreams, where he argued with Ghazali in the language of irreconcilables, the language of wholeheartedness, of going all the way, which would have doomed him to the executioner if he had used it in waking life.

As Dunia filled up with children and then emptied them into the small house, there was less room for Ibn Rushd's excommunicated "lies." Their moments of intimacy decreased and money became a problem. "A true man faces the consequences of his actions," she told him, "especially a man who believes in causes and effects." But making money had never been his forte. The horse-trading business was treacherous and full of cutthroats and his profits were small. He had many competitors in the *tinaja* market, so prices were low. "Charge your patients more," she advised him with some irritation. "You should cash in on your former prestige, tarnished as it is. What else have you got? It's not enough to be a baby-making monster. You make babies, the babies come, the babies must be fed. That is 'logic.' That is 'rational.'" She knew which words she could turn against him. "Not to do this," she cried triumphantly, "is 'incoherence.'"

(The jinn are fond of glittering things, gold and jewels and so on, and often they conceal their hoards in subterranean caves. Why did the jinnia princess not cry *Open* at the door of a treasure cave and solve their financial problems at a stroke? Because she had chosen a human life, a human partnership as the "human" wife of a human being, and she was bound by her choice. To have revealed her true nature to her lover at this late stage would have been to reveal a kind of betrayal, or lie, at the heart of their relationship. So she remained silent, fearing he might abandon her. But, in the end, he left her anyway, for human reasons of his own.)

There was a Persian book called *Hazar Afsaneh,* or *One Thousand Stories,* which had been translated into Arabic. In the Arabic version there were fewer than one thousand stories but the action was spread over one thousand nights, or, because round numbers were ugly, one thousand nights and one night more. He had not seen the book but several of its stories had been told to him at court. The story of the fisherman and the jinni appealed to him, not so much for its fantastic elements (the jinni from the lamp, the magic talking fishes, the be-witched prince who was half man and half marble), but for its tech-nical beauty, the way stories were enfolded within other stories and contained, folded within themselves, yet other stories, so that the story became a true mirror of life, Ibn Rushd thought, in which all our stories contain the stories of others and are themselves contained within larger, grander narratives, the histories of our families, or homelands, or beliefs. More beautiful even than the stories within stories was the story of the storyteller, a princess called Shahrazad or Scheherazade, who told her tales to a murderous husband to prevent herself from being executed. Stories told against death, to civilize a barbarian. And at the foot of the marital bed sat Shahrazad's sister, her perfect audience, asking for one more story, and then one more, and then yet another. From this sister's name Ibn Rushd got the name he bestowed on the hordes of babies issuing from his lover Dunia's loins, for the sister, as it happened, was called Dunyazad, "and what we have here filling up this house with no light and forc-ing me to impose extortionate fees on my patients, the sick and in-firm of Lucena, is the arrival of the *Dunia-zát,* that is, Dunia's tribe, the race of Dunians, the Dunia people, which, being translated, is 'the people of the world.'"

Dunia was deeply offended. "You mean," she said, "that because we are not married our children cannot bear their father's name." He smiled his sad crooked smile. "It is better that they be the Duni-azát," he said, "a name which contains the world and has not been judged by it. To be the Rushdi would send them into history with a mark upon their brow." She began to speak of herself as Schehe-razade's sister, always asking for stories, only her Scheherazade was a man, her lover not her brother, and some of his stories could get them both killed if the words were accidentally to escape from the darkness of the bedroom. So he was a sort of anti-Scheherazade,

Dunia told him, the exact opposite of the storyteller of *The Thousand Nights and One Night:* her stories saved her life, while his put his life in danger. But then the Caliph Abu Yusuf Yaqub was triumphant in war, winning his greatest military victory against the Christian king of Castile, Alfonso VIII, at Alarcos on the Guadiana River. After the Battle of Alarcos, in which his forces killed 150,000 Castilian soldiers, fully half the Christian army, the Caliph gave himself the name Al-Mansur, the Victorious, and with the confidence of a conquering hero he brought the ascendancy of the fanatical Berbers to an end, and summoned Ibn Rushd back to court.

The mark of shame was wiped off the old philosopher's brow, his exile ended; he was rehabilitated, un-disgraced, and returned with honor to his old position of court physician in Córdoba, two years, eight months and twenty-eight days and nights after his exile began, which was to say, one thousand days and nights and one more day and night; and Dunia was pregnant again, of course, and he did not marry her, of course, he never gave her children his name, of course, and he did not bring her with him to the Almohad court, of course, so she slipped out of history, he took it with him when he left, along with his robes, his bubbling retorts, and his manuscripts, some bound, others in scrolls, manuscripts of other men's books, for his own had been burned, though many copies survived, he told her, in other cities, in the libraries of friends, and in places where he had concealed them against the day of his disfavor, for a wise man always prepares for adversity, but, if he is properly modest, good fortune takes him by surprise. He left without finishing his breakfast or saying goodbye, and she did not threaten him, did not reveal her true nature or the power that lay hidden within her, did not say, I know what you say aloud in your dreams, when you suppose the thing that would be stupid to suppose, when you stop trying to reconcile the irreconcilable and speak the terrible, fatal truth. She allowed history to leave her without trying to hold it back, the way children allow a grand parade to pass, holding it in their memory, making it an unforgettable thing, making it their own; and she went on loving him, even though he had so casually abandoned her. You were my every-thing, she wanted to say to him, you were my sun and moon, and who will hold my head now, who will kiss my lips, who will be a father to our children, but he was a great man destined for the halls of the immortals, and these squalling brats were no more than the jetsam he left in his wake.

One day, she murmured to the absent philosopher, one day long after you are dead you will reach the moment at which you want to claim your family, and at that moment, I, your spirit wife, will grant your wish, even though you have broken my heart.

It is believed that she remained among human beings for a time, perhaps hoping against hope for his return, and that he continued to send her money, that maybe he visited her from time to time, and that she gave up on the horse business but went on with the *tinajas,* but now that the sun and moon of history had set forever on her house, her story became a thing of shadows and mysteries, so maybe it's true, as people said, that after Ibn Rushd died his spirit returned to her and fathered even more children. People also said that Ibn Rushd brought her a lamp with a jinni in it and the jinni was the father of the children born after he left her—so we see how easily rumor gets things upside down! And they also said, less kindly, that the abandoned woman took in any man who would pay her rent, and every man she took in left her with another brood, so that the Duniazát, the brood of Dunia, were no longer bastard Rushdis, or some of them were not, or many of them were not, or most; for in most people's eyes the story of her life had become a stuttering line, its letters dissolving into meaningless forms, incapable of revealing how long she lived, or how, or where, or with whom, or when and how—or if—she died.

Nobody noticed or cared that one day she turned sideways and slipped through a slit in the world and returned to Peristan, the other reality, the world of dreams whence the jinn periodically emerge to trouble and bless mankind. To the villagers of Lucena she seemed to have dissolved, perhaps into fireless smoke. After Dunia left our world the voyagers from the world of the jinn to ours became fewer in number, and then for a long time they stopped coming completely, and the slits in the world became overgrown by the unimaginative weeds of convention and the thornbushes of the dully material, until they finally closed up completely and our ancestors were left to do the best they could without the benefits or curses of magic.

But Dunia's children thrived. That much can be said. And almost three hundred years later, when the Jews were expelled from Spain, even the Jews who could not say they were Jews, the children of Dunia's children climbed into ships in Cádiz and Palos de Moguer, or walked across the Pyrenees, or flew on magic carpets or in giant urns like the jinni kin they were, they traversed continents and sailed the seven seas and climbed high mountains and swam mighty rivers and slid into deep valleys and found shelter and safety wherever they could, and they forgot one another quickly, or remembered as long as they could and then forgot, or never forgot, becoming a family that was no longer exactly a family, a tribe that was no longer exactly a tribe; adopting every religion and no religion, many of them, after the centuries of conversion, ignorant of their supernatural origins, forgetting the story of the forcible conversion of the Jews, some of them becoming manically devout while others were contemptuously disbelieving; a family without a place but with family in every place, a village without a location, but winding in and out of every location on the globe, like rootless plants, mosses or lichens or creeping orchids, who must lean upon others, being unable to stand alone.

History is unkind to those it abandons, and can be equally unkind to those who make it. Ibn Rushd died (conventionally, of old age, or so we believe) while traveling in Marrakesh barely a year after his rehabilitation, and never saw his fame grow, never saw it spread beyond the borders of his own world into the infidel world beyond, where his commentaries on Aristotle became the foundations of his mighty forebear's popularity, the cornerstones of the infidels' godless philosophy, called *saecularis,* meaning the kind of idea that only came once in a *saeculum,* an age of the world, or maybe an idea for the ages, and which was the very image and echo of the ideas he had only spoken in dreams. Perhaps, as a godly man, he would not have been delighted by the place history gave him, for it is a strange fate for a believer to become the inspiration of ideas that have no need for belief, and a stranger fate still for a man's philosophy to be victorious beyond the frontiers of his own world but vanquished within those borders, because in the world he knew it was the children of his dead adversary Ghazali who multiplied and inherited the kingdom, while his own bastard brood spread out, leaving his forbidden name behind them, to populate the earth. A high proportion of the survivors ended up in the great North American continent, and many others in the great South Asian subcontinent, thanks to the phenomenon of "clumping" that is a part of the mysterious illogic of random distribution; and many of those afterwards spread out west and south across the Americas, and north and west from that great diamond at the foot of Asia, into all the countries of the world, for of the Duniazát it can fairly be said that, as well as peculiar ears, they all have itchy feet. And Ibn Rushd was dead, but, as will be seen, he and his adversary continued their dispute beyond the grave, for to the arguments of great thinkers there is no end, the idea of argument itself being a tool to improve the mind, the sharpest of all tools, born of the love of knowledge, which is to say, philosophy.

Mr. Geronimo

Eight hundred and more years later, more than three and a half thousand miles away, and now more than one thousand years ago, a storm fell upon our ancestors' city like a bomb. Their childhoods slipped into the water and were lost, the piers built of memories on which they once ate candy and pizza, the boardwalks of desire under which they hid from the summer sun and kissed their first lips. The roofs of houses flew through the night sky like disoriented bats, and the attics where they stored their past stood exposed to the elements until it seemed that everything they once were had been devoured by the predatory sky. Their secrets drowned in flooded basements and they could no longer remember them. Their power failed them. Darkness fell.

Before the power died the TV showed images taken from the sky of an immense white spiral wheeling overhead like an invading alien spaceship. Then the river poured into the power stations and trees fell on the power cables and crushed the sheds where the emergency generators were housed and the apocalypse began. Some rope that moored our ancestors to reality snapped, and as the elements screamed in their ears it was easy for them to believe that the slits in the world had reopened, the seals had been broken and there were laughing sorcerers in the sky, satanic horsemen riding the galloping clouds.

For three days and nights nobody spoke because only the language of the storm existed and our ancestors did not know how to speak that awful tongue. Then at last it passed, and like children refusing

to believe in childhood's end they wanted everything to be as it was.
But when the light returned it felt different. This was a white light
they had not seen before, harsh as an interrogator's lamp, casting
no shadows, merciless, leaving no place to hide. Beware, the light
seemed to say, for I come to burn and judge.

Then the strangenesses began. They would continue for two years,
eight months and twenty-eight nights.

*This is how it has come down to us, a millennium later, as history infused
with and perhaps overwhelmed by legend. This is how we think of it now,
as if it were a fallible memory, or a dream of the remote past. If it's untrue, or partly untrue, if made-up stories have been introduced into the
record, it's too late to do anything about it. This is the story of our ancestors as we choose to tell it, and so, of course, it's our story too.*

It was on the Wednesday after the great storm that Mr. Geronimo
first noticed that his feet no longer touched the ground. He had
awoken an hour before dawn as usual, half-remembering a strange
dream in which a woman's lips were pressed against his chest, murmuring inaudibly. His nose was blocked, his mouth dry because he'd
been breathing through it in his sleep, his neck stiff thanks to his
habit of putting too many pillows beneath it; the eczema on his left
ankle needed to be scratched. The body in general was giving him
the familiar amount of morning grief: nothing to moan about, in
other words. The feet, in fact, felt fine. Mr. Geronimo had had trouble with his feet for much of his life, but they were being kind today.
From time to time he suffered the pain of his fallen arches, even
though he meticulously did his toe-clenching exercises last thing at
night before going to sleep and first thing after waking up, and he
wore insoles, and went up and down stairs on his toes. Then there
was the battle with gout, and the medication that brought on diarrhea. The pain came periodically and he accepted it, consoling him-

self with what he had learned as a young man: that flat feet allowed you to dodge the military draft. Mr. Geronimo was long past the soldiering age but this scrap of information still comforted him. And gout after all was the disease of kings.

Lately his heels had been forming thick, cracked calluses that needed attention, but he had been too busy to visit a podiatrist. He needed his feet, was on them all day. Also, they had had a couple of days of rest, no gardening to be done during a storm like this one, so perhaps they were rewarding him, this morning, by choosing not to make a fuss. He swung his legs out of bed and stood up. Something did feel different then. He was familiar with the texture of the polished wooden floorboards in his bedroom but for some reason he didn't feel them that Wednesday morning. There was a new softness underfoot, a kind of soothing nothingness. Maybe his feet had become numb, deadened by the thickening calluses. A man of his type, an older man with a day of hard physical work ahead of him, did not bother with such trifles. A man of his type, big, fit, strong, shrugged off niggles and got on with his day.

There was still no power and very little water, though the return of both was promised for the next day. Mr. Geronimo was a fastidious person and it pained him not to clean his teeth thoroughly, not to shower. He used some of the water that remained in his bathtub to flush the toilet. (He had filled it as a precaution before the storm began.) He climbed into his work overalls and boots and, ignoring the stalled elevator, ventured down into the ruined streets. At sixty-plus, he told himself, having reached an age at which most men would be putting their feet up, he was as fit and active as he'd ever been. The life he chose long ago had seen to that. It had taken him away from his father's church of miracle cures, of screaming women rising from wheelchairs because possessed by the power of Christ, and away too from his uncle's architectural practice where he might have spent long invisible sedentary years drafting that kindly gentleman's unrecognized visions, his floor plans of disappointments and frustrations and things that might have been.

Mr. Geronimo had left Jesus and drafting tables behind and moved into the open air.

In the green pickup truck, on whose sides the words *Mr. Geronimo Gardener* and a phone number and website URL were blocked out in yellow and drop-shadowed in scarlet, he couldn't feel the seat under him; the cracked green leather that usually poked comfortingly into the right cheek of his behind wasn't doing its thing today. He was definitely not himself. There was a general lessening of sensation. This was a worry. At his age, and given his chosen field of work, he had to be concerned about the small betrayals of the body, had to deal with them, to stave off the larger betrayals that awaited. He would have to get himself checked out, but not now; right now, in the aftermath of the storm, the doctors and hospitals had bigger problems to worry about. The accelerator and brake felt oddly cushioned beneath his booted feet, as if they needed a little extra pressure from him this morning. The storm had evidently messed with the psyches of motor vehicles as well as human beings. Cars lay abandoned, despondent, at odd angles beneath broken windows, and there was a melancholy yellow bus on its side. The main roads had been cleared, however, and the George Washington Bridge had reopened for traffic. There was a gas shortage but he had hoarded his own supply and reckoned he would be able to cope. Mr. Geronimo was a hoarder of fuel, gas masks, flashlights, blankets, medical supplies, canned food, water in lightweight packets; a man who expected emergencies, who counted on the fabric of society to tear and disintegrate, who knew that superglue could be used to hold cuts together, who did not trust human nature to build solidly or well. A man who expected the worst. Also a superstitious man, a crosser of fingers, who knew, for example, that in America wicked spirits lived in trees so it was necessary to knock on wood to drive them out, whereas British tree-spirits (he was an admirer of the British countryside) were friendly creatures so one touched wood to get the benefit of their benevolence. These things were important to know. One couldn't be too careful.

If you walk away from God you should probably try to stay in the good books of Luck.

He adjusted to the truck's needs and drove up the cast side of the island and over the reopened GWB. He had the radio tuned to the oldies station obviously. Yesterday's gone, yesterday's gone, the old timers were singing. Good tip, he thought. So it had. And tomorrow never comes; which leaves today. The river had fallen back into its natural course but all along the banks Mr. Geronimo saw destruction and black mud, and the drowned past of the city exhumed in the black mud, the funnels of sunken riverboats periscoping through the black mud, the haunted gap-toothed Oldsmobiles mud-crusted on the shore, and darker secrets, the skeleton of the legendary Kipsy river-monster and the skulls of murdered Irish longshoremen swimming in the black mud, and there was strange news on the radio too, the ramparts of the Indian fort of Nipinichsen had been raised by the black mud, and the bedraggled furs of ancient Dutch traders, and the original casket containing the actual trinkets worth sixty guilders with which a certain Peter Minuit bought an island of hills from the Lenape Indians, had been deposited at Inwood Hill Park, at the northern tip of Mannahatta, as if the storm was telling our ancestors, Fuck you, I'm buying the island back.

He made his way down broken storm-littered roads out to La Incoerenza, the Bliss estate. Outside the city the storm had been even wilder. Lightning bolts like immense crooked pillars joined La Incoerenza to the skies, and order, which Henry James warned was only man's dream of the universe, disintegrated beneath the power of chaos, which was nature's law. Above the gates of the estate a live wire swung dangerously, with death at its tip. When it touched the gates blue lightning crackled along the bars. The old house stood firm but the river had burst its banks and risen up like a giant lamprey all mud and teeth and swallowed the grounds in a single gulp. It had receded but left destruction in its wake. Mr. Geronimo looking at the wreckage felt that he was present at the death of his imagination, standing at the crime scene of its murder by the thick black mud and the indestructible shit of the past. It may be that he wept. And there on those formerly rolling lawns, hidden now beneath the black mud from the swollen Hudson, as weeping a little he surveyed the ruin of more than a decade of his best landscaping work, the stone spirals that echoed the Iron Age Celts, the Sunken Garden which put its Floridian cousin in the shade, the analemma sundial, a replica of the one at the Greenwich Meridian, the rhododendron forest, the Minoan labyrinth with the fat stone Minotaur at its heart, the secret hedge-hidden nooks, all of them lost and broken beneath the black mud of history, the tree roots standing up in the black mud like the arms of drowning men—it was there that Mr. Geronimo understood that his feet had developed a significant new problem. He stepped out onto the mud and his boots neither squelched nor stuck. He took two or three bewildered steps across the blackness and looked back and saw that he had left no footprints.

"Damn," he cried aloud in consternation. What kind of world had the tempest flung him into? Mr. Geronimo didn't think of himself as being easily scared but the missing footprints had him spooked. He stamped down hard, left boot, right boot, left boot. He jumped up and came down as heavily as he could. The mud was unmoved. Had he been drinking? No, though on occasion he did overdo things as an older man living alone sometimes does, and why not, but this time alcohol was not a factor. Was he still asleep, and dreaming of the estate of La Incoerenza lost beneath a mud sea? Maybe, but this didn't feel like a dream. Was this some unworldly river-bottom mud, some river-monsterish mud previously unknown to mud scientists whose deep-water mystery gave it the power to resist the weight of a leaping man? Or—and this felt the most plausible, though also the most alarming possibility—had there been a change in himself? Some inexplicable, personal gravitational lessening? Jesus, he thought, and at once also thought of his father frowning at the blasphemy, his father berating his child-self from two feet away as if threatening his congregation from his pulpit with his weekly fire and brimstone, Jesus! He would really have to get those feet looked at now.

Mr. Geronimo was a down-to-earth man, and so it did not occur to him that a new age of the irrational had begun, in which the gravitational aberration to which he had fallen victim would be only one of many outré manifestations. Further bizarreries in his own narrative were beyond his comprehension. It did not enter his mind, for example, that in the near future he might make love to a fairy princess. Nor did the transformation of global reality preoccupy him. He drew no broader conclusions from his plight. He did not imagine the imminent reappearance in the oceans of sea-monsters large enough to swallow ships in a single gulp, or the emergence of men strong enough to lift fully grown elephants, or the appearance in the skies over the earth of wizards traveling through the air at super-speed on magically propelled flying urns. He did not surmise that he could have fallen under the spell of a mighty and malevolent jinn.

However, he was methodical by nature, and so, undeniably concerned by his new condition, he reached into a pocket of his battered gardening jacket and found a folded sheet of paper, a bill from the power utility company. The power had been shut down but the bills continued to insist on prompt settlement. That was the natural order of things. He unfolded the bill and spread it out on the mud. Then he stood on it, stamped and jumped some more, tried to rub the document with his feet. It remained untouched. He reached down and tugged at it, and at once it slid out from beneath his feet. No trace of a footprint. He tried a second time, and was able to pass the utility bill cleanly under both boots. The gap between himself and the earth was tiny but unarguable. He was now permanently located at least a sheet of paper's thickness above the planet's surface. Mr. Geronimo straightened with the piece of paper in his hand. Giant trees lay dead around him, sinking into the mud. The Lady Philosopher, his employer the fodder heiress Miss Alexandra Bliss Fariña, was watching him through ground-floor French windows with tears streaming

down her beautiful young face and something else flowing from her
eyes that he couldn't make out. It might have been fear or shock. It
might even have been desire.

Mr. Geronimo's life up to this point had been a journey of a type that
was no longer uncommon in our ancestors' peripatetic world, in
which people easily became detached from places, beliefs, commu-
nities, countries, languages, and from even more important things,
such as honor, morality, good judgment, and truth; in which, we
may say, they splintered away from the authentic narratives of their
life stories and spent the rest of their days trying to discover, or forge,
new, synthetic narratives of their own. He had been born Raphael
Hieronymus Manezes in Bandra, Bombay, the illegitimate son of a
firebrand Catholic priest, more than sixty summers before the events
that concern us now, named on another continent in another age of
the world by a man (long deceased) who had come to seem as alien
to him as Martians or reptiles, but was also as close as blood could
make him. His holy father, Father Jerry, the Very Rev. Fr. Jeremiah
D'Niza, was in his own words a "huge orson of a man," a "whale-
sized moby," lacking earlobes but possessing, by way of compensa-
tion, the bellow of Stentor, the herald of the Greek army in the war
against Troy, whose voice was as strong as fifty men. He was the
neighborhood's leading matchmaker and its benevolent tyrant, a
conservative of the right type, everyone agreed. *Aut Caesar aut nullus*
was his personal motto as it had been Cesare Borgia's, either a Caesar
or a nobody, and as Father Jerry was definitely not a nobody it followed that he must be Caesar, and in fact so complete was his authority that nobody made a fuss when he surreptitiously (meaning
that everyone knew about it) made a match for himself with a grave-
faced stenographer, a slip of a thing named Magda Manezes who
looked like a fragile little twig next to the spreading banyan of the
Father's body. The Very Rev. Fr. Jeremiah D'Niza soon became a
little less than perfectly celibate, and fathered a fine male child, in-

stantly recognizable as his son by his distinctive ears. "The Hapsburgs and the D'Nizas are both lobeless," Father Jerry liked to say.
"Unfortunately, the wrong lot became emperors." (The rude street
boys of Bandra knew nothing of Hapsburgs. They said that Raphael's lack of earlobes was a sign that he was not to be trusted, a sign of
insanity, of being an exciting long word, a *psychopath*. But that was
ignorant superstition, obviously. He went to the movies like everyone else and saw that psychopaths—mad killers, mad scientists, mad
Mughal princes—had perfectly normal ears.)

Father Jerry's son could not be given his father's surname, of
course, the decencies had to be observed, so he received his mother's
instead. For Christian names the good pastor named him Raphael
after the patron saint of Córdoba, Spain, and Hieronymus after
Eusebius Sophronius Hieronymus of the city of Stridon, a.k.a. Saint
Jerome. "Raffy-'Ronnimus-the-pastor's-sonnimus" he was among
the rude boys playing French cricket in Bandra's sainted Catholic
streets—St. Leo St. Alexiou St. Joseph St. Andrew St. John St.
Roques St. Sebestian St. Martin—until he grew too big and strong to
be teased; but to his father he was always Young Raphael Hieronymus Manezes grandly and in full. He lived with his mother Magda
in East Bandra but was permitted to go over to the tonier west side
on Sundays to sing in his father's church choir and to listen to Father
Jerry preach without any apparent awareness of his own hypocrisy
about the fiery damnation that was the inevitable consequence of sin.

The truth was that Mr. Geronimo in later life had a poor memory, and so, much of his childhood was lost. Fragments of his father, however, remained. He remembered singing in church. Mr.
Geronimo had a bit of the Latin as a child, at Christmas in song
bidding the faithful come in the ancient Roman tongue, *w*-ing his
v's as his father commanded. *Wenite, wenite in Bethlehem. Natum
widete regem angelorum.* But it was Genesis that got him, the Vul-
gate that was his namesake Saint Jerome's work. Genesis, especially
chapter one, verse three. *Dixitque Deus: fiat lux. Et facta est lux.*
Translated by himself into his personal Bombay "Wulgate": *And*

God said, Cheap Italian motor car, beauty soap of the film star. And there was Lux. Please, Daddy, why did God want a small Fiat and a bar of soap, and also please, why did he get the soap only? Why couldn't he make the car? And why not a better car, Daddy? He could've asked for a Jesus Chrysler, no? Which brought down upon him a predictable jeremiad from Jeremiah D'Niza, plus a thunderous reminder of his wrong-side-of-the-blanketness, Don't call me Daddy, call me Father like everyone else, and he skipping with a giggle out of reach of the pastor's vengeful hand, singing *cheap Italian motor car beauty soap of the film star.*

That was his whole childhood right there. He always knew that church wasn't for him but he liked the songs. And on Sundays all the local Sandras came to church and he liked their flipped-up hairdos and their cheeky flouncing. *Hark the herald angels sing,* he taught them at Christmas, *Beecham's pills are just the thing. If you want to go to heaven, take a dose of six or seven. If you want to go to Hell, take the whole damn box as well.* The Sandras liked that and let him kiss them secretly on the lips behind the choir stall. His father so apocalyptic in the pulpit hardly ever hit him, mostly just let his son's mouth run out of blasphemous steam, understanding that bastards have their resentments and must be allowed to air them in whatever form they come out, and after Magda's death—she was a polio victim in those olden days when not everyone had access to the Salk vaccine—he sent Hieronymus to learn a trade from his architect uncle Charles in the capital of the world, but that didn't work either. Later, when the young man closed the architectural office on Greenwich Avenue and started the gardening business, his father wrote him a letter. *You'll never amount to anything if you can't stick to anything.* Mr. Geronimo unstuck in the grounds of La Incoerenza remembered his father's warning. The old man knew what he was talking about.

In American mouths "Hieronymus" quickly became "Geronimo" and he enjoyed, he had to admit, the Indian-chiefy allusion. He was a big man like his father with big competent hands a thick neck and hawkish profile and with his Indian-Indian complexion and all, it was easy for Americans to see the Wild West in him and treat him with the respect reserved for remnants of peoples exterminated by the white man, which he accepted without clarifying that he was Indian from India and therefore familiar with a quite different history of imperialist oppression, but never mind. Uncle Charles Duniza (he had changed the spelling of his surname, he said, to accommodate Americans' Italianate tastes) also lacked earlobes and had the family gift of height. He was white haired with bushy white eyebrows, his fleshy lips habitually stretched in a gentle disappointed smile, and in his modest architectural practice did not allow politics to be discussed. When he took twenty-two-year-old Geronimo to drink at an inn run by the Genovese family for drag queens and male hookers and transgendered persons, he wanted to speak only of sex, the love of men and men, which horrified and delighted his Bombay nephew who had never spoken of such matters before and to whom they had until now remained a mystery. Father Jerry, being a conservative of the right type, considered homosexuality a thing beyond the pale, to be treated as if it did not exist. But now young Geronimo was living in his homosexual uncle's run-down brownstone on St. Mark's Place and the house was full of Uncle Charles's protégés, half a dozen gay Cuban refugees whom Charles Duniza, with a lighthearted, dismissive wave of the hand, collectively referred to as the Raúls. The Raúls were to be found in the bathrooms at odd hours plucking their eyebrows or languidly shaving the body hair off their chests and legs before heading out in search of love. Geronimo Manezes had no idea how to speak to them but that was okay because they had no interest in speaking to him either. He had always exuded powerfully heterosexual pheromones which induced, in the Raúls, small moues of indifference that said, You can coexist in this space with us if you must, but please know that in all essential ways you don't exist for us at all.

As he watched them prance away into the night, Geronimo Manezes found that he envied them their carelessness, the ease with which they had shed Havana like an unwanted snakeskin, navigating this

new city with their ten words of bad English, diving into the poly-
glot urban sea and feeling instantly at home, or, at least, adding their
easy, brittle, angry, damaged misfittery to all the other square pegs in
the round holes all around them, using bathhouse promiscuity to
create the feeling of belonging. He wanted to be that way too, he
realized. He felt what the Raúls felt: now that he was here, in this
broke, dirty, inexhaustible, dangerous, irresistible metropolis, he was
never going home.

Like so many unbelievers Geronimo Manezes was looking for
paradise, but Manhattan Island then was anything but Edenic. After
the riots that summer Uncle Charles gave up the Mafia inn. A year
later he would march with the pride marchers, but uncomfortably.
He wasn't a natural protester. Reading Voltaire's *Candide,* he declared himself in agreement with the book's much-abused hero: *Il
faut cultiver son jardin.* "Stay home, go to work, attend to business,"
he advised his nephew Geronimo. "This solidarity cum activism
thing: I don't know." He was cautious by nature, a member of an
association of gay businesspeople which, as Charles Duniza took
pride in saying for years afterwards, had been addressed by Ed Koch
when he was on the city council, it was the first openly gay organization he spoke to, and everyone had been too courteous to ask the
future mayor anything about his own rumored sexual orientation.
Charles was a regular attendee at the association's suit-and-tie gath-
erings in the Village, and in his own way a conservative like his
brother Father Jerry back home. But when the call came to march he
put on his Sunday best and joined the wild parade, one of the few
formally dressed persons in that defiant carnival of self-assertion.
And Geronimo, straight as he was, went with him. By now they
were fast friends and it wouldn't have been right to let Uncle Charles
go into battle alone.

The years passed and the architectural practice began to struggle.
The walls of the Greenwich Avenue office were lined with dreams:
buildings Charles Duniza had never built and would never build. In
the late 1980s his friend the celebrated real estate developer Bento V.

Elfenbein bought a hundred acres of prime property in Big Ground-nut on the South Fork of Long Island—its name was taken from the Pequot Indian word later more usually translated as *potato*—and wanted a hundred "starchitects" to build signature homes on an acre each. One of these acres was promised to Charles—"Of course you, Charles! What do you think, I don't remember my friends?" Bento expostulated—but the project remained in the doldrums because of complex financing issues. Uncle Charles's smile faded a little, became a little sadder. Bento, a dandy with rakishly floppy brown hair and a colorful relationship with cravats, came across as absurdly glamorous and almost shockingly charming, the scion of a big Hollywood dynasty. He was flamboyantly intellectual, with a tendency to quote Thorstein Veblen's *Theory of the Leisure Class* with a bitter irony leavened somewhat by his own, indefatigable Hollywood grin, a Joe E. Brown dazzler full of big, bright, white teeth, inherited from a mother who had been on the screen with Chaplin. "The leisure class, a.k.a. the landed gentry, on whom my business depends," he told Geronimo Manezes, "are the hunters, not the gatherers; they make their way by the immoral road of exploitation, not the virtuous path of industry. But I, to make my way, have to treat the rich as the good guys, the lions, the creators of wealth and guardians of freedom, which naturally I don't mind doing because I'm an exploiter too and I also want to think of myself as virtuous."

Bento was proud to bear one version of the first name of the philosopher Spinoza. "In a translation of myself," he liked to say, "I would be Baruch Ivory. Maybe if I'd stayed in the motion picture business that would have been a better handle. Be that as it may. Here in New Amsterdam, I'm proud to be named after Benedito de Espinosa, Portuguese Jew of Amsterdam the Older. From him I take my famous rationalism, also my knowledge that mind and body are one and Descartes was wrong to separate them. Forget the soul. No such ghost in the machine. What happens to our mind befalls our body also. The condition of the body is also the state of the mind. Remember this. Spinoza said God had a body too, God's mind and

body were one just like ours. For this type of iconoclastic thinking
they flung him out of Jewish society. They issued against him in Amsterdam an excommunicating *cherem*. The Catholics took the hint,
put his immortal *Ethics* on their *Index Librorum Prohibitorum*. Which
doesn't mean he wasn't right. He in his turn was inspired by the An-
dalusian Arab Averroës, who was given a pretty rough ride too,
which also didn't mean he was wrong. In my opinion, by the way,
Spinoza's theory of mind-body union applies equally to nation-states.
The body politic and the ones in the control room are not separate
from one another. You remember that Woody Allen movie with the
operatives in the brain sending the sperm in their white outfits and
hoodies to work when the body is about to get laid. Same kind of
thing."

Bento owned a building on Park Avenue South and lunched most
days in the oak-paneled restaurant on its ground floor. Here he
sometimes invited Geronimo Manezes to talk about the real facts of
life. "A person like yourself," he said, "uprooted, not yet re-rooted, is
what my favorite, Thorstein V., called *an alien of the uneasy feet*. 'A
disturber of the intellectual peace, but only at the cost of becoming
an intellectual wayfaring man, a wanderer in the intellectual no-
man's-land, seeking another place to rest, farther along the road,
somewhere over the horizon.' Does that sound like you to you? Or
are you, as I'm guessing you are, seeking that resting place closer to
home? Not over the rainbow but in the company of, to be frank, my
beautiful daughter? Is Ella what you're looking for to stop you floating away? Your anchor, is that what you want her to be for you, the
one who makes your feet feel easy? She's a kid, twenty-one last
March. You're close to fourteen years her senior. I'm not saying that's
a bad thing. I'm a man of the world. And anyway my princess usually gets what she wants, so let's leave it to her to decide, okay?"
Geronimo Manezes nodded, not knowing what else to do. "So,
genug," Elfenbein said, smiling his Beverly Hills smile. "Try the
Dover sole."

That winter Uncle Charles suddenly announced he wanted to

make a trip back to India, and took Geronimo with him. After the long years away their hometown was a shock to the eyes, as if an alien city, "Mumbai," had descended from space and settled on top of the Bombay they remembered. But something of Bandra had survived, its spirit as well as its buildings, and Father Jerry too, still going strong at eighty, still surrounded by the adoring women of his congregation, though probably incapable of doing much about it. The old priest's mood had darkened with the passing years. His weight had dropped, his voice weakened. He had become, in many ways, a smaller man. "I am happy, Raphael, to have lived in my time and not in this one," he said over Chinese food. "In my time nobody ever dared say I was not a true Bombayite or a pukka Indian. Now, they say it." Geronimo Manezes, hearing his original given name after so long, felt a pang of a feeling he recognized as alienation, the sensation of not belonging anymore to a part of oneself, and he understood, also, that Father Jerry, shoveling chicken chow mein into his face as if it were the Last Supper, felt similarly alienated, comparably unnamed. In the new Mumbai, after a lifetime's service, he was newly inauthentic, excluded by the rise of extremist Hindutva ideology from full membership of his country, from his city, from himself. "I tell you a family story now I never told you before," Father Jerry said. "I did not tell you because I thought, in my error, you were not truly a part of the family and for this I ask your pardon." For Father Jerry to ask for forgiveness was a thunderbolt, a further indication that the place to which Geronimo Manezes had returned was no longer the place young Raphael Manezes had left so many years ago, while the hitherto-untold family story sounded, to Geronimo Manezes's Americanized ear, pretty garbled and irrelevant, a tale of ancient rumored origins in twelfth-century Spain, of conversions, expulsions, intermarriages, wanderings, illegitimate children, jinn, a mythical matriarch called Dunia, a baby-factory who might have been Scheherazade's sister or maybe a "genie without a bottle to pop or a lamp to rub" and a philosopher-patriarch, Averroës (Father Jerry used the Westernized version of Ibn Rushd's name and unwittingly

conjured up, before Geronimo's mind's eye, the face of Bento Elfenbein quoting Spinoza).

"I have little truck with Averroism, a deviant school of thought
descended from the priapic doctor of Córdoba," Father Jerry
growled, thumping the table with a little of his old fervor. "Even in
the Middle Ages it was considered a synonym for atheism. But if the
story of Dunia the fertile maybe-genie-with-the-dark-brown-hair is
true, if the Córdoban indeed planted his seed in that garden, then we
are his bastard brood, the 'Duniazát' from which maybe down the
centuries emerged our garbled 'D'Niza,' and the curse he laid upon
us all is our destiny and our doom: the curse of being out of step with
God, ahead of our time or behind it, who can say; of being weather-
cocks, showing how the wind blows, coal mine canaries, perishing to
prove the air is poisonous, or lightning rods, through whom the
storm strikes first. Of being the chosen people God smashes with his
fist to make an example of, whenever he wants to make a point."

So I'm being told at this point in my life that it's okay to be my
father's illegitimate son because we are all a wrong-side-of-the-
blanket tribe of bastards, Geronimo Manezes thought, and wondered if this too was part of the old man's idea of an apology. He
found it hard to take the story seriously, or to care about it very much.
"If the story is true," he said, making conversation to be polite, to
conceal his lack of interest in this old-time folderol, "we are a little
bit of everything, right? Jewslim Christians. Patchwork types." Father Jerry's heavy brow furrowed deeply. "Being a little bit of everything was the Bombay way," he muttered. "But it is out of fashion.
The narrow mind replaces the wide skirt. Majority rules and minor-
ity, look out. So we become outsiders in our own place, and when
trouble comes, and trouble is coming for sure, outsiders have a habit
of getting it in the neck before anyone else."

"By the way," Uncle Charles said, "the real reason you never heard
the family fairy tale from him is that he didn't want to admit his Jewish origins. Or maybe his genie origins, because genies don't exist, do
they, and if they do they come from the Devil, am I right? And the

reason you didn't hear it from me is that I forgot it years ago. My sexual orientation provided all the outsiderness I needed." Father Jerry glared at his brother. "I always thought," he said furiously, "you should have been beaten harder as a child, to thrash the buggery out of you." Charles Duniza pointed a noodle-wrapped fork at the priest. "I used to pretend to myself that he was joking when he came out with stuff like this," he told Geronimo. "Now, I can't pretend anymore." Lunch ended in a stiff, bad-tempered silence.

Chosen people, Geronimo thought. I've heard that term before.

Geronimo Manezes walking his formerly beloved streets realized that something had broken. When he left "Mumbai" a few days later he knew he would not return. He traveled the country with Uncle Charles, looking at buildings. They visited the home built by Le Corbusier in Gujarat for the matriarch of a textile dynasty. The house was cool and airy, protected by *brise-soleil* structures from the excesses of the sun. But it was the garden that spoke to Geronimo. It seemed to be clawing at the house, snaking its way inside, trying to destroy the barriers that separated exterior space from interior. In the upper regions of the house, flowers and grass successfully surmounted its walls, and the floor became a lawn. He left that place knowing he no longer wanted to be an architect. Uncle Charles went south to Goa but Geronimo Manezes made his way to Kyoto in Japan and sat at the feet of the great horticulturist Ryonosuke Shimura, who taught him that the garden was the outward expression of inner truth, the place where the dreams of our childhoods collided with the archetypes of our cultures, and created beauty. The land might belong to the landowner but the garden belonged to the gardener. This was the power of the horticultural art. *Il faut cultiver son jardin* didn't sound so quietist when viewed through Shimura's vision. But he had been named Hieronymus and knew from the great painter who was his mighty namesake that a garden could also be a metaphor of the infernal. In the end both Bosch's terrifying "earthly delights" and Shimura's murmurous mysticism helped him formulate his own thoughts and he came to see the garden, and his work in it, as somehow Blakean, a marriage of heaven and hell.

After the Indian trip Uncle Charles announced his decision to bring his small nest egg back to Goa and retire. He had bought a simple cottage there, and put up for sale the brownstone in St. Mark's (the Raúls of the 1970s were long gone). The proceeds would take care of his old age. As to the practice, "It's yours if you want it," he told Geronimo, who for perhaps the first time in his life knew exactly what he did want. He took over the Greenwich Avenue office and, with a little financial help from Bento Elfenbein, reconstituted it as a gardening-landscaping service, Geronimo Gardener, to which Bento's treasured daughter Ella added the *Mr.* that made it sing, that brought him into the fullness of his new American identity. Mr. Geronimo he was to everyone from then on.

Young Ella Elfenbein, of course, was what he really wanted, and unaccountably she wanted him too: motherless Ella, who had no memory of Rakel Elfenbein, lost to cancer when Ella was just two, but who was, for her father, her mother's very image and reincarnation. It was Ella's mysteriously unshakable love for Mr. Geronimo, whom, as she liked to say, she had after all partly invented, that led Bento to invest in the man she was going to marry. Ella was an olive-skinned beauty, her chin slightly too prominent, her ears, oddly, the same as his own, a little lacking in the lobes, and her maxillary central incisors a little too vampirishly long, but Mr. Geronimo wasn't complaining, he knew he was a lucky man. If he believed in souls he would have said she had a good one and he knew, from the stories she couldn't help telling him, how many men hit on her on a daily basis. But her loyalty to him was as unswerving as it was mysterious. She was, additionally, the most positive spirit Mr. Geronimo had ever encountered. She didn't like books with unhappy endings, faced every day of her life with joy, and believed that all reverses could be turned to one's advantage. She accepted the idea that positive thinking could help cure diseases whereas anger made you sick, and one day, searching idly through Sunday morning TV, she heard a tel-evangelist saying *God prospers the faithful, he's going to give you what-ever you want, all you have to do is truly want it,* and Mr. Geronimo heard her murmur under her breath, "That's true." She believed in God as firmly as she hated gefilte fish, she didn't think men de-scended from monkeys, and she knew, she told him, that there was a heaven, where she was going eventually, and also a hell, where un-fortunately he was probably bound, except that she was going to save him, so that he could have a happy ending too. He decided he would find all this not alien but delightful and their marriage was good. The years ran on. They had no children. Ella was barren. Maybe that was why she loved the idea of his being a gardener. At least there were some seeds he could plant and watch their flowers grow.

He told her in his black-comic way about lonely men in remote localities who fucked the earth, who made a hole in the soil and planted their own seed there to see if man-plants would grow, half human, half vegetal, but she made him stop, she didn't like stories like that, Why don't you tell me happy stories? she scolded him, That wasn't nice. He hung his head in mock apology and she for-gave him, nothing mock about her forgiveness, she meant it, as she meant everything she said or did.

The years ran on some more. The trouble Father Jerry had pre-dicted came to Bombay which had become Mumbai and there was a December and January of communal rioting during which nine hundred people died, mostly Muslims and Hindus, but, according to the official count, there were also forty-five "unknown" and five "others." Charles Duniza had come to Mumbai from Goa to visit the Kamathipura red-light district in search of Manjula, his favorite *hijra* "sex worker," to use the new morally neutral term, and found death instead of sex work. A mob angered by the destruction in Ayodhya of the Mughal emperor Babar's mosque ran through the streets and perhaps the first victims of the Hindu-Muslim troubles were a Christian "other" and his transgender whore, an "other" of another kind. Nobody cared. Father Jerry was off his turf, at the

Minara mosque in the Pydhonie district, trying, as a "third party," neither Muslim or Hindu, to use his long eminence in the city to calm the passions of the faithful, but he was told to leave, and maybe somebody followed him, somebody with murder in mind, and Father Jerry never got home to Bandra. After that there were two waves of killings, and Charles and Father Jerry became insignificant statistics. The city which once prided itself on being above communal troubles was above them no longer. Bombay was gone, dying with the Very Rev. Fr. Jeremiah D'Niza. All that remained was the new, uglier Mumbai.

"You're all I have now," Geronimo Manezes told Ella when the news about his uncle and father reached him. Then Bento Elfenbein died, struck by lightning out of a clear night sky while he was smoking an after-dinner cigar on his beloved hundred acres in Big Groundnut after a jovial dinner with good friends, and it emerged that his entrepreneurial dealings had led him to the edge of ruin, he had been involved in a lot of funny business, not actual Ponzi schemes but similar smoke-and-mirrors con games, home improvement and office supply scams, a Max Bialystock–type movie production swindle that gave him intense pleasure, *Who'd have thought,* he had written in an incriminating notebook found hidden in his bedroom after his passing, *that* Springtime for Hitler *idea would actually work in real life?* There was at least one giant pyramid con in the Midwest, and his whole operation was so heavily leveraged that immediately after his death the Elfenbein house of cards went tumbling into the humiliation of seizures and foreclosures. The Groundnut acres were forfeited and not one of Bento's dream houses was ever built. If Elfenbein had lived, he would have done jail time, Mr. Geronimo realized. The authorities were on Bento's trail, for tax fraud and a dozen other infractions, and they were closing in. The bolt from the blue gave him a dignified exit, or rather one as flamboyant as his life. "Now," said Ella, who inherited what she described as *next to nothing,* "you're all I have too." As he took her into his arms he felt a tremor of superstition shake his body. He remembered Father Jerry talking, at that strained Chinese lunch, about Ibn Rushd's household being cursed by God to be lightning rods or examples. Was it possible, he wondered, that those families who were joined to his family by marriage fell under the curse as well? *Stop it,* he admonished himself. *You don't believe in medieval curses, or in God.*

This, when she was thirty and he forty-four. She had made him a happy man. Mr. Geronimo the contented gardener, his weathered days spread out in the open like mysteries revealed, his spade trowel shears and glove speaking the language of living things as eloquently as any writer's pen, flower-pinking the earth in spring or fighting winter ice. Perhaps it is in the nature of workers to translate themselves into what they work upon, the way dog lovers come to look like their dogs, so perhaps Mr. Geronimo's little foible was not so peculiar after all—but often, if truth be told, he preferred to think of himself as a plant, perhaps even as one of those man-plants born of sexual congress between a human being and the earth; and, consequently, as the gardened rather than the gardener. He placed himself in the soil of time and wondered, godlessly, who might be gardening him. In these imaginings he cast himself always among the rootless plants, the epiphytes and bryophytes, who must lean upon others, being unable to stand alone. So he was, in his own fancy, a sort of moss or lichen or creeping orchid, and the one he leaned upon, the gardener of his nonexistent soul, was Ella Manezes. His loving and much-loved wife.

Sometimes when they made love she told him he smelled like smoke. Sometimes she said it was as if in the throes of his passion the edges of his body softened, became blurry, so that her body could melt into his. He told her he burned garden refuse every day. He told her she was imagining things. Neither of them suspected the truth.

Then, seven years after Bento's death, lightning struck again.

The thousand-and-one-acre La Incoerenza property had been named by a man dedicated to numbers who believed that the world didn't

add up, Mr. Sanford Bliss the animal-feed king, producer of the famous Bliss Chows for pigs, rabbits, cats, dogs, horses, cattle, and
monkeys. It was said of Sanford Bliss that there wasn't a line of poetry in his head but every dollar figure he'd ever encountered was
neatly filed away and readily accessible. He believed in cash; and in
the great vault in his library concealed behind a portrait painted in
the Florentine manner depicting him as a Tuscan grandee, he stored,
always, an almost comical amount of cash money, well over one million dollars in bricks of notes of different denominations, because, as
he said, *you never know.* He also believed in numerical superstitions,
such as the idea that round numbers were unlucky, you never charged
ten dollars for a bag of feed, you charged $9.99, and you never gave
a man a hundred-dollar tip, but always one hundred and one.

When he was a college student he spent a summer in Florence as
a guest of the Actons of La Pietra and at their dinner table in the
company of artists and thinkers for whom numbers were meaningless or at best common and therefore beneath consideration he encountered the extraordinarily un-American idea that reality was not
something given, not an absolute, but something that men made up,
and that values, too, changed according to who was doing the valu-
ing. A world that did not cohere, in which truth did not exist and
was replaced by warring versions trying to dominate or even eradicate their rivals, horrified him and, being bad for business, struck
him as a thing that needed altering. He named his home La Incoerenza, *incoherence* in Italian, to remind him daily of what he had
learned in Italy, and spent a sizable proportion of his wealth promoting those politicians who held, usually because of genuine or fake
religious convictions, that the eternal certainties needing protecting
and that monopolies, of goods, information and ideas, were not only
beneficial but essential to the preservation of American liberty. In
spite of his efforts the world's incompatibility levels, what Sanford
Bliss in his numerical way came to call its *index of incoherence,* continued inexorably to rise. "If *zero* is the point of sanity at which two
plus two always equals four, and *one* is the fucked-up place where

two and two can add up to any damn thing you want them to be," he told his daughter Alexandra, the adored child of his old age, born to his last, much more youthful, Siberian wife long after he had given up the dream of an heir, "then, Sandy, I'm sorry to tell you that we are currently located somewhere around zero point nine seven three."

When her parents suddenly died, when they fell out of the sky into the East River, the arbitrariness of their end finally proving to Sanford Bliss's daughter Alexandra that the universe was not only incoherent and absurd but also heartless and soulless, the young orphan inherited everything; and having neither business acumen nor entrepreneurial interest, she immediately negotiated the sale of the Bliss Chows to the Land O'Lakes agricultural cooperative of Minnesota, thus becoming, at nineteen years of age, America's youngest billionairess. She completed her studies at Harvard, where she revealed an exceptional gift for the acquisition of languages, becoming fluent, by the end of her time at the university, in French, German, Italian, Spanish, Dutch, Portuguese, Brazilian Portuguese, Swedish, Finnish, Hungarian, Cantonese, Mandarin, Russian, Pashto, Farsi, Arabic, and Tagalog, *she picked them up in no time,* people said in wonderment, *like shiny pebbles on a beach;* and she picked up a man too, the usual penniless Argentine polo player, a healthy slice of beef from the estancias named Manuel Fariña, picked him up and dropped him fast, married and quickly divorced. She kept his name, turned vegetarian, and sent him packing. After her divorce she retreated forever into the seclusion of La Incoerenza. Here she began her long inquiry into pessimism, inspired by both Schopenhauer and Nietzche, and, convinced of the absurdity of human life and the incompatibility of happiness and freedom, settled while still in the first bloom of youth into a lifetime of solitude and gloom, cloistered in abstraction and dressed in close-fitting white lace. Ella Elfenbein Manezes referred to her, with more than a little scorn, as the Lady Philosopher, and the name stuck, at least in Mr. Geronimo's head.

There was a streak of masochistic stoicism in the Lady Philosopher, and in bad weather she was often to be found out of doors, ignoring the wind and drizzle or rather accepting them as truthful representatives of the growing hostility of the earth towards its occupants, sitting under an old spreading oak reading a damp book by Unamuno or Camus. The rich are obscure to us, finding ways to be unhappy when all the normal causes of unhappiness are removed. But unhappiness had touched the Lady Philosopher. Her parents were killed in their private helicopter. An elite death but at the moment of dying we are all penniless. She never spoke of it. It would be generous to understand her behavior, willful, remote, abstract, as her way of expressing grief.

The Hudson at the end of its journey is a "drowned river," its fresh water pushed beneath the incoming salt tides of the sea. "Even the goddamn river makes no sense," Sanford Bliss told his daughter. "Look how often it flows the wrong goddamn way." The Indians had called it Shatemuc, the river that flows both ways. On the banks of the drowned river La Incoerenza likewise resisted order. Mr. Geronimo was called in to help. His reputation as a gardener and landscape artist had grown, and he was recommended to her manager, an avuncular British grizzlechops named Oliver Oldcastle with the beard of Karl Marx, a voice like a bassoon, a drink problem, and a Father Jerry–style Catholic upbringing that had left him loving the Bible and loathing the Church. Oldcastle ushered Mr. Geronimo into the grounds, looking like God showing Adam into Eden, and charged him with the task of bringing horticultural coherence to the place. When Mr. Geronimo started working for the Lady Philosopher tangles of thorns filled the ha-ha at the bottom of the garden as if surrounding a sleeping beauty's castle. Obstinate voles burrowed underground and popped up everywhere, ruining the lawns. Foxes raided the chicken coops. If Mr. Geronimo had run into a snake coiled around a branch of the tree of the knowledge of good and evil, he wouldn't have been surprised. The Lady Philosopher shrugged delicately at the state of things. She was barely twenty then but already spoke with the pitiless formality of a dowager. "To bring a country place to heel," the orphan châtelaine of La Incoerenza stiffly said, "one must kill and kill and kill, one must destroy and destroy. Only after years of mayhem can a measure of stable beauty be achieved. This is the meaning of civilization. Your eyes, however, are soft. I fear you may not be the murderer I need. But anyone else would probably be just as bad."

Because of her belief in the growing weakness and increasing incompetence of the human race in general, she agreed to put up with Mr. Geronimo, and suffer with a sigh the consequent imperfections of her land. She retreated into thought and left Mr. Geronimo to the war of the thorns and voles. His failures went unnoticed, his successes earned him no praise. A deadly oak blight struck the region, threatening Alexandra's beloved trees; he followed the example of scientists on the country's far western coast who were coating or injecting oaks with a commercial fungicide that kept the fatal pathogen, *Phytophthora ramorum,* at bay. When he told his employer that the treatment had succeeded and all her oaks were saved, she shrugged and turned away, as if to say, Something else will kill them soon enough.

Ella Manezes and the Lady Philosopher, both young, smart and beautiful, could have become friends, but did not: what Ella called Alexandra's "negativity," her insistence, when challenged by the ever-hopeful Ella, that it was "impossible, at this point in history, to adopt a hopeful view of humanity," drove them apart. Ella sometimes accompanied Mr. Geronimo to La Incoerenza and walked the grounds while he worked, or stood atop the estate's single green hill watching the river pass by in the wrong direction; and it was on that hill, seven years after her father died, that she too was hit by lightning out of a clear sky, and died on the spot. Among the many aspects of her death that Mr. Geronimo found unbearable was this: that of the two beauties at La Incoerenza that day, the lightning had singled out the optimist for death, and had let the pessimist live.

The phenomenon colloquially known as a "bolt from the blue" works like this: the lightning flash emanates from the rear of a

thundercloud and travels as many as twenty-five miles away from
the storm area, then angles down and strikes the ground, or a tall
building, or a lone tree in a high place, or a woman standing alone on
a hilltop watching the river pass by. The storm from which it came
is too far away to be seen. But the woman on the hilltop can be seen,
falling slowly to the ground, like a feather complying, very reluc-
tantly, with the law of gravity.

Mr. Geronimo thought of her dark eyes, the right eye with its
floaters that hampered her sight. He conjured up her talkativeness,
thinking of how she always had an opinion about everything, and
wondering what he would do without her opinions now. He remembered how she hated to be photographed and listed in his
thoughts all the foods she wouldn't eat, meat, fish, eggs, dairy, toma-
toes, onions, garlic, gluten, almost everything there was. And he
wondered again if lightning was stalking his family; and if, by mar-
rying into that family, Ella had called down the curse upon herself;
and if he might be next in line. In the weeks that followed he began
to study lightning as never before. When he learned that nine-tenths
of the people who were struck by lightning survived, sometimes developing mysterious ailments, but managing to live on, he understood that lightning really had it in for Bento and his girl. Lightning
wasn't letting them off the hook. Maybe it was because he had convinced himself that he wouldn't stand a chance if lightning ever
came for him that even after he was caught in the great storm that
first day, even after he discovered that his feet were suffering from
the mysterious ailment of refusing to touch the ground, it took him
a long time to think the obvious thought.

"Maybe lightning hit me during the hurricane and I lived but it
wiped my memory clean so I didn't remember being hit. And maybe
I'm now carrying around some sort of insane electric charge and
that's why I've lifted off the surface of the earth."

He didn't think that until quite a while later, when Alexandra
Fariña suggested it.

He asked the Lady Philosopher if he might bury his wife on her beloved green hill overlooking the drowned river and Alexandra said yes, of course. So he dug his wife's grave and laid her in it and for a moment he was angry. Then there was an end to anger and he shouldered his shovel and went home alone. On the day his wife died he had worked at La Incoerenza for two years, eight months and twenty-eight days. One thousand days and one day. There was no escape from the curse of numbers.

Ten more years passed. Mr. Geronimo dug and planted and watered and pruned. He gave life and saved it. In his mind every bloom was her, every hedge and every tree. In his work he kept her alive and there was no room for anyone else. But slowly she faded. His plants and trees resumed their membership of the vegetable kingdom and ceased to be her avatars. It was as though she had left him again. After this second departure there was only emptiness and he was certain the void could never be filled. For ten years he lived in a sort of blur. The Lady Philosopher, wrapped as she was in theories, dedicated to the triumph of the worst-case scenario while eating truffled pasta and breaded veal, her head full of the mathematical formulae that provided the scientific basis for her pessimism, became herself a sort of abstraction, his chief source of income and no more. It continued to be difficult not to blame her for being the one who lived, whose survival, at the cost of his wife's life, had not persuaded her to be grateful for her good luck and brighten her attitude to life. He looked at the land and at what grew upon it and could not raise his eyes to absorb the human being whose land it was. For ten years after his wife died he kept his distance from the Lady Philosopher, nursing his secret anger.

After a time, if you had asked him what Alexandra Bliss Fariña looked like, he would have been unable to answer with any precision. Her hair was dark like his late wife's. She was tall, like his late wife. She didn't like sitting in sunlight. Nor had Ella. It was said she walked her grounds at night because of her lifelong battle with insomnia. Her other employees, Manager Oldcastle and the rest, spoke of the persistent health problems that perhaps caused, or at least contributed to, her air of profound gloom. "So young, and so often sick," Oldcastle said. He used the antique word *consumption:* tuberculosis, the sickness of little tubers. The potato is a tuber and there are flowers like dahlias whose fleshy roots, properly called rhizomes, are known as tubers too. Mr. Geronimo had no expertise in the tubercles that formed in human lungs. Those were issues for the house to deal with. He was out in the open. The plants he tended contained the spirit of his deceased wife. The Lady Philosopher was a phantom, though she, and not Ella, was the one who was still alive.

Alexandra never published under her own name, or in the English language. Her pseudonym of choice was "El Criticón," taken from the title of the seventeenth-century allegorical novel by Baltasar Gracián which had greatly influenced her idol Schopenhauer, greatest of all pessimist thinkers. The novel was about the impossibility of human happiness. In a much-derided Spanish-language essay, *The Worst of All Possible Worlds,* "El Criticón" proposed the theory, widely ridiculed as sentimental, that the rift between the human race and the planet was approaching a tipping point, an ecological crisis that was metamorphosing into an existential one. Her academic peers patted her on the head, congratulated her on her command of *castellano,* and dismissed her as an amateur. But after the time of the strangenesses she would be seen as a kind of prophetess.

(Mr. Geronimo thought Alexandra Fariña's use of pseudonyms and foreign languages indicated an uncertainty about the self. Mr. Geronimo too suffered from his own kind of ontological insecurity. At night, alone, he looked at the face in the mirror and tried to see the young chorister "Raffy-'Ronnimus-the-pastor's-sonnimus" there, struggling to imagine the path not taken, the life not led, the other fork in the forked path of life. He could no longer imagine it. Sometimes he filled up with a kind of rage, the fury of the uprooted, the un-tribed. But mostly he no longer thought in tribal terms.)

The indolence of her days, the delicacy of her china, the elegance of her high-necked lace dresses, the amplitude of her estate and her carelessness regarding its condition, her fondness for *marrons glacés* and Turkish delight, the leather-bound aristocracy of her library, and the floral-patterned prettiness of the journals in which she made her almost military assault on the possibility of joy should have hinted to her why she was not taken seriously beyond the walls of La Incoerenza. But her small world was enough for her. She cared nothing for the opinions of strangers. Reason could not and would never triumph over savage, undimmed unreason. The heat-death of the universe was inevitable. Her glass of water was half empty. Things fell apart. The only proper response to the failure of optimism was to retreat behind high walls, walls in the self as well as in the world, and to await the inevitability of death. Voltaire's fictional optimist, Dr. Pangloss, was, after all, a fool, and his real-life mentor, Gottfried Wilhelm Leibniz, was in the first place a failure as an alchemist (in Nuremberg he had not managed to transmute base metal into gold), and in the second place a plagiarist (*vide* the damaging accusation leveled at Leibniz by associates of Sir Isaac Newton—that he, G. W. Leibniz, inventor of the infinitesimal calculus, had sneaked a look at Newton's work on that subject and pinched the Englishman's ideas). "If the best of all possible worlds is one in which another thinker's ideas can be purloined," she wrote, "then perhaps it would be better after all to accept the advice of Candide, and withdraw to cultivate one's garden."

She did not cultivate her garden. She employed a gardener.

It was a long time since Mr. Geronimo had considered sex, but recently, he had to confess, the subject had begun to cross his thoughts again. At his age such thinking veered towards the theoretical, the practical business of finding and conjoining with an actual partner being, given the ineluctable law of *tempus fugit,* a thing of the past. He hypothesized that there were more than two sexes, that in fact each human being was a gender unique to himself or herself, so that maybe new personal pronouns were required, better words than *he* or *she*. Obviously *it* was entirely inappropriate. Amid the infinity of sexes there were a very few sexes with which one could have congress, who wished to join one in congress, and with some of those sexes one was briefly compatible, or compatible for a reasonable length of time before the process of rejection began as it does in transplanted hearts or livers. In very rare cases one found the other sex with whom one was compatible for life, permanently compatible, as if the two sexes were the same, which perhaps, according to this new definition, they were. Once in his life he had found that perfect gender and the odds against doing so again were prohibitive, not that he was looking, not that he ever would. But here, now, in the aftermath of the storm, as he stood on the sea of mud full of the indestructible shit of the past, or, to be precise, as he somehow failed to stand on that sea, hovering just a fraction above it, just high enough to allow a sheet of paper to pass without difficulty under his boots, now, as he wept for the death of his imagination and was filled with fears and doubts on account of the failure of gravity in his immediate vicinity, at this absolutely inappropriate moment, here was his employer, the Lady Philosopher, the fodder heiress Alexandra Bliss Fariña, beckoning to him from her French windows.

Mr. Geronimo arriving at the French windows noted the estate manager Oliver Oldcastle positioned behind Alexandra's left shoulder. If he had been a hawk, thought Mr. Geronimo, he would have perched upon that shoulder, ready to attack his mistress's foes and rip their hearts out of their chests. Mistress and servant stood together, surveying the ruin of La Incoerenza, Oliver Oldcastle looking like Marx observing the fall of Communism, Alexandra her customary enigmatic self in spite of the drying tears on her cheeks. "I can't complain," she said, addressing neither Mr. Geronimo nor Manager Oldcastle, rebuking herself as if she were her own governess. "People have lost their homes and have nothing to eat and nowhere to sleep. All I have lost is a garden." Mr. Geronimo the gardener understood that he was being put in his place. But Alexandra was looking at his boots now. "It's a miracle," she said. "Look, Oldcastle, a real miracle. Mr. Geronimo has taken leave of solid ground and moved upwards into, let us say, more speculative territory."

Mr. Geronimo wanted to protest that his levitation was neither his doing nor his choice, to make it plain that he would be happy to subside to the ground again and get his boots dirty. But Alexandra had a glitter in her eye. "Were you struck by lightning?" she asked. "Yes, that's it. Lightning hit you during the hurricane and you lived, but it wiped your memory clean, so you don't remember being hit. And now you're filled with an unspeakably large electric charge and that's why you've lifted off the surface of the earth." This silenced Mr. Geronimo, who considered it gravely. Yes, perhaps. Though in the absence of any evidence it was no more than a supposition. He found it difficult to know what to say but there was nothing he needed to say. "Here's another miracle," Alexandra said, and her voice was different now, no longer imperious but confidential. "For most of my life I have set aside the possibility of love, and then, just now, I realized that it was waiting for me right here, at home, out-side my French windows, stamping its boots towards the mud, but untouched by that evil filth." Then she turned and vanished into the shadows of the house.

He feared a trap. Appointments of this sort were not on his sched-ule anymore, never had been, really. Manager Oldcastle jerked his head, ordering him to follow the lady of the house. So Mr. Geronimo understood that he had his orders and moved indoors, not knowing where the lady of the house had gone. But he followed the trail of her discarded clothing and found her easily enough.

His night with Alexandra Bliss Fariña began strangely. Whatever force was preventing him from touching the ground was also at work in her bed, and when she lay beneath him his body hovered above hers, just a fraction of an inch above, but there was a definite separation that made things awkward. He tried placing his hands beneath her buttocks and lifting her towards him but that was uncomfortable for them both. They solved the problem soon enough; if he was beneath her then things worked well enough, even if his back didn't quite touch the bed. His *condition* seemed to arouse her, and that in turn excited him, but the moment their lovemaking was over she appeared to lose interest and swiftly fell asleep, leaving him to stare at the ceiling in the dark. And when he got out of bed to dress and leave, the gap between his feet and the floor was distinctly greater. After his night with the mistress of La Incoerenza he had lifted almost a full inch off the ground.

He left her bedchamber to find Oldcastle outside with murder in his eyes. "Don't imagine you're the first," the manager told Mr. Geronimo. "Don't imagine that at your ridiculous age you are the only love she has ever found waiting right outside her window. You pathetic old fungus. You sickening parasite. You growth, you blunted thorn, you bad seed. Get out and don't come back." Mr. Geronimo understood at once that Oliver Oldcastle had been driven mad by unrequited love. "My wife is buried on that hill," he said firmly, "and I will visit her grave whenever I choose. You will have to kill me to stop me, unless I kill you first."

"Your marriage ended last night in milady's bedchamber," retorted Oliver Oldcastle. "And as to which of us kills the other, that bloomin' remains to be seen."

There had been fires, and buildings our ancestors had known all their lives stood charred among them, staring into the pitiless brightness through the hollow sockets of their blackened eyes, like the undead on TV. As our ancestors emerged from their places of safety and lurched through the orphaned streets, the storm began to feel like their fault. There were preachers on television calling it God's punishment for their licentious ways. But that was not the point. It did feel, at least to some of them, that something they had made had escaped their grasp and, freed, had raged around them for days. When the earth, air and water calmed down they feared that force's return. But for a time they were busy with repair work, with feeding the hungry and caring for the old and weeping for the fallen trees, and there was no time to think about the future. Wise voices calmed our ancestors, telling them not to think of the weather as a metaphor. It was neither a warning nor a curse. It was just the weather. This was the soothing information they wanted. They accepted it. So most of them were looking in the wrong direction and did not notice the moment when the strangenesses arrived to turn everything upside down.

The Incoherence
of the
Philosophers

One hundred and one days after the great storm, it seems that Ibn Rushd lying forgotten in his family tomb in Córdoba somehow began to communicate with his equally deceased opponent, Ghazali, in a humble grave on the edge of the town of Tus, in the province of Khorasan; initially in the most cordial of terms, afterwards less jovially. We accept that this statement, difficult as it is to verify, may be met with some scepticism. Their bodies had decayed long ago, so that the notion of *lying forgotten* contains a kind of untruth, and the further notion of some sort of sentient intelligences remaining in the locations of their interments is patently absurd. Yet in considering that strange era, the era of the two years, eight months and twenty-eight nights which is the subject of the present account, we are forced to concede that the world had become absurd, and that the laws which had long been accepted as the governing principles of reality had collapsed, leaving our ancestors perplexed and unable to fathom what the new laws might be. It is in the context of the time of the strangenesses that the dialogue between the dead philosophers should be understood.

Ibn Rushd in the darkness of the tomb heard a familiar female voice whisper in his ear. *Speak.* With a sweet nostalgia seasoned with bitter guilt he remembered Dunia, the stick-thin mother of his bastards. She was tiny, and it occurred to him that he had never seen her eat. She suffered from regular headaches because, he told her, of her dislike of water. She liked red wine but had no head for it and after two glasses became a different person, giggling, gesticulating,

talking without stopping, interrupting others, and, always, wanting
to dance. She climbed on the kitchen table and when he declined to
join her she stamped out a pouting solo piece containing equal parts
of petulance and release. She clung to him at night as if she would
drown in the bed if he let her go. She had loved him without holding anything back and he had left her, had walked out of their home
without looking back. And now in the dank blackness of his crum-
bling tomb she had returned to haunt him in the grave.

Am I dead? he asked the phantom wordlessly. No words were
necessary. There were no lips to shape them anyway. Yes, she said,
dead for hundreds of years. I woke you up to see if you were sorry. I
woke you up to see if you could defeat your enemy after almost a
millenium of rest. I woke you up to see if you were ready to give your
children's children your family name. In the grave I can tell you the
truth. I am your own Dunia, but I am also a princess of the jinnias or
jiniri. The slits in the world are reopening, so I can come back to see
you again. And so at last he understood her inhuman origin, and
why, sometimes, she had looked a little smudged at the edges, as if
she were drawn in soft charcoal. Or smoke. He had ascribed the
blurriness of her outline to his bad eyesight and dismissed it from his
thoughts. But if she was whispering to him in his grave and had the
power to waken him from death then she was from the spirit world,
a thing of smoke and magic. Not a Jew who could not say she was a
Jew but a female jinn, a jinnia, who would not say she was of unearthly descent. So if he had betrayed her, she had deceived him. He
wasn't angry, he noted, without finding the information very important. It was too late for human anger. She, however, had a right to be
angry. And the anger of the jiniri was a thing to be feared.

What do you want? he asked. That's the wrong question, she
replied. The question is, what do *you* desire? You can't grant my
wishes. Maybe I can grant yours, if I want to. That's the way this
works. But we can discuss this later. Right now, your enemy is awake.
His old jinni has found him, just as I found you. What is the jinni of
Ghazali? he asked her. The most potent of all the jinn, she answered.

A fool without an imagination, whom nobody ever accused of intelligence, either; but with ferocious powers. I do not even want to speak his name. And your Ghazali seems to me an unforgiving, narrow man, she said. A puritan, whose enemy is pleasure, who would turn its joy to ash.

Her words felt chilling, even in the tomb. He felt something stir in a parallel darkness, faraway, so close. "Ghazali," he murmured soundlessly, "can that possibly be you?"

"It wasn't enough that you tried and failed to demolish my work when you were alive," the other replied. "Now, it would appear, you think you can do better after death."

Ibn Rushd pulled together the shards of his being. "The barriers of distance and time no longer pose a problem," he greeted his foe, "so we may begin to discuss matters in the proper way, courteously as to the person, ferociously as to the thought."

"I have found," Ghazali replied, sounding like a man with a mouth full of worms and dirt, "that the application of a degree of ferocity to the person usually brings his thinking into line with my own."

"At any rate," said Ibn Rushd, "we are both beyond the influence of physical deeds, or, if you prefer, misdeeds."

"That is true," Ghazali answered, "if, one must add, regrettable. Very well: proceed."

"Let us think of the human race as if it were a single human being," Ibn Rushd proposed. "A child understands nothing, and clings to faith because it lacks knowledge. The battle between reason and superstition may be seen as mankind's long adolescence, and the triumph of reason will be its coming of age. It is not that God does not exist but that like any proud parent he awaits the day when his child can stand on its own two feet, make its own way in the world, and be free of its dependence upon him."

"As long as you argue from God," Ghazali replied, "as long as you feebly try to reconcile the rational and the sacred, you will never defeat me. Why don't you just admit you're an unbeliever and we can take it from there. Observe who your descendants are, the godless scum of the West and East. Your words resonate only in the minds of *kafirs*. The followers of truth have forgotten you. The followers of truth know that it is reason and science that are the true juvenilia of the human mind. Faith is our gift from God and reason is our adolescent rebellion against it. When we are adult we will turn wholly to faith as we were born to do."

"You will see, as time goes by," said Ibn Rushd, "that in the end it will be religion that will make men turn away from God. The godly are God's worst advocates. It may take a thousand and one years but in the end religion will shrivel away and only then will we begin to live in God's truth."

"There," said Ghazali. "Good. Now, father of many bastards, you begin to speak like the blasphemer you are." Then he turned to matters of eschatology, which, he said, was now his preferred topic, and he spoke for a long time about the end of days, with a kind of relish that puzzled and distressed Ibn Rushd. Finally the younger man interrupted his elder in spite of the requirements of etiquette. "Sir, it feels as though, now that you yourself are nothing but oddly sentient dust, you are impatient for the rest of creation to plunge into its grave as well."

"As all true believers should," Ghazali replied. "For what the living call life is a worthless triviality when compared to the life to come."

Ghazali thinks the world is ending, Ibn Rushd told Dunia in the dark. He believes that God has set out to destroy his creation, slowly, enigmatically, without explanation; to confuse Man into destroying himself. Ghazali faces that prospect with equanimity, and not only because he himself is already dead. For him, life on earth is just an anteroom, or a doorway. Eternity is the real world. I asked him, in that case, why has your eternal life not begun, or is this all it is, this consciousness lingering in an uncaring void, which is, for the most part, boring. He said, God's ways are mysterious, and if he asks patience of me, I will give him as much as he desires. Ghazali has no desires of his own anymore, he says. He seeks only to serve God. I suspect him of being an idiot. Is that harsh? A great man, but an idiot too. And you, she said softly. Do you have desires still, or new desires you did not have before? He remembered how she would lay her head on his shoulder and he would cradle the back of it in the palm of his hand. Now they had passed beyond heads and hands and shoulders and lying together. The disembodied life, he said, is not worth living.

If my enemy is correct, he told her, then his God is a malicious God, for whom the life of the living has no value; and I would desire my children's children to know that, and to know my enmity towards such a God, and to follow me in standing against such a God, and defeating his purposes. So you acknowledge your bloodline, she whispered. I acknowledge it, he said, and I beg your forgiveness for not doing so before. The Duniazát is my race and I am its forefather. And this is your wish, she softly pressed him, that they may become aware of you, and your desire, and your will. And of my love for you, he said. Armed with that knowledge, they may yet save the world.

Sleep, she said, kissing the air where his cheek once lay. I'll be off now. I don't usually care very much about the passage of time, but right now, time is short.

The existence of the jinn posed problems to moral philosophers from the beginning. If men's deeds were motivated by benevolent or malignant sprites, if good and evil were external to Man rather than internal, it became impossible to define what an ethical man might be. Questions of right and wrong action became horribly confusing. In the eyes of some philosophers, this was a good thing, reflecting the actual moral confusion of the age, and, as a happy side effect, giving students of morality a task that had no ending.

At any rate, in the old days before the separation of the Two Worlds, they say everyone had his or her personal jinni or jinnia whispering in an ear, encouraging good deeds or bad. How they chose their human symbiotes, and why they took such an interest in us, remains obscure. Maybe they just didn't have much else to do. Much of the time the jinn seem to be individualists, even anarchists, acting purely on their own personal impulses, caring nothing for social organization or group activity. But there are also stories of wars between rival armies of jinn, dreadful conflicts which shook the jinn world to its foundations, and which, if true, may account for the decline in the number of these creatures and of their long retreat from our own sweet dwelling place. Tales abound of sorcerer-jinn, the Grand Ifrits, streaking across the skies in their giant flying urns to deal colossal blows, possibly even deadly ones, to lesser spirits, although, in contradiction, it is sometimes rumored that the jinn are immortal. This is untrue, though they are hard to kill. Only a jinni or a jinnia can kill another of the jinn. As will be seen. As we shall tell. What can be said is that the jinn, when they intervened in human affairs, were gleefully partisan, setting this human against that one, making this one rich, turning that one into a donkey, possessing people and driving them mad from inside their heads, helping or hindering the path of true love, but always holding themselves aloof from actual human companionship, except when trapped inside a magic lamp; and then, obviously, against their will.

Dunia was an exception among the jinnias. She came down to earth and fell in love, so deeply that she would not allow her beloved to rest in peace even after eight and a half centuries and more. To fall in love a creature must possess a heart, and whatever we may mean by a soul, and certainly such a creature must possess the group of traits we humans call *character*. But the jinn, or most of them, are—as you'd expect of beings made of fire and smoke—heartless, soulless, and above mere character, or perhaps beyond it. They are essences: good, bad, sweet, naughty, tyrannical, demure, powerful, whimsical, devious, grand. Dunia the lover of Ibn Rushd must have lived a long time among human beings, in disguise, clearly, to absorb the idea of *character* and begin to show signs of it. One might say that she caught *character* from the human race the way children catch chicken pox or mumps. After that she began to love love itself, to love her capacity for love, to love the selflessness of love, the sacrifice, the eroticism, the glee. She began to love her beloved in her and she in him, but beyond that she started loving the human race for its ability to love, and then for its other emotions too; she loved men and women because they could fear, and rage, and cower, and exult. If she could have given up being a jinnia she might even have chosen to become human, but her nature was what it was and she could not deny it. After Ibn Rushd left her and made her, yes, *sad,* she *pined,* and *grieved,* and was shocked by her deepening humanity. And then one day before the slits in the world closed she left. But not even hundreds of years in her palace in the jinn world, not even the endless promiscuity that is the everyday norm of life in Fairyland, could cure her; and so when the slits broke open she returned to renew her bonds. Her beloved asked her from beyond the grave to reunite their scattered family and help it fight the coming world cataclysm. Yes, she would do it, she said, and sped off on her mission.

Unfortunately, she was not the only citizen of the jinn world who had reentered the human levels, and not all of them had good deeds in mind.

The Strangenesses

Natraj Hero naaching down the avenue like dancing god Lord Shiva, lord of dance, bringing world into being as he prance. Natraj young&beautiful, scorns old dudes, laughs at all the painfoot-limpy-with-heavy/bhaari-body-types. Girls, but, don't give him a second look. Not knowing his superpowers, Creator and Destroyer of Universe, they are ignoring. That's okay: theek thaak. He is in disguise. Just now he is being tax accountant Jinendra going for grocery to Subzi Mandi store, Jackson Heights, Quveens. Jinendra Kapoor a.k.a. Brown Clark Cunt. Wait till he rips off his outer garment yaar. Then they'll dekho him all right, they'll be checking him proper. Until dat time, hinting only at secret mightiness, he is prancing Thirty-Seventh Avenue like king from Desh, the old country, shahenshah or maharana or wat. Natraj dance to the bulbul tune. He is like dis only. He is Dil-ka-Shehzada. A.k.a. Jack of Hearts.

Natraj Hero did not exist. He was the fictional alter ego of a young would-be graphic novelist, Jimmy Kapoor. Natraj's superpower was dancing. When he "ripped off his outer garment" his two arms turned into four, he had four faces too, front, back and sides, and a third eye in the middle of his front forehead, and when he began to dance the bhangra or bust out his best disco moves—he was from Queens, after all—he was able literally to shape reality, to create or destroy. He could make a tree grow in the street or make himself a Mercedes convertible or feed the hungry, but he could also knock down houses and blow bad guys to bits. It was a mystery to Jimmy why Natraj hadn't leapt up into the divine pantheon with Sandman and Watchmen and the Dark Knight and Tank Girl and the Punisher and the Invisibles and Dredd and all the other Marvel, Titan and DC greats. Sadly, Natraj had remained obstinately earthbound, and tax accountancy in Jimmy's cousin's practice on Roosevelt Avenue was beginning, at his low points, to feel like the young artist's fate.

He had begun to post episodes from the career of Natraj Hero online but the big boys had notably failed to call. Then, one hot night—one hundred and one nights after the storm, though he hadn't worked that out—up there in his third-floor bedroom with a red moon shining through his window, he woke up with a start of terror. There was somebody in the room. Somebody . . . *big.* As his eyes grew accustomed to the darkness he observed that the far wall of his bedroom had disappeared completely and been replaced by a swirl of black smoke at whose heart was what looked like a black tunnel leading into the depths of the unknown. It was hard to see the tunnel clearly because a gigantic many-headed multi-limbed individual was in the way, trying to fold those limbs into the cramped space of Jimmy's room, looking like it—he—was about to knock down the other bedroom walls, and complaining loudly.

The individual did not look as if he—it—was made of flesh and blood. It—he—looked *drawn, illustrated,* and Jimmy Kapoor recognized, with a shock, his own graphic style, Frank Milleresque (he hoped), sub-Stan-Lee-universe (he conceded), post-Lichtensteinian (this when in the company of snobs, himself included). "You've come to life?" he asked, being incapable at that moment of depth or wit. Natraj Hero's voice, when he—it—spoke, sounded familiar, a voice he'd heard somewhere before, a snarling multi-mouthed echo-chamber voice of divine authority, ruthlessness and wrath, the very antithesis of Jimmy's own voice, a poor thing filled with fears, insecurities and uncertainty. The correct response to this voice was to quail before it. Jimmy Kapoor made the correct response.

Fuck yaar no space in here sala having to make self smaller, chhota like fucking ant, or I will take roof off your pathetic ghar. Okay, better. See me? Check me? One two three four arm, four three two one face, third eye looking straight into your piddling soul. No, no, please to excuse, respect must be shown, because you are my creator, isn't it? HA HA HA HA HA. As if great Natraj was dreamed up by tax accountant in Quveens and hasn't been around and dancing since Start of Time. Since, to be precise, I personally have danced Time and Space into being. HA HA HA HA HA. You think you have summoned me maybe. You think you are a wizard maybe. HA HA HA HA HA. Or you think it's a dream? No, baba. You just woke the fuck up. Also me. Returning after absence of eight-nine hundred years, featuring many long snoozes.

Jimmy Kapoor shook with terror. "How didid you get hehere?" he stammered. "Ininto my bebedrooroom?" *You have seen* Ghostbusters *fillum?* responded Natraj Hero. *This is like that only.* That was it, Jimmy understood. It was one of his favorite films, and Natraj's voice was like the voice of the Sumerian destruction-god, Gozer the Gozerian, speaking through the lips of Sigourney Weaver. Gozer with kind of an Indian accent. *Portaal is busted open. Border between what imagineers are imagining and what imaginees are desiring is leaky now like Mexico-USA, and we-all, who before were caged in Phantom Zone, can go fast now through wormholes and land up here like General Zod with superpowers. So many wanting to come. Soon we will be taking over. Hundred and one percent. Forget about it.*

Natraj began to flicker and dim. This was not to his liking. *Portaal not functioning just now at full efficiency. Okay. Tata for now. But please be assured, I will return.* Then he was gone and Jimmy Kapoor alone wide-eyed in bed watched the black clouds spiral inward until the dark tunnel was gone. After that his bedroom wall reappeared, with the photos of Don Van Vliet a.k.a. Captain Beefheart, Scott Pilgrim, Lou Reed, the defunct Brooklyn hip-hop group Das Racist, and the Faustian comic-book hero Spawn pinned to the corkboard unaltered, as if they hadn't just voyaged to the fifth dimension and back, and only Rebecca Romijn, in the large pin-up poster of the blue-skinned shapeshifter Raven Darkhölme a.k.a. Mystique, looked a little put out, as if to say, Who was that who shifted my shape out of the way, fucking nerve of some people, I'm the only one who decides when I change form.

"Now *sabkuch* changes, Mystique," Jimmy told the blue creature in the poster. "Meaning to say, *everything*. Now the world itself is shape-shifting, looks like. Vow."

Jimmy Kapoor was the first to discover the wormhole, and after that, as he correctly intuited, everything shifted form. But in those last days of the old world, the world as we all knew it before the strangenesses, people were reluctant to admit that the new phenomena were truly occurring. Jimmy's mother pooh-poohed her son's account of his transformative night. Mrs. Kapoor was stricken with lupus, and rose only to feed the exotic birds, the peahens, the toucans, the ducks. These she obstinately reared for sale and profit in the concrete-and-dirt wasteland behind their building, an empty plot where something had fallen down long ago and nothing had risen in its place. She had been doing this for fourteen years and nobody had objected, but there were thefts, and in the winter some birds froze to death. Rare breeds of duck were pilfered and ended up on somebody's dinner table. An emu fell over shivering and was gone. Mrs. Kapoor accepted these events uncomplainingly, as manifestations of the world's unkindness and her personal karma. Holding a newly laid ostrich egg, she scolded her son for confusing dreams and reality, as he always did.

"Unusual thing is never the true thing," she told him, while a toucan on her shoulder nuzzled her neck. "Those flying saucers always turn out to be fakes, na, or ordinary lights, isn't it. And if people are coming here from another world, why only show themselves to crazy hippies in the desert? Why they are not landing at JFK like all others? You think a god with so-many arms legs and what-all would come to you in your bedroom before visiting president in

Oval Office? Don't be mad." By the time she had finished Jimmy had begun to doubt his own memory. Maybe it really had been a nightmare. Maybe he was such a loser that he had started swallowing his own shit. In the morning there had been no trace of Natraj Hero, right? No disarranged furniture or fallen coffee mug. No torn photographs. The bedroom wall felt solid and real. As always, his ailing mother was right.

Jimmy's father had flown the coop with a secretary bird some years back and Jimmy did not as yet possess the funds to get a place of his own. There was no girlfriend. His sick mother wanted him to marry a thin-thin girl with a big nose that was always stuck in a book, college girl, nice manner on surface nasty behavior underneath, the way those girls were, No thank you, he thought, better off on my own until I hit the big time and then look out major babeland. The tall pretty girls lived in New York and the short pretty girls lived in LA; Jimmy was glad he lived on the glamazon coast. He aspired to be worthy of a personal glamazon. But right now there was no girlfriend. Fuck. Never mind. Right now he was at the office quarreling as usual with his cousin Normal, boss of accountancy firm.

He hated that his cousin Nirmal wanted to be normal so badly that he changed his name to Normal. He hated even more that Nirmal—Normal—spoke such bad normal *Amreekan* that he thought the word for *name* was Monica. Jimmy told his cousin that nowadays *moniker* meant a graffiti artist's drawing on a freight train. Normal ignored him. Look at Gautama Chopra son of famous Deepak, Normal said, he changed his Monica to Gotham because he wanted so bad to be New Yorker. Also basketball players: Mr. Johnson wanted to be Magic, isn't it, and Mr. Ron or Wrong Artist, don't correct me, please—okay—Mr. Ar*test* preferred to be Mr. World Peace. And don't forget those actresses so famous in before-time, Dimple and sister Simple, if those Monicas are acceptable then what you talking. Me, I just want to be Normal, and so what's wrong with it, Normal by name, normal by nature. Gotham Chopra. Simple Kapadia. Magic

Johnson. Normal Kapoor. Same to bloody same. You should focus on
the figures and keep your head out of the dreams, isn't it. Your good
mother told me your dream. Shiva Natraj in your bedroom as drawn
by Jinendra K. Keep going on that way, why not? Keep going on and
you will come to a grief. You want a life? Wife? No strife? Focus on
figures. Take care of your mother. Stop dreaming. Wake up to reality.
That is Normal practice. You will do well to follow suit.

Outside, when he left work, it was Halloween. Children, marching bands et cetera, parading. He had always been kind of a Halloween party-pooper, never got into the whole dressing-up Baron-Samedi
thing, and half admitted to himself that the killjoy attitude was related to the absence of a girlfriend, was both an effect of said absence
and also the partial cause of it. Tonight, with his thoughts full of last
night's manifestation, Halloween had completely slipped his mind.
He walked down streets filled with dead people and tits-out prosti-
tutes, readying himself for his mother's infirmity, her guilt-trip
monologues and her doddering birdseed duties, I'll do it, Ma, he told
her, but she shook her head weakly, No, son, what am I good for
now except to keep my birds alive and wait for death, her usual
speech, a little more macabre given the context, the dead rising from
their tombs to perform their *danses macabres,* the night of skeleton-
masked figures in hooded monks' habits carrying the Sickles of the
Reaper and drinking vodka from the bottle through the gaping
mouths of their skulls. He passed a woman with astonishing face
makeup, a zipper running down the middle of her face, "unzipped"
around her mouth to reveal bloody skinless flesh all the way down
her chin and neck, You really went all out, darling, he thought, that's
really full on, but I don't think anybody will want to kiss you tonight. Nobody wanted to kiss him either but he had a superhero-
slash-god to meet. Tonight, he told himself, filled with both dread
and joy. Tonight we'll see who's dreaming and who's awake.

And sure enough, at midnight, the pictures of Captain Beefheart,
Rebecca/Mystique and the rest were swallowed up by the swirling
dark cloud, which slowly spiraled open to reveal the tunnel to some-

where infinitely strange. For some reason—Jimmy supposed that supernatural beings weren't required to abide by the laws of reason, that reason was one of the things they defied, held in contempt, and sought to overthrow—Natraj Hero didn't bother on this occasion to visit the bedroom in Queens. And, again for some reason—though Jimmy himself would have admitted afterwards that rational thought had very little to do with his decision—the young would-be graphic novelist moved slowly towards the cloud spiral and gingerly, as if testing the temperature of bathwater, put his arm into the black hole at its heart.

Now that we know about the War of the Worlds, the main event to which the strangenesses were the prologue, the bizarre cataclysm which many of our ancestors did not live through, we can only marvel at the courage of young Jinendra Kapoor in the face of the terrifying unknown. When Alice fell down the rabbit hole, it was an accident, but when she stepped through the looking glass, it was of her own free will, and a braver deed by far. So it was with Jimmy K. He had no control over the wormhole's first appearance, or the entry into his bedroom of the giant Ifrit, the dark jinn, disguised as Natraj Hero. But on this second night, he made a choice. Men like Jimmy were needed in the war that followed.

When Jimmy Kapoor plunged his arm into the wormhole, as he afterwards told his mother and his cousin Normal, a number of things happened at *mind-blowing speed*. In the first place, he was instantly sucked into that space where the laws of the universe ceased to operate, and in the second place, he at once lost his sense of where the first place might be. In the place where he found himself the idea of *place* ceased to have meaning and was replaced by *velocity*. The universe of pure and extreme velocity required no point of origin, no big bang, no creation myth. The only force at work here was the so-called g-force, under whose influence acceleration is felt as weight. If time had existed here he would have been crushed to nothing in a millisecond. In that timeless time he had time to perceive that he had entered the transportation system of the world behind the veil of the real, the subcutaneous subway network operating just below the skin of the world he knew, which allowed such beings as the dark jinn and he had no idea who or what else besides to move at FTL speeds—speeds faster than light—around their lawless land for which the word *land* seemed inappropriate. He had time to hypothesize that for whatever reasonless reason this, the underground railroad of Fairyland, had been sequestered from terra firma for a long time, but had now begun to burst through into the dimension of the actual to wreak miracles or havoc amongst human beings.

Or it may be that he did not have time for these thoughts and that they actually formed in his mind after he was rescued, because what he felt there in the tunnel of swirling black smoke was a rushing towards him of something or someone he could not see or hear much less name, and then he was tumbling backwards into his bedroom with his pajamas ripped off his body so that he was obliged to shield his nakedness with his bare hands from the woman standing before him, a beautiful young woman dressed in the casual uniform of young women her age, skinny black jeans, a black tank top and lace-up ankle boots, a person even more thin-thin than the girl his mother wanted him to marry but with a far more attractive nose, the kind of girl he would have loved to date obviously, except that she was not glamazon shaped, but he found he didn't care so much about that, but in spite of or because of her stick-thin beauty he knew she was far out of his league, *forget about it, Jimmy, don't make a fool of yourself, stay loose, play it cool.* And this was the girl who had saved him from the vortex of velocity and who apparently was a being from the other world, a fairy or peri from Peristan, and she was talking to him. This stuff that was happening to him now: it did his head in. Vow, *yaar.* No words. Just . . . vowee.

The jinn are not noted for their family lives. (But they do have sex. They have it all the time.) There are jinn mothers or fathers, but the generations of the jinn are so long that the ties between the generations often erode. Jinn fathers and daughters, as will be seen, are rarely on good terms. Love is rare in the jinn world. (But sex is incessant.) The jinn, we believe, are capable of the lower emotions—anger, resentment, vindictiveness, possessiveness, lust (especially lust)—and even, perhaps, some forms of affection; but the high noble sentiments, selflessness, devotion, and so on, these elude them. In this, as in so much else, Dunia proved herself exceptional.

Nor do the jinn alter greatly with the passage of the years. For them existence is purely the business of being, never becoming. For this reason, life in the jinn world can be tedious. (Except for the sex.) Being, by its nature, is an inactive state, changeless, timeless, eternal, and dull. (Except for the nonstop sex.) This is why the human world was always so attractive to the jinn. The human way was *doing*, the human reality was *alteration*, human beings were always growing and shriveling and striving and failing and yearning and envying, acquiring and losing and loving and hating, and being, in sum, interesting, and when the jinn were able to move through the slits between the worlds and meddle in all this human activity, when they could tangle or untangle the human web and accelerate or hold back the endless metamorphosis of human lives, human relations, and human societies, they felt, paradoxically, more like themselves than they ever did in the static world of Fairyland. It was human beings who allowed the jinn to express themselves, to create immense wealth for lucky fishermen, to imprison heroes in magic webs, to thwart history or enable it, to take sides in wars, between the Kurus and Pandavas, for example, or the Greeks and Trojans, to play Cupid or to make it impossible for a lover ever to reach his beloved, so that she grew old and sad and died alone at her window waiting for him to arrive.

We now believe that the long age in which the jinn were unable to interfere in human affairs contributed to the ferocity with which they reentered it when the seals between the worlds were broken. All that pent-up creative and destructive power, all that good and bad mischief, burst upon us like a storm. And between the jinn of white magic and the jinn of black magic, the bright jinn and the dark, an enmity had grown in their Peristan exile, and human beings became the surrogates upon whom that hostility played itself out. With the return of the jinn the rules of life on earth had changed, had become capricious where they should have been stable, intrusive where privacy would have been better, malicious to a fault, preferential with scant regard for fairness, secret according to their occult origins, amoral for that was the nature of the dark jinn, opaque with no care for transparency, and accountable to no citizenry on the planet. And the jinn, being jinn, had no intention of teaching mere humans what the new rules might be.

In the matter of sex, it is true that the jinn have on occasion had intercourse with human beings, adopting whatever form they chose, making themselves pleasing to their mate, even altering gender on occasion, and having little regard for propriety. However, there are very few cases in which a jinnia bore human children. That would be as if the breeze were to be impregnated by the hair it ruffled and gave birth to more hair. That would be as if a story mated with its reader to produce another reader. The jinnias have been for the most part infertile and uninterested in such human problems as motherhood and family responsibility. It will readily be apparent, then, that Dunia, the matriarch of the Duniazát, was, or became, very unlike the vast majority of her kind. Not only had she produced offspring the way Henry Ford learned to produce motor cars, the way Georges Simenon wrote novels, which is to say, like a factory, or industriously; she also continued to care for them all, her love for Ibn Rushd transferring itself naturally, *maternally,* towards their descendants. She was perhaps the only true mother of all the jinnias that existed, and as she embarked on the task the great philosopher had given her, she also became protective of what remained of her dispersed brood after the cruelty of the centuries, missed them bitterly during the long separation of the Two Worlds, and yearned to have them back under her wing.

Do you understand why you are still alive, she asked Jimmy Kapoor, as, blushing, he pulled a bedsheet around himself. "Yes," he replied, his eyes filled with wonder. "Because you saved my life." That is so, she conceded, inclining her head. But you would have been dead before I reached you, crushed to bits in the great Urn, if it wasn't for the other reason.

She saw his fear, his disorientation, his inability to process what was happening to him. She couldn't help it. She was about to make his life even harder for him to grasp. I am going to tell you some things you will find hard to believe, she said. Unlike almost any other human being you have entered the Urn, the pathway between the worlds, and survived, so you already know that another world exists. I am a person from that world, a jinnia, a princess of the tribe of the bright jinn. I am also your great-great-great-great-great-great-great-grandmother, though I may have omitted a *great* or two. Never mind. In the twelfth century I loved your great-great-et-cetera-grandfather, your illustrious ancestor the philosopher Ibn Rushd, and you, Jinendra Kapoor, who can't trace your family history back further than three generations, are a product of that great love, maybe the greatest love there ever was between the tribes of men and jinn. This means that you, like all the descendants of Ibn Rushd, Muslim, Christian, atheist or Jew, are also partly of the jinn. The jinni part, being far more powerful than the human part, is very strong in you all, and that is what made it possible for you to survive the otherness in *there;* for you are Other too.

"Vow," he cried, reeling. "It isn't bad enough being a brown dude in America, you're telling me I'm half fucking goblin as well."

How young he was, she thought, and stronger than he knew. Many men, seeing what he had seen in the last two nights, would have lost their minds, but he, for all his panic, was holding himself together. It was the resilience in human beings that represented their best chance of survival, their ability to look the unimaginable, the unconscionable, the unprecedented in the eye. This was the kind of thing young Jinendra confronted regularly in his art, through his somewhat derivative (and therefore unsuccessful) Hindu-deity-transplanted-to-Queens superhero: the monster rising from the deep, the destruction of your home village and the rape of your mothers, the arrival of a second sun in the sky and the consequent abolition of the night, and in the voice of his Natraj Hero he answered horror with scorn, Is that all you've got, is that your best shot, because guess what, we can deal with you, motherfucker, we can take you down. Now, having practiced courage in fiction, he was discovering it in his real life. And his own comic-book creation was the first monster he had to confront.

She spoke gently, maternally, to this brave young man. Be calm, your world is changing, she told him. At times of great upheaval when the wind blows and the tide of history surges, cool heads are needed to navigate a path to calmer waters. I will be here with you. Find the jinni within yourself and you may be a bigger hero than your Natraj. It's in there. You will find it.

The wormhole closed. He was sitting on his bed holding his head in his hands. "This is what happens to me now," he muttered. "They build a transworld railway station three feet from my *bed*. No construction permit, yo? There's no, like, zoning laws in hyperspace? Imma *complain* 'bout that. Imma call 3-1-1 *right now*." His hysteria was talking. She let it play itself out. It was his way of dealing with the situation. She waited. He flung himself down on his bed and his shoulders shook. He was trying to hide his tears from her. She pretended she did not see them. She was there to tell him he was not alone, to introduce him to his cousins. Quietly, she planted the information in his mind. The jinn part of him absorbed, understood, knew. You know where they are now, she told him. You can help one another in the time that is to come.

He sat up, clutched his head again. "I don't need all this contact info at present," he said. "I need *Vicodin*."

She waited. He would come back to her soon. He looked up at her and attempted a smile. "It's a lot," he said. "Whatever *that* was . . . whatever you are . . . whatever you're saying I am. I'm going to need some time."

You don't have time, she told him. I don't know why the portal opened in your room. I know that what appeared last night was not your Natraj Hero. Somebody took that form, to frighten you, or just because it was funny. Somebody you should hope never to meet again. Move out. Take your mother to a safe place. She won't understand. She won't see the swirling black smoke because she is not of the Duniazát. That comes from your father's side.

"That bastard," Jimmy said. "He sure disappeared like a jinni or wat. Didn't grant us wishes, but. Just, went off in a puff of smoke with Secretary Bird."

Take your mother away, Dunia told him. It isn't safe for either of you here anymore.

"Vow," Jimmy Kapoor marveled. "Worst. Halloween. Ever."

The discovery of a girl baby in the office of the recently elected mayor Rosa Fast, swaddled in the national flag of India and gurgling contentedly in a bassinet on the mayoral desk, was thought by the superstitious and sentimental citizenry to be, on the whole, a good thing, especially when it was announced that the baby was approximately four months old and must have been born at the time of the great storm, and survived it. Storm Baby, the media called her, and the name stuck. She became Storm Doe, conjuring up the image of a Bambi-like fawn bravely facing down the tempest on unsteady legs: an instant short-term heroine for those instant and forgetful times. It won't be long, many of our ancestors surmised, considering her apparent South Asian ethnicity, before she's old enough to become the national spelling bee champion. She made the cover of *India Abroad* and was the subject of an exhibition of "imaginary portraits" of her future, adult self, commissioned from prominent New York artists by an Indo-American arts organization and auctioned off as a fundraising ploy. But the mystery of her arrival enraged those who were already outraged by the election of a second consecutive woman mayor of progressive inclinations. It would never have happened, these nostalgists cried, back in the tough-guy days. Whether the rest of our ancestors agreed with that or not, it was true that in the age of maximum security her arrival on Mayor Fast's desk felt like a small miracle.

Where did Storm Doe come from and how did she get into City Hall? The evidence from the battery of security cameras that constantly swept City Hall showed a woman in a purple balaclava strolling through every checkpoint late at night, carrying the bassinet, without attracting a single flicker of attention, as if she had the power to make herself invisible, if not to the cameras, then at least to people in her immediate vicinity; but also, obviously, to the duty officers whose responsibility it was to monitor the security screens. The woman simply walked into the mayor's office, deposited the baby, and departed. Our ancestors speculated a good deal about this female. Did she somehow catch the system napping or did she possess some sort of invisibility cloak? And if the cloak, would she not also have been invisible to the cameras? Normally down-to-earth people began to have serious dinner-table conversations about superpowers. But why would a woman with superpowers abandon her baby? And if she was the child's mother, might Storm Doe possess some sort of magic qualities as well? Might she . . . because it was important not to shy away from unpleasant possibilities in the time of the war on terror . . . might she be dangerous? When an article appeared under the headline *Is Storm Baby a Human Time Bomb?* our ancestors realized that many of them had abandoned the laws of realism long ago and felt at home in the more glamorous dimensions of the fantastic. And as things turned out little Storm was indeed a visitor from the country of improbability. But at first everyone was more concerned with finding her a home.

Rosa Fast came from a prosperous Ukrainian-Jewish family based in Brighton Beach, and dressed smartly in Ralph Lauren power suits, "because his people were our neighbors," she liked to say, "but not in Sheepshead Bay," meaning that Ralph Lifshitz from the Bronx had ancestors in Belarus, adjacent to "her" Ukraine. Fast's star rose as Mayor Flora Hill's fell, and there was no love lost between her and the outgoing mayor. Mayor Hill's term had been beset by allegations of financial improprieties, of money rerouted into secret slush funds, and two of her closest colleagues had been indicted, but the dirt had stopped short of the mayor's office, though some of the stench had penetrated it. Rosa Fast's successful election campaign, which hinged on her promise to clean up City Hall, had not endeared her to her predecessor, while Flora Hill's suggestion, made after she left office, that her successor was a "closet atheist" had irritated Rosa Fast, who had, in fact, fallen far away from the faith of her ancestors, but felt that what she did in the closet of godlessness was her own business and nobody else's. Divorced, presently unattached, fifty-three years old and childless, Fast confessed herself deeply touched by the plight of Baby Storm and made it her business to see the little girl safely into a new life, if possible out of the reach of the tabloid press. Storm was fast-tracked for adoption and successfully transferred to her new parents to make a new, anonymous beginning under a new name, or that was the idea, but within weeks the new parents approached reality-TV producers and pitched a show to be called *Storm Watch* which would follow the star baby as she grew. When Rosa Fast heard the news she exploded with rage and shouted at the adoption services that they had delivered an innocent child into the hands of exhibitionist pornographers who would probably take a dump on television if somebody sponsored them to do it.

"Get her away from those bravoes," she cried, using the slang term for reality wannabes that had become common usage even though the television network from which the term originated had ceased broadcasting, because programming of mendacious artifice that presented itself as actuality had invaded so much of the cable-sphere that the original purveyor of such programming had become redundant. Everyone had learned that it was worth giving up privacy for the merest possibility of fame, and the idea that only a private self was truly autonomous and free had been lost in the static of the airwaves. So Baby Storm was in danger of being bravoed and

Mayor Fast was furious; but as it happened the very next day the wannabe reality-star adoptive father brought the baby back to the adoption services, saying, Take her back, she's diseased, and literally ran out of the room, but not before everyone had seen the sore on his face, the putrescent, decaying area that looked as if a part of his cheek had died and begun to rot. Baby Storm was taken back to hospital for checks but given a clean bill of health. The next day, however, one of the nurses who had held her began to rot as well, patches of malodorous decaying flesh sprang up on both forearms, and as she was rushed weeping hysterically into the emergency room she confessed that she had been stealing prescription meds and fencing them to a dealer in Bushwick to make a little extra money on the side.

It was Mayor Rosa Fast who first understood what was happening, who brought the strangeness into the arena of what could be properly spoken about, of *news*. "This miracle baby can identify corruption," she told her closest aides, "and the corrupt, once she has fingered them, literally begin to show the signs of their moral decay on their bodies." The aides warned her that kind of talk, belonging as it did to the archaic old-Europe world of dybbuks and golems, probably didn't sit too well in the mouth of a modern politician, but Rosa Fast was undeterred. "We came into office to clean this place up," she declared, "and chance has given us the human broom with which we can sweep it clean." She was the kind of atheist who could believe in miracles without conceding their divine provenance, and the next day the foundling, now in the care of the foster care agency, came back to the mayor's office for a visit.

Baby Storm reentered City Hall like a tiny human minesweeper or drug-sniffing Alsatian. The mayor enfolded her in a big Brooklyn-Ukrainian hug, and whispered, "Let's go to work, baby of truth." What followed instantly became the stuff of legend, as in room after room, department after department, marks of corruption and decay appeared on the faces of the corrupt and decaying, the expenses cheats, the receivers of backhand payments in return for civic contracts, the accepters of Rolex watches and private airplane flights and Hermès

bags stuffed with banknotes, and all the secret beneficiaries of bureau-
cratic power. The crooked began to confess before the miracle baby
came within range, or fled the building to be hunted down by the law.

Mayor Fast herself was unblemished, which proved something.
Her predecessor was on TV deriding the mayor's "occult mumbo
jumbo" and Rosa Fast issued a brief statement inviting Flora Hill to
"come on down and meet this little sweetheart," which invitation Hill
did not take up. The entry of Baby Storm into the council chamber
induced a panic among the individuals seated therein, and a desperate rush for the exits. Those who remained proved immune to the
baby's powers and were revealed as honest men and women. "I guess
we finally know," said Mayor Fast, "who's who around these parts."

Our ancestors were fortunate in such an hour to have a leader like
Rosa Fast. "Any community that cannot agree on a description of
itself, of how things go in the community, of *what is the case,* is a community in trouble. It is plain that events of a new kind, events of a
type we would have described until very recently as fantastic and
improbable, have begun, provably and objectively, to occur. We need
to know what this means, and to face the changes that may be taking
place with courage and intelligence." The 311 phone lines, she declared, would for the time being be available to people wishing to
report unusual occurrences of any kind. "Let's get the facts," she
said, "and move forward from there." As for Baby Storm, the mayor
herself adopted her. "Not only is she my pride and joy, she's also my
secret weapon," she told us. "Don't try any BS on me or my baby girl
here will get medieval on your face."

There was one disadvantage to being the adoptive mother of the
baby of truth, she told her fellow citizens on breakfast television. "If
I tell the smallest little white lie in her presence, well! My whole face
begins, just dreadfully, to itch."

Two hundred and one days after the great storm, the British composer Hugo Casterbridge published an article in *The New York Times*

that announced the formation of a new intellectual group whose purpose was to understand the radical shifts in the world conditions and to devise strategies for combating them. This group, widely derided in the days following the article's publication as a bunch of semi-eminent though undeniably telegenic biologists, mad-professor climatologists, magic-realist novelists, idiot movie actors and renegade theologians, was responsible—in spite of all the jeering—for popularizing the term *strangenesses,* which caught on quickly, and stuck. Casterbridge had long been a divisive cultural figure on account of his firebrand hostility to American foreign policy, his fondness for certain Latin American dictators, and his aggressive hostility to all forms of religious belief. There was also a never-proven rumor concerning the end of his first marriage, a rumor as persistent and damaging as the notorious gerbil rumor which attached itself to a Hollywood leading man of the 1980s. As a struggling young cellist— with, at the time, a serious dependency on dangerous narcotics— Casterbridge had met and quickly married a beautiful fellow musician, a violinist with star potential, who, soon afterwards, also caught the eye of a certain industrial tycoon, who began to pursue her without regard for her marital status, and, according to the rumor, confronted Casterbridge in the composer's small Kennington Oval apartment with the blunt question "What would it take to make you disappear from her life?" Whereupon Casterbridge, heavily under the influence of opium or something worse, replied, "One million pounds," and passed out. When he awoke his wife was gone without leaving a note, and he found, when he checked, that one million pounds had been deposited in his bank account.

His wife refused to have anything to do with him after that, divorced him quickly and went on to marry the industrial tycoon. He never took drugs again and his career blossomed, though he never remarried. "He sold his wife as if she was a Stradivarius, and lived off the cash," people said of him behind his back. Casterbridge was a capable boxer with a famously short fuse, so nobody repeated the slander to his face.

The strangenesses are multiplying, he wrote in his article, *though the world before they began was already a strange place, so often it's difficult to know if an event falls into the category of the old, ordinary strangenesses or the new, extraordinary variety. Superstorms have devastated Fiji and Malaysia, and as I write giant fires are spreading across Australia and California. Perhaps this extreme weather is just the new normal, giving rise to the usual arguments between the proponents and opponents of climate change. Or perhaps this is evidence of something much worse. Our group takes what I'll call a Post-Atheist stance. Our position is that god is a creation of human beings, who only exists because of the clap-hands-if-you-believe-in-fairies principle. If enough people were sensible enough not to clap hands, then this Tinker Bell god would die. However, unfortunately, billions of human beings are still prepared to defend their belief in some sort of god-fairy, and, as a result, god exists. What's worse is that he is now running amok.*

On the day that Adam and Eve invented god, the article continued, *they at once lost control of him. That is the beginning of the secret history of the world. Man and Woman invented god, who at once eluded their grasp and became more powerful than his creators, and also more malevolent. Like the supercomputer in the film* Terminator: *"Skynet," sky-god, same thing. Adam and Eve were filled with fear, because it was plain that for the rest of time god would come after them to punish them for the crime of having created him. They came into being simultaneously in a garden, Eve and Adam, fully grown and naked and enjoying you could say the first Big Bang, and they had no idea how they got there until a snake led them to the tree of the knowledge of good and evil and when they ate its fruit they both simultaneously came up with the idea of a creator-god, a good-and-evil decider, a gardener-god who made the garden, otherwise where did the garden come from, and then planted them in it like rootless plants.*

And lo, there, immediately, was god, and he was furious, "How did you come up with the idea of me," he demanded, "who asked you to do that?" and he threw them out of the garden, into, of all places, Iraq. "No good deed goes unpunished," said Eve to Adam, and that ought to be the motto of the entire human race.

The name "Casterbridge" was an invention. The great composer came from an immigrant family of Iberian Jews, and was a strikingly handsome man with a grand, sonorous voice and the bearing of a king. He also shared the most unusual physical characteristic of his kin: he had no earlobes. He was not a man to be trifled with, though his loyalties were as fierce as his enmities, and he was capable of profound loyalty and friendship. His smile was a thing of menacing, almost feral sweetness, a smile that could bite your head off. His politeness was terrifying. His two most endearing qualities were his Rottweiler obstinacy and his rhinoceros-thick hide. Once he had an idea between his teeth, nothing would induce him to yield it up, and the ridicule with which the new Post-Atheism was received did not deter him in the slightest. He was asked on late-night American TV if he was actually saying that the Supreme Being was fictional, and that this fictional divinity had now decided, for undisclosed reasons, to torment the human race. "Exactly," he said with great firmness. "That's exactly right. The triumph of the destructive irrational manifests itself in the form of an irrationally destructive god." The talk-show host whistled between the famous gap in his central upper incisors. "Whew," he said. "And here I was thinking the Brits were better educated than us."

"Suppose," said Hugo Casterbridge, "that one day god sent a storm, such a storm as could shake loose the moorings of the world, a storm which told us to take nothing for granted, not our power, not our civilization, not our laws, because if nature could rewrite its laws, break its bounds, change its nature, then our constructs, so puny in comparison, stood no chance. And this is the great test we face—our world, its ideas, its culture, its knowledge and laws, is under attack by the illusion we collectively created, the supernatural monster we ourselves unleashed. Plagues will be sent, like those sent to Egypt. But this time, there will be no request to *let my people go*. This god is not a liberator but a destroyer. He has no commandments. He's over all that. He's sick of us, the way he was in Noah's time. He wants to make an example. He wants to do us in."

"And we'll be right back," said the talk-show host, "after these messages."

In certain quarters the quest for scapegoats had begun. It was important to know whose fault all this was. It was important to know if things were going to get worse. Maybe there were identifiable persons, destabilizing persons, who were somehow responsible for the destabilized world. Maybe these were persons carrying within themselves some sort of genetic mutation that gave them the power to induce paranormal happenings, persons who posed a threat to the rest of the normal human race. It was interesting that the so-called storm baby had been wrapped in the Indian flag. It might be necessary to look at the South Asian immigrant community to see if answers could be found. Maybe the *disease*—the strangeness was a social disease now, it seemed—had been brought to America by some of these persons, Indians, Pakistanis, Bangladeshis, just as the devastating AIDS epidemic had originated somewhere in Central Africa and arrived in the United States in the early 1980s. A public murmuring began, and Americans of South Asian origins began to fear for their safety. Many taxi drivers put up stickers in their cabs reading *I'm not that strange* or *Normalness not strangeness is the American way.* There were a few, worrying reports of physical attacks. Then another scapegoat group was identified, and the laser beam of public attention swung away from brown-skinned folks. This new group was harder to identify. They were lightning-strike survivors.

During the great storm the lightning strikes multiplied in frequency and ferocity. It seemed like a new kind of lightning, not just electrical but eschatological. And when the machines told our ancestors that there had been over four thousand strikes per square mile, they began to understand how much danger they had been in, how much danger they might still be in. In an average year in the city there were fewer than four lightning strikes per square mile, just about all of which were absorbed by the lightning rods and radio masts on the tall buildings. Four-thousand-plus strikes per square mile meant almost ninety-five thousand strikes on the island of Manhattan alone. It was impossible to understand what the long-term consequences of such an assault might be. Approximately three thousand dead bodies were found in the wreckage of the streets. Nobody had any idea how many survivors of the strikes were still walking around, or how the voltage might have changed them on the inside. They didn't look any different, they looked exactly like everyone else, but they were no longer like everyone else, or so everyone else feared. Perhaps they were everyone else's enemies. Perhaps, if they were angry, they could stretch out their arms and unleash the thunderbolts they had absorbed, sending tens of thousands of amperes at our ancestors, frying them to a crisp. They could murder our ancestors' children, or the president. Who were these people? Why were they still alive?

People were close to panicking. But nobody, at that time, was looking for men and women with unusual ears. Everyone was listening to lightning tales.

The word that the hedge fund nabob and self-styled "shareholder activist" Seth Oldville had taken up with a notorious libertine and fisher-for-rich-men named Teresa Saca Cuartos came as a shock and disappointment to his wide circle of friends. A fellow like Oldville, a big clubbable guy who knew what he wanted, what he expected the world to make available to him, and how he expected the universe to adjust to the shape he chose to impose upon it, had the edge over most of his peers, and even after successive presidential elections emphatically rejected his preferred conservative ticket, which was incomprehensible to him, running counter to his understanding of the country he loved, he remained undeflected from the aggressive pursuit of his political and economic goals. In business you could ask the folks at Time Warner, Clorox, Sony, Yahoo or Dell about his methods and you'd get an earful, some of it unprintable. As to politics, like his late friend and mentor the great, if a little crooked, Bento Elfenbein, he dismissed the sequence of presidential routs as errors by the electorate, "turkeys voting for Thanksgiving," and set about picking candidates for the future, a governor to back here, a mayoral race to fund there, a young congressman on the rise to bankroll, backing his horses, preparing for the next battle. He called himself an atheist Jew who would have preferred to have been an opera singer or a great surfer, and in his early fifties he was still physically fit enough to go each summer in search of the big wave. Also after dinner in his townhouse he might treat the guests to an aria sung in his fine Joycean tenor, "E lucevan le stelle," perhaps, or "Ecco ridente in cielo," and everybody agreed he could give an excellent account of the music.

But Teresa Saca! Nobody had gone near that girl for years, not since she snared AdVenture Capital's iconic chief Elián Cuartos. She latched onto him in his senior years when all he wanted to do was leave AVC to his protégés and have a little overdue fun; got the ring; had his baby thanks to the miracle of in vitro; and waited him out. Now old Elián was gone and she had his cash, sure, but she had the bad rep to go with it also. For a brief moment the financial titan Daniel "Mac" Aroni tried her out "just to see what all the fuss was about" but he ran from her after a couple of weeks, complaining that she was the most bad-tempered, foulmouthed bitch he'd ever laid hands on. "She called me words I'd never heard, and I have a pretty good personal thesaurus in that area," he told everyone. "She'll try to tear your heart out and eat it raw, right on the sidewalk, and me, I was brought up right, I don't talk to women that way no matter the provocation, but that woman, in five minutes you're over the body and the sex, which they're both something, this is undeniable, but nothing's good enough to make up for her bad character, you just want to throw her out the car door on the Turnpike and go home to eat meatloaf with your wife."

Seth Oldville as it happened had a perfectly good wife at home, Cindy Sachs as was, a wife widely admired for her beauty, taste,

charitable work, and great goodness of heart. She could have been a
dancer, she had the gift, but when he asked for her hand she made
him her career instead, "Like Esther Williams," she told their
friends, "giving up her Hollywood career for the man she loved,
who wanted her at home." *Big mistake,* Seth used to joke, *settling for
me,* but lately there was no humor in her answering little smile. They
had married young, had a string of children quickly, and remained,
it must be said, each other's closest friends. But Oldville was a man
of a certain standing and type for whom the taking of a mistress was
par for the course. Teresa Saca must have seemed like perfect mistress material, she had her money now so she wouldn't be after his,
she had lived in the world of discretion for long enough to understand the consequences of kissing and telling, and she was lonely, so
a little companionship from a big man would please her and encour-
age her to do a lot of pleasing in return. But Oldville soon learned
what his friend Aroni already knew. Teresa was a raven-haired Floridian firecracker with an anger in her towards men whose origins
didn't bear examining, and her gift for verbal abuse was tiring. In
addition there were, as he told her in their break-up conversation,
just too many things she disliked. She would only eat in five restau-
rants. She disliked clothes in any color other than black. She was
unimpressed by his friends. Modern art, modern dance, movies with
subtitles, contemporary literature, all types of philosophy, these she
abhorred, but the mediocre neoclassicist nineteenth-century American pictures at the Met, those she much admired. She loved Disney
World but when he wanted to take her to Mexico for a romantic
getaway at Las Alamandas she said, "It's not my kind of place. Plus,
Mexico is dangerous, it would be like vacationing in Iraq." This,
with zero self-irony, from the daughter of Spanish immigrants living just one step up from the trailer park in Aventura, Florida.

Six weeks after he took up with her he kissed her goodbye on the
lawn of his place on Meadow Lane, Southampton (Cindy Oldville
loathed the seaside and stayed firmly planted in the city). There was

a man mowing the lawn riding a garden tractor wearing a wind-breaker with the words *Mr. Geronimo* on the back but he didn't exist for the fragmenting couple. "You think I'm sorry? I have options," Teresa told him. "I won't be shedding a tear over you. If you knew who wanted to date me right now you would die." Seth Oldville began to shake with repressed laughter. "So we're fourteen years old again?" he asked her but she was burning with injured pride. "I'm getting lipo next week," she said. "My doctor says I'm a great candidate, he doesn't have to do much and after that my body will be *insane*. This I was doing for you, to perfect myself, but my new boyfriend, he says he can. Not. Wait." Oldville began to walk away. "I'll send you photographs of what you can't have," she shouted after him. "You will *die*." That wasn't the end of it. In the weeks that followed a vengeful Teresa called Seth's wife repeatedly and even though Cindy Oldville hung up on her right away she left voicemail messages so sexually explicit and detailed that they pushed the Oldvilles towards divorce. Super-lawyers geared up for the fight. Wildenstein-divorce-settlement-type numbers were bruited about. People settled down to watch. For this bout you wanted a ringside seat. Seth Oldville looked crushed in those days. It wasn't about the money. The guy was genuinely sorry to have hurt his wife, who had done nothing but good things for him. He didn't want the war; but now, she did. She had spent a lifetime turning a blind eye, she told girlfriends, but now she had new glasses and saw everything in sharp focus, and enough, really, with her husband's entitled alpha-male crap. "Go get him," the girlfriend chorus sang.

On the weekend before the storm Seth was out at the beach place by himself and fell asleep in a reclining chair on the lawn. While he was asleep somebody came up to him and drew a red bull's-eye target on his forehead. It was the gardener fellow, Mr. Geronimo, who pointed it out to him when he woke up. In the mirror it looked like somebody was trying to simulate a Lyme disease tick bite but no, that wasn't it, it was plainly a threat. The security personnel were embarrassed. Yes, Miss Teresa had talked her way past them. She was a persuasive lady. It was a judgment call and they had gone the wrong way on this one. It wouldn't happen again.

Then the hurricane struck, and there followed the falling trees, the thunderbolt overload, the outages, all of it. "All of us were distracted by our own affairs in those days," Daniel Aroni said at the memorial service at the Society for Ethical Culture, "and none of us thought she was truly capable of fulfilling her threat, and in the middle of the storm at that, when the whole city was trying to survive, it was, let me confess, unexpected. As his friend I am ashamed that I wasn't more alert to the danger, that I didn't warn him to raise his guard." After the eulogies the same image was in everyone's mind's eye as they spilled out onto Central Park West: the rain-bedraggled woman at the door of the townhouse, the first security man blown away, a second coming at her and sent toppling backwards, the woman running through the house, up towards his sanctum, screaming *Where are you, motherfucker,* until he just walked out in front of her, sacrificing himself to save his wife and children, and she murdered him right there and he toppled down the red-carpet stairs like an oak. For a moment she knelt by his body soaked to the skin as she was and weeping uncontrollably and then she ran from the house; nobody stopped her, nobody dared approach.

But the question nobody could answer, not at the time, not at the memorial, was the question of the nature of the weapon. No bullet holes were found in any of the three dead bodies. All the bodies, when the police and the emergency medical teams arrived, smelled strongly of burning flesh, and their garments too had been burned. Cindy Oldville's testimony was scarcely credible, and many people discounted it as the forgivable error of a woman in a state of extreme terror, but she was the only eyewitness and what she said her eyes witnessed was what the less reputable parts of the news media seized upon and magnified into two-inch headlines, the lightning bolts streaming from Teresa Saca's fingertips, the white forking voltage pouring out of her, doing her deadly work. One tabloid called her *Madame Magneto*. Another preferred a *Star Wars* reference: *The Empress Strikes Back*. Things had reached a point at which only science fiction gave people a way of getting a handle on what the formerly real world's non-CGI mundanity seemed incapable of making comprehensible.

And at once there was more electricity news: at the terminus of the 6 train at Pelham Bay Park, an eight-year-old girl fell onto the tracks and the steel melted like ice cream, allowing the girl to be rescued unharmed. At a safe deposit facility near Wall Street burglars succeeded in using an unidentified weapon to "burn open" the doors of safes, vaults and boxes, and made off with an unspecified sum in the "multiple millions of dollars," according to a spokesman for the facility. Mayor Rosa Fast, under political pressure to act, called a joint press conference with the police commissioner and grimly declared all recent lightning-strike survivors to be "persons of interest," which was, in her own ashamed opinion, clearly written across her face, a betrayal of her progressive liberalism. Her statement was predictably condemned by civil liberties groups, political rivals and many newspaper columnists. But the old liberal-conservative opposition lost its meaning when reality gave up being rational, or at least dialectic, and became willful, inconsistent, and absurd. If a boy rubbing a lamp had summoned a genie to do his bidding, that would have been a credible event in the new world our ancestors had begun to inhabit. But their senses had been dulled by long exposure to the everydayness of the everyday and it was hard for them even to accept that they had entered an age of wonders, much less to know how to live in such a time.

They had so much to learn. They had to learn to stop saying *genie* and associating the word with pantomime, or with Barbara Eden in pink harem pants on TV, blonde "Jeannie" in love with Larry Hagman, an astronaut who became her "master." It was extremely unwise to believe that such potent, slippery beings could have masters. The name of the immense force that had entered the world was *jinn*.

She, Dunia, had also loved a mortal man—never her "master"—and many lobeless children were the consequence of that love. Dunia searched out her earmarked descendants wherever they were. Teresa Saca, Jinendra Kapoor, Baby Storm, Hugo Casterbridge, many more. All she could do was plant in their minds the knowledge of who they were and of their scattered tribe. All she could do was awaken the bright jinn within them and guide them towards the light. Not all of them were good people. In many of them human weakness proved more potent than jinni strength. This was a problem. As the slits between the worlds broke open the mischief of the dark jinn began to spread. At first, before they began to dream of conquest, the jinn had no grand design. They created havoc because it was in their nature. Mischief and its senior sibling, real harm, they foisted without compunction upon the world; for just as the jinn were not real to most human beings, so also human beings were not real to the jinn, who cared nothing for their pain, any more than a child cares for the pain of a stuffed animal she bangs against a wall.

The influence of the jinn was everywhere, but in those early days, before they fully revealed themselves, many of our ancestors did not see their hidden hands at work, in the collapse of a nuclear reactor, the gang rape of a young woman, or an avalanche. In a Romanian village a woman started laying eggs. In a French town the citizenry began turning into rhinoceroses. Old Irish people took to living in trash cans. A Belgian man looked into a mirror and saw the back of his head reflected in it. A Russian official lost his nose and then saw it walking around St. Petersburg by itself. A narrow cloud sliced across a full moon and a Spanish lady gazing up at it felt a sharp pain as a razor blade cut her eyeball in half and the vitreous humor, the gelatinous matter filling the space between the lens and the retina, flowed out. Ants crawled out of a hole in a man's palm.

How were such things to be understood? It was easier to believe that Chance, always the hidden principle of the universe, was joining forces with allegory, symbolism, surrealism and chaos, and taking charge of human affairs, than it was to accept the truth, namely the growing interference of the jinn in the daily life of the world.

When the rake, restaurateur and man-about-town Giacomo Donizetti first left his hometown of Venice, Italy, as a young fellow of thirteen and set out on his travels, his mother, a Black Jew of Cochin who had married his Italian Catholic father at the Sri Aurobindo ashram in Pondicherry when they were both spiritual and young—with the Mother herself, Mirra Alfassa, performing the ceremony at the age of ninety-three!—gave him a parting gift: a square of chamois leather folded into the shape of an envelope and tied with a scarlet bow. "Here is your city," she told him. "Never open this package. Your home will always be with you, safe inside, wherever you may roam." So he carried Venice with him across the world until news reached him of his mother's death. That night he got the folded leather down from its place of safekeeping and undid the scarlet bow, which fell to pieces in his fingers. He opened the chamois envelope and found nothing inside, because love has no visible form. At that moment love, shapeless invisible love, fluttered up and away from him and he couldn't have it anymore. The idea of home too, of feeling at home in the world wherever he was, that illusion vanished as well. After that he seemed to live as other men did but he could not fall in love or settle down and in the end he began to think of those losses as advantages, because in their stead came the conquest of many women in many places.

He developed a specialty: the love of unhappily married ladies. Almost every married woman he met was to some degree unhappy in her marriage, though the majority of them were unprepared to end it. For his own part, he was determined never to be caught in any woman's matrimonial web. So they had the right things in common,

Signor Donizetti and the *Malmaritate,* as he privately called them, the borderless nation of the gloomily espoused. The ladies felt gratitude for his attentions and he in his turn was unfailingly grateful to them. "Gratitude is the secret of success with women," he wrote in his secret journal. He kept a record of his conquests in this oddly ledger-like book, and if his claims were to be believed they numbered many thousands. Then one day his luck changed.

After a night of strenuous lovemaking, Donizetti liked to seek out a well-run Turkish bathhouse, or *hammam,* and allow himself to be heated, steamed and scrubbed. It is probable that it was in one such establishment in Nolita that a jinn whispered to him.

The dark jinn were whisperers. Becoming invisible, they placed their lips against the chests of human beings and murmured softly into their hearts, overpowering their victims' will. On occasion the act of possession was so profound that the individual self dissolved and the jinn actually inhabited the body of his victim. But even in cases of less-than-full possession, good people, when whispered to, became capable of bad deeds, bad folk of worse. The bright jinn whispered too, steering humanity towards acts of nobility, generosity, humility, kindness and grace, but their whispers were less effective, which may suggest that the human race falls more naturally towards the dark, or, alternatively, that the dark jinn, especially the handful of Grand Ifrits, are the most powerful of all the members of the jinn world. That is a matter for philosophers to argue about. We can only record what happened when the jinn, after a long absence, returned to the lower of the Two Worlds—our world—and declared war upon it, or rather *within* it. The so-called War of the Worlds which wrought such havoc upon the earth was not only a battle between the jinn world and our own but became, in addition, a civil war among the jinn fought out on our territory, not theirs. The human race became the battleground for the struggle between the bright and the dark. And, it must be said, on account of the essentially anarchic nature of the jinn, between brightness and brightness, and the dark and the dark.

Our ancestors learned, during those two years, eight months and twenty-eight nights, to be constantly on their guard against the dangers of the jinn. The safety of their children became a deep concern. They began to leave lights on in their children's bedrooms and locked their windows even if the boys and girls complained that the rooms were airless and stuffy. Some of the jinn were child snatchers and no one could say what became of the children they seized. Also: it was a good idea, when entering an empty room, to go in right foot first while muttering *excuse me* under one's breath. And above all: it was wise not to bathe in the dark because the jinn were attracted to darkness and moisture. The *hammam,* with its low light levels and high humidity, was a place of considerable danger. All this our ancestors came to know gradually during those years. But when Giacomo Donizetti entered the well-appointed Turkish baths on Elizabeth Street, he did not know the risk he was taking. A mischievous jinn must have been waiting for him, because when he left the *hammam* he was a changed man.

In short: women no longer fell in love with him, no matter how gratefully he wooed them; whereas he had only to glance at a woman to tumble helplessly, hopelessly into a horrible puppyish love. Wherever he went, at work or play or in the street, he dressed with his familiar sharpness, in a three-thousand-dollar bespoke suit, Charvet shirt and Hermès tie, yet no woman swooned, while every female who crossed his path set his heart pounding, turned his legs to jelly and inspired in him an overwhelming desire to send her a large bouquet of pink roses. He wept in the street as three-hundred-pound pedicurists and ninety-pound anorexics rushed past him ignoring his protestations as if he were a drunk or panhandler and not one of the most sought-after bachelors on at least four continents. His business colleagues asked him to stay away from work because he was embarrassing the hatcheck girls, waitresses and maîtresses d' at his various nightlife hotspots. Within a few days his life became a torment to him. He sought medical help, willing to be declared a sex addict if necessary, though fearing the cure. However, in the doctor's waiting room he felt obliged to fall to one knee and ask the homely Korean American receptionist if she would consider doing him the honor of becoming his wife. She showed him her wedding band and pointed to the photograph of her children on her desk and he burst into tears and had to be asked to leave.

He began to fear both the randomness of the sidewalk and the erotic thrum of enclosed spaces. In the city streets the overload of women to fall in love with was so great that he genuinely feared a heart seizure. All interiors were dangerous because so few of them were single-sex. Elevators were particularly humiliating because he was trapped with ladies who spurned him with expressions of faint, or not so faint, disgust. He sought out all-male clubs where he could sleep fitfully in a leather armchair, and he seriously considered the monastic life. Alcohol and narcotics offered an easier and less taxing escape, and he spiraled downwards towards self-destruction.

One night as he staggered towards his Ferrari he understood with the true clarity of the drunk that he was friendless, that nobody loved him, that everything on which he had based his life was tawdry and as cheap as fool's gold, and that he almost certainly ought not to be driving a motor vehicle. He remembered being taken by one of his amours, back in the day when he was the one in the driving seat, to see the only Bollywood movie of his life, in which a man and a woman contemplating suicide on the Brooklyn Bridge see each other, like what they see, decide not to jump, and go to Las Vegas instead. He wondered if he should drive to the bridge and prepare to jump and hope to be rescued by a beautiful movie star who would love him forever as deeply as he loved her. But then he remembered that thanks to the occult consequences of the new strangeness that gripped him, he would continue to fall in love with every woman who crossed his path on the bridge or in Vegas or wherever they ended up, so that the movie goddess would undoubtedly dump him and he would be even more miserable than before.

He was no longer a man. He had become a beast in the thrall of the monster Love, *la belle dame sans merci* herself, multiplying herself and inhabiting the bodies of all the world's *dames* whether *belles* or not, and he needed to go home and lock the door and hope that he was suffering from a curable illness that would eventually run its course and allow him to resume his normal life, although at that moment the word *normal* seemed to have lost its meaning. Yes, home, he urged himself, accelerating towards his Lower Manhattan penthouse, the Ferrari adding its own dose of recklessness to the driver's, and at a certain moment on a certain intersection in the least fashionable part of the island there was a pickup truck with on its sides the words *Mr. Geronimo Gardener* and a phone number and website URL blocked out in yellow and drop-shadowed in scarlet and the Ferrari jumping the light was clearly in the wrong and then there were frantic turnings of driving wheels and screechings of brakes and it was okay, nobody died, the Ferrari took some heavy damage to a fender and there was gardening equipment spilling onto the roadway from the back of the pickup, but both drivers were ambulatory, they got out without assistance to examine the damage, and that was when Giacomo Donizetti, dizzy and trembling, finally knew he had lost his mind, and fainted right there in the street, because the physically imposing older man coming towards him was walking on air, several inches off the ground.

More than a year had passed since Mr. Geronimo lost contact with the earth. During that time the gap between the soles of his feet and solid horizontal surfaces had increased and was now three and a half, perhaps even four inches wide. In spite of the obviously alarming aspects of his condition, as he had begun to call it, he found it impossible to think of it as permanent. He envisaged his condition as an illness, the product of a previously unknown virus: a gravity bug. The infection would pass, he told himself. Something inexplicable had happened to him, whose effects would surely fade. Normality would reassert itself. The laws of nature could not be defied for long, even by a sickness unknown to the Centers for Disease Control. In the end he would certainly descend. This was how he sought to reassure himself every day. Consequently the inescapable signs of the worsening of his condition hit him hard and it took much of his remaining willpower to suppress feelings of panic. Frequently, without any warning, his thoughts began to swim wildly about, even though he prided himself on being for the most part a stoical individual. What was happening to him was impossible, but it was happening, so it was possible. The meanings of words—*possible, impossible*—were changing. Could science explain it to him? Could religion? The idea that there might be no explanation and no cure was a notion he was not willing to entertain. He began to delve into the literature. Gravitons were elementary particles with no mass that somehow transmitted gravitational pull. Maybe they could be created or destroyed and if so that could account for an increase or decrease in gravitational force. That was the news according to quantum physics. But, PS, there was no proof that gravitons actually existed. Quantum physics, thanks a lot, he thought. You've been a great help.

Like many older persons, Mr. Geronimo led a relatively isolated life. There were no children or grandchildren to fret about his condition. This was a relief to him. He felt relieved also that he had not remarried, so that there was no woman to whom he was a cause of grief or concern. Over the long years of his widowerhood his few friends had responded to his taciturn ways by withdrawing from him, becoming mere acquaintances. After his wife died he sold their home and moved into modest rental accommodation in Kips Bay, the last forgotten neighborhood in Manhattan, whose anonymity suited him perfectly. Once he had had a friendly relationship with his barber on Second Avenue but nowadays he cut his hair himself, becoming, as he preferred to put it, the gardener of his own head.

The Koreans at the corner bodega were professionally cordial, though lately, as a younger generation took over from its parents, he was sometimes received with blank stares that revealed the ignorance of youth, instead of the faint smiles and small acknowledging nods with which the bespectacled elders had greeted a longtime customer. The many medical institutions along First Avenue had infected the neighborhood with a plague of doctors but he was contemptuous of the medical profession. He no longer went to see his own doctor and the admonitory texts from that gentleman's assistant, *We need to see you at least once a year if you want to continue the relationship with Dr.——,* had stopped coming. What use did he have for doctors? Could a pill cure his condition? No, it could not. American medical care invariably failed those who needed it most. He wanted nothing to do with it. Your health was what you had until the day you didn't have it and after that day you were screwed and it was better not to let doctors screw you before that day came.

On the rare occasions that his phone rang, it was invariably a gardening matter, and the longer his condition continued, the harder it was for him to work. He had handed off his clientele to other gardeners and was living now off his savings. There was the nest egg he had accumulated over the years, which was not insubstantial, on account of his thrifty lifestyle and the proceeds from the sale of the marital home, but, on the other hand, nobody ever went into the gardening business to accumulate a fortune. There was Ella's inheritance too, which she had described as "next to nothing," but that was because she had grown up rich. It was in fact quite a tidy sum and had passed to him after her death and he had never touched it. So he had time, but a moment would inevitably come, if things remained as they were, when the money would be gone and he would be at fortune's mercy—Fortune, that merciless hag. So yes, he worried about money, but, again, he was happy he was not inflicting those worries on anyone else.

It was no longer possible to conceal what was happening from his neighbors, from people on the sidewalk, or in the stores he had to enter from time to time to buy provisions, though he had his hoarded supplies of soups and cereals, and he raided that larder to minimize his excursions. When he needed to restock he shopped online, often ordered for delivery when he was hungry, and went out less and less, except, occasionally, under cover of darkness. In spite of all his precautions, however, his condition was known to the neighborhood. He was lucky to live amongst people with a low boredom threshold, famous for their jaundiced, seen-it-all uninterest in their fellow citizens' eccentricities. Hearing of his levitation, the neighborhood was largely unimpressed, assuming, with minimal discussion, that it must be some kind of trick. The fact that he continued to perform the same trick day after day made him tiresome, a stilt walker who never got off his stilts, an exhibitionist whose "wow" factor had long since evaporated. Or, if he was in some way damaged, if something had gone wrong, it was probably his fault. Probably he had been meddling in stuff that was best not meddled with. Or, the world was sick of him and was kicking him out. Whatever. The bottom line was, his shtick had gotten old, like him.

So for a time he was ignored, which made things a little easier, because he had no desire to explain himself to strangers. He stayed home and made calculations. Three and a half inches in one year meant that in three years' time, if he was still alive, he would still be less than a foot off the ground. At that rate, he comforted himself, he should be able to work out survival techniques that would give him a livable life—not a conventional or easy existence, but one that should be workable. There were practical problems to be solved, however, some of them very awkward. Taking a bath was out of the question. Fortunately there was a shower cubicle in the bathroom. Performing his natural functions was trickier. When he tried to sit down on the toilet his behind obstinately hovered above the seat, maintaining exactly the same distance from it as his feet insisted on keeping from the ground. The higher he got, the harder it would be to shit. This needed to be considered.

Travel was already a problem, and would become a much bigger one. He had already ruled out air travel. He might strike a TSA officer as constituting some sort of threat. Only aircraft were permitted to take off at airports. A passenger trying to do so without boarding a plane could very easily be seen as acting improperly and needing to be restrained. Other forms of public transportation were also problematic. In the subway his levitation might be mistaken for an illegal effort to vault the turnstiles. Nor could he drive safely anymore. The accident had made that clear. That left walking, but even nocturnal walking was too visible and vulnerable, no matter how indifferent people acted. Perhaps it would be best to stay put in his apartment. An enforced retirement until the condition eased and he could go back to what remained of everyday life. But that was difficult to contemplate. After all, he was a man accustomed to life in the outdoors, doing hard physical work for many hours a day, in sunshine and in rain, in heat and cold, adding his own small sense of beauty to the natural beauty of the earth. If he could not work, he would still have to exercise. To walk. Yes. To walk at night.

Mr. Geronimo lived on the lowest two floors of The Bagdad, a narrow apartment building on a narrow block which might have been the least fashionable block in that least fashionable of neighborhoods, his narrow living room at the level of the narrow street and his narrow bedroom in the narrow basement below. During the great storm The Bagdad had been inside the evacuation zone but the floodwaters had not quite reached his basement. It had been a narrow escape; the adjacent streets, broader, opening their arms to the elements, had been battered. Perhaps there was a lesson to be learned, Mr. Geronimo thought. Perhaps narrowness survived attacks better than breadth. But that was an unattractive lesson and he didn't want to learn it. Capaciousness, inclusiveness, everything-at-once-ness, breadth, width, depth, *bigness:* these were the values to which a tall, long-striding, broad-shouldered man like himself should cleave. And if the world wanted to preserve the narrow and to destroy the expansive, favoring the pinched mouth over wide fleshy lips, the emaciated body over the ample frame, the tight over the loose, the whine over the roar, he would prefer to go down with that big ship.

His own narrow home might have withstood the storm, but it had not protected him. For unknown reasons the storm had affected him uniquely—if indeed the storm was responsible—separating him to his growing alarm from the home soil of his species. It was hard not to ask *why me,* but he had begun to grasp the difficult truth that a thing could have a cause but that was not the same as having a purpose. Even if you could work out how a certain thing had come about—even if you answered the *how* question—you would be no closer to solving the *why.* Anomalies of nature, like diseases, did not respond to inquiries about their motivation. Still, he thought, the *how* bothered him. He tried to present a brave face to the mirror—he had to stoop uncomfortably, now, to see himself while he shaved—but the fear mounted daily.

The apartment in The Bagdad was a kind of absence, not only narrow but minimally furnished. He had always been a man of few needs and after his wife's death he needed nothing except what he could not have: her presence in his life. He had discarded possessions, shedding burdens, keeping nothing but what was essential, lightening his load. It did not occur to him that this process of divesting himself of the physical aspects of his past, of letting go, might be related to his condition. Now, as he rose, he began to clutch at scraps of memory, as though their cumulative weight might bring him back down to earth. He remembered himself and Ella with microwaved popcorn in a bowl and a blanket across their laps, watching a movie on TV, an epic in which a Chinese boy-king was raised in the Forbidden City in Beijing believing himself to be God but, after many changes, ended up as a gardener working in the very palace in which he had formerly been a deity. The god/gardener said he was happy with his new life, which may have been true. Maybe, thought Mr. Geronimo, it's the other way around with me. Maybe I am slowly ascending towards the divine. Or maybe this city, and all cities, will soon be forbidden to me.

When he was a child he often had a flying dream. In the dream he was lying in his own bed in his own bedroom and was able to rise lightly up towards the ceiling, his bedsheet dropping from him as he rose. Then in his pajamas he floated about, carefully avoiding the slowly rotating blades of the ceiling fan. He could even turn the room upside down and sit on the ceiling giggling at the furniture down there on the inverted floor and wondering why it didn't fall down, that is to say up, towards the ceiling, which was now the floor. As long as he stayed in his room the flying was effortless. But his room had long high windows which stayed open at night to let in the breeze and if he was foolish enough to fly out through them he found that his house was on top of a hill (it wasn't, in his waking hours) and that he immediately began to lose height—slowly, not frighteningly, but inexorably—and he knew that if he didn't fly back inside the moment would come when his bedroom would be lost to him and he'd descend slowly to the bottom of the hill, where there were what his mother called "strangers and dangers." He always managed to make it back through the bedroom windows but sometimes it was a close-run thing. This memory too he turned upside down. Maybe now groundedness depended on him staying in his room, while every foray into the outdoors led to his becoming more detached.

He turned on the television. The magic baby was on the news. He noticed that the magic baby and he both had the same ears. And both of them now lived in the universe of magic, having become detached from the old, familiar, grounded continuum. He took comfort from the magic baby. Its existence meant that he was not alone in departing from what he was beginning to understand was no longer the norm.

The car accident hadn't been his fault, but driving was awkward and uncomfortable now and his reflexes were not what they should be. He was lucky to have escaped without serious injury. After the accident the other driver, a playboy type called Giacomo Donizetti, had regained consciousness in a kind of delirium and had shouted at him like a man possessed, "What are you doing up there? You think you're better than the rest of us? Is that why you hold yourself apart? The earth isn't good enough for you, you have to be higher than everyone else? What are you, some kind of fucking *radical*? Look what you did to my beautiful car with your pathetic truck. I hate people

like you. Fucking *elitist.*" After delivering these words Signor Donizetti passed out again and the paramedics arrived and took care of
him.

Shock made people behave strangely, Mr. Geronimo knew, but he
was beginning to be aware of a certain budding hostility in the eyes
of at least some people who observed his condition. Perhaps he was
more alarming at night. Perhaps he should just bite the bullet and
walk around in the daylight hours. But then the objections to his
condition would multiply. Yes, the familiar indifference of the citizenry had protected him thus far, but it might not guard him against
the accusation of a bizarre type of snobbery, and the further he rose,
the greater the antagonism might be. This idea, that he was setting
himself apart, that his levitation was a judgment on the earthbound,
that in his extraordinary state he was looking down on ordinary people, was beginning to be visible in the eyes of strangers, or he was
beginning to think he saw it there. Why do you imagine I consider
my condition an improvement? he wanted to cry out. Why, when it
has ruined my life and I fear it may bring about my early death?

He longed for a way "down." Could any branch of science help
him? If not quantum theory, maybe something else? He had read
about "gravity boots" that allowed their wearers to hang down from
the ceiling. Could they be adjusted to allow their wearers to cling to
the floor? Could anything be done, or was he beyond the reach of
medicine and science? Had real life simply become irrelevant? Had
he been captured by the surreal, and would he soon be devoured by
it? Was there any way of thinking about his plight that made any
ordinary kind of sense? And was he in fact infectious or contagious
or capable in some other way of transmitting his condition to others?

How long did he have?

Levitation was not an entirely unknown phenomenon. Small living creatures, frogs for example, had been levitated in laboratory
conditions by electromagnets that used superconductors and produced something he did not understand, the diamagnetic repulsion
of body water. Human beings were mostly made up of water, so

might this be a clue to what was happening to him? But in that case where were the giant electromagnets, the huge superconductors that were creating the effect? Had the earth itself become a gigantic electromagnet/superconductor? And if so why was he the only living creature to be affected? Or was he for some biochemical or supernatural reason preternaturally sensitive to the changes in the planet—in which case, would everyone else soon be in the same boat as he was? Was he the guinea pig for what would eventually be the earth's rejection of the entire human race?

Look, here on his computer screen was something else he didn't understand. The levitation of ultrasmall objects had been achieved by manipulating the Casimir Force. As he struggled to explore the subatomic world of this force, he understood that at the deeper levels of the essence of matter the English language disintegrated under the immense pressure of the foundational forces of the universe and was replaced by the language of creation itself, *isospin doublet, Noether's theorem, rotation transformation, up and down quarks, Pauli exclusion principle, topological winding number density, De Rham cohomology, hedgehog space, disjoint union, spectral asymmetry, Cheshire Cat principle,* all of which was beyond his comprehension. Maybe Lewis Carroll who created the Cheshire Cat knew that its principle was somewhere near the roots of matter. Maybe something Casimirish was at work in his personal circumstances, and then again maybe not. If he saw himself in the eye of the cosmos then he might well be an ultrasmall object upon whom such a Force could work.

He understood that his mind, like his body, was detaching itself from solid ground. This had to stop. He had to concentrate on simple things. And the simple thing on which he had most particularly to concentrate was that he was hovering several inches above all solid planes: the ground, the floor of his apartment, beds, car seats, toilet seats. Once and once only he attempted a handstand and found that when he tried a trick like that his hands instantly developed the same condition as his feet. He fell heavily, and lay flat on his back, winded, hovering an inch above the rug. The empty space barely cushioned the fall. After the fall he moved more carefully. He was, and had to treat himself as, a seriously sick man. He was feeling his age, and there was something even worse to be faced. His condition was not only affecting his health, weakening his muscles, making him old; it was also erasing his character, replacing it with a new self. He was no longer himself, no longer Raffy-'Ronnimus-the-pastor's-sonnimus, no longer Uncle Charles's nephew or Bento Elfenbein's son-in-law or his beloved Ella's heartbroken husband. He was no longer Mr. Geronimo of the Mr. Geronimo Gardener landscaping firm, nor even his most recent self, the Lady Philosopher's lover and her manager Oldcastle's enemy. History had slipped away from him, and in his own eyes as well as others' he was becoming, he had become, nothing more or less than the man who was three and a half inches off the ground. Three and a half inches, and rising.

He was paying his rent promptly but he worried that Sister would find a pretext to expel him from the building. Sister C. C. Allbee, the super or—her preferred title—"landlady" of The Bagdad, was, at least in her own opinion, a broad-minded woman, but she did not care for what was happening on the news. Storm Doe, the baby of truth, for example—that little child freaked her out just like all the other horror-movie kids, Carrie White, Damien Thorn, all that demon seed. And what came after Baby Storm was just crazy. A woman pursued by a would-be rapist turned into a bird and made her escape. The video was embedded on the kind of news websites Sister followed and was also up on YouTube. A peeping tom spying on one of the city's favorite "angels," the Brazilian lingerie goddess Marpessa Sägebrecht, was turned by magic into an antlered stag and pursued down Avenue A by a pack of ravenous phantom hounds. Then things got even worse right in Times Square, where, for a period of time variously described by different witnesses as "a few seconds" and "several minutes," the clothes worn by every man in the square disappeared, leaving them shockingly naked, while the contents of their pockets—cellphones, pens, keys, credit cards, currency, condoms, sexual insecurities, inflatable egos, women's underwear, guns, knives, the phone numbers of unhappily married women, hip flasks, masks, cologne, photographs of angry daughters, photographs of sullen teenage boys, breath-freshening strips, plastic baggies containing white powder, spliffs, lies, harmonicas, spectacles, bullets, and broken, forgotten hopes—tumbled down to the ground. A few seconds (or maybe minutes) later the clothes reappeared but the nakedness of the men's revealed possessions, weaknesses and indiscretions unleashed a storm of contradictory emotions, including shame, anger and fear. Women ran screaming while the men scrambled for their secrets, which could be put back into their revenant pockets but which, having been revealed, could no longer be concealed.

Sister wasn't and had never been a nun but folks called her Sister because of her religious temperament and a supposed resemblance to the actress Whoopi Goldberg. Nobody had called her C.C. since her late husband departed this life with a buxom younger person of the Latina persuasion and ended up in hell, or Albuquerque, which were just two names for the same one place, Sister said. Seemed like ever since his New Mexican "demise" the whole world was going to hell in sympathy with that loser. Sister Allbee had had enough of it. She was familiar with a certain type of American crazy. Gun crazy was normal to her, shooting-kids-at-school or putting-on-a-Joker-mask-and-mowing-people-down-in-a-mall or just plain murdering-your-mom-at-breakfast crazy, Second Amendment crazy, that was just the everyday crazy that kept going down and there was nothing you could do about it if you loved freedom; and she understood knife crazy from her younger days in the Bronx, and the knockout-game type of crazy that persuaded young black kids it was cool to punch Jews in the face. She could comprehend drug crazy and politician crazy and Westboro Baptist Church crazy and Trump crazy because those things, they were the American way, but this new crazy was different. It felt 9/11 crazy: foreign, evil. The devil was on the loose, Sister said, loudly and often. The devil was at work. When one of her tenants started floating several inches off the floor at all times of day and night, then it was plain that the devil had come into her own building, and where was Jesus when you needed him. "Jesus," she said aloud standing right in the little hallway of The Bagdad, "you got to step down to earth one more time, I got God's work right here for you to do."

That was where Blue Yasmeen, the artist (performance, installations, graffiti) living on the top floor of The Bagdad, came in. Mr. Geronimo didn't know her, hadn't cared to get to know her, but all of a sudden he had an ally, a friend speaking on his behalf who had the Indian sign on Sister, or so it seemed. "Leave him alone," Blue Yasmeen said, and Sister made a face and did as she was asked. Sister's fondness for Yasmeen was as surprising as it was deep, it was one of the myriad improbable liaisons of the great city, the loves that caught the lovers by surprise, and maybe it had its roots in talk, Yasmeen being quite the talker and Sister hypnotized by her words. Baghdad, Iraq, that's a tragedy, Blue Yasmeen liked to say, but Bagdad-with-no-*h,* that's a magic location, that's the Aladdin-city of stories that winds around actual cities like a creeper, in and out of actual city streets, whispering in our ears, and in that parasite-city stories are the fruit hanging from every tree, tall tales and short ones, thin tales and fat, and nobody who hungers for an anecdote goes unsatisfied. That rich fruit falls from branches to lie bruised in the street and anyone can pick it up. I build that flying-carpet city wherever I can, she said, I grow it in the paved backyards of downtown condominiums and the stairwell graffiti of the projects. That Bagdad is my city and I am both its monarch and its citizen, its shopper and its storekeeper, its drinker and its wine. And you, she told Sister Allbee, you are its caretaker. The landlady of The Bagdad: superintendent of storyland. Here you stand at its very heart. That kind of talk melted Sister's heart. Mr. Geronimo is turning out to be one hell of a story, Blue Yasmeen told her. Let him be so we can see how he comes out.

Blue Yasmeen's hair wasn't blue, it was orange, and her name wasn't Yasmeen. Never mind. If she said blue was orange that was her right, and Yasmeen was her nom de guerre and yeah, she lived in the city as if it were a war zone because even though she had been born on 116th Street to a Columbia literature professor and his wife she wanted to recognize that *originally, before that,* which was to say *before fucking birth,* she came from Beirut. She had shaved off her eyebrows and tattooed new ones in their place, in jagged lightning-bolt shapes. Her body too was a tat zone. All the tattoos except the eyebrows were words, the usual ones, *Love Imagine Yeezy Occupy,* and she said of herself, unintentionally proving that there was more in her of Riverside Drive than Hamra Street, that she was intratextual as well as intrasexual, she lived between the words as well as the sexes. Blue Yasmeen had made a splash in the art world with her Guantánamo Bay installation, which was impressive if only for the powers of persuasion required to make it happen at all: she somehow got that impenetrable facility to allow her to set a chair in a room with a video camera facing it, and linked that to a dummy sitting in a Chelsea art gallery, so that when inmates sat in the Guantánamo chair room and told their stories their faces were projected onto the head of the Chelsea dummy and it was if she had freed them and given them their voices, and yeah, the issue was freedom, mother-fuckers, freedom, she hated terrorism as much as anyone, but she hated miscarriages of justice too, and, FYI, just in case you were wondering, just in case you had her down as a religious-fanatic ter-rorist in waiting, she had no time for God, plus she was a pacifist and a vegan, so fuck *you.*

She was something of a downtown celebrity, *world famous on twenty blocks,* she said, at the story-slam sessions run by the "Day of the Locusts" people, who took their name not from Nathanael West's novel (which was *locust* singular) but from the Dylan song (*locusts* plural): *the locusts sang, and they were singing for me.* The Locusts story events were movable feasts, switching locations around the city, and though they were called Days the events took place, obviously, at night, and Blue Yasmeen was a star at the mic, telling her tales of Bagdad-with-no-*h*.

Once in old Bagdad, Blue Yasmeen said, *a merchant was owed money by a local nobleman, really quite a lot of money, and then unexpectedly the nobleman died and the merchant thought, This is bad, I'm not going to get paid. But a god had given him the gift of transmigration, this was in a part of the world in which there were many gods, not just one, so the merchant had the idea of migrating his spirit into the dead lord's body so that the dead man could get up from his deathbed and pay him what he owed. The merchant left his body in a safe place, or so he thought, and his spirit jumped into the dead man's skin, but when he was walking the dead man's body to the bank he had to pass through the fish market and a large dead codfish lying on a slab saw him go past and started to laugh. When people heard the dead fish laughing they knew there was something fishy about the walking dead man and attacked him for being possessed by a demon. The dead nobleman's body quickly became uninhabitable and the merchant's spirit had to abandon it and make its way back to its own abandoned shell. But some other people had found the merchant's aban-doned body and, thinking it the body of a dead man, had set it on fire ac-cording to the customs of that part of the world. So the merchant had no body and had not been paid what he owed and his spirit is probably still wandering somewhere in the market. Or maybe he ended up migrating into a dead fish and swam away into the ocean of the streams of story. And the moral of the story is, don't push your fucking luck.*

And also:

There was once, in Old Bagdad, a very, very tall house, a house like a vertical boulevard leading upwards to the glass observatory from which its owner, a very, very rich man, looked down upon the tiny swarming human anthills of the low sprawling city far below. It was the tallest house in the city, set upon the highest hill, and it was not made of brick, steel or stone but, rather, of the purest pride. The floors were tiles of highly polished pride that never lost its sheen, the walls were of the noblest hau-teur, and the chandeliers dripped with crystal arrogance. Grand gilded mirrors stood everywhere, reflecting the owner not in silver or mercury but in the most flattering of reflective materials, which is amour propre. *So great was its owner's pride in his new home that it mysteriously infected all those who were privileged to visit him there, so that nobody ever said a word against the idea of building such a tall house in such a short city.*

But after the rich man and his family moved in they were plagued by bad luck. Feet were accidentally broken, precious vases dropped, and somebody was always sick. Nobody slept well. The rich man's business was unaffected, because he never conducted it at home, but the jinx on the house's occupants led the rich man's wife to call in an expert on the spiritual aspects of homes, and when she heard that the house had been permanently cursed with ill fortune, probably by a jinni friendly to the ant people, she made the rich man and their family and their one thousand and one minions and their one hundred and sixty motor cars leave the tall house and move into one of their many shorter residences, houses built of the ordinary sort of materials, and they lived happily thereafter, even the rich man, although injured pride is the hardest of all injuries to recover from, a fracture to a man's dignity and self-regard is much worse than a broken foot, and takes much longer to heal.

After the rich family moved out of the tall house the ants of the city began to swarm up its walls, the ants and the lizards and the snakes, and the wilderness of the city invaded the living spaces, creepers twined around the four-poster beds, and spiky grass grew up through the priceless silk Bukhari rugs. Ants everywhere, making the place their own, and gradually the fabric of the place was worn down by the marching the grasping the sheer presence *of the ants, a billion ants, more than a billion, the arrogance of the chandeliers splintered and broke under their collective weight, shattered shards of arrogance plummeted to the floors whose pride had grown dim and dirty, the fabric of pride of which the carpets and tapestries were made had been eroded by those billion tiny feet, marching, marching, grasping, grasping, and simply being* present, *existing, ruining the whole point of the pride of the tall building, which could no longer deny their existence, which crumbled under the fact of their being, of their billion tiny feet, of their ant-ness. The hauteur of the walls gave way, fell away like cheap plaster, and revealed the flimsiness of the building's frame; and the mirrors of* amour propre *cracked from side to side, and all was ruin, that glorious edifice had become a wormhole, an insectarium, an anthillia. And of course in the end it fell, it crumbled like dust and was blown away, but the ants lived, and the lizards and mosquitoes and snakes, and the rich family lived too, everybody lived, everyone remained the same, and soon enough everyone forgot the house, even the man who built it, and it was as if it had never been, and nothing changed, nothing had changed, nothing could change, nothing would ever change.*

Her father the professor, so handsome, so smart, a little vain, was dead but she tried every day to bring his ideas to life. We were all trapped in stories, she said, just as he used to say, his wavy hair, his naughty smile, his beautiful mind, each of us the prisoner of our own solipsistic narrative, each family the captive of the family story, each community locked within its own tale of itself, each people the victims of their own versions of history, and there were parts of the world where the narratives collided and went to war, where there were two or more incompatible stories fighting for space on, to speak, the same page. She came from one such place, his place, from which he had been forever displaced, they exiled his body, but his spirit, never. And maybe now every place was becoming that place, maybe Lebanon was everywhere and nowhere, so that we were all exiles, even if our hair wasn't so wavy, our smiles not so naughty, our minds less beautiful, even the name *Lebanon* wasn't necessary, the name of every place or any place would do just as well, maybe that's why she felt nameless, unnamed, unnameable, Lebanonymous. That was the nameless name of the one-woman show she was developing, which might (she hoped) also become a book, and (she really hoped) a movie and (if everything went really, really well) a musical (though in that case she would probably have to write parts for a few other people). The thing I'm thinking is that all these stories are fictions, she said, even the ones that insist on being facts, like who was where first and whose God had precedence over whose, they're all make-believe, fantasies, the realist fantasies and the fantastic fantasies are both *made up,* and the first thing to know about made-up stories is that they are all untrue in the same way, Madame Bovary and the quarreling Lebanonymous histories are fictional *in the same way as flying carpets and genies are,* she was quoting him there, nobody ever said things better than he could, and she was his daughter, so his words belonged to her now, this is our tragedy, she said in his words, our fictions are killing us, but if we didn't have those fictions, maybe that would kill us too.

According to the Unyaza people of the Lâm mountain range which almost encircles Old Bagdad, Blue Yasmeen said at The Locusts, *the story parasite entered human babies through the ear within hours of their birth, and caused the growing children to demand much that was harmful to them: fairy tales, pipe dreams, chimeras, delusions, lies. The need for the presentation of things that were not, as if they were things that were, was dangerous to a people for whom survival was a constant battle, requiring the maintenance of an undimmed focus on the actual. Yet the story parasite proved hard to eradicate. It adapted itself perfectly to its host, to the contours of human biology and the human genetic code, becoming a second skin upon human skin, a second nature to human nature. It seemed impossible to destroy it without also destroying the host. Those who suffered excessively from its effects, becoming obsessed with the manufacture and dissemination of the things that were not, were sometimes executed, and that was a wise precaution, but the story parasite continued to plague the tribe.*

The Unyaza were a small, dwindling mountain people. Their environment was harsh, their mountainous terrain rocky and infertile, their enemies brutal and plentiful, and they were prone to wasting sicknesses that made their bones disintegrate into powder, and to fevers that rotted the brain. They worshipped no gods, even though the story parasite infected them with dreams of rain-deities who brought them water, meat-deities who gave them cows, and war-deities who struck their foes down with diarrhea and made them easier to kill. This delusion—that their triumphs, such as the finding of water, the rearing of livestock and the poisoning of their enemies' food, were not their own doing, but gifts from invisible supernatural entities—was the last straw. The headman of the Unyaza ordered that the ears of babies be stopped with mud to prevent the story parasite from entering.

After that the story disease began to die out and the young Unyaza learned sadly as they grew older that the world was all too real. A spirit of deep pessimism began to spread, as the new generation understood that comfort, ease, gentleness *and* happiness *were words that had no meaning in the world as it was. Having considered the profound dreadfulness of reality, they concluded that there was, additionally, no place in their lives for such debilitating weaknesses as emotion, love, friendship, loyalty, fellowship or trust. After that the last insanity of the tribe began. It is believed that after a period of bitter quarrels and violent dissension, the Unyaza youths, in the grip of the mutinous pessimism which had replaced the story infection, murdered their elders and then fell upon one another until the tribe was lost to Man.*

In the absence of sufficient field data it is not possible to say for certain whether or not the story parasite ever truly existed, or if it was itself a story, a parasitical invention that attached itself to the consciousness of the Unyaza: a thing that was not, which, on account of its insidious persuasiveness, created the consequences that such a fictional parasite might have created had it been a thing that was; in which case the Unyaza, who loathed paradoxes almost as much as fictions, may, paradoxically, have been exterminated by their certainty that an illusion which they had collectively created was the truth.

And why did she care about mysterious Mr. Geronimo, Yasmeen asked her mirror at night, that silent old man who made no attempt to be cordial, was it because he was tall and handsome and stood up straight the way her father used to and was the age her father would have been if he had lived? Yes, probably, she conceded, her daddy issues were at work again, and maybe she would have been annoyed with herself for indulging in a form of transferred nostalgia if she had not been severely distracted at that moment by the appearance behind her, clearly reflected in her bedroom mirror, of a beautiful, skinny young-looking woman dressed all in black and seated cross-legged upon a flying carpet, which was hovering, like the gardener downstairs, approximately four inches above the floor.

Even though the normality of the city had been disrupted, most people hadn't been able to get their heads around it, and were still dumbfounded by the irruption of the fantastic into the quotidian, even people like Blue Yasmeen, who had, after all, just encouraged Sister Allbee to be tolerant of the levitation going on month after month in the basement. Yasmeen unleashed an almost canine yelp and turned to face Dunia, who, it must be said, looked as startled as the orange-haired human female before her.

"In the first place," Dunia said, tetchily, "you ought to be a person with whom I have important business, Mr. Raphael Manezes known as Geronimo, and you plainly are not. And in the second place, you have perfectly ordinary ears."

Blue Yasmeen opened her mouth but was unable to produce a sound from it. "Geronimo Manezes?" the woman on the flying carpet repeated, still sounding irritable. It had been a long day. "Which is his apartment?" Yasmeen jabbed a finger at the floor. "One," she managed to say. The woman on the flying carpet looked disgusted.

"This is why I prefer not to use carpets," she said. "Their blasted positioning system is always going wrong."

Ma, we have to move, we have to leave this house immediately, tonight if possible.

Why, my son, because a monster is in your bedroom? Normal, tell him to be normal.

What, even you are calling him Normal now?

Why not, Jinendra, this is America, everyone's name gets shifted. You also are Jimmy now so get off your high horse.

Okay, never mind. Nirmal, tell Ma we have to leave here, it isn't safe to stay.

Call me Normal. I'm serious.

Then I'll call you Serious.

Jinendra, stop upsetting your cousin who gives you good job, good money. Why you don't give him respect?

Ma. We have to get out of here before it's too late.

And I should just leave my birds? What about the birds?

Forget the birds, Ma. He will return in full force and if we are here it will be a bad business.

I checked your bedroom. Your ma asked me to check so I checked. Nothing is out of ordinary. All is normal. No hole in the wall, no bhoot, *everything A-1 tip-top.*

Ma. Please.

My boy. Where to go? There is nowhere to go. Your mother is sick. Gallivanting god-knows-where is out of the question.

There's Nirmal's place.

What, you want to move in with me now? For how long? One night? Ten years? And what about this house?

This house is a danger zone.

Enough. Too much bakvaas. *We will stay here only. Subject is closed.*

And so on for many months, until he began to believe his mother was right, what he feared would never happen, the wormhole and Dunia and Natraj Hero had been hallucinations of the sort that, in ancient times, were caused by psychotropic wine, or mushrooms, or moldy bread, and he needed psychiatric help, maybe, medication, maybe, he was crazy. Until finally the night arrived, in the winter, in the snow, the deep unnatural snow, more snow than had fallen in living memory, the snow which people had started treating as a judgment or a curse, because lately everyone was treating all the weather that way, when it rained in California everyone started building arks, when an ice storm hit Georgia people abandoned their cars on the interstate and fled as if pursued by a gigantic ice-monster, and in Queens where people whose origins and dreams were all located in hot countries, people to whom snow still felt like a fantasy, no matter how many years they had lived here, no matter how often and how hard it fell, snow was surrealist, it was like black magic disguised as white, and so, yeah, on the night the black magic became real, the night when the monster actually showed up, it had snowed pretty hard, and that made it harder to run.

That was the night he had to run, he ran home from Normal's office as fast—slipping, falling, rising again to run—as he could, with Normal puffing, wheezing, holding his ribs some distance behind, because of the fire, there it was, the fire instead of the house, the flames where the house used to be, the birds roasted or flown, and on a hard chair on the opposite sidewalk, with the feathers of her incinerated birds floating in the air above her head, facing the flames that were consuming her old life, the flames melting the snow so that her chair stood in a small pool of water, there was his mother, charred and soot-stained but alive, surrounded by a few of her possessions, a floor lamp standing by the chair, a peacock-feather fan, three framed photographs lapped by the melting slush, his mother immobile and wordless, red flames behind her, red flames that were somehow smokeless, *why isn't there any smoke,* he asked himself, and as he raced up to her there were firemen saying, Poor lady, turn the chair around so she doesn't have to watch, poor madam, she looks so cold, move her closer to the fire.

And no argument now about the cause, everybody saw the giant jinni who emerged from the fireball, born like all male jinn from smokeless fire, toothy, pockmarked, wearing his long flame-red battle shirt decorated with its ornate golden motifs, with his great black beard tied around his waist like a belt, his sword in its green and gold scabbard tucked into that hairy waistband on the left side, Zumurrud Shah no longer bothering to take the shape of Natraj Hero just to mess with little Jimmy's head, but appearing in his full terrible glory: Zumurrud the Great, grandest of the Grand Ifrits astride his flying urn, whose explosion into the world, followed by three of his closest cohorts, signaled the end of the time of random strangenesses. This was the beginning of the so-called War.

Zumurrud the Great

and

His Three Companions

The Grand Ifrit Zumurrud Shah, on whose head was a golden crown taken from the head of a prince he had accidentally or not so accidentally decapitated once upon a time, had at a certain point in history become the philosopher Ghazali's personal jinni: a terrifying entity whose name even Dunia the jinnia had been afraid to utter. Ghazali was not, however, the jinni's master. The words *master* and *servant* are inappropriate when applied to the relationship between human beings and the jinn, for any service a jinni may perform for a human being is a boon rather than evidence of enslavement, an act of generosity, or, in the case of a jinni liberated from some sort of trap, a lamp, for example, a gesture of gratitude. The story goes that Ghazali had in fact freed Zumurrud Shah from just such a trap, a blue bottle in which a forgotten sorcerer had trapped him. Long, long ago, wandering in the streets of his native Tus, Ghazali had spotted the opaque bottle lying abandoned in the heaps of trash which unfortunately disfigured that old town of salmon minarets and enigmatic walls, and had intuited at once, as philosophers with the proper training are able to intuit, the presence of a captive spirit therein. He scooped up the bottle casually, but with the guilty expression of a novice burglar, and pressing his lips against the royal blue glass whispered a little too loudly the occult incantation that is the required opening for all dialogues with captured jinn:

Jinni great and jinni grand,
Now I hold you in my hand.

Tell me ere I set you free
What reward you'll offer me.

A miniaturized jinni speaking through glass sounds like a talking mouse in a cartoon. Many human beings have been deceived by this feeble squeakety-squeak into swallowing the poisoned pill the captured jinni will invariably offer them. Ghazali, however, was made of sterner stuff.

This was the jinni's reply:

Never bargain. Let me go.
Weak men bargain. Strong men know
Those who freely set me free
Evermore will blessed be.

But Ghazali knew the proper retort to this childish deception.

Well I know your tribe and kin!
Make your promise while you're in!
Without a sacred vow to keep
Only fool lets jinni leap.

Zumurrud Shah, knowing he had little choice, offered the usual three-wishes formula. Ghazali replied, sealing the contract, accepting in words that deviated somewhat from the usual formula.

Any time, 'neath any moon,
I may ask you for a boon.
Any time, these one two three
Swiftly will fulfillèd be.

Released, expanding at once to his full immensity, the jinni was struck by two things that marked out Ghazali as a most unusual mortal. Firstly, he did not quail. Quailing—as young Jimmy Kapoor was to discover centuries later—was not only de rigueur, it was also, in most cases, the instinctive reaction to the sight of Zumurrud in his dark glory. However, "this mortal," the Grand Ifrit noted with some perplexity, "quaileth not." That was firstly. And secondly, he didn't ask for something right away! That was unprecedented. Infinite wealth, a bigger sexual organ, unlimited power . . . these wishes were at the top of any jinni's list of the top demands of the human male. The human male wishing mind was surprisingly unimaginative. But *no wish*? The deferral of all *three* wishes? That was almost indecent. "You ask for *nothing*?" Zumurrud Shah roared. "Nothing is a thing I cannot give." Ghazali inclined his philosopher's head and put a hand around his chin. "I see that you give to nothing the quality of a thing. Nothing is the thing that cannot be given precisely because it is not a thing, yet in your view it's not-thingness is itself a form of thingness. This, perhaps, we may discuss. Understand, jinni, that I am a man of few personal needs. I need neither infinite wealth, nor a bigger sexual organ, nor unlimited power. However, the time may come when I ask for some larger service. I'll let you know. In the meantime, be off. You're free to go."

"When will this time come?" Zumurrud Shah demanded. "I'm going to be busy, you know. After being stuck in that bottle for so long there are many things to be done."

"The time will come when it's time," Ghazali said, infuriatingly, and turned away to his book. "I spit upon all philosophers," Zumurrud Shah told him, "also artists, and the rest of humanity as well," and he whirled himself into a funnel of rage, and was gone. And then time passed, years passed, decades passed, and Ghazali was dead, and with him died the contract, or so the jinni believed. And the slits between the world silted up, and closed, and Zumurrud in Peristan which is Fairyland forgot for a time all about the world of men, all about the man who refused to make a wish; and centuries passed, and a new millennium began, and the seals which separated the worlds began to break, and then boom! Here he was again in the world of these feeble beings, and suddenly there was a voice in his head commanding his presence, the voice of a dead man, the voice of dust, of less than dust, the voice of the void where the dust of the dead man had been, a void that was somehow animated, somehow possessed of the sensibility of the dead man, a void that was ordering him to present himself to be told its first great wish. And he, having no option, being bound by the contract, even though he intended to argue that the contract did not apply posthumously, he remembered Ghazali's unusual language, *any time, 'neath any moon, any time these one two three,* and he knew that as he had forgotten to insert a death clause (a detail he should make it a point to remember if at any point in the future he needed to grant the three-wishes contract again!), the obligation still lay upon him like a shroud, and he had to do whatever the void desired.

He remembered and summoned up in a rush all his unassuaged rage, the wrath of a Grand Ifrit who has spent half an eternity bottled up in blue, and conceived the desire to be avenged against the entire species from which his captor came. He would rid himself of this puny obligation to a dead man, and then it would be time for vengeance. This, he swore.

Regarding the rage of Zumurrud Shah: in the sixteenth century a group of brilliant Indian court artists in the employ of the Grand Mughal, Akbar the Great, had belittled and offended him. Four hundred and forty years ago, give or take, he appeared several times in the Hamzanama sequence of paintings depicting the adventures of the hero Hamza. Here Zumurrud is—here in this picture!—with his cronies, Ra'im Blood-Drinker and Shining Ruby, plotting their next evil move. Whisper whisper cackle hiss. An orange and white canopy above them, and behind them a mountain made of puffy boulders like stone clouds. Men with long-horned bullocks kneel, swearing fealty, or maybe just swearing, because Zumurrud Shah in person is a sight scary enough to make good men use bad language. He is a monster, is a terror, is a giant, ten times bigger than anyone else and twenty times nastier. Light skin, long black beard, ear-to-ear grin. A mouthful of man-eater teeth, mordant as Goya's Saturn.

And yet the painting slights him. Why? Because it depicts him as a mortal. A giant, certainly, but no jinni. Blood and flesh, not smokeless fire. Quite an insult to hand a Grand Ifrit.

(And, as events would show, he was not the Grand Ifrit with a taste for human flesh.)

In the paintings made by the brilliant artists assembled at Akbar's jeweled court, there are several images of horrible Zumurrud Shah, but few that show him triumphant. Most often he is the defeated opponent of Hamza, the semi-mythical hero. Here he is along with his soldiers fleeing from Hamza's army on his famous flying urns. Here, ignominiously, he has fallen into a hole dug by some gardeners to catch people who have been robbing their fruit groves, and is being badly beaten by the angry horticulturists. In their eagerness to glorify Hamza the warrior—and, through his fictional figure, the real-life emperor-hero who commissioned the pictures—the artists give Zumurrud Shah a hard time. He's big, but a boob. Even the magic of the airborne urns is not his; they are sent to fly him to safety from Hamza's attacks by his friend the sorcerer Zabardast. This *Zabardast,* which is to say "Awesome," is and was like Zumurrud Shah one of the mightiest members of the tribe of the dark jinn; a sorcerer, yes, but one with special gifts regarding levitation. (And snakes.) And had their true nature been revealed by the Mughal court artists, they would have given Hamza a far tougher fight than he actually got.

That was one thing. But even if the Mughal painters had not misrepresented him Zumurrud Shah would still have been the enemy of the human race because of his contempt for human character. It was as if he took the complexity of human beings as a personal affront, the maddening inconsistency of human beings, their contradictions which they made no attempt to wipe out or reconcile, their mixture of idealism and concupiscence, grandeur and pettiness, truth and lies. They were not to be taken seriously any more than a cockroach deserves serious consideration. At best they were toys; and he was as close as any of them would ever get to a wanton god, and he would, if he so chose, kill them for his sport. In other words, even if the philosopher Ghazali had not unleashed him upon the unsuspecting world, he would have unleashed himself upon it. His inclination was in accordance with his instructions. But the instructions from the dead philosopher were clear.

"Instill fear," Ghazali told him. "Only fear will move sinful Man towards God. Fear is a part of God, in the sense that it is that feeble creature Man's appropriate response to the infinite power and punitive nature of the Almighty. One may say that fear is the echo of God, and wherever that echo is heard men fall to their knees and cry mercy. In some parts of the earth, God is already feared. Don't bother about those regions. Go where Man's pride is swollen, where Man believes himself to be godlike, lay waste his arsenals and fleshpots, his temples of technology, knowledge and wealth. Go also to those sentimental locations where it is said that God is love. Go and show them the truth."

"I don't have to agree with you about God," replied Zumurrud Shah, "about his nature or even his existence. That is not and never will be my business. In Fairyland we do not speak of religion, and our daily life there is utterly alien to life on earth, and, if I may say so, far superior. I can tell that even in death you are a censorious prude, so I will not go into details, though they are juicy. At any rate, philosophy is a subject of no interest except to bores, and theology is philosophy's more tedious cousin. I'll leave such soporific matters to you in your dusty grave. But as to your wish, I not only accept it as my command. It will be my pleasure to comply. With the proviso that, as you are in fact asking for a series of acts, this will redeem the entirety of my three-wishes pledge."

"Agreed," the void that was Ghazali replied. If the dead could giggle with delight then the dead philosopher would have chortled with glee. The jinni perceived this. (Jinn can be perceptive at times.) "Why so mirthful?" he inquired. "Unleashing chaos upon the unsuspecting world is not, or is it, a joke."

Ghazali was thinking of Ibn Rushd. "My adversary in thought," he told Zumurrud Shah, "is a poor fool who is convinced that with the passage of time human beings will turn from faith to reason, in spite of all the inadequacies of the rational mind. I, obviously, am of a different mind. I have triumphed over him many times, yet our argument continues. And it is a fine thing in a battle of wits to be in possession of a secret weapon to fire, an ace in the hole to play, a trump card to use at an opportune time. In this particular case, mighty Zumurrud, you are that trump. I relish the fool's imminent discomfiture and his further, inevitable defeat."

"Philosophers are children," the jinni said. "And I've never liked children myself."

He departed in scorn. But the time would come when he returned to Ghazali, to listen to what the dead man's dust had to say. The time would come when he was less contemptuous of religion, and of God.

A note regarding Zabardast. He too had once been captured by a mortal sorceress, which was even more humiliating to him than imprisonment by a male wizard would have been. It is said by those who study such matters that this may have been the same witch spoken of in the Matter of Britain, the vile Morgana le Fay, who lay with her brother between incestuous sheets and seized, also, the wizard Merlin, sealing him in a crystal cave. It's a story we have heard from certain storytellers. We cannot say if it's true. Nor is it recorded how he escaped. However, what is known is that Zabardast carried in his heart a fury towards the human race at least the equal of Zumurrud's. But Zumurrud's was a hot anger. Zabardast's ire was cold as polar ice.

In those days, the days of the strangenesses and the War of the Worlds that followed them, the president of the United States was an unusually intelligent man, eloquent, thoughtful, subtle, measured in word and deed, a good dancer (though not as good as his wife), slow to anger, quick to smile, a religious man who also thought of himself as a man of reasoned action, handsome (if a little jug-eared), at ease in his own body like a reborn Sinatra (though reluctant to croon), and color-blind. He was practical, pragmatic, and had his feet firmly planted on the ground. Consequently he was utterly incapable of responding appropriately to the challenge flung down by Zumurrud the Great, which was surreal, whimsical and monstrous. As has already been mentioned, Zumurrud did not attack alone, but came in force, accompanied by Zabardast the Sorcerer, Shining Ruby the Possessor of Souls, and Ra'im Blood-Drinker, he of the sharply serrated tongue.

Ra'im was prominently involved in the first assaults. He was a nocturnal metamorph, in his normal daytime state a small, nondescript, dark-complexioned, fat-assed jinni, but able, when he could be persuaded to rouse himself from his habitual arrack-induced torpor, to mutate under cover of darkness into enormous, long-fanged beasts of land, sea and air, female as well as male, all thirsting for human or animal blood. It is probable that this Jekyll-and-Hyde jinni, one of the first of such spirits to show up in the historical record, and the cause of much terror wherever he appeared, was the single entity responsible for all the vampire stories in the world, the legend of the Gaki of Japan, a blood-drinking corpse that could take the shape of living men and women, and animals too, the Aswang of the Philippines with its long tubular tongue, who often took female form and preferred to suck the blood of children, the Irish Dearg-Due, the German Alp, the Polish Upier with its tongue of barbs, a vile creature who sleeps in a blood-bath, and, of course, the Transylvanian vampire Vlad Dracul, which is to say "dragon," about whom most readers and filmgoers are already somewhat (albeit mostly inaccurately) informed. At the beginning of the War of the Worlds, Ra'im took to the water, and one lightless afternoon he arose as a giant sea-monster from the winter harbor and swallowed the Staten Island Ferry. A tide of horror spread across the city and beyond and the president went on TV to calm the nation's fears. That night even this most articulate of chief executives looked ashen and at a loss; his familiar nostrums, *we will not sleep until, those responsible will be, you harm the United States of America at your peril, make no mistake, my fellow Americans, this crime will be avenged,* sounded hollow and impotent. The president had no weapons that could deal with this attacker. He had become a president of empty words. As many of them are, as they all have been, for so very, very long. But we had expected better of him.

As for Shining Ruby, the second of Zumurrud's three mighty cohorts, he was, in his own opinion, the greatest of the whispering jinn (although it must be said that the sorcerer Zabardast considered himself to be far superior; the egotism and competitiveness of the great jinn cannot be overemphasized). Shining Ruby's forte was to make trouble by first whispering against a man's heart and then entering his body, subduing his will, and forcing him into acts either dreadful or humiliating or revelatory or all of those at once. At first, when Daniel Aroni, the über-boss of the world's most powerful nongovernmental financial institution, began to talk like a crazy man, people did not guess at the presence of Shining Ruby inside him, did not grasp that he was quite literally behaving like a man possessed. It was only when Ruby released "Mac" Aroni's body after four days of possession, leaving him a poor husk of a man sprawled like a broken puppet on the finely carpeted floor of the great lobby in the sky of his corporate headquarters, that our ancestors understood. The jinni, a long skinny fellow so slender that he disappeared when he turned sideways, pranced and capered around the fallen financial titan. "All the money in the world," cried the jinni, "will not be too much. All the gold, men, in your sacks will not save you from my clutch." Traders on the six immense trading floors of the world's most powerful nongovernmental financial organization wept copiously and shivered with fear as the image of their unconscious leader shimmered like an intimation of doom on hundreds of giant high-definition flatscreen monitors. Tasked with helping Zumurrud Shah to grant the wishes of the dead philosopher, Shining Ruby had done an excellent job.

Ever since the death of his friend Seth Oldville at the hands of the still-missing Teresa Saca Cuartos, Daniel "Mac" Aroni had entered a dark place. Life was hard and dealt men many blows and a strong man could take those eventualities on the chin and move on. He thought of himself as a strong man, a man with two fists, who could punch his weight, and there were seven thousand five hundred people in a glass tower who needed him to be that guy, the enforcer, the creator and defender of the world as his employees wanted it to be. He made the picture of the world and the world lived in it. That was his job. Along the way there were bumps in the road. The infidelity of women on the hustle, the promiscuous nature of powerful men exposed in the public prints, revelations of corrupt business dealings by close associates, cancer, car crashes at speed, skiing deaths on off-piste black slopes, coronaries, suicides, the aggression of rivals and underlings on the make, the excessive manipulation of public servants for personal gain. He shrugged at these things. They went with the territory. If somebody had to take the fall, somebody took the fall. Even taking the fall could be a scam. Kim Novak in *Vertigo,* she took the fall twice, the second time for real. This crap happened. Happened all the time.

He was aware that the way things really were was far different than most people believed. The world a wilder, more feral, more abnormal environment than ordinary civilians were able to accept. Ordinary civilians lived in a state of innocence, veiling their eyes against the truth. The world unveiled would scare them, destroy their moral certainties, lead to losses of nerve or retreats into religion or drink. The world not just as it was but as he had made it. He lived in that picture of the world and could handle it, knew the levers and engines of it, the strings and keys, the buttons to push and the ones to avoid pushing. The real world which he created and controlled. If it was a rough ride, that was okay. He was a rough rider among and above seven and a half thousand of the same. Many, maybe most of the rough riders in his employ liked to live large, they went for the Casa Dragones tequila, the high-end girls, the ostentation. He did not live in that way but he stayed in shape, on the judo mat he was as feared as he was in the boardroom, and he could bench-press more weight than guys half his age, the guys who didn't have windows yet, who worked in the interior space of the tower like members of an A-list typing pool, the guys in the belly of his beast. Youth was not the exclusive preserve of the young anymore. "Mac" Aroni did golf, tennis, the old guy things, but then, just to throw in a curve ball, he had made himself a beach boy, a surfing master, he had gone in search of the Yodas of the big wave and learned their ways and he got his kicks, now, gleaming the cube. He had no need to beat his chest like Weissmuller's Tarzan. He could handle whatever came his way. He was the big ape. He was the king of the apes.

But what happened to Seth Oldville was different. That eventuality had crossed a line. Lightning from a woman's fingertips. That did not accord with the rules of his universe; and if somebody else was redrawing the picture of how things were, then he needed to have a word with that person, to reason with that person, to make that person understand that it was not for others to alter the laws of possibility. This was at first offensive to him, an angering thing, and then as the strangenesses multiplied he sank into a thunderous silence, his neck withdrawing into his collar so that his bull head sat right on his shoulders like a toad's. In the tower overlooking the river, men looked out at the Statue of Liberty and the empty harbor, the harbor all boats had fled since the eating of the ferryboat and its passengers, and listening to the unnatural silence of the water they understood that it echoed Aroni's equally unaccustomed muteness. Something bad was bubbling to the surface, and then Aroni began to speak, and the bad thing was out in the open, and it was worse than the seven and a half thousand could have imagined.

This was what Daniel "Mac" Aroni said and did under the power of the dark jinn. On the first day of his possession he informed *The Wall Street Journal* that he and his corporation were involved in a global conspiracy, and that their partners were the International Monetary Fund, the World Bank, the U.S. Treasury and the Federal Reserve. On the second day, with the media furore boiling up around him, he was on Bloomberg giving details of the first prong of the conspirators' strategy, which was "the destruction of America's domestic economy through the introduction of derivative debt which is sixteen times greater than the world's GDP. This I can say we already accomplished," he said proudly, "proved by the fact that America now has more workers on welfare, 101 million, as opposed to actual full-time workers—97 million." On day three, with demands for his resignation or summary dismissal being made on every side, he appeared on the liberally inclined MSNBC network to speak of "setting the chessboard in such a fashion that World War III becomes a one hundred percent sure thing." Gasps were audible in the studio as he added, "This we have near completion. The U.S. and Israel we got cranking up to go to war with China and Russia for two reasons, apparent and actual, numero uno, the apparent cause, that's Syria and Iran, and numero two, the actual, being the preservation of the value of the petrodollar." On day four, he addressed his own staff, looking unshaven and wild-haired and very much like a man who hadn't slept in a bed for several nights, and with his eyes lolling lazily from side to side asked for their support, whispering madly into his handheld microphone, "Soon we will initiate a false-flag event which will culminate in the abolition of the presidency, the imposition of martial law and the elimination of all opposition to the coming apocalypse. What you get in the endgame is a strongman world government accompanied by a one-world economic system. This is the outcome we all want, am I correct? I say, do I have this right?"

He was frightening his audience. His employees began drifting away from him, mushroom clouds in their eyes, mourning the destruction of their hopes of country club memberships and good marriages. They were seeing the deaths of their children and the annihilation of their homes, and even before any of that came to pass, the collapse of this great institution as the inevitable hurricane of umbrage burst upon it, and the consequent termination of their wealth. But before they could leave the scene of Daniel Aroni's meltdown they saw the dark jinni Shining Ruby emerge from his crumpling body crowing in triumph as the kingpin fell. The sight of a supernatural being stopped many of them in their tracks while others ran screaming for the stairs. Shining Ruby laughing in their faces induced seizures in some traders and there were two terminal heart failures and for all who survived it was a sign—just as Seth Oldville's death had been for his friend "Mac" Aroni—that everything they had worked for had just come to an end and they were living, now, on somebody else's dread unspeakable terms. And had Aroni been uttering the devil-words this possessor-devil had put in his mouth, or did the real devilry of the creature lie in the fact that he had made the great man reveal his insane secrets? In which case . . . was the end of the world actually nigh? Shining Ruby certainly wanted them to think so. "Ba-boom ka-boom!" he cried joyfully, turning sideways and vanishing. "Prepare to meet thy doom doo-doom!"

For a long time the sorcerer Zabardast had looked the way a sorcerer should look: the long beard, the high hat, the staff. The sorcerer to whom Mickey Mouse was apprenticed, Gandalf the Grey, and Zabardast would all have recognized kindred spirits in one another. However, Zabardast was conscious of his image and, now that the seals were broken and the slits between the worlds had reopened, now that the jump gate to a wormhole to Peristan stood open day and night in Jackson Heights, he studied films and magazines to keep his look relevant. Above all others he liked the edginess of Jet Li falling in love with a thousand-year-old white snake. He wished briefly that he looked like Jet Li, and for a time he considered a radical modernization of his look, and putting on the Buddhist monk's white robe and necklace of beads and shaving his head like a chopsocky movie hero. In the end he rejected this change. *Act your age,* he told himself. He didn't want to look like a kung fu star after all. He wanted to look like a god.

Levitation—antigravity—was Zabardast's specialty. The creator of the famous flying urns which served many jinn as their personal private aircraft, he had also provided enchanted brooms, magicked slippers, and even self-raising hats to witches who wanted to fly, and had amassed a considerable fortune in gold and jewels by providing these services. The well-known and much-documented fascination of the jinn for rare metals and precious stones has its origins, according to the greatest scholars, in the wild and incessant orgies conducted in Fairyland, and the love of many jinnias for all that glitters and gleams. Lying on beds of gold, heavily ornamented, their hair, ankles, necks and waists bedecked with gemstones, the jinnia voluptuaries saw no need for other clothing, and gratified their jinni counterparts with an inexhaustible will. Zabardast, one of the wealthiest of the jinn, was also one of the most sexually active. His flying magic funded his often extreme needs.

In that first phase of the War of the Worlds, Zabardast set out to spread fear by a spate of poltergeist activity, sending sectional settees flying across the chic, fragile interiors of high-design showrooms, encouraging yellow taxis to fly over the roofs of other vehicles instead of swerving dangerously into their paths, lifting up manhole covers and sending them skidding at head height along the city's sidewalks, turning them into flying giant discuses looking to decapitate the ungodly. It was the ungodly who had been specified as the targets but, Zabardast complained to Zumurrud, this place was not at all ungodly. In point of fact it was excessively godly. Atheists were few and far between and gods of all types were being adored and worshipped constantly in every neck of the woods. "Never mind," Zumurrud retorted. "They come from this benighted place or have chosen to live here. That will suffice."

In between his feats of levitation, just for pleasure, the sorcerer Zabardast liked to watch the effect of releasing large numbers of venomous serpents upon an unsuspecting public. The snakes were jinn too, but jinn of a lower order; more like his servants, or even his pets. The sorcerer Zabardast's love of the snakes he unleashed was genuine, but superficial. He was not a jinni of profound emotions. Profound emotions do not interest the jinn. In this, as in so much else, the jinnia Dunia was an exception.

One of Zabardast's snakes coiled itself around the Chrysler building from top to bottom like a helter-skelter slide. One distraught or possibly drug-addled and certainly bespectacled office worker was seen leaping from a window on the sixty-seventh floor, the middle floor of the three occupied by the reborn Cloud Club. Round and round the snake he slid until he hit the back of its head and fell to the sidewalk, in excellent physical condition, with his spectacles, if not his dignity, intact. He fled towards the railway station and was lost to history. His descent was filmed by at least seven different camera phones but it proved impossible to identify him. We are happy to leave him to his privacy. We have what we need of him, the digital images, much enhanced, on which, for ever and a day, he reenacts, a thousand and one times, whenever we desire him to do so, his great helix of a slide.

The snake's flickering tongue was twenty feet long and whipped at the ankles of fleeing pedestrians, causing falls and injuries. Another great worm, patterned in diamond-shaped lozenges colored yellow black and green like the Jamaican flag come to life, was simultaneously seen in Union Square, dancing on its tail, scattering the chess players and skateboarders, the dealers and the protesters, the teenagers in their new sneakers, the mothers and children heading down to the chocolate store. Three oldsters fled slowly uptown on Segways, past the second and third locations of the Warhol Factory, and in quavering voices they wondered what Andy would have made of the dancing snake, a silver silkscreen *Double Ouroboros,* perhaps, or a twelve-hour film. It had been a hard winter and there was still snow piled at the edges of the square but when the snake danced people forgot about the weather and ran. The people of the city did a lot of running that winter, but whatever horror they fled from, they were also fleeing towards a different terror, rushing from frying pan to fire.

Emergency supplies were running out. Bug Out Bags, also known as GOODbags or INCHbags—acronyms for Get Out of Dodge bags and I'm Never Coming Home bags—became de rigueur that season. There was much argument about what your go-bag needed. Did it, for example, need a gun to repel crackheads who didn't have go-bags? The exits to the city were jammed with honking cars full of INCHbag-bearing adults and children, heading for the hills. Lane closures were ignored and this led to accidents and even longer traffic jams. Panic was the order of the day.

As for Zumurrud the Great himself, if the truth be told, he was feeling a little upstaged by his illustrious companions. He did his best, appearing in full panoply in the plaza at Lincoln Center bellowing *You are all my slaves* but even in those days of hysteria there were some innocents who thought he was promoting a new opera at the Met. He flew one night to the top of One World Trade Center and balanced on one foot on its high pinnacle, unleashing his finest ear-splitting yodel; but in spite of the horror that filled many New Yorkers' hearts there were still puzzled citizens down below by the sad rectangular waterfalls who assumed his lofty presence was an advertising stunt for a bad-taste remake of the famous old gorilla movie. He smashed a hole in the celebrated façade of the old post office building but such destruction could be seen every summer in the movie theaters, and had lost its effect by being portrayed too frequently. So it was also with extreme weather conditions: snow, ice and so on. This was a species with an exceptional ability to ignore its approaching doom. If one sought to be the embodiment of the doom that was approaching, this was a little frustrating. All the more so when the jinn he had brought along as his supporting cast seemed to have cast themselves, somewhat ungratefully, in leading roles. It was enough to make the great Zumurrud wonder if he might be losing his touch.

If the dark jinn have a fault, it is—but no! One should rather, less sloppily, more accurately, say *Among the many faults of the dark jinn is*—well then, a certain purposelessness about their behavior. They live in the moment, have no grand designs, and are easily distracted. Do not go to a jinni for strategy, for there are no jinni Clausewitzes, no Sun Tzu jinn among their ranks. Genghis Khan, conquering all he saw, based his strategy on maintaining herds of horses that accompanied his army. His archers on horseback were a dreaded cavalry. His soldiers lived on a diet of horse milk, blood and meat, so that even a dead horse was useful. The jinn do not think in this way, are not accustomed to collective action, being arch individualists. Zumurrud Shah, who enjoyed mayhem as much as any jinni, was, to be absolutely frank, disenchanted. How many cars could one transform into giant porcupines prickling down the West Side Highway, how much real estate could one damage with the swipe of an arm, before one's thoughts turned to the superior delights of the infinitely extended sexual activity plentifully awaiting one back in Fairyland? In the absence of a worthy adversary, was the game worth the candle?

Humanity had never been an enemy worth fighting for long, Zumurrud Shah grumbled to himself. It was enjoyable to mess around with these puny entities for a while—so pompous they were! So self-important! So unwilling to recognize their irrelevance to the universe!—and to upset their much-prized applecarts, but after a while, three-wish promise to a dead philosopher or not, prolonged engagement was unappealing. The opening of the wormhole which linked his world to theirs had been his most impressive feat, and to underline its significance he appeared on the jumbotron in Times Square to reveal himself as the leader of a mighty invasion which would shortly subjugate the entire human race, *You are all my slaves now,* he cried again, *forget your history, a new time begins today.* But a true student of the jinn would have noted that even though the wormhole in Queens stood scarily open, there was no invading army pouring through it. The jinn in Peristan were just too busy having sex.

It is necessary to speak briefly of the extreme laziness of the great jinn. If you wish to understand how it can be that so many of these extremely powerful spirits have been so frequently captured in bottles, lamps and so on, the answer lies in the immense indolence that comes over a jinni after he has performed more or less any action. Their periods of sleep greatly exceed their waking hours and, during these times, so deeply do they slumber that they can be shoved and pushed into any enchanted receptacle without waking them up. So, for example, after the great feat of swallowing and digesting the ferry, Ra'im Blood-Drinker, still in the guise of a mighty sea-dragon, fell asleep on the harbor bed and did not awaken for several weeks; and the possession and manipulation of the financial titan Daniel Aroni similarly exhausted Shining Ruby for a couple of months. Zabardast and Zumurrud were less easily exhausted but after a while they too were ready to doze. A sleepy jinni is an irritable spirit and it was in this condition that Zumurrud and Zabardast, sitting on clouds over Manhattan, quarreled about who had done what to whom, who had been the standout performer and who the also-ran, which of them should henceforth defer to which, and who had come closest to fulfilling the promise made by Zumurrud the Great to the philosopher Ghazali centuries ago. When Zumurrud bombastically claimed responsibility for the cruel winter that had the city in its grip, Zabardast issued a peal of malicious laughter. "The fact that you take credit for bad weather," he said, "only serves to show how desperate you are to prove your potency. I myself argue only from cause and effect. I do this, the result is that. Perhaps tomorrow you will take responsibility for the sunset, and claim to have plunged the world into darkness."

This must be said again: the competitiveness of even the mightiest of the jinn is often petty and childish, and leads to childish feuds. These are usually, as is the way with childishness, quarrels of short duration, but they can be bitter and spiteful while they last. When the jinn fight the results can be spectacular to the human eye. They throw things which are not things as we understand them, but the products of enchantment. Looking up at the sky from the earth, human beings would read these enchanted not-things as comets, meteors, shooting stars. The more powerful the jinni, the hotter and more fearsome the "meteor." Zabardast and Zumurrud were the strongest of all the dark jinn, so their magic fire was dangerous, even to each other. And the slaying of the jinn by the jinn is a crucial part of our story.

At the height of the quarrel, up there in the white clouds over the city, Zabardast pummeled his old friend in Zumurrud's weakest spot: his immense *amour propre,* his pride. "If I so chose," Zabardast cried, "I could make myself a larger giant than you, but I am unimpressed by size. If I so chose, I could be a more dazzling metamorph than Ra'im Blood-Drinker, but I prefer to retain my own shape. When I want, I am a more potent whisperer than Shining Ruby, and my whispering has more lasting and dramatic results." Zumurrud, never the most verbal of the jinn, roared his anger and hurled a large fireball, which Zabardast turned into a harmless snowball and threw back at his rival like a boy in a winter park. "What's more," Zabardast shouted, "let me tell you, who are so puffed up about the creation of your wormhole, that after the long separation of the worlds, when the first seals broke and the first slits reopened, I came back to earth long before you dreamed of doing so. And what I did then sowed a seed that will soon bear fruit and inflict a wound upon humanity deeper than any injury you could manage. You hate the human race because it is not like us. I hate it for its possession of the earth, the beautiful, damaged earth. I have gone far beyond the tiny fanatical vengeance of your dead philosopher. There is a gardener from whom a whole garden of horrors will grow. What I have begun with a whisper will become a roar that will expel the human race from the planet forever. Then Fairyland will seem dull and plain, and the whole blessed earth, purified of Man, will be the province of the jinn. This is what I can do. I am *Awesome.* I am *Zabardast.*"

"Unreason defeats itself," Ibn Rushd said to Ghazali, dust to dust, "by reason of its unreasonableness. Reason may catnap for a time, but the irrational is more often comatose. In the end it will be the irrational that is forever caged in dreams, while reason gains the day."

"The world men dream of," replied Ghazali, "is the world they try to make."

There followed a period of calm, during which Zabardast, Shining Ruby and Ra'im Blood-Drinker returned to Fairyland. The jump-gate to the wormhole in Queens closed and only the ruined house remained. Our ancestors allowed themselves to believe the worst was over. The clocks went forward. Spring sprang. Everywhere men went they stood in the shadow of young girls in flower, and they were glad. We were in those days a people with no memory, especially the young, and there was so much to divert the young. They permitted themselves to be happily diverted.

Zumurrud the Great did not return to Peristan. He went to sit at the feet of Ghazali's grave, to ask questions. After all his protests against philosophy and theology, he decided to listen. Maybe he was sick of jinn chatter and malice. Perhaps the purposeless anarchy of jinn behavior, the making of mayhem for its own sake, was finally too empty and he understood that he needed a flag to fight under. Maybe, in the end, he *grew,* not physically but inwardly; and, having grown, felt that for him to respect a cause, it had to be bigger than himself, and he was a giant, so it would have to be very large indeed; and the only outsize cause on the market was the one Ghazali was trying to sell him. At this distance in time, we cannot fully know his mind. We only know that he bought it.

Beware the man (or jinni) of action when he finally seeks to better himself with thought. A little thinking is a dangerous thing.

Dunia in Love, Again

When Dunia first saw Geronimo Manezes he was floating on
his side in his bedroom in the almost-dark, wearing a sleep
mask, in the exhausted, heavily drowsy condition that was as close to
sleep as he got these days, with the light from a single still-illuminated
lamp on a nightstand flowing up towards him, casting horror-movie
shadows across his long, bony face. A blanket hung down from both
sides of his body, making him look like a magician's assistant, levitated while hypnotized by some top-hatted trickster, and about to be
sawn in half. Where have I seen that face before, she thought, and
immediately answered herself, even though the memory was more
than eight hundred years old. The face of her one true human love,
even though there was no cloth wound around his head, and the
gray beard was less carefully managed, rougher, wilder than in her
remembering of it, not the beard of a man who has chosen to have a
beard, but the unkempt growth on the face of one who has simply
given up shaving. Eight centuries and more since she had seen that
face, yet here it was, as if it were yesterday, as if he had not abandoned her, as if he were not reduced to dust, dust to which she had
spoken, animate dust, but dust nevertheless, disembodied, dead. As
if he had been waiting for her here all this time, in the dark, for eight
hundred years and more, waiting for her to find him and renew
their ancient love.

The floating was not a puzzle to a jinnia princess. This had to be
the work of Zabardast the sorcerer jinni. Zabardast had slipped
through the first slits to reopen and curse Geronimo Manezes: but

why? That was a mystery. Was this random malice, or had Zabardast somehow intuited the existence of the Duniazát and understood that if properly marshaled they might prove to be an obstacle to the power of the dark jinn, a resistance, a counterforce? Dunia did not believe in chance. The jinn believe in the purposive nature of the universe, in which even the random has a goal. She needed to answer the question of Zabardast's motives, and in time she found what she needed, she learned about Zabardast's plan to spread the dual diseases of rising and crushing which would, once and for all, remove humanity from the surface of the earth. In the meanwhile, however, she was impressed by Geronimo Manezes's resistance to the spell. Ordinary men would simply have floated off into the sky to die, suffocated for lack of oxygen, frozen by the low temperature, attacked by territorial birds incensed by a land creature's elevation into the air. But here was Geronimo, after quite a while, still only a relatively small distance off the ground, still able to occupy interiors and perform his natural functions without leaving a humiliating mess. This was an individual to admire, she thought. A tough customer. But mostly she was distracted by that face. She had not thought to see that face again.

Ibn Rushd caressing her body had often praised its beauty to the point at which she grew irritated and said, You do not think my thoughts worth praising, then. He replied that the mind and body were one, the mind was the form of the human body, and as such was responsible for all the actions of the body, one of which was thought. To praise the body was to praise the mind that ruled it. Aristotle had said this and he agreed, and because of this it was hard for him, he whispered blasphemously in her ear, to believe that consciousness survived the body, for the mind was of the body and had no meaning without it. She did not want to argue with Aristotle and said nothing. Plato was different, he conceded. Plato thought the mind was trapped in the body like a bird and only when it could shed that cage would it soar and be free.

She wanted to say, I am made of smoke. My mind is smoke, my

thoughts are smoke, I am all smoke and only smoke. This body is a garment I put on, which by my magic art I have made capable of functioning as a human body functions, it's so biologically perfect that it can conceive children and pop them out in threes, fours and fives. Yet I am not of this body and could, if I chose, inhabit another woman, or an antelope, or a gnat. Aristotle was wrong, for I have lived for aeons, and altered my body when I chose, like a garment of which I had grown tired. The mind and body are two, she wanted to say, but she knew it would disappoint him to be disagreed with, so she held her tongue.

Now in Geronimo Manezes she saw Ibn Rushd reborn and wanted to murmur, You see, you have entered a new body as well. You have moved through time, down the dark corridor that some say the soul travels between lives, shedding its old consciousness as it goes, relieving itself of its selfhood, until finally it is pure essence, the pure light of being, ready to enter another living thing; and nobody can deny that here you are again, different, yet the same. Imagine that you came into the world blindfolded, in the dark, and floating in the air, just as you are now. You would not even know you had a body and yet you would know that you were you. Your selfhood, your mind, that would be there as soon as you were conscious. It is a separate thing.

But, she thought, arguing with herself, maybe it's not so. Maybe it is different with human beings, who cannot change their form, and this sleeping figure's echo of a man long dead can be ascribed to a freak of biology and nothing more. Maybe in the case of true humans, their mind, their soul, their consciousness flows through their bodies like blood, inhabiting every cell of their physical being, and so Aristotle was right, in humans the mind and body are one and cannot be separated, the self is both with the body and perishes with it too. She imagined that union with a thrill. How lucky human beings were if that was the case, she wanted to tell Geronimo who was and was not Ibn Rushd: lucky and doomed. When their hearts pounded with excitement their souls pounded too, when their pulses raced their spirits were aroused, when their eyes moistened with tears of happiness it was their minds that felt the joy. Their minds touched the people their fingers touched, and when they in turn were touched by others it was as if two consciousnesses were briefly joined. The mind gave the body sensuality, it allowed the body to taste delight and to smell love in their lover's sweet perfume; not only their bodies but their minds, too, made love. And at the end the soul, as mortal as the body, learned the last great lesson of life, which was the body's death.

A jinnia took human form but the form was not the jinnia and so it could not taste or smell or feel, and her body was not made for love because it was not the symbiotic partner and possessor of the mind. When the philosopher touched her intimately it was as though someone were fondling her while she was dressed in heavy winter garments, many-layered, so that she felt no sensation except a distant susurration, as if of a hand brushing an overcoat. But she had loved her philosopher so strongly that she had made him believe that her body was aroused and ecstatic. Ibn Rushd had been fooled. Men were easily deceived in such matters because they wanted to believe they had the power to arouse. She wanted to make him believe he pleased her. But the truth was that she could give physical pleasure to a man but not receive it, she could only imagine what such pleasure might be like, she could watch and learn, and offer up to her lover the outward signs of it, while trying to fool herself, as well as him, that yes, she was being pleasured too, which made her an actress, a phony, and a self-deceiving fool. Yet she had loved a man, had loved him for his mind and put on a body so that he could love her back, she had borne his children, and carried the memory of that love down eight centuries and more, and now, to her surprise and excitement, here he was, reborn, given new flesh, new bones, and if this floating Geronimo was old, what of it? Ibn Rushd too had been "old." Human beings, brief candles that they were, had no idea what the word meant. She was older than both these men, so much older that it would horrify them if she aged as humans do.

She remembered the dinosaurs. She was older than the human race.

The jinn rarely admitted to one another how interested they were in human beings, how fascinating the human race actually was to those who were not human. Yet in the time before Man, in the age of the first single-cell organisms, the fishes, the amphibians, the first walking creatures, the first flying things, the first things that slithered, and then the ages of the larger beasts, the jinn rarely ventured forth from Fairyland. The earthly jungle, the desert, the mountaintop, these savage things were of no concern. Peristan revealed the obsession of the jinn with the patterning of things which only civilization provides; it was a place of formal gardens, elegantly terraced, with cascading streams of water, neatly channeled. Flowers grew in flower beds, trees were planted symmetrically to create pleasing avenues and clusters, to provide easeful shade and a sense of gracious amplitude. There were pavilions of red stone in Fairyland, many-cupolaed, with silken walls within which could be found the carpeted boudoirs, with bolsters to lie against and handy samovars of wine, where the jinn retired for pleasure. They were made of smoke and fire, yet they preferred shapely things to the formlessness of their natures. This led them frequently to take human form. This fact alone revealed the degree of—yes!—their indebtedness to poor, mortal humanity, which provided them with a template, helping them to impose physical, horticultural, architectural order upon their essentially chaotic selves. Only in the act of sex—the major activity of Fairyland—did the jinn, male and female, abandon their bodies and fall into one another as essences, smoke entwining fire, fire billowing smoke, in long ferocious union. Otherwise, they had actually come to prefer to use their "bodies," the shells in which they cased their wildness. These "bodies" formalized them, much as the formal garden formalized the wilderness. "Bodies," the jinn agreed, were good.

Princess Dunia—or, to be precise, the princess who had adopted the name "Dunia," *the world,* on her visits to the world of men—had gone further than most of her kind. So deep had her fascination with human beings become that she had found a way to discover human emotion in herself. She was a jinnia who could fall in love. Who had fallen in love once, and was now on the verge of doing so again, with the same man, reincarnated in a different time. What was more, if he had asked her, she would have told him that she loved him for his mind, not his body. He himself was the proof that the mind and body were two, not one: the extraordinary mind in, frankly, an unexceptional casing. Nobody could truly love Ibn Rushd for his physique, in which there were, to be blunt, elements of flabbiness, and, by the time she met him, other signs of the decrepitude of old age. She noted with some satisfaction that the body of this sleeping man, Geronimo Manezes, the reincarnation of the beloved, was a considerable improvement on the original. This body was strong and firm, even if it was also "old." It was Ibn Rushd's face placed in a better setting. Yes, she would love him, and maybe this time she could work some extra magic upon herself and acquire sensation. Maybe this time she would be able to receive as well as give. But what if his mind was idiotic? What if it was not the mind she had fallen in love with? Could she settle for the face and the body alone? Maybe, she thought. Nobody was perfect, and reincarnation was an inexact procedure. Maybe she could settle for less than everything. He looked right. That might well be enough.

One thing did not cross her mind. Geronimo Manezes was of the tribe of the Duniazát, which made him her descendant, very possibly her great-great-great-great-great-great-great-grandson, give or take a *great* or two. Technically, sex with Mr. Geronimo would be an incestuous union. But the jinn do not recognize an incest taboo. Child-bearing is so rare in the jinn universe that it never seemed necessary to place descendants off-limits, so to speak. There were almost no descendants to speak of. But Dunia had descendants; many of them. However, in the matter of incest she followed the example of the camel. The camel will gladly have sex with its mother, daughter, brother, sister, father, uncle, or what you will. The camel observes no decencies and never thinks of propriety. He, or she, is motivated solely by desire. Dunia, like all her people, was of the same persuasion. What she wanted, she would have. And to her surprise she had found what she wanted here in this narrow house, in this narrow basement, where this sleeping man floated several inches above his bed.

She watched him sleeping, this mortal for whom his body was not a choice, who belonged to it and it to him, and she hesitated to wake him. After her awkwardly embarrassing intrusion into the apartment upstairs and the alarm of its occupant Blue Yasmeen, Dunia had made herself invisible, preferring, this time, to see before being seen. She moved slowly towards the recumbent form. He was sleeping poorly, on the edge of wakefulness, mumbling in his sleep. She would need to be careful. She needed him to stay asleep so that she could listen to his heart.

Something has already been said about the skill of the jinn at *whispering,* overpowering and controlling the will of human beings by murmuring words of power against their chests. Dunia was a consummate whisperer, but she possessed, additionally, a rarer skill: the gift of *listening,* of approaching a sleeping man and placing her ear very gently against his chest and, by deciphering the secret language that the self speaks only to itself, discovering his heart's desire. As she *listened* to Geronimo Manezes, she heard first his most predictable wishes, *please let me sink down towards the earth so that my feet touch solid ground again,* and beneath that the sadder unfulfillable wishes of old age, *let me be young again, give me back the strength of youth and the confidence that life is long,* and beneath that the dreams of the displaced, *let me belong again to that faraway place I left so long ago, from which I am alienated, and which has forgotten me, in which I am an alien now even though it was the place where I began, let me belong again, walk those streets knowing they are mine, knowing that my story is a part of the story of those streets, even though it isn't, it hasn't been for most of a lifetime, let it be so, let it be so, let me see French cricket being played and listen to music at the bandstand and hear once more the chil-*

dren's back-street rhymes. Still she *listened* and then she heard it, below everything else, the deepest note of his heart's music, and she knew what she must do.

Mr. Geronimo awoke at dawn feeling the daily dull bone-ache that he was learning to think of as his new normal condition, the consequence of his body's involuntary struggle against gravity. Gravity was still there, he could not at this point muster sufficient egotism to believe it had somehow diminished in his immediate vicinity. Gravity was gravity. But his body in the grip of an inexplicable and very slightly stronger counterforce was tugging against it, moving him slowly upwards, and it was exhausting. He thought of himself as a tough man, hardened by work, grief and time, a man not easily dismayed, but these days when he woke from his uneasy half-rest the first thoughts in his head were *worn down worn out* and *not long to go.* If he died before his condition subsided could he be buried, or would his corpse refuse the grave, push earth aside and, rising slowly, burst through the surface to hover above his final plot of ground while he decayed? If he was cremated would he be a small cloud of ash clustering obstinately in the air, ascending gravely like a swarm of indolent insects, until at some point it was dispersed by the winds or lost among the clouds? These were his morning concerns. But on this particular morning sleep's heaviness was quickly dispelled because something felt wrong. The room was in darkness. He did not remember turning off the table lamp by his bed. He had always liked a dark room to sleep in but in these strange times he had started leaving a small light on. His blanket often fell off him while he slept and he needed to reach several inches down to find it and he hated groping for it in the dark. So, usually, a light, but this morning he woke in shadow. And as his eyes grew accustomed to the dark he realized that he was not alone in the room. A woman was slowly *materializing,* his mind formed that impossible word, *materializing* in the darkness as he watched; a woman who was recognizable, even in the deep shadows where she was manifesting herself, as his dead wife.

Ella Elfenbein in the years since lightning took her from him at the old Bliss place, La Incoerenza, had not ceased to come to him in dreams, forever optimistic, forever gorgeous, forever young. In this time of his fear and melancholy she, who had gone before him into the great incoherence, came back to comfort and reassure. Awake, he had never been in any doubt that life was followed by nothingness. If pressed, he would have said that, in fact, life was a coming-into-being out of the great sea of nothingness from which we briefly emerged at birth and to which we must all return. His dreaming self, however, wanted nothing to do with such doctrinaire finality. His sleep was troubled and unsettled, but still she came, in all her loving physicality, her body swarming around his to enfold him in its warmth, her nose nuzzling into his neck, his arm encircling her head, his hand resting on her hair. She talked too much, as she always had, *your nonstop chat-a-tat,* he had called it in the good old days, *Radio Ella,* and there had been times when, laughing but just a little irritated, he had asked her to try being silent for sixty seconds, and she hadn't been able to do it, not even once. She advised him on healthy eating, admonished him about drinking too much alcohol, worried that in his increasingly confined condition he was not getting the exercise to which he was accustomed, discussed the latest skin-friendly cosmetics (dreaming, he didn't ask how she kept abreast of such matters), pontificated about politics, and, of course, had much to say about landscape gardening; talked about nothing, and everything, and nothing again, at length.

He thought of her monologues the way music lovers thought of beloved songs. They had provided their own kind of musical accompaniment to his life. His days had fallen silent now but his nights, some of them at least, still bulged with her words. But now he was awake and there was a woman standing over him and here was another impossible thing to set alongside the impossible thing his life had become, maybe this was an even more impossible impossibility, but he could recognize her body anywhere, even in the dark. He must have entered some sort of delirium, he thought, maybe he was at the end of his life and in the chaos of his last moments he had been granted this vision.

Ella? he asked. Yes, came the answer. Yes and no.

He turned on the light and jumped, if not out of his skin, then at least out of bed. Out of his supine position four inches above his mattress. His blanket fell away. And, facing mutated Dunia, now the spit and image of Ella Elfenbein Manezes, he trembled with true fear and the birth of an impossible joy.

They couldn't stop looking at each other. They were both looking at reincarnations, both falling in love with surrogates. They were not originals but copies, each an echo of the other's loss. From the beginning each knew the other to be a counterfeit, and from the beginning each was willing to suppress the knowledge; for a while, at least. We live in the age of coming after, and think of ourselves not as prime movers, but consequences.

"My wife is dead," said Mr. Geronimo, "and there are no ghosts, so either I am in the grip of a hallucination or this is a cruel prank."

"The dead don't walk, that's true," Dunia replied, "but the miraculous exists."

"First levitation," he said, "and now resurrection?"

"As to levitation," Dunia coquettishly answered, rising to his level, and inducing, in Mr. Geronimo, a loud, old-fashioned gasp, "two can play at that game. And as to resurrection, no, not exactly."

He had been trying hard to cling to his belief in the reality of the real, to treat his own condition as exceptional, and not a sign of a more general breakdown. The magic baby on television, whose existence had at first comforted him, had soon begun to worsen the disturbance in his spirit, and he tried to force her out of his thoughts. He had stopped listening to the news. If there were more surreal manifestations being reported, he didn't want to know about them. Solitude, uniqueness, these things had come to feel more desirable than the alternatives. If he could accept that he alone was or had become an aberration, a freak, then he could also still define the rest of the known world, the city, the country, the planet, by the known or credibly hypothesized principles of post-Einsteinian science, and could therefore dream of his own return to that lost, that yearned-for state. Aberrations occurred even in perfect systems. Such phenomena need not indicate the total failure of the system. Glitches could be unglitched, rebooted, fixed.

Now, confronted by Ella risen from the dead, he had to let go of that last scrap of hope, of what he had thought of as sanity, for here was Ella revealing herself as Dunia, princess of the jinn, who had adopted his wife's appearance to please him, or so she said; but perhaps it was to deceive him, to seduce and destroy him as the sirens destroyed mariners, or as Circe did, or some other fictional enchantress. Here was Elladunia, Duniella, in his beautiful wife's beautiful voice telling him wonder tales of the existence of the jinn, bright and dark, fairies and Ifrits, and of Fairyland, where the sex was incredible, and of metamorphs and whisperers; and of the breaking of the seals, the opening of the slits in reality; the first wormhole in Queens (there were more now, all over the place), the coming of the dark jinn and the consequences of their arrival. He was a skeptical and godless man and this kind of story unleashed a churning in his stomach and a sort of babbling in his brain. I'm losing my mind, he told himself. He no longer knew what to think, nor how to think it.

"The fairy world is real," she said soothingly, *listening* to his inner confusion, "but it does not follow that God exists. On that subject I am as skeptical as you."

She was still in the room, going nowhere, floating in the air just as he was, allowing him to touch her. He touched her first to see if he could touch her, because there was a part of his brain that believed his hand would pass right through. She was wearing a black tank top he actually remembered, a black tank over cargo pants like a photographer in a combat zone, her hair pulled back in a high ponytail, and there were her lean muscular bare arms, olive-skinned.

People had often asked Ella if she was Lebanese. His fingertips touched her arms and felt warm skin, familiar to his touch, Ella's skin. She moved towards him and then it was impossible for him to resist her. He became aware that there were tears streaming down his face. He held her and she allowed herself to be held. His hands cradled her face, and suddenly, unbearably, it felt wrong. Her chin: an unexpected lengthening. You're not her, he said, whoever or whatever you are, you're not her. She *listened* beneath his words and made an alteration. Try again, she said. Yes, he said, his palm curved tenderly under her jaw. Yes, that feels good.

At the beginning of all love there is a private treaty each of the lovers makes with himself or herself, an agreement to set aside what is wrong with the other for the sake of what is right. Love is spring after winter. It comes to heal life's wounds, inflicted by the unloving cold. When that warmth is born in the heart the imperfections of the beloved are as nothing, less than nothing, and the secret treaty with oneself is easy to sign. The voice of doubt is stilled. Later, when love fades, the secret treaty looks like folly, but if so, it's a necessary folly, born of lovers' belief in beauty, which is to say, in the possibility of the impossible thing, true love.

This man in his sixties, detached from the earth from which he had made his living, torn away by a lightning bolt from the only woman he had ever loved, and this princess of the otherworld, nursing in her bosom the memory of a centuries-old loss, across an ocean, far away, were both in pain, the unique anguish born of lost or broken love. Here, in a darkened basement bedroom in a house called The Bagdad, they agreed with themselves and with each other to renew two loves destroyed long ago by Death. She took on the clothing of his beloved wife's body, and he chose not to notice that Dunia's voice was not Ella's, that her manner was not his wife's, and that the shared memories that unite a loving couple were largely missing from her thoughts. She was a magnificent *listener* and had set herself the task of being the woman he wanted her to be, but, in the first place, *listening* takes time and care and, in the second place, a jinnia princess wants to be loved for herself, and so the desire to be loved as Dunia fought with her attempt to impersonate a dead woman and made the simulacrum less perfect than it might have been. And as for Geronimo Manezes, yes, she admired his strong, lean, old man's physique, but the man she had loved had been all mind.

"What do you know," she finally asked him, "about philosophy?"

He told her about the Lady Philosopher and her Nietzschean, Schopenhauerian pessimism. When he mentioned that the name of Alexandra Bliss Fariña's home was La Incoerenza, Dunia drew in her breath sharply, thinking of the battle of the books that had taken place long ago between Ghazali and Ibn Rushd, *The Incoherence of the Philosophers* versus *The Incoherence of the Incoherence*. Here was a third incoherence. Dunia saw, in coincidence, the hidden hand of kismet, which was also karma. Destiny was in that name. In names are concealed our fates.

Geronimo Manezes also told her Blue Yasmeen's fable about the pessimism of the Unyaza. "At this point, and in my present condition," he said, surprising himself by finding a version of one of Alexandra Fariña's mottoes issuing from his lips, "to say nothing of the state of the planet in general, it is difficult not to have a tragic view of life." It wasn't a bad answer, Dunia thought. It was the answer of a thinking man. She could work with that. "I understand," she replied, "but that attitude comes from the days before you met a fairy princess."

Time stopped. Mr. Geronimo was in a highly charged, enchanted place which was both his basement room and that room transformed into a jinni's smoke-scented love-lair, a place where no clock ticked, no second hand moved, no digital number changed. He could not have said if minutes passed during the timeless time of their love-making, or weeks, or months. Already, ever since his detachment from the earth, he had been obliged to set aside most of what he believed he knew about the nature of things. Now he was coming loose from the few fragments of his old beliefs that still remained. Here after a long interval was a woman's body which was and was not his wife's. It had been so long that his sense memory of Ella's flesh had weakened and though he was ashamed to admit it his more recent recollections of Alexandra Fariña were jumbled up with what he remembered about making love to his wife. And now this entirely new feeling was supplanting it, was becoming what he agreed with himself to think of as the feeling of Ella Elfenbein moving beneath him like a sweet warm tide, he, who had never believed in reincarnation or any such mumbo jumbo, was helpless, in the grip of the fairy princess's enchantments, and plunged into the sea of love, where everything was true if you said so, everything was true if the enchantress *whispered* it in his ear, and he could even accept in his confusion that his wife had been a fairy princess all along, that even during Ella's lifetime, *my first lifetime,* the jinnia whispered, *and this is my second,* yes, even in her first lifetime she had been a jinnia in disguise, so that the fairy princess was neither a counterfeit nor an imitation, it had always been her, even though he had not known it until now, and if this was delirium, he was okay with that, it was a delirium he chose and wanted, because all of us want love, eternal love, love returning beyond death to be reborn, love to nourish and enfold us until we die.

In that darkened room, no news reached them of the mayhem being wrought on the city outside. The city was screaming with fear but they could not hear it, boats were refusing to venture onto the water of the harbor, people were afraid to come out of their homes and go to work, and the panic was showing up in the money, stocks were crashing, banks were shuttered, supermarket shelves were empty and deliveries of fresh produce were not being made, the paralysis of terror held the city in its grip and catastrophe was in the air. But in the darkness of the narrow bedroom in the basement of The Bagdad the television was off and the crackle of the calamity could not be heard.

There was only the act of love, and lovemaking had a surprise in store for them both. "Your body smells of smoke," she said. "And look at you. When you're aroused you become blurred, smudged, there's smoke at the edges of you, didn't your human lovers ever tell you that?" No, he lied, remembering Ella telling him exactly that, but concealing the memory, correctly intuiting that Dunia would not like to know the truth. No, he said, they did not. This pleased her, as he had suspected it would. "That's because you never made love to a jinnia before," she told him. "It's a different level of arousal." Yes, he said, it was. But she was thinking, with mounting excitement, that it was his jinn self revealing itself, the jinn self that had come to him, down the centuries, from her. This was the sulfurous smokiness of the jinn when they made love. And if she could release the jinn with him then many things became possible. "Geronimo, Geronimo," she murmured in his smoky ear, "it looks like you are a fairy too."

Something unexpected happened to Dunia in their lovemaking: she enjoyed it, not as much as the bodiless sex of Fairyland, that ecstatic union of smoke and fire, but there was (as she had hoped there might be) a definite—no, a strong!—sensation of pleasure. This showed her not only that she was becoming more human but that her new lover might contain more of the jinn than she first suspected. So it was that their mimic love, their love born of the memory of others, their post-love that *came after,* became true, authentic, a thing in and of itself, in which she almost stopped thinking about the dead philosopher, and Mr. Geronimo's dead wife whose copy she had allowed herself to be was slowly replaced in his fantasy by this unknown magical creature who had come to him so improbably in his hour of need. The time might even come, Dunia allowed herself to think, when she could show herself to him as she truly was—neither the sixteen-year-old waif who had materialized at Ibn Rushd's door, nor this replicant of a lost love, but her royal self in all its glory. In the grip of that unexpected hope she began to tell Geronimo Manezes things she had never told Ibn Rushd.

"Around the borders of Fairyland," she said, "there stands the circular mountain of Qâf, where, according to legend, a bird-god once lived, the Simurgh, a relative of the Rukh of Sindbad. But that's just a story. We, the jinn and jiniri, we who are not legend, know that bird, but it does not rule over us. There is, however, a ruler on Qâf Mountain, not a thing of beak, feather and claw but a great fairy emperor, Shahpal son of Shahrukh, and his daughter, most powerful of the jinnias, *Aasmaan Peri,* which is to say, "Skyfairy," known as the Lightning Princess. Shahpal is the Simurgh King and that bird sits on his shoulder and serves him.

"Between the emperor and the Grand Ifrits there is no affection. Mount Qâf is the most desirable location in all of Fairyland and the Ifrits would dearly love to possess it but the thunderbolt magic of the emperor's daughter, a great jinnia sorceress, is equal to that of Zabardast and Zumurrud Shah, and it maintains a wall of sheet lightning that surrounds Qâf and protects the circular mountain against their greed. However, they are always on the lookout for an opportunity, fomenting trouble among the *devs,* or lesser spirits who populate the lower slopes of Qâf, trying to persuade them to rebel against their rulers. At this moment there is a hiatus in the endless struggle between the emperor and the Ifrits, which, to tell the truth, has been in a condition of stalemate for many millennia, because the storms, earthquakes and other phenomena that broke the long-closed seals between Peristan and the world of men have permitted the Ifrits to make their mischief here, which has the attraction for them of a novelty, or at least a thing long denied. They haven't been able to do this for a long time, and they believe there is no magic on earth capable of resisting them, and, being bullies, they like the idea of destroying an overmatched opponent. So while they think of conquest my father and I get a little respite."

"You?" Mr. Geronimo asked. "It's you, the princess of Qâf?"

"That's what I'm trying to tell you," she said. "The battle beginning here on earth is a mirror of the battle that has been going on in Fairyland for all time."

Now that she had learned the trick of pleasure, she was indefatigable in its pursuit. One of the reasons she preferred an "older" human lover, she murmured to Geronimo Manezes, was that they found it easier to control themselves. With young men it was over in a flash. He told her he was glad that age had a few advantages. She wasn't listening. She was discovering the joys of climax. And for the most part he was lost in a sweet confusion, hardly knowing to which of three women, two human, one not, he was making love, and as a result neither of them noticed at first what was happening to him, until at a certain moment when he was beneath and she above he felt something unexpected, something almost forgotten, under his head and back.

Pillows. Sheets.

The bed took his weight, the pocketed springs of the mattress sighing a little beneath him like a second lover, and then he felt her weight come down on him too, as the law of gravity reasserted itself. When he understood what had happened he began to weep, though he was not a man who found it easy to cry. She came off him and held him but he was unable to stay lying down. He climbed out of bed, gingerly, still half in disbelief, and allowed his feet to move towards the bedroom floor. When they touched it he cried out. Then stood, almost falling at first. His legs were weak, the muscles softened by lack of use. She stood beside him and he put an arm around her shoulder. Then he steadied, and released her, and was standing by himself. The room, the world, fell back into its familiar and long-lost shape. He felt the weights of things, of his body, his emotions, his hopes. "It seems I must believe you," he marveled, "and that you are who you say you are, and Fairyland exists, and you are its most powerful sorceress, for you have broken the curse that was laid upon me and rejoined me to the earth."

"What is more extraordinary than that," she rejoined, "is that, although I am indeed who I say I am, not only Dunia mother of the Duniazát but also the Princess Skyfairy of Qâf Mountain, I am not responsible for what has happened here, except that in our lovemaking I helped to unleash a power in you which neither of us suspected you possessed. I didn't bring you back down to earth. You did it by yourself. And if the jinni spirit in your body is capable of overcoming the sorcery of Zabardast, then the dark jinn have an enemy to reckon with in this world as well as the other one, and the War of the Worlds can perhaps be won instead of ending, as Zumurrud and his gang believe, in the inevitable victory of the dark jinn, and the establishment of their tyranny over all the peoples of the earth."

"Don't get carried away," he said. "I'm just a gardener. I shovel and plant and weed. I don't go to war."

"You don't have to go anywhere, my dearest," she said. "This war is coming to you."

Oliver Oldcastle the estate manager of La Incoerenza heard a scream of terror coming from his mistress's bedroom and immediately understood that what had happened to him must also have happened to her. "Now I really will kill that bastard hedge clipper," he roared and ran barefoot to help the Lady Philosopher. His hair was loose and wild and his shirt hung out of his worn cord trousers and with his arms windmilling as he ran he was more ungainly Bluto or Obélix moving at speed than leonine latter-day Marx. He passed the boot room with its faint ineradicable odor of horseshit, galloping along old wooden floors that on another day would have delivered splinters into his pounding feet, watched by the angry tapestries of imaginary ancestors, narrowly avoiding the Sèvres porcelain vases uneasy on their alabaster tables, running with his head down like a bull, ignoring the disapproving whispers of the supercilious shelves of books, and burst into Alexandra's private wing. At the door of her bedroom he gathered himself, smacked uselessly at his tangled hair, tugged his beard into shape, and stuffed his shirt into his trousers like a schoolboy asking for an audience with the head teacher, and "May I enter now, milady," he cried, the volume of his voice betraying his fear. Her loud answering wail was all the invitation he needed and then they stood facing each other, mistress and servant, she in a long archaic nightdress and he in shambles, with the same horror in their eyes, which turned slowly towards the floor, and saw that not one of their four bare feet, his sprouting hair at the ankle and from each toe, hers tiny and well formed, was in contact with the floor. A good inch of air stood between them and the ground.

"It's a bastard disease," Oldcastle bellowed. "That superfluous growth of a person, that fungus, that weed, came into your home bearing this blighty infection, and he has transmitted it to us."

"What kind of infection could possibly produce such a result?" she wept.

"This sodding kind, milady," cried Oldcastle, clenching his fists. "This turfing variety, pardon my French. This Dutch elm beetle you took into your private flower bed. This fatal oak killer *Phytophthora*. He's left us bloomin' diseased."

"He's not answering his phone," she said, waving her instrument uselessly in his face.

"He'll answer to me," said Oliver Oldcastle monumentally. "Or I'll landscape his ill-formed rump. I'll horticulture his savage bastard skull. He'll answer to me all right."

Separations of all sorts were being reported in those incomprehensible nights. The separation of human beings from the earth was bad enough. However, in certain parts of the world it had not begun or ended there. In the world of literature there was a noticeable separation of writers from their subjects. Scientists reported the separation of causes and effects. It became impossible to compile new editions of dictionaries on account of the separation of words and meanings. Economists noted the growing separation of the rich from the poor. The divorce courts experienced a sharp increase in business owing to a spate of marital separations. Old friendships came abruptly to an end. The separation plague spread rapidly across the world.

The detachment from the ground of a growing number of men, women and their pets—chocolate Labradors, bunny rabbits, Persian cats, hamsters, ferrets, and a monkey named E.T.—caused global panic. The fabric of human life was beginning to unravel. In the Menil Collection gallery in Houston, Texas, a shrewd curator named

Christof Pantokrator suddenly understood for the first time the pro-
phetic nature of René Magritte's masterwork *Golconda,* in which
men in overcoats, wearing bowler hats, hang in the air against a
background of low buildings and cloudless sky. It had always been
believed that the men in the picture were slowly falling, like well-
dressed rain. But Pantokrator perceived that Magritte had not
painted human raindrops. "They are human balloons," he cried.
"They rise! They rise!" Foolishly he made his discovery public and
after that the Menil buildings had to be protected by armed guards
against local people incensed by the great work of the prophet of
antigravity. Some of the guards began to rise, which was alarming,
and so did several of the protesters, the would-be vandals.

"The places of worship are full of terrified men and women seeking
the protection of the Almighty," Ghazali's dust said to the dust of Ibn
Rushd. "Just as I expected. Fear drives men to God."

There was no response.

"What's the matter?" Ghazali scoffed. "You finally ran out of hollow arguments?"

At length Ibn Rushd answered in a voice full of masculine com-
plication. "It's hard enough to discover that the woman who bore
your children is a supernatural being," he said, "without also having
to bear the knowledge that she is lying with another man." He knew
this because she had told him. In her jinnia way she thought he
would take it as a compliment that she had fallen for his copy, his
echo, his face on another body, revealing that in spite of her love for
human beings there were things about them she absolutely didn't
understand.

Ghazali laughed as only dust can laugh. "You're dead, you fool,"
he said. "Dead for eight centuries and more. This is no time for jeal-
ousy."

"That is the kind of inane remark," Ibn Rushd snapped back from
his grave, "which shows me that you have never been in love; from

which it follows that even when you were alive you never truly lived."

"Only with God," Ghazali replied. "That was and is my only lover, and he is and was more than enough."

When Sister Allbee discovered that her feet were an inch and a half off the ground she was angrier than at any point in her life since her father ran off with a gravel-voiced Louisiana chanteuse the week before he was supposed to take his daughter to the new Disney park in Florida. On that occasion she had gone through the second-floor apartment in the Harlem River Houses destroying all trace of her delinquent parent, tearing up photographs, shredding his hat, and making a bonfire of his abandoned clothes in the play space outside, watched silently by her mother flapping her arms and silently opening and shutting her mouth but making no attempt to dial back her daughter's rage. After that her father no longer existed and young C. C. Allbee gained a reputation as a girl never to be crossed.

Her favorite tenant, Blue Yasmeen, had taken off too, and was found sobbing uncontrollably in the hallway a full two inches up in the air. "I always defended him," she wailed. "Whenever you said something against him, I stuck up for the guy, because he was kind of a silver fox and he reminded me of my dad. Then a female on a flying rug shows up and I'm like am I going crazy and now this. I stuck up for the dude. How did I know he would pass his fuckin' sickness on to me?"

That made two betrayals by father figures to be mad about, and a few minutes later Sister Allbee used her master key to enter Mr. Geronimo's apartment with a loaded shotgun in her hand, with Blue Yasmeen fretful close behind her. "You're out of here," she bellowed. "Walk out by nightfall or be carried out feet first before dawn."

"He's standing on the floor!" Blue Yasmeen screamed. "He's cured, but he's left us sick."

Fear changed the fearful, thought Mr. Geronimo looking down

the barrel of the gun. Fear was a man running from his shadow. It was a woman wearing headphones and the only sound she could hear in them was her own terror. Fear was a solipsist, a narcissist, blind to everything except itself. Fear was stronger than ethics, stronger than judgment, stronger than responsibility, stronger than civilization. Fear was a bolting animal trampling children underfoot as it fled from itself. Fear was a bigot, a tyrant, a coward, a red mist, a whore. Fear was a bullet pointed at his heart.

"I'm an innocent man," he said, "but your gun makes an excellent argument."

"You are the spreader of the plague," said Sister Allbee. "Patient Zero! Typhoid Mary! Your body should be wrapped in plastic and buried a mile underground so you can't ruin any more lives."

Fear had Blue Yasmeen by the throat as well. "My father betrayed me by dying and abandoning me to the world, when he knew how much I needed him. You betrayed me by ripping the world away from beneath my feet. He was my father, so I love him anyway. You? You should just go."

The fairy princess had disappeared. When she heard the key turning in the lock she had turned sideways and disappeared through a slit in the air. Maybe she would help him, maybe not. He had heard all about the whimsical untrustworthiness of the jinn. Maybe she had just used him to feed her sexual hunger, for it was said that the jinn are insatiable in that department, and now that she was done he would never see her again. She had brought him down to earth and that was his reward, and all the rest, about his own jinn powers, was nonsense. Maybe he was alone, about to be homeless, faced with the unarguable truth of a shotgun in the hands of a woman enraged by her fear.

"I'll go," he said.

"One hour," said Sister.

And in the city of London, far from Mr. Geronimo's bedroom, a mob had gathered outside the home of the composer Hugo Casterbridge in Well Walk, in the sylvan borough of Hampstead. He was surprised to see it, because he had of late become a laughingstock, and public anger seemed an inappropriate response to his new reputation. It had become conventional to ridicule Casterbridge ever since his ill-advised television appearance in which he threatened the world with plagues sent down upon humanity by a god in whom he did not believe, the classic idiocy of the artist, everyone said, he should have stayed home and tinkled and tootled and clanked and banged and kept his mouth shut. Casterbridge was a man shored up by an immense, solid and hitherto impermeable self-belief but he had been unnerved by the ease with which his previous eminence had been obliterated by what he thought of as the new philistinism. There was apparently no room for the idea that the metaphorical sphere could be so potent that it affected the actual world. So he was a joke now, the atheist who believed in divine retribution.

Very well. He would indeed stay home with his strange Schoenbergian music which few people understood and even fewer enjoyed. He would think about hexachordal inversional combinatoriality and multidimensional set presentations, he would brood on the properties of the referential set, and let the rotting world go hang. He was more and more of a recluse anyway these days. The doorbell of the Well Walk mansion had gone wrong and he saw no need to have it fixed. The Post-Atheist group he had briefly assembled had melted away under the heat of public obloquy but he stuck, silently, angrily, with gritted teeth, to his guns. He was accustomed to being thought incomprehensible. Laugh! he mutely instructed his critics. He would see who had the last laugh of all.

But apparently there was a new preacher in town. There was a wildness in the city, fires on council estates in the poor boroughs to the north, looting of high-street stores in the usually conservative regions south of the river, and mutinous crowds in the main square that didn't know what to demand. Out of the flames came the turbaned firebrand, a small man with Yosemite Sam saffron beard and eyebrows, wrapped in a strong smell of smoke; he appeared from nowhere one day as if he stepped through a slit in the sky, Yusuf Ifrit was his name, and suddenly he was everywhere, a *leader,* a *spokesman,* he was on government committees, there was talk of a knighthood. There is indeed a plague spreading, he thundered, and if we do not defend ourselves against it we will all be infected for sure, it's infecting us already, the impurity of the disease has touched the blood of many of our weaker children, but we are ready to defend ourselves, we will fight the plague at its roots. The plague had many roots, Yusuf said, it was carried by books, films, dances, paintings, but music was what he feared and hated most, because music slid beneath the thinking mind to seize the heart; and of all music makers, he hated one the worst of them all, the plague personified as cacophony, evil transmuted into sound. And so here was a police officer visiting the composer Casterbridge, I'm afraid you'll have to move out, sir, until things cool off, we can't guarantee your safety at this location, and there are your neighbors to consider, sir, innocent bystanders could be hurt in an affray, and he bridled at that, Let me understand you, he said, let me be perfectly clear what you're telling me here, what you're saying to me now is that if *I* get hurt in this putative *affray* of yours, if the injury is to *me,* then I'm not an innocent bystander, is *that* your fucking point? There's no need for that kind of language, sir, I won't stand for it, you need to take on the situation as it is, I won't endanger my officers by reason of your egotistical intransigence.

Go away, he said. This is my home. This is my castle. I'll defend myself with cannons and boiling oil.

Is that a threat of violence, sir?

It's a fucking figure of speech.

Then, a mystery. The gathering mob, words of hate, aggression disguised as defensiveness, the threatening claiming to be under threat, the knife pretending to be in danger of being stabbed, the fist accusing the chin of attacking it, all that was familiar, the loud malevolent hypocrisy of the age. Even the preacher from nowhere wasn't much of a puzzlement. Such unholy holy men cropped up all the time, created by some form of sociological parthenogenesis, some weird bootstrap operation that made authorities out of nonentities. That was stuff to shrug at. Then on the night of the mystery there were reports of a woman seen with the composer, silhouetted against the living room window, an unknown woman who appeared as if from nowhere and then disappeared, leaving the composer alone at the night window, opening it in defiance of the gathered mob, his painful dissonant music clanging behind him like an alarm system, his arms outstretched as if crucified, what was he doing, was he inviting death into his home, and why was the crowd suddenly hushed, as if some giant invisible cat had got its tongue, why wasn't it moving, it looked like a waxwork tableau of itself, and where were those clouds coming from, the weather in London was clear and mild, but not in Hampstead, in Hampstead that night all of a sudden there was rolling thunder, and then bolts of lightning, wham, crash, and the mob didn't wait around for another strike, the lightning broke the spell and the mob ran screaming for its life, down Well Walk and on to the Heath, nobody killed thank goodness, except for the idiot who decided the best place to shelter from thunderbolts was under a tree, he got fried. The next day the mob didn't come back, or the next, or the next.

Quite a coincidence, sir, that oddly localized storm, almost as if you brought it on, you wouldn't have an interest in meteorology, would you, sir? There wouldn't be some weather-altering contraption in your attic, now would there? You'll excuse us if we just take a look?

Inspector, be my guest.

On the way back to Mr. Geronimo from Hugo Casterbridge, flying east not west, for the jinn move so swiftly that there's no need to take the shortest route, Dunia flew over ruins, hysteria, chaos. Mountains had begun to crumble, snows to melt and oceans to rise, and the dark jinn were everywhere—Zumurrud the Great, Shining Ruby, Ra'im

Blood-Drinker, and Zumurrud's old ally, increasingly his rival for jinn supremacy, the sorcerer-jinni Zabardast. Water reservoirs turned to urine and a baby-faced tyrant, after Zabardast *whispered* in his ear, ordered all his subjects to have the same ridiculous haircut as himself. Human beings did not know how to handle the irruption of the supranormal into their lives, Dunia thought, most of them simply fell apart or had the haircuts and wept with love for the baby-faced tyrant, or under Zumurrud's spell they prostrated themselves before false gods who asked them to murder the devotees of other false gods, and that too was being done, statues of These gods destroyed by followers of Those gods, lovers of Those gods castrated stoned to death hanged sliced in half by the lovers of These. Human sanity was a poor, fragile thing at best, she thought. Hatred stupidity devotion greed the four horsemen of the new apocalypse. Yet she loved these wrecked people and wanted to save them from the dark jinn who fed, watered and made manifest the darkness within themselves. To love one human being was to begin to love them all. To love two was to be hooked forever, helpless in the grip of love.

Where did you go, he said. You disappeared just when I needed you.

I went to see someone who also needed me. I had to show him what he was capable of.

Another man.

Another man.

Did you look like Ella when you were with him. Are you making my dead wife fuck men she never met is that it.

That isn't it.

I have my feet on the ground again so you're done with me this was some sort of jinn therapy is that it.

That isn't it.

What do you really look like. Show me what you really look like. Ella is dead. She's dead. She was a beautiful optimist and believed in an afterlife but this wasn't it, this zombie of my darling wife inhabited by you. Stop. Please stop. I'm being thrown out of this apartment. I'm losing my mind.

I know where you need to go.

It is dangerous for human beings to enter Peristan. Very few have ever done so. Until the War of the Worlds only one man, as far as we know, ever stayed there for any length of time, and married a fairy princess, and when he returned to the world of men he discovered that eighteen years had passed even though he believed himself to have been away for a much shorter period. A day in the jinn world is like a month of human time. Nor is that the only danger. To look upon the beauty of a jinnia princess in her true uncloaked aspect is to be dazzled beyond the capacity of many human eyes to see, minds to grasp or hearts to bear. An ordinary man might be blinded or driven insane or killed as his heart burst with love. In the old days, a thousand years ago, a few adventurers managed to enter the jinn world, mostly with the assistance of well- or evil-intentioned jinn. To repeat: only one human being ever returned in good shape, the hero Hamza, and the suspicion remains that he may have been part jinni himself. So when Dunia the jinnia, aka Aasmaan Peri the Lightning Princess of Qâf Mountain, suggested to Mr. Geronimo that he return with her to her father's kingdom, suspicious minds might have concluded that she was luring him to his doom like the sirens singing on the rocks near Positano or Lilith the night monster who was Adam's wife before Eve, or John Keats's merciless beauty.

Come with me, she said. I will reveal myself to you when you're ready to see me.

Then,

just as the inhabitants of the city were discovering the true meaning of being without shelter, even though they had always believed themselves to be experts in shelterlessness, because the city they hated and loved had always been bad at providing its inhabitants with protection against the storms of life, and had inculcated in its citizens a certain fierce loving-hating pride at their own habits of survival in spite of everything, in spite of the not-enough-money issue and the not-enough-space issue and the dog-eat-dog issue and so on;

just as they were being forced to face the fact that the city or some force within the city or some force arriving in the city from outside the city might be about to expel them from its territory forever, not horizontally but vertically, into the sky, into the freezing air and the murderous airlessness above the air;

just as they began to imagine their lifeless bodies floating out beyond the solar system, so that whatever alien intelligences might be out there would meet dead human beings long before living ones and wonder what stupidity or horror had pushed these entities out into space without so much as protective clothing;

just as the screams and weeping of the citizens began to rise above the noise of such traffic as continued to ply the streets, because the plague of rising had broken out in many neighborhoods, and those individuals who believed in such things began to shout in the frightened streets that the Rapture had begun, as foretold in Paul's first epistle to the Thessalonians, when the living and the dead would be caught up in the clouds and meet the Lord in the air, it was the end of days, they cried, and as people began to float upwards away from the metropolis it was getting to be hard even for the most diehard skeptic to disagree;

just as all this was going on, Oliver Oldcastle and the Lady Philosopher arrived at The Bagdad with murder in his eyes and terror in hers, having had to struggle into the city without the benefit of a car or bus or train, it was, Oldcastle told Alexandra, just about the distance traveled by Pheidippides from the battlefield of Marathon to Athens, at the end of which, by the way, he dropped dead, and they too were exhausted, at the end of their strength, and irrationally believing that a confrontation with Geronimo Manezes could re-

solve everything, that if they could just frighten him enough or seduce him enough he would be able to reverse what he had set in
motion;

just at that precise moment a great light flooded outwards and
upwards from the basement bedroom in which the greatest of the
jinnia princesses was revealing herself in her true glory for the first
time ever in the human world, and the revelation opened the royal
gate into Fairyland, and Mr. Geronimo and the Lightning Princess
were gone, and the gate closed and the light went out and the city
was left to face its fate, C. C. Allbee and Blue Yasmeen floating
balloon-fashion in the stairwell of The Bagdad, and Manager Oldcastle in his great wrath and the chatelaine of La Incoerenza who
had left her estate for the first time in many years standing impotent
in the street, already a foot or so off the ground, without any hope of
redress.

There was too much light and when it diminished so that he could
see again, Mr. Geronimo to his consternation found himself a child
in a long-forgotten but familiar street playing French cricket with
chanting boys, Raffy 'Ronnimus once more, and all of a sudden and
quite inexplicably and there winking at him looking like any other
Sandra from Bandra was a young girl in whose wicked delighted
eyes he saw the jinnia princess. And his mother Magda Manezes and
Father Jerry himself also watching him at play, hand in hand and
happy, as they never did and rarely were in life. And a warm evening, but not too hot, and the shadows lengthening away from the
cricketing boys, showing them in silhouette pictures of the men they
might grow up to be. His heart filled with something that might
have been happiness, but poured out of his eyes as grief. The tears
were uncontrollable and his whole body shook with the sadness of
what was, *there are tears in things,* said pious Aeneas in Virgil's words
long ago, *and mortal things touch the mind.* His feet were on the
ground now but where was this ground, in Fairyland or Bombay or
an illusion, it was just another way of being adrift, or in the clutches
of the jinnia princess. As he looked around at the dream of an old

street scene, this occult hologram, he was in the grip of everything sad that ever happened to him, he wished he had never become detached from the place he was born, wished his feet had remained planted on that beloved ground, wished he could have been happy all his life in those childhood streets, and grown into an old man there and known every paving stone, every betel-nut vendor's story, every boy selling pirated novels at traffic lights, every rich man's car rudely parked up on the sidewalk, every girl at the bandstand aging into a grandmother and remembering when they kissed furtively at night in the churchyard, he wished he could have roots spreading under every inch of his lost soil, his beloved lost home, that he could have been a part of something, that he could have been himself, walking down the road not taken, living a life *in context* and not the migrant's hollow journey that had been his fate; ah, but then he would never have met his wife, he argued with himself, and that deepened his grief, how could he bear the idea that by remaining joined to the line of the past he might never have had his one true passage of joy, maybe he could dream her into his Indian life, maybe she would have loved him there as well, she would have walked down this street and found him here and loved him just the same, even though he would have been the self he never became, maybe she would have loved that self too, Raphael Hieronymus Manezes, that lost boy, that boy which the man had lost.

I thought you'd like it, said the little girl with the jinnia's eyes, puzzled. I *listened* to your heart and *heard* your sorrow at what you had left behind and I thought this would be a welcome gift.

Take it away, he said, choking on his tears.

Bombay vanished and Peristan appeared, or rather Mount Qâf the circular mountain that encloses the fairy world. He was in a white marble courtyard of the curved palace of the Lightning Princess, its red stone walls and marble cupolas around and above, its soft tapestries rippled by a breeze, and the curtain of sheet lightning that guarded it hanging like the aurora in the sky. He did not want to be here. Anger replaced grief in him. Until a few hundred days ago, he reminded himself, he had had no interest whatsoever in the supra-normal or fabulous. Chimeras or angels, heaven or hell, metamor-phoses or transfigurations, a pox on them all, he had always thought. Solid ground beneath his feet, dirt under his fingernails, the hus-bandry of growing things, bulbs and roots, seeds and shoots, this had been his world. Then all of a sudden, levitation, the arrival of an absurd universe, strangenesses, cataclysm. And just as mysteriously as he rose, so he had descended, and all he wanted now was to re-sume. He didn't want to know what it meant. He wanted not to be a part of the place, the *thing*—he didn't have the word for it—in which all those things existed, he wanted to re-create the real world around himself, even if the real world was an illusion and this continuum of the irrational was the truth, he wanted the fiction of the real back. To walk, jog, run and jump, to dig and grow. To be earth's creature and not, like some devil, a creature of the powers of the air. That was his only desire. Yet here was Fairyland. And a goddess of smoke before him who was obviously not his dead wife exhumed from the grave by his memory of her. Comprehension failed him. He had no more tears to cry.

Why have you brought me here, he asked. Couldn't you have just left me alone.

She dissolved into a whirl of white with a shining light at its heart. Then she took shape again, no longer skinny Dunia the love of Ibn Rushd but Aasmaan Peri, Skyfairy, splendid with lightning crack-ling like a victor's wreath at her brow, adorned with jewels and gold and clad in wisps of smoke with a gaggle of handmaidens behind her in half-moon formation, awaiting her command. Don't ask a jinnia princess for reasons, she said, her turn to be angry now, maybe I brought you here to be my slave, to pour my wine or oil my feet, or perhaps even, if I so please, you could be my lunch, fricasseed on a platter with a little wilted kale, these ladies will cook you if I decide to crook my little finger against you, do not imagine they won't. You fail to praise a princess's beauty and then ask her for reasons! Reasons are human follies. We have only pleasures and what we will.

Return me to my ordinary life, he said. I'm not a dreamer and am out of place in castles in the air. I have a gardening business to run.

Because you are my great-great-great-great-great-great-great-grandson, give or take a *great* or two, she said, I forgive you. But, in the first place, mind your manners, especially if my father enters the room, he may be less generous than I. And in the second place, stop being a fool. Your ordinary life no longer exists.

What did you say? I'm your what?

She had so much to teach him. He didn't even know how lucky he was. She was Skyfairy the Beautiful and could have had anyone in the Two Worlds and she had chosen him because his face was the echo of a great man she once loved. He didn't understand that he was standing on Mount Qâf as if it was the most normal thing in the world, even though just setting foot in Peristan would drive many mortal men out of their minds. He didn't know himself, the great jinni spirit he bore in his blood, because of her. He should be thanking her for this gift and instead he looked disgusted.

How old *are* you, anyway? he asked.

Be careful, she said, or I will send a thunderbolt to melt your heart so that it runs down your body inside your clothes and fills your foolish human shoes with goo.

She snapped her fingers and Father Jerry materialized beside her, and scolded Geronimo Manezes as he always did. I told you so, he wagged a finger at Mr. Geronimo. You heard this from me first, and you wouldn't believe it. The Duniazát, the brood of Averroës. Turns out I was spot-on. What do you have to say to me now?

You're not real, said Mr. Geronimo. Go away.

I was thinking more along the lines of an apology, but never mind, said Father Jerry, and vanished in a puff of smoke.

The seals between the Two Worlds are broken and the dark jinn ride, she said. Your world is in danger and because my children are everywhere I am protecting it. I'm bringing them together, and together we will fight back.

I'm not a fighter, he told her. I'm not a hero. I'm a gardener.

That is a pity, she said, a little scornfully, because right now, as it happens, heroes are what we need.

It was their first lovers' quarrel, and who knows where it might have ended up, for it destroyed the last vestiges of the illusions which had brought them together, she was no longer the avatar of his lost wife and he was plainly an inadequate substitute for the great Aristotelian, the father of her clan. She was smoke made flesh and he was a disintegrating clod of earth. Maybe she would have dismissed him then and there; but then calamity came to Mount Qâf too, and a new phase of the War of the Worlds began.

A cry went up in a distant chamber, and then came a relay of louder and louder cries, the shrieks being passed from mouth to mouth like dark kisses, until the running figure of the royal household's chief spy, Omar the Ayyar, could be seen approaching at speed along the curved length of the great court where Mr. Geronimo stood with the jinnia princess, to tell her, in a voice bursting with horror, that her father, the fairy emperor, mighty Shahpal the son of Shahrukh, had been poisoned. He was the Simurgh King, and the holy bird of Qâf, the Simurgh, stood guard over him on his bedpost, sunk in its own enigmatic form of sadness; and after a reign lasting many thousands of years Shahpal found himself approaching lands to which few of the jinn ever traveled, lands ruled over by an even mightier king than Shahpal himself, who stood waiting for the mountain emperor at the gates of his own twin kingdoms, with two giant four-eyed dogs at his side: Yama, the lord of death, the guardian of heaven and hell.

When he fell it was as if the mountain itself had fallen, and, in fact, cracks were reported to have appeared in the perfect circle of Qâf, trees split down the middle, birds fell from the sky, the lowest *devs* on the lowest slopes felt the tremors, and even his most disloyal subjects were shaken, even the *devs* most ready to be seduced by the blandishments of the dark jinn, the Ifrits, the immediate prime suspects in the matter of his poisoning, because the question on everyone's lips was, how can a king of the jinn be poisoned, the jinn are creatures of smokeless fire, and how do you poison a fire, are there occult extinguishers of some kind that can be fed to a jinni, anti-inflammatory agents created by the black arts that will kill him, or magic spells that suck the air out of his immediate vicinity so that the fire cannot burn, everyone was clutching at straws as he lay dying, because all explanations sounded absurd, but good answers were nowhere to be had. There are no doctors among the jinn because sickness is unknown to them and deaths are extremely rare. *Only a jinni can kill a jinni* is a truism among the jinn and so when King Shahpal clutched at himself and cried *Poison* everyone's first thought was that there had to be a traitor in their midst.

Omar the Ayyar—*ayyar* means "spy"—had come a long way in the royal service from humble beginnings. He was a good-looking fellow, full-lipped, large-eyed, a little effeminate in fact, and a long time ago he had been obliged to wear women's clothing and take up residence in the harems of earthly princes so that he could smooth the path for his jinni master to visit the ladies at night, when the princes' attention was elsewhere. On one occasion, the Prince of O. unexpectedly showed up while King Shahpal was dallying with the bored O. wives, for whom a jinni lover made a spirited and welcome change. Omar unfortunately misheard his master's command, Away with us at once, as, Do away with him at once, and so alas and alack he cut off the royal head of the Prince of O. After that in Peristan the ayyar was known as Omar the Cloth-Eared and it had taken him two years, eight months and twenty-eight nights in earth time to live down that mistake. Since then he had risen to the top, trusted above all others both by Shahpal and by his daughter Skyfairy known as Dunia, becoming the unofficial head of the intelligence services of Qâf. But he had been the first to find the fallen monarch and so the cold fingertip of suspicion naturally came to rest upon his brow. When he came running to the princess he was not only bringing the news. He was also fleeing a mob of angry palace servitors, and carrying a Chinese box.

She was the princess of Qâf and the heir apparent, so of course she could quell the misdirected wrath of her angry people, she raised a palm and they froze like children playing grandmother's footsteps, she waved her hand and they scattered like crows, all that was straightforward, her faith in Omar the no-longer-cloth-eared was complete, and what was that in his hand, maybe an answer, he was trying to tell her something. Your father is a strong man, he said, he's not dead yet, he's fighting with all his power and maybe his magic will be stronger than the dark magic attacking him. She understood all of this very well but what caught her off guard and was harder for her to grasp was that when the dreadful news reached her ears, *poison, the king, your father,* she neither reacted with majestic restraint as she had been bred to do, nor did she fall weeping into the arms of her handmaidens, who had gathered behind her clucking their unease, no, she had turned to him, Geronimo Manezes, the ungrateful gardener, the human being, and needed his embrace. And as for him, as he held in his arms the loveliest female entity he had ever seen, and felt simultaneously drawn to this fairy princess and disloyal to his dead wife, simultaneously intoxicated by Fairyland and even less grounded than when his feet left the ground of his own city in his own world, an existential bewilderment, as if he were being asked to speak a language without knowing any of its words or syntax, what was right action, what was wrong action, he no longer had any idea, but here she was nestling sadly into his chest, and that, he could not deny it, felt good. And behind her and beyond her he saw a cockroach scuttle under a chaise-longue and a butterfly hover in the air, and the thought occurred to him that *these were memories,* that he had seen this specific cockroach and this particular butterfly before, elsewhere, in his lost country, and that the ability of Peristan to read his mind and bring his deepest memories to life was in danger of driving him insane. Turn away from yourself, he said, look outwards through your eyes and let your interior world take care of itself. There's a poisoned king here, and a frightened spy, and a shocked and saddened princess, and a Chinese box.

What's in the box, he asked the spy.

It dropped from the king's hands when he fell, Omar said. I believe the poison is inside.

What sort of poison, said Mr. Geronimo.

Verbal, said Omar. A fairy king can only be poisoned by the most dreadful and powerful of words.

Open the box, Dunia said.

Within the
Chinese Box,

like layers of rectangular skin, were many other boxes, disappearing into the center of the enclosed space as if tumbling into an abyss. The outermost layer, the box containing all the other boxes, actually seemed to be alive, and Mr. Geronimo wondered with a small shudder of disgust if it, and all that it contained, might actually be made of living, perhaps human, skin. He found it impossible even to think of touching the accursed thing, but the princess handled it easily, displaying her long familiarity with recursive skin-onions of this type. The six surfaces of the Chinese box were intricately decorated—the word *tattooed* came to Mr. Geronimo's mind—with images of mountainous landscapes and ornate pavilions by babbling streams.

In such boxes, now that contact between the Two Worlds had been reestablished, the emperor's spies sent him detailed and varied accounts of the world below, the human reality, which Shahpal found endlessly fascinating. The centuries of separation had created in the monarch of Qâf a profound feeling of enervation which often made it difficult for him to get out of bed, and even the jinnia harlots who ministered to him there found him sexually sluggish, a shocking thing in the jinn world, where sex provides the one, unceasing entertainment. Shahpal remembered the story about how the Hindu deity Indra had responded to the boredom of heaven by inventing the theater and staging plays for the amusement of his underemployed pantheon of gods, and he toyed for a moment with the idea of bringing the dramatic art to Peristan as well, but abandoned the idea because everyone he asked about it ridiculed the notion of watching imaginary people doing imaginary things that did not end in sexual intercourse, though a few of his sample conceded that make-believe might be a useful way of jazzing up their smoke-and-fire sex lives. The jinn, Shahpal concluded, were uninterested in fiction, and obsessed by realism, no matter how dull their realistic lives might be. Fire burned paper. There were no books in Fairyland.

These days the Ifrits, or dark jinn, had retreated from the so-called Line of Control that separated Qâf from their savage territory, and busied themselves with an attack on the human world that distressed Shahpal, who was an earth-lover, a terraphile. The consequent near-cessation of hostilities at the borders of Qâf, while providing a welcome respite, had also lessened the flow of incident, and increased the tedium of the days. Shahpal envied the freedom of his daughter the Lightning Princess, who, having set her protective barriers in place, could be absent from Qâf for long periods, exploring the pleasures of the world below, and battling the dark jinn while she was there. The king had to stay on his throne. That was the way of it. The crown was a prison. A palace did not need barred windows to hold its resident within its walls.

We tell this story still as it has come down to us through many retellings, mouth to ear, ear to mouth, both the story of the poisoned box and the stories it contained, in which the poison was concealed. This is what stories are, experience retold by many tongues to which, sometimes, we give a single name, Homer, Valmiki, Vyasa, Scheherazade. We, for our own part, simply call ourselves "we." "We" are the creature that tells itself stories to understand what sort of creature it is. As they pass down to us the stories lift themselves away from time and place, losing the specificity of their beginnings, but gaining the purity of essences, of being simply themselves. And by extension, or by the same token, as we like to say, though we do not know what the token is or was, these stories become what we know, what we understand, and what we are, or, perhaps we should say, what we have become, or can perhaps be.

As carefully as a sapper defusing a bomb, Omar the Ayyar peeled away the outer skin of the box, and poof! the onion skin dematerialized, and at once a story began, released from its wafer-thin layer of cornered space: a murmur rising to become a mellifluous female voice, one of the many voices the Chinese box contained and made available for the use of the messenger. This voice, husky, low, soothing, made Mr. Geronimo think of Blue Yasmeen, and of The Bagdad-without-an-*h* where she lived, the home from which he had been evicted. A wave of melancholy washed over him and then receded. The story flung its hook at him, which lodged in his lobeless ear, and caught his attention.

"That morning after the general election, O illustrious King, a certain Mr. Airagaira of the distant city of B. was awoken like everyone else by loud sirens followed by a megaphone announcement from a flag-waving white van. Everything was about to change, the megaphone cried, because it was what the people had demanded. The people were sick of corruption and mismanagement and above all sick of the family that had had a stranglehold on power for so long that they had become like the relatives everyone hates and can't wait until they leave the room. Now the family was gone, the megaphone said, and the country could finally grow up without the detested National Relatives. Like everyone else, the megaphone said, he was to stop working immediately at his present job, a job which as a matter of fact he enjoyed—he was an editor of books for young adults, at a prominent publishing company in the city—and report for duty at one of the new assignment stations that had been set up overnight, where he would be informed of his new employment, and become a part of the new grand national enterprise, the construction of the machine of the future.

"He got dressed quickly and went downstairs to explain to the officer with the megaphone that he possessed neither the necessary engineering skills nor mechanical aptitude for such a task, being a person *from arts side not science side,* and besides, he was content to allow things to remain as they were, he had made his choices, and selected career satisfaction over the accumulation of wealth. As a confirmed bachelor of a certain age, he had more than enough for his needs, and the work was valuable: the challenging, entertaining, and shaping of young minds. The megaphone officer shrugged indifferently. 'What's that to me?' he said in a curt, discourteous manner. 'You'll do as the new nation requests unless you want to be thought of as an antinational element. That is an element for which there is no longer any place in our periodic table. It is, as the French say, though I do not speak French, believing it to be alien to our traditions and therefore unimportant to know, *hors de classification.* The trucks will be here soon. If you insist on making your objection, take it up with the transportation officer.'

"His colleagues in the publishing company said of Mr. Airagaira, not always in complimentary tones, that he possessed an innocence that exceeded the knowing cynicism of most children, and therefore failed to grasp the disappointed bitterness of a world that had lost its innocence long ago. Gentle, bespectacled, confused, he waited for the promised trucks. If René Magritte had painted Stan Laurel in shades of light brown the result might have resembled Mr. Airagaira, grinning his vague, goofy grin at the gathering crowd, and blinking myopically at the herders corralling them, men with orange marks on their foreheads and long sticks in their hands. The convoy of trucks duly arrived, curving down the old seaside promenade like ink blots dripping down an old painting, and when Mr. Airagaira finally found himself face to face with the transportation officer, a burly thick-haired young man plainly proud of his muscly arms and barrel chest, he was sure that the misunderstanding would soon be cleared up. He began to speak but the transportation officer interrupted him and asked for his name. He gave it and the officer consulted a sheaf of documents attached to a clipboard in his hands. 'Here it is,' he said, showing a paper to Mr. Airagaira. 'Your employers have let you go.' Mr. Airagaira shook his head. 'That's impossible,' he explained reasonably. 'In the first place, I'm valued at the office, and in the second place, even if this were true, I would have first received oral and then written warnings and finally a letter of dismissal. That is the proper way of doing things and that procedure has not been followed, plus, I repeat, I have every reason to believe I am well regarded at work, and in line, not for dismissal, but for promotion.' The transportation officer pointed to a signature at the bottom of the sheet. 'Recognize that?' Mr. Airagaira was shocked to note that he did recognize his boss's unmistakable hand. 'Then that's an end to it,' the transportation officer said. 'If you've been fired, you must have done something very wrong. You can play the innocent, but your guilt is written on your face, and this signature which you have verified is the proof. Get in the truck.'

"Mr. Airagaira allowed himself one sentence of dissent. 'I would never have believed,' he said, 'that such a thing could happen, here in my own beloved hometown of B.'

"'The name of the city has been changed,' the transportation officer said. 'It will now be known once again by its ancient name, which the gods gave it long ago: Deliverance.'

"Illustrious King: Mr. Airagaira had never heard that name, and knew nothing about the gods' involvement in naming the city in ancient times, when the city had not even existed, it being one of the newer cities of the country, not an ancient metropolis like D. to the north but a modern conurbation, but he made no further protest, and along with everyone else climbed meekly into one of the trucks and was driven away to the new factories in the north where the machine of the future was being constructed. In the weeks and months that followed his bewilderment grew. At his new workplace, among the forbidding resonances of the turbines and the staccato sizzle of the drills, in between the silent enigma of the conveyor belts upon which nuts, bolts, elbow joints and cogs moved smoothly past quality control points towards unknown destinations, he saw to his surprise that workers even less skilled than himself had been drafted into the great work, that small children were gluing together contraptions of wood and paper and these too were somehow being incorporated into the immensity of the whole, that cooks were making patties which were being stuck to the sides of the machine the way cow dung was used in the villages on the walls of mud houses. What kind of machine was this, Mr. Airagaira asked himself, that the entire nation was required to build? Seamen had to insert their ships into the machine and tillermen their plows; as he was moved from place to place along the gigantic construction site of the machine he saw hoteliers building their hotels into the machine and there were motion picture cameras in there and textile looms, but there were no clients in the hotels or film in the cameras or cloth on the looms. The mystery grew as the machine expanded, whole neighborhoods were demolished to make room for the machine, until it began to seem to Airagaira Sahib that the machine and the country had become synonymous, because there was no longer room in the country for anything except the machine.

"In those days food and water rationing had been imposed, hospitals ran out of medication and stores out of things to sell, the machine was everything and everywhere and everyone went to their appointed workstations and did the work they were allotted, screwing, drilling, riveting, hammering, and went home at night too exhausted to speak. The birthrate began to drop because sex was too much of an effort, and that was presented as a national benefit by the radio and television and megaphones. Mr. Airagaira noticed that the managers of the construction program, the orderers and pointers and herders, all seemed to be viciously angry all the time, and intolerant too, particularly of people like himself, people who had previously gone about their lives quietly and been happy for others to do the same. Such people were deemed to be simultaneously weak and dangerous, simultaneously useless and subversive, in need of a heavy disciplinary hand, which, make no mistake, the megaphones said, would be used wherever and whenever necessary, and how strange, Mr. Airagaira thought, that those who were on top in this new dispensation were angrier than those who were underneath.

"One day, O illustrious King, Mr. Airagaira saw a terrible sight. There were men and women carrying building materials in metal pans on their heads, which was normal, but something was wrong with the shape of these women and men, they looked—he groped for the word—squashed, as though something far heavier than the building materials they carried were weighing down on them, as if gravity itself had increased in their vicinity and they were literally being crushed into the earth. Was that even possible, he asked his neighbors on the quality control belt to which he had been assigned, could it be that they were being tortured, and everyone he asked said no with their mouths but yes with their eyes, no, what a suggestion, our country's free, said their tongues, while their eyes said don't be a fool, it's frightening to utter such thoughts aloud. The next day the squashed people had gone and the pans of construction materials were being borne by new carriers, and if Mr. Airagaira saw something a little compressed about these persons too he kept his mouth shut about it and only his eyes spoke to his fellow workers, whose eyes spoke silently back. But keeping your mouth shut when there's something you need to spit out is bad for the digestion, and Mr. Airagaira went home feeling nauseous and close to throwing up explosively in the transportation truck, which would have been, to use one of the new words of those days, inadvisable.

"That night Mr. Airagaira must have been visited, or even possessed, by a jinni, because the next morning on the production line he seemed like a different person, and there seemed to be a kind of electricity crackling around his ears. Instead of going to his workstation he marched right up to one of the construction management team, the senior-most orderer in sight, and said in a loud voice that made many of his fellow workers pay attention, 'Excuse me, sir, but I have an important question for you concerning the machine.'

" 'No questions,' said the orderer. 'Go about your appointed tasks.'

" 'The question is this,' Airagaira Sahib continued, having abandoned his gentle, confused, myopic voice for these new, stentorian, even megaphonic tones. 'What does the machine of the future produce?'

"Many people were listening now. An assenting murmur rose from their ranks, *Yes, what does it produce.* The orderer narrowed his eyes and a group of herders closed in on Mr. Airagaira. 'That is obvious,' the orderer answered. 'It produces the future.'

" 'The future is not a product,' shouted Mr. Airagaira. 'Rather, it is a mystery. What does the machine actually make?'

"The herders were close enough to seize Mr. Airagaira now, but a crowd of workers was gathering, and it was plain the herders were not sure how best to proceed. They looked for guidance to the orderer.

" 'What does it make?' the orderer screamed. 'It makes glory! Glory is the product. Glory, honor and pride. Glory is the future, but you have shown that there is no place in that future for you. Take this terrorist away. I will not allow him to infect this sector with his diseased mind. Such a mind is a bearer of the plague.'

"The crowd was unhappy as the herders made a grab for Mr. Airagaira but then people began to scream, because the electricity that had been crackling around the ears of the former publisher of books for young adults was seen flowing down his neck and arms, all the way to his fingertips, and then bolts of high-voltage electricity poured out of his hands, killing the orderer instantly, sending the herders running for cover, and striking the machine of the future with a violence that caused a sizable sector of the colossal behemoth to buckle and explode."

The box began to move in the princess's hands. A layer of the rectangular onion skin peeled away and vanished into smoke just as the first layer had, and another voice, this one a fine baritone, began to speak. "This mention of a plague," said the Chinese box, "reminds me of another story which you may be interested to hear." But before the tale could progress very far Dunia gave a start and a little cry. She let go of the box and lifted her hands up to cover her ears. Omar cried out also and his hands flew also to his ears and it was Mr. Geronimo who caught the box before it hit the ground and stared at the two Peristanis with concern.

"What was that?" Dunia said. But Geronimo Manezes had heard nothing. "A sound like a whistle," she told him. "The jinn can hear higher frequencies than dogs and obviously human beings. But it was only a noise."

"A noise may contain a hidden curse," Omar said. "The box should be closed, Princess. It may be poisonous to you and me as well as your father."

"No," she said, her expression unwontedly grim. "Continue. If I don't understand the curse I won't find the counter-curse and the king will die."

Mr. Geronimo set the box down on a small table of walnut inlaid with an ivory chessboard and it resumed its storytelling. "It was a time of plagues," said the box in its new male voice, "and in the village of I. a man named John was being held responsible for the spread of a disease of silence. Quiet John, a short man with powerful forearms, worked as a blacksmith in I., as picturesque a country hamlet as you could wish to see lost in an idyll of green fields, rolling hills, dry stone walls, thatched roofs and nosy neighbors. After his marriage to the local schoolteacher, a girl more learned and refined of manner than her husband, it became well known that once he had had a few drinks at night he shouted at his wife, using the ugliest words anyone in the village had ever heard and so increasing his wife's vocabulary as well as her misery. This went on for many years. By day he was a diligent worker in his forge of fire and smoke, and a good companion to his wife and friends, but in the darkness the monster within came out. Then one night when his son Jack was sixteen years old and grown taller than his father, the boy stood up to

John and commanded him to be silent. Some in the village said that
the boy made a fist and struck his father in the face, because the man
had a swollen cheek for some days after that, but others put the
swelling down to toothache.

"Whatever the cause, there was general agreement on two points:
firstly, that the father did not strike the son in return, but retreated to
his bedroom in shame, and secondly, that from that moment on his
words, always few and far between except during the nocturnal tor-
rents of cursing, dried up altogether and he simply ceased to speak.
As the distance between his tongue and the words it used to utter
grew greater, he seemed to calm down. The drinking stopped, or at
least diminished to manageable levels. As Quiet John he turned into
his best self, people said, gentle and generous and honorable and
kind, so that it became obvious that language itself had been his
problem, language had poisoned him and damaged his intrinsically
noble humanity, and that, having given up words the way some people gave up cigarettes or masturbation, he could at last be what he
should have been: a good man.

"His neighbors, noticing the change in him, began to experiment
with wordlessness themselves, and sure enough the less they spoke,
the more cheerful and better natured they became. The idea that
language was an infection from which the human race needed to
recover, that speech was the source of all dissension, wrongdoing and
character decay, that it was not as many had often declared the bed-
rock of liberty but rather the seedbed of violence, spread rapidly
through the cottages of I. and soon children were being dissuaded
from singing playground songs and old-timers discouraged from
reminiscing about antique exploits while sitting on their accustomed
benches under the tree in the main square. A division appeared and
deepened in the formerly harmonious hamlet, fostered, according to
the newly silent, by the new young village schoolteacher, Yvonne,
who posted signs everywhere warning that speechlessness, not
speech, was the real disease. 'You may think it's a choice,' she wrote,
'but soon you won't be able to talk even if you want to, while we talk-

ers actually can choose to converse or to keep our mouths shut.' At first people were angry with the schoolteacher, a pretty, chatty woman with an annoying habit of cocking her head to the left when she talked, and these militants wanted the school shut down, but then they discovered she was right. They could no longer make any sort of sound, even if they wanted to, even if they wanted to warn a loved one to avoid an oncoming truck. Now the village's anger turned away from Yvonne the teacher and focused instead on Quiet John, whose decision had foisted upon the community a muteness they could no longer escape. Dumbly, inarticulately, the villagers gathered outside the blacksmith's forge, and only their fear of his immense physical strength and hot horseshoes held them back,"

—and here Omar the Ayyar interjected, Why, this is just like the story of the composer Casterbridge and the preacher Yusuf Ifrit, each accusing the other of being the pestilence, so maybe this is a new kind of sickness, a sickness that prevents human beings from knowing when they are sick and when they are in good health,

—but the jinnia princess had found her own story hidden within these other stories. She was thinking about her stricken father, about their own troubled story, more troubled than the story of the blacksmith and his wife or the composer and the preacher, and by accident her thoughts spilled out of her mouth, He never loved me, she said, I always worshipped my father but I knew I wasn't the son he wanted. My inclination was towards philosophy, and if I had had my way I would have built myself a library life, happily lost in the labyrinth of language and ideas, but he needed a warrior, so I became one for him: the Lightning Princess, whose defenses shielded Qâf from the dark. The dark jinn didn't scare me. When we were young I played with all those guys, Zumurrud and Zabardast and Shining Ruby and Ra'im back in the days before he started drinking blood. In the back alleys of Fairyland we played kabaddi and seven tiles and not one of them was ever a match for me because I was busy becoming superboygirl, the daughter whose father wanted a son. At mealtimes the disappointment burned in his eyes and curdled the milk.

When I told him I was studying the art of the thunderbolt he grunted, making it clear he would have preferred a swordsman to a witch. When I learned to wield a sword he complained that in his old age he needed a statesman by his side to negotiate the complex politics of Peristan. When I became a scholar of the law of the jinn he said, If only I had a son to hunt with me. In the end his disappointment in me became my disillusion with him and we were no longer close. But still, though I never admitted it, he was the only person in either of the Two Worlds I wanted to please. For a time I left him and in the other world I launched the dynasty that became my fate. After that, when I returned to Qâf and the doors between the worlds were sealed and the human centuries passed, he moved even further away from me, and his feelings went beyond disapproval and arrived at distrust, You don't know who your people are anymore, he said, and here in Peristan you long only for the world you have lost, where your human children are. Those words, *human children,* were heavy with his distaste, and the longer I bore the weight of his criticism, the more ardently I hoped to be rejoined to that earthly family, which Ibn Rushd had named the Duniazát.

It is I, she cried, who have spent long ages laboring on the construction of a machine without a purpose, or a purpose so farfetched, like glory, that the attempt to achieve it is self-defeating, and the machine is my life and the purpose which no machine could ever fulfill was the glory of capturing my father's love. It is I, not a blacksmith or a teacher or a philosopher, who have failed to learn the difference between sickness and health, between pestilence and cure. In my unhappiness I persuaded myself that my father's disdain for his daughter was the natural state of affairs, the healthy state, and my female nature was the plague. But here we are at the truth, and it is he who is sick and I who am well. What is the poison in his body? Maybe it's himself.

She was sobbing by this time, and Geronimo the gardener was holding her, offering what puny human comfort he could to his non-human lover, caught up himself in profound existential confusion.

What did it mean that he had ascended into the air and then softly descended as he had, beyond his own volition—that the earth had rejected him and then as mysteriously accepted him again—and that he found himself here in a world that had no meaning for him, meaning being a thing human beings constructed out of familiarity, out of what scraps they possessed of the known, like a jigsaw puzzle with many pieces missing. Meaning was the frame human beings placed around the chaos of being to give it shape; and here he was in a world no frame could contain, clinging to a supernatural stranger who had for a time posed as his departed wife, holding to her as desperately as she, now, held to him, drawn to him because he looked like a long-dead philosopher, each hoping that an alien surrogate could, by embracing them, allow them to believe that the world was good, this world or that world or simply the world in which two living things held one another and said the magic words.

I love you, said Mr. Geronimo.

I love you too, the Lightning Princess replied,

—and inside her distress about her father who was impossible to please, the king wearing the Simurgh Crown who was so invested in his kingship that his daughter had to call him Your Majesty, the king who had forgotten how to love, lay the memories of her own first loves, or at least of the first boys who loved her, and who were not, at that time, the feared dark jinn and her father's deadly foes. In those days Zabardast had the sweet seriousness of the child magician, pulling with the gravest of faces the most improbable rabbits—insane chimera-rabbits and gryphon-rabbits that had never existed in nature—out of one of his wide selection of absurd fools' caps. Zabardast with his nonstop patter, his jokes, his easy grin, was the one she liked best. Zumurrud Shah, always Zabardast's muscle-bound opposite, tongue-tied, mumbling, made permanently bad-tempered by his own inarticulacy, was the more beautiful of the two, no doubt about that, a gorgeous dumb giant possessed of a sort of surly innocence, if that was the sort of thing you liked.

They were both crazy about her, of course, which was less of a

problem in the jinn world than it would have been on earth, because
of the jinn's contempt for monogamy, but they competed for her fa-
vors just the same, Zumurrud brought her giant jewels from the giants' jewelry hoards (he came from the wealthiest of the jinn
dynasties, the builders of the palaces and aqueducts, the gazebos and
terraced gardens that made Peristan what it was), while Zabardast
the technician of magic, the artist of the occult, was also clownish by
temperament and made her laugh, and she couldn't remember, she
probably had sex with them both, but if she did it didn't leave much
of an impression, and she began to turn her attention from these inadequate Fairyland suitors to the more tragic figures of men. When
she abandoned them and broke the triangle of their infatuations,
leaving them to their own devices, both Zumurrud and Zabardast
began to change. Zabardast slowly became a darker, colder personal-
ity. He had loved her the most, she supposed, and so felt her loss most
keenly. Something vengeful crept into his nature, to her surprise,
something bitter and thwarted. Zumurrud, by contrast, moved on,
away from love and towards manly things. As his beard grew longer
he grew less interested in women and jewels and became obsessed
with power. He became the leader and Zabardast the follower,
though Zabardast continued to be the deeper thinker, in part because it would have been hard to be shallower. And so they remained
friends until, during the War of the Worlds, they fell out once again.

Zumurrud, Zabardast and Aasmaan Peri the Lightning Princess:
how long had their dalliance lasted? The jinn are poor judges of
duration. In the jinn world time does not so much pass as remain. It
is human beings who are the prisoners of clocks, their time being
painfully short. Human beings are cloud-shadows, moving rapidly,
gone with the wind, which was why Zabardast and Zumurrud were
filled with disbelief when Dunia first took the name Dunia and
adopted, along with the name, a human lover, and not a young one
either: the philosopher Ibn Rushd. They approached her together,
one last time, for her own sake. "If it's intellect that excites you," said
Zabardast, "then I must remind you that in all of Peristan there is no

greater scholar of the arts of sorcery than I." "Is sorcery a branch of ethics?" she replied. "Are magic tricks related to reason?" "Right and wrong, and an interest in the rational, are human afflictions, like fleas on dogs," said Zabardast. "The jinn act as they choose and do not bother with the banalities of good and evil. And the universe is irrational, as every jinn knows." She turned her back on him then and forever and the bitterness which had been growing within him possessed him like a flood. "Your human, your philosopher, your wise fool," Zumurrud scoffed. "You realize that he will die very soon, whereas I will live, if not forever, then for the next best length of time." "You say that as if it's a good thing," she answered him. "But a year of Ibn Rushd is worth more to me than an eternity of you."

After that they were her enemies, and, because of the humiliation of being rejected in favor of a human being who, like a mayfly, lived for a day and was then snuffed out forever, they had new reasons for hating the human race,

—and while she was remembering her youth, Mr. Geronimo found his way within the story of her youthful flirtations into the memory of his one true love, Ella Elfenbein his beautiful chatterbox, kind to all comers, proud of her body, and more in love with her father Bento than with him, he sometimes thought. She called Bento Elfenbein five times an hour every day until his last day, and in every call she used the words *I love you* as a way of saying hello and good-bye to him. After Bento died and not until then she started doing the same when she called Geronimo, *you're my everything,* she said, then and not until then. It was ridiculous to be jealous of a daughter's love for her brilliant, rakish, slightly crooked father with his joker's smile like a happy fiend constantly finding a way to outsmart the Batman, but sometimes I couldn't help it, Mr. Geronimo admitted to himself, even now he couldn't help it, she even found a way to die just as Bento had died, she found her way to a lightning bolt just like his.

And what am I doing now, he asked himself, I'm holding in my arms a supernatural creature who is the fairy queen of the

thunderbolt, the possessor and incarnation of the power that murdered my beloved, and I'm murmuring words of love into her ear,
as if I'm allowing myself to love what killed my wife, to whisper *I
love you* as hello and goodbye into the queen of what destroyed
Ella, and what does that say about me, what does that mean, who
am I. Her ear by the way as lacking in lobe as my own. An ancient
creature out of fantasy who says she's my distant ancestor, get a
grip, he told himself, you're lost in illusion, your feet may be back
on the ground but now your head's far, far up in the clouds. But
even as he admonished himself he felt Ella fading, felt her slipping
towards nothingness, while the warm body in his arms became
more solidly real, even if he knew it was made of smoke.

He realized that he did not feel well. His heart pounded in his
chest and the rarefied air of Mount Qâf made him light-headed; he
was nursing what felt like an altitude headache. His thoughts turned
to his lost trade, which felt more and more like a lost self, and to La
Incoerenza, so beautiful until the storm came, he remembered the
digging, the weeding, the planting of seeds, the trimming of hedge-
rows, the battle against the groundhogs who ate the rhododendrons,
the victory over the tree parasites, the building of the labyrinth, stone
on stone, the thick sweat on his brow, the happy ache in his muscles,
the days of good work in sun and rain and frost, summer and winter,
heat on heat, snow on snow, the thousand acres and one acre, the
drowned river, the hill where his wife lay under the rippling grass.
He wanted to turn back the clock to that time of innocence, before
thunderbolts and strangenesses broke the world, and he understood
that what ailed him was homesickness.

He sickened for his home lost both in space and time. Home too
was now estranged, and needed to be fixed. Blue Yasmeen and Sister
Allbee, Oliver Oldcastle and the Lady Philosopher, had been left
hanging in a stairwell at The Bagdad-without-an-*h*, in suspended
animation, and that picture needed to start moving again. Two of
those four he cared about and two were foes but all four deserved a
cure, deserved to be unstranged, as did the city, the country and the

whole world of men. This Fairyland of curved palaces defended by sheets of lightning, this fable of love-sick jinn, dying kings and magic boxes unspooling their stories in the tricky hands of spies, this was not for him. He was a denizen of the lower world and had had enough of fabulous heights.

As for us, looking back at him, seeing him as if from a great distance, held there in a motionless tableau of three figures, lost in fantasy: it is hard for us too to see him clearly there amidst the cloud-capp'd towers, the gorgeous palaces. We too need him back on earth, himself and his new beloved, fairy though she be. Their love story, and this was, even if only briefly, their love story, only makes sense to us here below. There, above, it's an airiness, as insubstantial as a dream. Their true love story, the one that has meaning for us and weight, comes wrapped up in a war. For our future places too, in that past time, had been made strange, and we know, we who come after and reflect, that we could not be who we are or lead the lives we live had these two not fallen back to earth to make things right, or as right as things can ever be, if indeed our time is right, as we say it is, if it be not simply a different kind of wrong.

And by this time the Chinese box was peeling crazily, and as each layer fell away a new voice told a new tale, none of the tales finished because the box inevitably found a new story inside each unfinished one, until it seemed that digression was the true principle of the universe, that the only real subject was the way the subject kept changing, and how could anyone live in a crazy situation in which nothing remained the same for five minutes and no narrative was ever driven through to its conclusion, there could be no meaning in such an environment, only absurdity, the unmeaningness that was the only sort of meaning anyone could hold on to. So here at one moment was the tale of the city whose people stopped believing in money, they went right on believing in God and country because those stories made

sense but these scraps of paper and plastic cards were obviously val-
ueless; and at the next moment inside that story there began (but did
not end) the story of Mr. X who woke up one day and began, for no
reason at all, to speak a new language that nobody understood, and
the language began to change his character, he had always been a
sullen fellow but the less comprehensible his words were, the more
voluble he became, gesticulating and laughing, so that people liked
him a lot better than they did when they had followed what he was
saying; and just as that was getting interesting another layer peeled
off and the story changed again,

*and we, remembering, see in our minds' eyes the tableau unfreeze, a star-
burst of parrots exploding from the palace balcony at the marble courtyard's edge, the scent of white lilies on the breeze rippling the princess's
garments, and somewhere in the distance the sweet mourning of a wooden
flute. We see her jerk away from Mr. Geronimo while pointing at the
Chinese box unspooling on its table, and then fall to the floor with her
hands over her ears and Omar the spy, too, falling, his body jerked by
strong spasms, while Geronimo Manezes hears nothing, feels nothing, sees
only the jinn and the jinnia in convulsions on the palace floor, and this is
where, according to our histories, he showed the presence of mind on
which the future hinged, our future as well as his own, snatching up the
Chinese box and running with it to the balcony overlooking the slopes of
Qâf and throwing the lethal object with all his strength into the high
empty air.*

After a moment Dunia and Omar recovered and rose from the floor.
Thank you, she said to Mr. Geronimo. You saved our lives and we
are in your debt.

   The jinn can be formal at such moments. It is their way. Do a service for a jinni or jinnia and he or she owes you service in return. In
these matters, even with lovers, the behavior of the jinn is scrupu-

lously correct. Dunia and Omar may even have bowed to Geronimo Manezes, for that would be the correct ritualistic gesture, but on this subject the records are silent. If they had, he, being the strong silent type, would have been embarrassed by their display.

I know what the spell is now, she said. Let's go quickly to my father and I will try to undo it.

No sooner had the words left her lips than they heard the loud noise.

At the last moment of his life the lord of Qâf opened his eyes and in his final delirium demanded to see a book that had never been written, and after that immediately began to recite its invisible contents as if he were reading it aloud. It was an account of the posthumous quarrel between the philosophers Ghazali and Ibn Rushd, reignited long after their deaths by the revivifying actions of the jinn Zumurrud and Shahpal's own daughter, the Princess Aasmaan Peri, a.k.a. Skyfairy, Dunia, and the Lightning Princess. Zumurrud the powerful giant who had awakened Ghazali in his grave was Shahpal's enemy and far beyond his reach, but the knowledge that his daughter too had meddled with matters of life and death, which he acquired from the words magically emanating from his own mouth, caused the old monarch in his terminal moments to utter a roar of disapproval so magnificent that the tapestries in his bedchamber fell from the walls and a crack appeared in the marble floor that ran like a wriggling snake all the way from his bedside to the princess's feet and told her that the end had come. She flew to her father along the length of the crack as fast as she could go, leaving Geronimo Manezes far behind, and by the time he reached the royal bedchamber she was screaming the counter-spell as loudly as she could into her father's ear, but it was too late.

The master of Mount Qâf had left Peristan forever. The Simurgh rose up from its place on the king's bedpost and burst into flames. The courtiers in the chamber of death, not one of whom had ever seen the death of any jinn before, let alone the passing of their king, fell into attitudes of mourning, and there was undoubtedly much rending of garments and tearing of hair, but in spite of their careful attention to their dutiful ululations and chest beatings they did not fail to mention to their new queen that it was Shahpal's discovery of her misdeed that had finally broken his heart. She had raised a spirit from the grave, an action far beyond the permitted boundaries of jinn activity, and while it proved her to be a jinnia of rare and formidable power it was also profoundly sinful, and the knowledge of her grievous sin had been the last straw that ended Shahpal's life. So his death was somewhat her fault, the courtiers obsequiously wanted her to know, while of course bowing, genuflecting, pressing their foreheads to the floor, and giving her all the honor due to their new monarch, yes, they murmured, and the proof of her responsibility was the crack in the floor which had sped without pause for reflection towards her guilty feet.

Omar the Ayyar defended her and pointed to her risking of her own life to discover the nature of the poisonous spell embedded in the Chinese box and her rush to the king's bedside to save his life, and of course everyone agreed that yes, that had been heroic, but their eyes were shifty and the awkwardness of their bodies showed their lack of conviction, because after all, the king was dead, so she had failed, that was the bottom line, she had failed in this as well. And as the word of the king's death rustled outwards from the deathbed into the avenues and gullies of Qâf, as it was bruited up and down the slopes of the mountain kingdom, the whisper of her guilt attached itself to the news, never, of course, causing any to express the slightest doubt regarding her claim to the succession, but the whispers tarnished her nonetheless, the whispers like vocal mud, and the mud sticking, as mud always does; and as the crowds of her subjects who had loved her father almost as much as she had gathered outside the palace walls, she could hear with her powerful jinnia hearing the sound, mixed up in the keening sobs of her people, of a small but significant number, we must regretfully admit, of boos.

She was calm. She neither weakened nor wept. What she felt about her father's last moments she kept to herself and showed to no one. From a balcony of the palace she addressed the people of Qâf. In her cupped palms were the gathered ashes of the Simurgh and as she blew them out into the crowd they gathered themselves into the shape of the mighty bird and burst back into squawking magnificent life. With the magic bird on her shoulder and the Simurgh Crown on her head, she commanded their respect and the whispers ceased. She made her vow to her people. Death had entered Peristan, and death would have death. She would not rest until her father's killers were no more. Zumurrud Shah and his cohorts, Zabardast, Ra'im Blood-Drinker and Shining Ruby, would be removed forever from the Two Worlds. Thus the War of the Worlds would end and peace return above and below.

This, she swore. Then she screamed.

Geronimo Manezes felt the scream as a hammer blow to the head and passed out cold. It had been many millennia since anyone in either of the Two Worlds had heard the scream of the Skyfairy. It was so loud that it filled the entire jinn world with sound and penetrated also into the world below where Zumurrud and his three cohorts heard it and understood that it was a declaration of war. Death had come into the jinn world and before the war was over more of the jinn would die.

She returned to her father's bedside and for a long time she found it impossible to leave. She sat on the floor beside him and talked. Geronimo Manezes, having recovered consciousness but with his ears unstoppably ringing, sat down on a brocaded chair a little way away with his eyes closed, nursing the worst headache of his life, still shaken, still groggy, and became unconscious again, falling into a deep sleep filled with dreams of death and thunder. While he slept the dead king's daughter told her father all her secret thoughts, the ones he never had time to listen to while he was alive, and she had the impression that she had his full attention for the first time. The courtiers melted away and Omar the Ayyar stood guard in the doorway of the room of death and Mr. Geronimo slept. Dunia spoke and spoke, words of love, anger and regret, and when she had finished pouring out her heart she told the dead king about her plan for revenge, and the dead king did not attempt to dissuade her, not only because he was dead but also because the jinn are like that, they do not believe in turning the other cheek, if they are wronged they get even.

Zumurrud and Zabardast and their followers knew that Dunia would come after them, they would have been expecting her assault even before she screamed, but that did not deter her in the least from making it. They had underestimated her because of her femaleness, she knew that, and she would teach them a harsh lesson, she would give them much more than they bargained for. Over and over she promised her father that he would be avenged until finally he believed her and at that point his body did what the bodies of the jinn do on those rare occasions when they die, they lose their corporeal form and a flame rises into the air and goes out. After that the bed was empty but she could see the impression of his body in the sheet he had been lying on, and his favorite old slippers were there on the floor next to the bed, lying there expectantly, as if he might come back into the room at any moment and put them on.

(In the days that followed Dunia told Mr. Geronimo that her father appeared to her often, during the periods of hiatus which are the jinn equivalent of sleep, and that during these appearances he was curious about her, interested in everything she was doing, warm in his manner and loving in his embraces; that, in short, her relationship with him after his death was a big improvement on the way things had been during his lifetime. I still have him, she told Geronimo Manezes, and this version of him is better than the one I had before.)

When she stood up at last she was different again, no longer a princess or even a daughter but a dark queen terrible in anger, golden eyed and trailing clouds of smoke from her head instead of hair. Geronimo Manezes, waking up in his armchair, understood that this was what his life had always had in store for him, the uncertainty of being, the bewilderment of change—he dozed off in one reality and woke up in another. The illusion of Ella Elfenbein's return had both unnerved and overjoyed him and it had been easy to sink towards belief in it but his portage to Peristan had fatally undermined that and now the sight of the Queen of Qâf revealed in angry beauty finished off Ella's ghost. And in Dunia too, Skyfairy the Lightning Queen, there was a change of heart. She had seen Ibn Rushd reborn in Geronimo but the truth was that she was leaving the old philosopher behind at last, recognizing that that antique love had turned to dust and its reincarnation, while pleasing, could not rekindle the old fire, or only momentarily. She had clung to him for a moment but now there was work to do and she knew how she would try to do it.

You, she said to Geronimo Manezes, not as a lover might address her lover but as an imperious matriarch, a grandmother with hair growing out of a mole on her chin, for example, might address a junior member of her dynasty. Yes. Let's start with you.

He was a boy in shorts shuffling his feet before his grandmother and answering her in a scolded mumble. I can't hear you, she said. Speak up.

I'm hungry, he said. Is it possible to eat first, please.

In Which
the Tide Begins
to Turn

A few words about ourselves. It is hard for us as we look back to put ourselves in the shoes of our ancestors, for whom the arrival in the midst of their everyday life of the implacable forces of the metamorphic, the descending avatars of transformation, represented a shocking disruption in the fabric of the real; whereas in our own time such activity is the commonplace norm. Our mastery of the human genome allows us chameleon powers unknown to our predecessors. If we wish to change sex, well then, we straightforwardly do so by a simple process of gene manipulation. If we are in danger of losing our tempers, we can use the touch pads embedded in our forearms to adjust our serotonin levels, and we cheer up. Nor is our skin color fixed at birth. We adopt our hue of choice. If, as passionate football fans, we decide to acquire the pigmentation of our favorite team, the Albiceleste or the Rossonero, then hey presto! we colorize our bodies in blue and white stripes, or dramatic red and black. A woman artist in Brazil long ago asked her countryfolk to name their own skin colors and produced tubes of paint to represent each shade, each pigment named as the possessors of the color wished, Big Black Dude, Light Bulb, and so on. Today she would run out of tubes before she ran out of color variations; and it is widely believed and generally accepted by all of us that this is an excellent thing.

This is a story from our past, from a time so remote that we argue, sometimes, about whether we should call it history or mythology. Some of us call it a fairy tale. But on this we agree: that to tell a story about the past is to tell a story about the present. To recount a fantasy, a story of the imaginary, is also a way of recounting a tale about the actual. If this were not true then the deed would be pointless, and we try in our daily lives to eschew pointlessness whenever possible.

This is the question we ask ourselves as we explore and narrate our history: how did we get here from there?

A few words, too, on the subject of lightning. Being a form of celestial fire, the thunderbolt was considered historically to be the weapon of powerful male deities: Indra, Zeus, Thor. One of the few female deities to wield this mighty weapon was the Yoruba goddess Oya, a grand sorceress who, when in a bad mood, which she often was, could unleash both the whirlwind and the sky-fire, and who was believed to be the goddess of change, called upon in times of great alteration, of the rapid metamorphosis of the world from one state to the next. She was a river goddess too. The name of the river Niger in Yoruba is Odo-Oya.

It may be, and it seems to us probable, that the story of Oya had its origin in an earlier intervention into human affairs—perhaps several millennia ago—of the jinnia Skyfairy, in the present narrative known mostly by her later name of Dunia. In those ancient times Oya was believed to have had a husband, Shango the Storm King, but eventually he disappeared from view. If Dunia had once had a husband, and if he had been killed in some previous, unrecorded battle of the jinn, that may account for her fondness for the similarly bereaved Geronimo. That is one hypothesis.

As to Dunia's power over water as well as fire, it may well have existed, but it is not a part of our present narrative and we have no information about it. As for the reason why she was partly responsible for just about everything that happened to people on earth during the time of the strangenesses, the tyranny of the jinn and the War of the Worlds, however, that will be made plain before we're done.

When African traditions made their way into the New World on the slave ships, Oya came along for the ride. In the Brazilian rites of

Candomblé she became Yansa. In syncretic Caribbean Santería her image was merged with that of the Christian Black Madonna, the Virgin of Candelaria.

However, Dunia, like any jinnia, was far from virginal. She was the fecund matriarch of the Duniazát. And as we well know by now, her descendants too had the gift of lightning in their hands, although almost none of them knew it until the strangenesses began and such things became thinkable. In the battle against the dark jinn, this lightning became a crucial weapon. And so it was that lightning freaks, a group accused during the mighty paranoia of those days of being behind the disruptions that became known as the strangenesses, in fact became the prominent and eventually legendary front line of the resistance to the Zumurrud gang of dark jinn as it set out to colonize, even to enslave, the peoples of the earth.

And just a very few words about the Zumurrud project. Conquest was something entirely new for the jinn, to whom empire does not come naturally. The jinn are meddlesome; they like to interfere, to lift this one up, to cast that one down, to plunder a treasure cave or throw a magic spanner in a rich man's works. They like the making of mischief, mayhem, anarchy. They have traditionally lacked management skills. But a reign of terror cannot be effective through terror alone. The most effective tyrannies are characterized by their excellent powers of organization. Efficiency had never been Zumurrud the Great's long suit; scaring people was his game. Zabardast the sorcerer jinni, however, turned out to be an excellent nuts-and-bolts person. But he wasn't perfect, and nor were his lesser cohorts, and so the new scheme of things was (fortunately) full of holes.

Before they returned to the lower world Dunia opened the secret doors in Mr. Geronimo's head that led to the jinn nature hidden within him. If you could cure yourself of the weightlessness plague and bring yourself back to earth without even knowing who you were, she told him, then imagine what you'll be able to do now. Then she put her lips to his temples, first the left one, then the right, and *whispered,* "Open." Immediately it was as if the universe itself opened and spatial dimensions whose existence he had never known about became visible and usable, as if the frontiers of the possible had been pushed outwards and much became feasible that had been unfeasible before.

He felt as a child must feel as it masters language, as the first words form and are spoken, as phrases come, then sentences. The gift of language, as it arrives, allows one not only to express thoughts but to form them, it makes the act of thinking possible, and so it was that the language which Dunia opened to him and in him allowed him forms of expression he had never before been able to rescue from the cloud of unknowing in which they had been hidden from his sight. He saw how easy it was to have influence over the natural world, to move objects, or change their direction, or accelerate them, or arrest their movement. If he blinked quickly three times the extraordinary communications systems of the jinn unfurled before his mind's eye, as complex as the synaptic circuits of the human brain, as easy to operate as a megaphone. To travel almost instantly between anywhere and anywhere he had only to clap his hands together, and to bring objects into being—platters of food, weapons, motor vehicles, cigarettes—a simple twitch of the nose would suffice. He began to understand time in a new way, and here his human self, urgent, transient, watching the sand run out of the hourglass, was at odds with his new jinn self, which shrugged at time, which saw chronology as a disease of tiny minds. He understood the laws of transformation, both of the external world and of himself. He felt increasing within him the love of all shining things, the stars and precious metals and gemstones of all kinds. He began to understand the allure of harem pants. And he knew he was just at the borderland of the jinn reality, and that he might, as the days progressed, be shown marvels for the comprehension and articulation of which the language had not yet been granted him. "The universe has ten dimensions," he said, gravely. Dunia grinned as a parent does at a child who is quick to learn. "That's one way of looking at it," she replied.

But for Dunia herself existence was narrowing. The jinn have multitrack minds and are the best of multitaskers but all of Dunia's consciousnesses were fixed on a single goal: the annihilation of those who had destroyed her father. And it was on account of the death of her father that she succumbed to an extreme version of the antinomian heresy, according herself powers of grace and exculpation normally reserved for deities, and claiming that nothing she commanded her tribe to do in the war against the dark jinn could be considered wrong or immoral because she had given her blessings to those actions. Geronimo Manezes, whom she had appointed her lieutenant in the struggle, was increasingly obliged to be her cautionary spirit, the cricket on her shoulder questioning her headlong certainties, worrying about the absolutism that gripped her as, driven by unspeakable grief, she unleashed her immense force.

"Come on," she ordered Mr. Geronimo. "The meeting is about to begin."

There continues to be much dispute among scholars of the subject concerning the total size of the jinn (male) and jinnia (female) populations of Peristan. On one side of the debate are those eminences who still contend, in the first place, that the number of jinn and jinnia is a constant, and, in the second place, that the species is sterile and cannot reproduce, and, in the third place, that both males and females are blessed with immortality and cannot die. Across the debating chamber are those who, like ourselves, accept the information that has come down to us concerning the ability of jinnias like the Lightning Princess not only to reproduce but to do so in quantity, and also regarding the mortality (albeit only in extreme circumstances) of the jinn. The history of the War of the Worlds is itself our best evidence in this regard; as will be seen, as will very soon be seen.

Consequently we cannot accept that the total numbers of jinnia and jinn are immutably fixed for all time.

The traditionalists insist that that number itself must be the number of magic, which is to say, one thousand and one; or one thousand and one male, one thousand and one female. That is how it should be, they reason, and therefore it must be so. We, for our part, accept that the population is not large, and that the numbers proposed by the traditionalists are probably close to the truth, but we are willing to admit that there is no way for us to know the precise jinn population at any given point in time, and so to fix the numbers arbitrarily based on some sort of theory of appropriateness is little more than mere superstition. And in any case, as well as the jinn, there were and probably still are lower forms of life in Fairyland, the most numerous of which were the *devs,* though there were also *bhoots.* In the War of the Worlds both *bhoots* and *devs* were pressed into service in the lower world and marched in the armies of the four Grand Ifrits.

As to the jiniri: the historic jinnia gathering convened by the orphaned Lightning Princess in the great hall of Qâf included almost all the female spirits that existed and so ranks as the largest such assembly on record. The horrifying news of the murder of the King of Qâf Mountain had spread rapidly throughout Fairyland, generating outrage and sympathy in almost every breast, and when the orphaned Lightning Princess sent word there were very few who failed to heed the call.

When Dunia addressed the gathering and called for an immediate and comprehensive sex boycott to punish the dark jinn for Shahpal's murder and force them to end their improper campaign of conquest on the earth below, however, her audience's sympathy for her loss was not sufficient to prevent many of the gathered jinnia from expressing their shocked disapproval. Her childhood friend Sila, the Princess of the Plain, articulated the general feeling of horror. "If we can't have sex at least a dozen times a day, darling," she cried, "we might as well be nuns. You always were the bookish one," she added, "and quite frankly a leetle too much like humans, I love

you darling but it's true, so maybe you can do without sex more easily than the rest of us and just read a book instead, but we, darling,
most of us, it's what we do."

There was a mutinous murmur of assent. A second princess, Lay-
lah of the Night, brought up the old rumor that if jinn and jinnias
stopped having sexual relations for any length of time then the entire
jinn world would crumble and fall and all its inhabitants perish.
"There's no smoke without fire, and no fire without smoke," she said,
quoting the old jinn proverb, "so if the two are not conjoined, then
the flame will surely die." At which her cousin Vetala, Princess of the
Flame, unleashed a frightening, and frightened, ululation. But Dunia
would not be denied. "Zumurrud and his gang have lost their heads
and betrayed all the rules of right behavior, not only between the jinn
and human beings, but also between jinn and jinn," she replied. "My
father is already dead. Why do you imagine your kingdoms—your
fathers, your husbands, your sons, and you yourselves—are safe?" At
which the gathered queens and princesses, of the Plain, the Water, the
Cloud, the Gardens, the Night, and the Flame, stopped complaining
about feeling horny, and paid attention; and their entourages too.

However, as we know, the sexual rejection of the dark jinn by
the entire female population of Fairyland, designed to bring Zumurrud the Great and his followers to heel, proved strangely
counterproductive—strange, that is, to the jinnia ladies who enforced it, who abstained and refrained, even though it was as hard
for them as for any addict, and there were withdrawal symptoms,
irritability and trembling and insomnia, because the union of
smoke and fire was an ontological requirement of both genders of
the jinn. "If this goes on for long," the desperate Sila told Dunia,
"the whole of Fairyland will come crashing down about our ears."

We, looking back on these events, see them through the perspec-
tive of our hard-won knowledge, and understand that the practice of
extreme violence, known by the catch-all and often inexact term *terrorism,* was always of particular attraction to male individuals who
were either virgins or unable to find sexual partners. Mind-altering

frustration, and the damage to the male ego which accompanied it, found its release in rage and assaults. When lonely, hopeless young men were provided with loving, or at least desirous, or at the very least willing sexual partners, they lost interest in suicide belts, bombs, and the virgins of heaven, and preferred to live. In the absence of the favorite pastime of every jinni, human males turned their thoughts to orgasmic endings. Death, being readily available everywhere, was often an alternative pursuit to unavailable sex.

So it was with human beings. The dark jinn, however, did not consider self-immolation. Their response to the sex boycott was not surrender to the wishes of their erstwhile jinnia partners, but rather an increase in violent activity of the nonsexual kind. Ra'im Blood-Drinker and Shining Ruby, inflamed by the denial of physical pleasure, embarked in the lower world on a savage rampage of subjugation by force, displaying an intemperate abandon which at first alarmed even Zumurrud and Zabardast; then, after a time, the same red mist rose in the eyes of the two senior jinn, and the human race paid the penalty for the jinnias' punishment of the Grand Ifrits. The war entered a new phase. It was time for Dunia and Geronimo Manezes to return to earth.

She made him swear a solemn oath, the mirror of her own. "Now that I have opened your eyes to your true nature and given you power over it, you must promise to fight at my side until what has to be done is done, or we perish in the attempt." Her eyes blazed. Her will was too great to be resisted. "Yes," he said. "I swear."

She kissed his cheek to show him her approval. "There's a boy you need to meet," she told him. "Jimmy Kapoor, who also goes by the name of Natraj Hero. A brave boy, and your cousin. Speaking of cousins, there's also a bad girl."

Her name, Teresa Saca, was unusable. She had killed a man, and that used up all the credit in her name. She cut it in half like dead plastic and tossed it in the trash, she spat it out like gum. Fuck her name. She was on the run and went now by many names, the names on stolen debit cards and fake IDs bought from street corner hustlers, the names in the smudged registers of one-night cheap hotels. She was not good at this, the low life. She needed service industries. In the good times a day away from the wellness spa or yoga shala was a day wasted. But those days were gone and she had to live by her wits, fuck that, Jack, and her a college dropout. Luckily for her everything was in a mess, law enforcement wasn't what it used to be, and the chaos of the times allowed her to slip through the cracks. So far, anyway. Or maybe she had been forgotten. The people's attention was elsewhere and she was yesterday's news.

So Teresa or Mercedes or Silvia or Patrizia or whatever she went by that evening: sitting solo in a sports bar in Pigeon Forge, Tennessee, spurning the advances of well-muscled men with military haircuts, doing tequila shots, watching the latest school killings on outsize flat-screen HDTV. Ag god, she mumbled in a voice made imprecise by alcohol, it is an age of killing and you know what that's all right with me. It's slaughterhouse time out there and you look to be getting in on the act yourself god whatever your name is you got more aliases than me. Yeah you god I'm talking to you. You with this name that name in that country this country, always big on the killing thing, you okay with people getting killed for a Facebook post, or not being circumcised, or fucking the wrong guy. I have no problem with that because guess what god I'm a killer too. Little me. I got me some action myself.

In those times when suspicion fell on lightning-strike survivors some of them gathered furtively here and there to bemoan their fate. She sought them out wanting to listen to their tales, in case any of them turned out to be like her, masters of the thunderbolt and not just victims. When you're a freak it's good to know you're not alone. But here in the Center of Fun in the Smoky Mountains the survivors' gathering was a cluster of sad sacks. They huddled in a small room behind the sports bar, a poorly lit room situated in a small street off the main drag where tourists formerly did what tourists liked to do, eating tourist food and driving tourist bumper cars and posing for tourist pictures with a picture of Dolly Parton and mining in a tourist mine for tourist gold. For those with more ghoulish tastes, there had been a Titanic Museum Attraction where you could see the violin that had belonged to the ship's bandleader, Wallace Hartley, and enjoy the tributes to the 133 children who went down with the ship, the "littlest heroes." All that was shut down now that the world had changed, now that everywhere was the *Titanic* and everyone was going down. The sports bar stayed in business because men will drink in hard times, that doesn't change, only the games on the screens were reruns, all the famous initials had shut down operations, MLB NBA NFL, all gone. Their ghosts moved on the big screens between the occasional news broadcasts when such items were flickeringly able to come online thanks to those brave journalists in the field who knew how to uplink to the satellites.

The survivors of thunderbolt attacks were of two types. The first type had a lot to say. This one had been hit by lightning four times, but that one held the record with seven strikes. Many said they felt confused, they had headaches and panic attacks. They sweated too much, they couldn't sleep, one leg mysteriously began to shrink. They wept when there was nothing to cry about, they walked into doors and bumped into furniture. They remembered that the strike had literally blown them out of their shoes and their clothes had exploded off their bodies, leaving them naked as well as stunned. The absence of burn marks meant that people accused them of protesting too much, or for too long. They spoke with awe of the bolts from the blue. Many of them called it a religious experience. They had witnessed, at first hand, the devil's work.

The second type was silent. These survivors sat alone in corners, locked into their secret worlds. The lightning had sent them somewhere far away and they either could not or chose not to share their own mysteries. When Teresa or Mercedes or whoever she was now tried to talk to them, they looked frightened and moved away or responded with sudden, extreme hostility, baring their teeth and clawing at their questioner.

This was of no use to her. These people were weak and broken. She left the gathering and hit the tequila and near the bottom of the bottle a voice spoke to her inside her head, and she thought she should probably stop doing shots. It was a woman's voice, quiet and measured, and she could hear it very clearly, even though nobody was talking to her. I'm your mother, the voice said, and before she could open her mouth to say No you're not because my mother never calls me not even on my fuckin' birthday not unless she gets cancer, then I probably get a fuckin' text asking for help with medical expenses, before she could say any of that, the voice said, No, not that mother, your mother from nine hundred years ago, give or take, the mother who put the magic in your body, and now you're going to put it to good use. That was good tequila, she said aloud admiringly, but the so-called mother in her head was undeterred, I'll show myself to you when I'm ready, she said, but if it helps to establish my credibility I can tell you the name and number on your stolen card and the location and combination number of the pathetic deposit box where you stored your so-called valuables. If you want me to do it I can tell the story of what your dad said when you told him you wanted to study English, what are you going to do with that, he said, be a paralegal or a secretary, or maybe you want to hear how you took that old used red convertible you stole when you were seventeen and drove it as fast as you could west and south from Aventura to Flamingo not caring if you lived or died. You have no secrets from me but fortunately I love you as a daughter whatever you did, even though you killed that gentleman, that doesn't matter now because now there's a war and I want you as a soldier and you already showed me you're good at what I need you to do.

You mean you don't care if I kill people, Teresa Saca said without speaking. What am I doing, she asked herself, I'm talking to a voice in my head, I'm hearing voices now? What am I, Joan of Arc? I saw the TV show. They burned her.

No, said the voice in her head. You're no saint and neither am I.

You want me to kill people, she asked again, silently, inside her head, knowing it was beyond drunk, it was insane.

Not people, the voice said. We're hunting bigger game.

When Mr. Geronimo found himself standing once again at the entrance to The Bagdad, he was armed with the new knowledge that until that day he had known nothing, not only about the world but about himself, and his place in it. But now he knew something; not everything, but it was a start. He had to begin again and he knew where he wanted to do it, and had asked Dunia to return him to this place, to attempt his first cure. She left him there and went about her own business, but he had access, now, to the communications system of the jinn, and could locate her precisely at any moment on that extraordinary internal positioning system, so her physical absence was a mere detail. He rang the doorbell and waited. Then he remembered that he still had the key. It still worked, turning in the lock as if nothing had happened, as if he hadn't been expelled from this place for being the bringer of a terrifying disease.

How long had he spent in Peristan? A day, a day and a half? But here in the lower world eighteen months had passed, or perhaps more. Much changes in eighteen months on earth, in the age of acceleration that began around the turn of the millennium and still continues to this day. All our stories are told more quickly now, we are addicted to the acceleration, we have forgotten the pleasures of the old slownesses, of the dawdles, the browses, the three-volume novels, the four-hour motion pictures, the thirteen-episode drama series, the pleasures of duration, of lingering. Do what you have to do, tell your story, live your life, get out quickly, *spit spot*. Standing on the doorstep of The Bagdad, he seemed to see a year and a half of his hometown rush before his eyes, the screaming terror as the risings multiplied, and alongside their opposites, the crushings, people squashed flat by a local increase in gravitational force, just like the story in the Chinese box, Mr. Geronimo thought, and there were swooping random attacks on groups of citizens by the Grand Ifrits astride their flying urns, the Grand Ifrits offering rewards, great chests of jewels, to anyone who could point a finger at men or women without earlobes. Martial law had been declared and the emergency services had done an astonishing job, the fire department ladder crews ministering to the floating people, the police keeping some semblance of order in the streets, helped by the National Guard.

Religious gangs had been roaming the city, looking for people to blame. Some of these mobs had targeted the mayor, whose adopted child Storm, the miraculous arbiter of honesty, was slandered as demon seed. A crowd of the faithful, for whom hostility seemed to be the necessary sidekick of fidelity, Hardy to its Laurel, gathered around the mayoral residence—converging on it from three directions, the ferry terminal, East End Avenue and the FDR—and then, shockingly, succeeded in storming the historic building and setting it ablaze. The successful attack on Gracie Mansion was news even in those disorderly times, because the frontline group of assailants, faced with troopers firing heavy-duty assault weapons, did not fall even when shot multiple times, in the head as well as the torso, or so the story went, and in spite of the decay of communications it was a story that spread rapidly. An unusual detail of some accounts added that several vehicles were assaulted, among them a fishmonger's van, and when its back doors were pulled open and the dead fish on ice—albacore, sockeye, chinook, coho and pink salmon, pollock, haddock, sole, whiting—were able to stare glassily at the bloodied demonstrators, several of the fish commenced, in spite of being dead, to laugh uproariously. The story of the parasite fanatics immediately reminded Mr. Geronimo of Blue Yasmeen's folktale of a laughing fish and he understood once again that many things formerly believed to be fantastic were now commonplace.

He had not known about the parasite-jinn until Dunia *whispered* to him and opened his eyes to the reality of his jinn inheritance. One of the Grand Ifrits, Shining Ruby, was the lord of the parasite-jinn, a master of possessing bodies for a time and then releasing them alive, as he had shown by his sensational occupation of the financial titan Daniel Aroni, and all the lesser parasites were foot soldiers serving under General Ruby's command. But whereas Shining Ruby was able to function without a living being to occupy, his parasite followers were both less potent and clumsier. When on earth they needed hosts—dogs, snakes, vampire bats, human beings—and destroyed their temporary homes when they moved on.

The Zumurrud gang was evidently waging war on many fronts, Mr. Geronimo thought. It would not be easy to defeat.

The mayor and her little daughter Storm had fled the burning building unharmed. Again, the stories that circulated about their escape preferred a supernatural explanation. According to this version (and there is no other, more plausible account that has come down to us) the unknown mother of the storm baby was a jinnia who, unwilling to raise her half-human love child, had abandoned her at the mayor's door, but had kept a watchful eye on her child from a distance, and, seeing that child's life threatened, had entered the burning mansion and thrown a protective shield around Rosa Fast and young Storm and given them safe passage out of the house. *Faute de mieux,* this is the story we have.

How treacherous history is! Half-truths, ignorance, deceptions, false trails, errors, and lies, and buried somewhere in between all of that, the truth, in which it is easy to lose faith, of which it is consequently easy to say, it's a chimera, there's no such thing, everything is relative, one man's absolute belief is another man's fairy tale; but about which we insist, we insist most emphatically, that it is too important an idea to give up to the relativity merchants. Truth exists, and Toddler Storm's magic powers provided, in those days, the visible proof of it. In her illustrious memory we refuse to allow truth to become "truth." We may not know what it is, but it's out there. We can't be sure how Rosa Fast and Storm escaped the burning mayoral mansion, but we can accept our zone of unknowing and hold fast to what is known: they did escape. And after that the mayor, accepting the recommendation of the security services, went into a secret facility and governed the city from an undisclosed location. That location is unknown; her heroic governance is known. She marshaled the fight against the chaos inflicted by the Grand Ifrits; she made broadcasts to the citizenry to reassure them that everything possible was being done to help them and more would be done soon. She became the face and voice of the resistance and kept her invisible finger on the city's pulse. This is known, and what is not known does not undermine it. This is the scientific way. To be open about the limits of one's knowledge increases public confidence in what one says is known.

The city was a war zone and the war had spilled into The Bagdad. Graffiti tags, obscene writings, fecal matter, a broken place outside and in. The windows boarded up and many panes of glass long gone. He entered the darkened foyer and at once felt metal pressed to the side of his head and heard a high, wired voice threatening death, this house be *occupy,* muthafucka, open your shirt, open your goddam shirt, he had to show them he wasn't wearing a grenade belt, he wasn't a bomb somebody told to walk in here and spring-clean the building, who sent you, muthafucka, who you *from.* It was interesting, he thought, that he was moving at his normal leisurely rate but everything around him could be slowed right down, the voice of the man with the gun could be stretched out, becoming slo-mo-low, and he could slow things down further just by wanting to, just like *this,* and now the tough guys in the dark of the foyer were like statues, and he could reach up to the muzzle of the gun and pinch it, *so,* and squash it shut like a Plasticine toy, this was almost fun. He could do *this,* and now all the weapons in the possession of the occupiers had been turned into carrots and cucumbers. Oh, and he could do *this,* and now they were all naked. He allowed them to speed up—or himself to decelerate—and had the satisfaction of watching another transformation, from gang lords into frightened kids, who the what the let's get outta here. As they backed away from him clutching at their manhood, he had a question for them: Sister Allbee, Blue Yasmeen, those names mean anything to you? And the man who had held a gun to his head now delivered a dagger to his heart. Those be the floatin' bitches? The *balloons*? He removed his hands from his private parts and made a spreading gesture. Kapow, man. It was a mess. What do you mean, Mr. Geronimo asked, even though he knew what the man meant. Like a fuckin' piñata, the naked man said. *Boom.* Dat some wack shit.

That was not how this part of the story was supposed to go. He was supposed to come home from Fairyland with superpowers and rescue Yasmeen and Sister. He was supposed to use his newly harnessed skills and bring them gently back to earth, hear their complaints, accept the blame, apologize, hug them, give them back the dailiness of their lives, save them from the madness and celebrate their salvation, like friends. It was supposed to be the moment when good sense began to return to the world and he, along with the others, was to be the bringer of that sense. The madness that had gotten into the world had had its way long enough. It was time for sanity to return and this was where he had wanted the process to begin. Them being dead—did they starve to death or were they killed, shot at for sport by the madness, maybe by those naked kids when the madness took them, and then their bodies left floating in the stairwell, filling up with the gases of death, until the explosion, until their insides like sticky rain—that wasn't it at all.

He searched the house, which was now close to dereliction. There was blood on the walls. Maybe some of it had come from the exploding bodies of Sister and Yasmeen. In one room a naked wire sparked, which could start a fire at any time. Almost all the toilets were clogged. Almost all the chairs were broken and there were ripped mattresses on the floors of several units. In his own apartment there had been extensive looting. He owned nothing now except the clothes he was wearing. Outside, he did not expect to find his truck where he had left it, and so it was no surprise to find it gone. None of this mattered to him. He left The Bagdad in the grip of a new force, a rage that allowed him to understand Dunia's blazing wrath after her father's murder. The war had just become personal.

The phrase *to the death* formed in his thoughts and he realized, with some surprise, that he meant it.

The Lady Philosopher and Oliver Oldcastle were nowhere to be seen. Maybe they were still alive. Maybe they had found their way back home. He had to go to La Incoerenza at once. That, before anything else. He didn't need the green pickup truck. He had a new way to get around.

He was only slowly grasping what his life had become. That he had risen, he well knew. He had faced that and accepted it. The descent had been involuntary, as unexpected as the rising, and it was, he understood, the consequence of an opening within himself of a secret self whose existence he had not previously suspected. But perhaps there was also a human dimension to his descending, his overcoming of what he had often thought of as a fault, his fault. In those lonely pendant hours he had faced the darkest things in his life, the pain of separation from what that life had once been, the agony of the rejected path, the path that rejected him. By embracing his grave wound, showing it to himself, he became stronger than his affliction. He had earned his gravity, and came down to earth. Thus Patient Zero became a source not only of the disease but of the cure.

He felt as if he had entered another skin. Or as if he, who was another, had become the new occupant of his body, which was other to him. Age had slipped from his thoughts and a great field of possibility stood before his inner eye, filled with white flowers, each one the enabler of a miracle. The white asphodel was the flower of the afterlife but he had never felt more alive. It also occurred to him that the curse of rising had this in common with his present condition: that its local effects transcended the laws of nature. For example, this ability to move very rapidly while the world seemed to stand still, a power over relative motion which he did not begin to understand but which was surprisingly easy to use. One does not have to know the secrets of the internal combustion engine, he reminded himself, to be able to drive a car. This kind of local sorcery, he understood, was the essence of the jinn. He was still flesh and blood, and that slowed him down somewhat—he could not move at anything like the speed of the Lightning Princess—but she had released into his body the secrets of smoke and fire and they carried him pretty swiftly along.

And so after a brief moment of blurred space and altered time he stood once again on the ravaged lawns of La Incoerenza and the gardener in him knew that there was one small victory, at least, that was within his reach. If there was one story of the jinn that everyone knew it was the tale of the jinni of the lamp who built Aladdin a palace with beautiful grounds fit for him to live in with his love the beautiful princess Badralbudur, and even though the story was probably a French fake the fact was that any jinni worth his salt could rustle up a decent palace and grounds in less time than it took to snap your fingers or clap your hands. Mr. Geronimo closed his eyes and there before him was the field of white asphodel. As he leaned down to smell their enchanted aroma the whole of the La Incoerenza estate appeared before him in miniature, perfect in every detail as it had been before the great storm, and he was a giant kneeling down to blow into it the breath of renewed life while the white flowers, also gigantic in comparison to the tiny house and grounds, waved gently all around.

When he opened his eyes the spell had done its work. There was La Incoerenza restored to its former glory, no trace anymore of the mud and detritus deposited there by the river, the indestructible shit of the past was gone and the great uprooted trees stood again as if their roots had never clawed at air, coated in black mud, and all his work of so many years was remade, the stone spirals, the Sunken Garden, the analemma sundial, the rhododendron forest, the Minoan labyrinth, the secret hedge-hidden nooks, and from the golden wood he heard a great cry of happiness, which told him that the Lady Philosopher was alive, and was discovering that pessimism was not the only way of looking at the world, that things could change for the better as well as the worse, and that miracles did happen.

They had been living like birds, Alexandra and her Oldcastle, fluttering at first in empty rooms but then as they rose higher they were obliged to leave the house and float under cover of foliage. But they were birds with money: Alexandra Fariña had continued her father's practice of keeping an absurd amount of cash locked up in the vault behind the Florentine painting, and that money had enabled her and her estate manager to survive. Cash money had provided a measure of security, though there had been burglaries, much had been taken, perhaps by the security personnel themselves, but at least there had been no physical or sexual violence in those lawless months, the perimeter had been more or less guarded and only occasionally breached, and after all they had only been robbed, not killed or raped. Cash money had paid the emergency services to visit regularly to bring fresh food and drink and whatever other supplies they needed. They had risen, now, to a height of about a dozen feet, and kept what they needed in an elaborate network of boxes and baskets slung from broad branches in the wood, built by local workmen and paid for, of course, in cash. The wood allowed them to perform their toilettes unobserved and without shame and there were moments when it was almost enjoyable.

But the sadness grew, and as the months passed Alexandra Bliss Fariña found herself hoping for an ending, wishing for it to come soon, and painlessly, if possible. She had not yet used any of her cash supply to purchase the substances that could make her wish come true, but she thought about it often. And then here instead of death was Mr. Geronimo and the lost world miraculously restored, time turned back, and hope given—lost hope, improbably rediscovered, like a precious ring, mislaid for eighteen months, found in a long-unopened drawer—that perhaps all could be as it had been. Hope. She cried out to him with improbable hope in her voice. *We're here. Over here. Here we are.* And then, almost pleading, fearing a negative answer that would burst this tiny balloon of optimism, *Can you get us down?*

Yes, he could, he could close his eyes and imagine their tiny figures descending onto the restored lawns of the repaired property, and then there she was, running towards him, embracing him, and Oliver Oldcastle who had once threatened his life now standing hat in hand with head bowed in gratitude and not protesting at all as the Lady Philosopher covered Mr. Geronimo's face in kisses. Much obliged, Oldcastle mumbled. Damned if I know how you did it, but still. Very much obliged.

And this, all of this, Alexandra cried, whirling about and about. You're a wonder worker, Geronimo Manezes, that's what you are.

If he had given in to his jinn self he would have made love to her on the spot, right there on the magically renewed grass with Oliver Oldcastle watching, and yes, the desire was in him all right, but he had sworn himself to a cause, he was in the service of Dunia the new jinnia Queen of the Mountain and his human part insisted he remember his oath; before life, his life, human life, could be properly renewed, her banner had to be planted in triumph on the battlefield.

I have to go, he said, and Alexandra Bliss Fariña's disappointed pout was the perfect opposite of Oliver Oldcastle's grumpy grin of joy.

In the faraway country of A. there once lived a gentle king known to all his subjects as the Father of the Nation. He was progressively inclined, so he helped to bring his country into the modern age, introducing free elections, defending women's rights, and building a university. He was not a rich king, and made ends meet by allowing half his palace to be used as a hotel, where he often took tea with the guests. He endeared himself to the young people of his own country and of the West by permitting the legal manufacture and sale of hashish, quality controlled and stamped with government seals of approval, gold, silver and bronze, denoting grades of purity and price. Those were good years, the years of the king, innocent years, perhaps, but sadly his health was poor; his back hurt and his eyes were weak. He traveled to Italy to undergo surgery but while he was away his former prime minister performed some surgery of his own, cut the king away from the state and took over the kingdom himself. In the next three decades while the king was in exile, contenting himself, as was his way, with the quiet pursuits of chess, golf and gardening, all hell broke loose in his former kingdom. The prime minister didn't last long, and a period of tribal faction fighting followed, which made at least one of A.'s powerful neighbors think the country was ripe for the picking.

So there was a foreign invasion. This was a mistake foreigners repeatedly made—the attempted conquest of the land of A.—but they invariably left with their tails between their legs, or just lay dead on the battlefield for the benefit of scavenging wild dogs, who weren't choosy about what they ate and were willing to digest even this type of horrible foreign food. But when the foreign invasion was repelled what replaced it was even worse, a murderous gang of ignoramuses who called themselves the Swots, as if the mere word would earn them the status of true scholars. What the Swots had studied deeply was the art of forbidding things, and in a very short time they had forbidden painting, sculpture, music, theater, film, journalism, hashish, voting, elections, individualism, disagreement, pleasure, happiness, pool tables, clean-shaven chins (on men), women's faces, women's bodies, women's education, women's sports, women's rights. They would have liked to have forbidden women altogether but even they could see that that was not entirely feasible, so they contented themselves with making women's lives as unpleasant as possible. When Zumurrud the Great visited the land of A. in the early days of the War of the Worlds, he saw at once that it was an ideal place to set up a base. It is an interesting and little-known detail that Zumurrud the Great was an aficionado of golden-age science fiction, and could have discussed with friends, if he had had any friends, the work of such masters of the genre as Simak, Blish, Henderson, Van Vogt, Pohl and

Kornbluth, Lem, Bester, Zelazny, Clarke, and L. Sprague de Camp. Among his favorites was Isaac Asimov's classic novel of the 1950s, *Foundation,* and he decided to name his operation in A. after that novel. "The Foundation" he set up and ran—originally with the assistance of Zabardast the Sorcerer, but, after their quarrel, by himself—quickly acquired a foothold in A. by the simple procedure of purchasing the country's new rulers.

"I bought the country," he boasted to his followers. "It's ours now."

It didn't take much. The underground jewel caves of Zumurrud the Great are celebrated in the lore of the jinn. Perhaps, and we believe this to be probable, at least one of these caverns was situated in the harsh mountainous eastern borderlands of A., deep below the mountains, hidden from human eyes by gates of stone. When Zumurrud presented himself to the leadership of the Swots they were overawed by his gigantic size, made witless with fear by being in the presence of a fire-born jinni—but they were also driven mad with desire by the golden bowls of diamonds and emeralds he bore, casually, as if they were nothing, one bowl in each immense hand. Diamonds larger than the Kohinoor fell from the bowls and rolled along the floor, coming to rest at the Swots' trembling feet. "You can have as many of these little trinkets as you want," said Zumurrud in his giant's voice, "and you can do what you like with this godforsaken land, you can ban the wind, for all I care, you can forbid the clouds to rain or the sun to shine, go right ahead. But from now on the Foundation owns you, Swots, so you had better swot up how to keep me happy. If not, then bad things can happen, such as this." He snapped his fingers and one of the Swots, a skinny, bent fellow with rotten teeth and a deep hatred of dance music, was transformed instantly into a pile of smoldering ash. "Just a demonstration," murmured Zumurrud the Great, setting down the bowls of jewels. And that was that.

While Dunia and Mr. Geronimo were away in Fairyland the Zumurrud group launched a series of such "demonstrations," albeit on a larger scale, designed to cow the human race and bring it meekly to heel. We say "the Zumurrud group" because, as has previously been mentioned, the Grand Ifrit himself was a person of considerable natural indolence, who preferred to let others do the dirty work while he reclined in an arbor, drinking, eating grapes, watching pornography on TV, and being serviced by his personal cohort of jinnia females. He had brought down a small army of lesser jinn from the upper world and mostly pointed them in the directions he desired, and off they went, assassinating prominent individuals, sinking ships, bringing down airliners, interfering with the computer operations of the stock markets, cursing some people with the rising curse, others with the crushing curse, and using the jewels he had in such quantities to bribe governments and bring other countries into his sphere of influence. However, the total number of fully fledged dark jinn who descended to the lower world almost certainly never exceeded one hundred individuals, to which the lesser species of parasite-jinni must be added. So, perhaps two or three hundred conquerors, on a planet of seven billion souls. At the height of the British Empire in India, there were no more than twenty thousand Britishers in that vast land, ruling successfully over three hundred million Indians, but even that impressive achievement was as nothing when compared with the rise of the dark jinn. The Grand Ifrits were in no doubt that the jinn were superior to the human race in every way, that human beings for all their pretensions of civilization and advancement were little better than bow-and-arrow primitives, and that the best thing that could happen to these lowlifes would be to spend a millennium or two in thrall to, and learning from, a superior race. This, Zabardast went so far as to say, was the burden the dark jinn had taken upon themselves, a duty which they were determined to discharge.

The Grand Ifrits' contempt for their subjects was only increased by the ease with which they recruited human beings to assist them in the maintenance of their new empire. "Greed and fear," Zumurrud told his three fellow leaders, who met, as was their custom, on a dark cloud circling the earth at the Equator, from which they watched and judged the mere mortals below them, "fear and greed, are the tools by which these insects can be controlled with almost comical ease," a remark which made Zabardast the Sorcerer laugh loudly, because Zumurrud was well known not to possess anything that even slightly resembled a sense of humor. Zumurrud glared at him with open hostility. The gulf between the two senior Ifrits was growing wider every day. They had patched up their quarrel, made a truce and joined forces again, but trouble continued to rumble between them. They had known one another too long, and their friendship was nearing its end.

Lightning crackled in the heart of the cloud. Ra'im Blood-Drinker and Shining Ruby did their best to change the subject. "What about religion?" asked Blood-Drinker. "What should we do about that? The believers are multiplying down there even faster than before." Shining Ruby, the self-styled Possessor of Souls, had never had any time for God or heaven. Fairyland was paradise enough and there was no reason to suppose the existence of a higher and better-perfumed garden. Showing a somewhat Swot-like fondness for proscription, he said, "We should ban it immediately. It's a circus."

This remark caused Zumurrud the Great and Zabardast the Sorcerer actually to sizzle with wrath. They crackled at the edges like a hundred eggs frying in a pan, and Shining Ruby and Ra'im Blood-Drinker understood that something had changed in the two senior Ifrits. "What's the matter with you two?" Blood-Drinker wanted to know. "Since when did you join the halo brigade?"

"Don't be a fool," Zabardast told him slyly. "We are in the process of instituting a reign of terror on earth, and there's only one word that justifies that as far as these savages are concerned: the word of this or that god. In name of a divine entity we can do whatever the hell we like and most of those fools down there will swallow it like a bitter pill."

"So it's a strategy, a ruse," said Shining Ruby. "That, I can understand."

But now Zumurrud the Great rose up in wrath, and the rage of the huge giant was a little frightening even to his fellow jinn. "There will be no more blasphemy," he said. "Fear God's word, or you too will be numbered among its enemies."

This came as a shock to the other three. "Well, you're singing a new song," Blood-Drinker said, refusing to sound impressed. "Who taught you that one?"

"You've spent your whole life carousing, killing, gambling, fucking, and then sleeping it off," added Shining Ruby, "so sainthood sits as uncomfortably on you as that golden crown, which, by the way, is far too small, having been made for a human head which, if you recall, you quite unnecessarily severed from its body."

"I've been studying philosophy," muttered the giant, reddening, more than a little embarrassed by his admission. "It's never too late to learn."

The transformation of the skeptical giant Zumurrud into a soldier for a higher power was the last achievement of the dead philosopher of Tus. Ghazali was dust and the jinni was fire but the thinker in his grave still knew a trick or two. Or, to put it another way: when a being who, all his life, has defined himself by deeds finally opens his ears to words, it isn't hard to make him accept whichever words you pour into them. Zumurrud had come to him. He was ready to receive what the dead man had to say.

"Every being which begins has a cause for its beginning," said Ghazali, "and the world is a being which begins; therefore, it possesses a cause for its beginning."

"That doesn't include the jinn," Zumurrud said. "We don't need a cause."

"You have mothers and fathers," said Ghazali. "Therefore you began. Therefore you also are beings who begin. Therefore you must have a cause. It's a question of language. When the language insists, we can only follow."

"Language," Zumurrud repeated slowly.

"Everything boils down to words," Ghazali said.

"What about God?" Zumurrud, genuinely puzzled, asked at their next encounter. "Didn't he have a beginning too? If not, where did he spring from? If so, who or what was *his* cause? Wouldn't God have to have a God and so on backwards forever?"

"You're not as stupid as you look," Ghazali conceded, "but you must understand that your confusion arises, again, out of a problem of language. The term *begins* supposes the existence of linear time. Both human beings and the jinn live in that time, we have births, lives and deaths, beginnings, middles and endings. God, however, lives in a different kind of time."

"There's more than one kind?"

"We live in what can be called Becoming-Time. We are born, we become ourselves, and then, when the Destroyer of Days comes to call, we unbecome, and what's left is dust. Talkative dust, in my case, but dust nonetheless. God's time, however, is eternal: it's just Being-Time. Past, present and future all exist together for him, and so those words, *past, present, future,* cease to have meaning. Eternal time has neither beginning nor end. It does not move. Nothing begins. Nothing finishes. God, in his time, has neither a dusty end, nor a fat, bright middle, nor a mewling beginning. He just *is*."

"Just is," Zumurrud repeated doubtfully.

"Yes," Ghazali confirmed.

"So God is a sort of time traveler," Zumurrud proposed. "He moves from his kind of time to ours, and by doing so becomes infinitely powerful."

"If you like," Ghazali agreed. "Except that he doesn't *become*. He still just *is*. You have to be careful how you use words."

"Okay," Zumurrud said, confused again.

"Think about it," Ghazali urged him.

"This god, Just-Is," Zumurrud said on a third occasion, after thinking about it, "he doesn't like being argued with, right?"

"He is *essential,* that is to say, pure essence, and as such, he is also *inarguable,*" Ghazali told him. "The second proposition unavoidably follows the first. To deny his essence would be to call him *inessential*, which would be to argue with him, who is, by definition, *inarguable*. Thus to argue with his inarguability is self-evidently to misuse language, and, as I told you, you have to be careful what words you use and how you use them. Bad language can blow up in your face."

"Like explosives," Zumurrud said.

"Worse," Ghazali said. "This is why wrong words are not to be tolerated."

"I have the feeling," Zumurrud mused, "that these wretched mortals of the lower world are even more confused about language than I was."

"Teach them," Ghazali said. "Teach them the tongue of the divine Just-Is. The instruction should be intensive, severe, even, one could say, fearsome. Remember what I told you about fear. Fear is man's fate. Man is born afraid, of the dark, of the unknown, of strangers, of failure, and of women. Fear leads him towards faith, not as a cure for fear, but as an acceptance that the fear of God is the natural and proper condition of man's lot. Teach them to fear the improper use of words. There is no crime the Almighty finds more unforgivable."

"I can do that," said Zumurrud the Great. "They'll be speaking my way soon enough."

"Not *yours*," Ghazali corrected him, but only mildly. When one was dealing with a Grand Ifrit one had to make certain allowances for his vast egotism.

"I understand," said Zumurrud the Great. "Rest now. No more words are necessary."

There ended the lesson. As Ghazali would soon discover, sending the most potent of the dark jinn down the path of extreme violence could have results that alarmed the sender. The student soon surpassed the master.

Dunia awakened Ibn Rushd in his grave for the last time. I've come to say goodbye, she told him. I won't be back to see you after today.

What has taken my place in your affections? he asked, his voice heavy with sarcasm. A pile of dust knows its limitations.

She told him about the war. The enemy is strong, she said.

The enemy is stupid, he replied. That is ground for hope. There is no originality in tyrants, and they learn nothing from the demise of their precursors. They will be brutal and stifling and engender hatred and destroy what men love and that will defeat them. All important battles are, in the end, conflicts between hatred and love, and we must hold to the idea that love is stronger than hate.

I don't know if I can do that, she said, for now I too am full of hatred. I look at the jinn world and see my dead father there, yes, but beyond that I see its shallowness: its obsession with shiny baubles, its amorality, its widespread contempt for human beings, which I must call by its true name, racism. I see the narcissistic malice of the Ifrits and I know that a little of that is in me too, there is always darkness as well as light. I don't see any light in the dark jinn now but I sense the darkness in myself. It's the place from which the hate comes. So I question myself as well as my world but I also know that this is no time for discussions. This is war. In wartime one must not ask, but do. So our discussions too must end, and what has to be done must be done.

That is a sad speech, he said. Reconsider. You need my guidance now.

Goodbye, she answered.

You're abandoning me.

You abandoned me once.

Then this is your revenge. To leave me conscious and impotent in my grave for all eternity.

No, she said, kindly. No revenge. Only farewell. Sleep.

Natraj Hero dancing the destruction dance. Find the jinni within yourself, the hot girl told him, the skinny little chick who said she was his great-great-great-great-and-more-*great*s-granny. His home was gone his mother didn't last much longer his mother who so far in life was the only woman he had truly loved. The shock of the night of the giant and the burning house did her in. He buried her and then was stuck on his cousin Normal's couch missing her more every minute of every day. His cousin who he fuckin' hated more every minute of every day. When I get in charge of my inner goblin, Normal, you jus might be the first a-hole I blast. Jus waitonly, waitansee.

The whole world gone to hell in a handcart and he, Jimmy Kapoor, spending his nights hittin' the graveyards with, because he's a funny guy, a lightning bolt painted on his *matha* like Harry P. He uses St. Michael's mostly, cradled in the outstretched arms of the Brooklyn-Queens Expressway or the way he really thinks of it the fuck-you V-sign of the BQE, all those headstones with lady angels perched on top looking down sad-faced at the stiffs. He's different now, ever since his hot granny whispered against his body, first his temples then his heart, bleeve it bruh she put her lips against my chest and worked her Hogwarts magic. *Bam* his head blew open like in that Kubrick flick like a rushing towards somewhere very cool and he's seeing shit he never dreamed, the grid of jinn knowledge and capability. It's actually mind-blowing, fuck, his mind is literally blown, but hey, interestingly, it hasn't made him crazy. Guess why. Guess that inner goblin is awake inside him and can handle this stuff. This must be what it feels like when people say, I feel like another person, or, I feel like a new man.

So now he's another person who has no other name, just his own. And that other person is him.

First there was the wormhole and the giant pretending to be his cartoon character just to fuck with his head but now his hot granny *really* fucked with his head and whaddya know it's like he's the superhero. The magic dancing king. *Having the time of your life.*

And oh yeah he's getting it. He can move really fast, slow the world down and speed himself up, that is sick. He can turn this into that. A handful of pebbles, hey presto, jewelry. A fallen branch when he squeezes it becomes a block of gold, who needs you Normal with your lousy couch I'm rich. But then Dunia's voice in his head, as if she hears every thought, if you don't concentrate on the fighting you'll be dead sooner than you think. He thinks about his mother and that gives him the anger. That puts the rage in him. Dunia says she's putting together an army. In different cities different Jimmys. He looks into his new brain and sees the network spreading. He reaches out his arm and the juice flows down it and wham, the thunderbolt, and one less sad-face angel. This he can't believe. It's his dream.

Somebody left pumpkins over there at that last resting place, well, thas jus askin' for it dude I'm sorry. *Boom*. Pumpkin soup.

When he got into it, it wasn't lightning with him. It was metamorphosis. Sure he blew the heads off a few stone angels, that was fun, he was exercising his Second Amendment right to bear arms, though probably the Founding Fathers didn't mean *actual arms*— but he discovered soon enough that he was better at the transformation thing. It didn't have to be jewelry, that was the key. Not just pebble into ruby. It has to be admitted that he tried his powers out on living things. Birds. Stray cats. Mangy curs. Rats. Well, nobody minds if you turn rats into rat turds or rat sausages, but birds, cats, dogs, there are people who care about those entities, starting with his late mother the bird-keeper, so, sorry, people, sorry, Mom.

The best bit was when he found out he could turn his targets into, for example, *sounds*. Whoa. He could turn a bird into birdsong, no bird, just the song hanging there, he could turn a cat into a meow. Once he got the hang of that he started getting playful, he zapped a headstone and then there was just a kind of sobbing sound hanging in that space, yeah, he was discovering kind of a sick streak, maybe inside every tax accountant there was a sicko superhero trying to get out, and hey, he thought, what about *colors*, can I turn roaches or flags or cheeseburgers into just colors hanging in space and then, yeah, *dissipating*. He needed to practice on larger animals. Any sheep around here? Nobody's gonna miss a few sheep, right? Maybe the metamorphoses were reversible, in which case, hey, no sheep were harmed in the making of this superpower. But the sheep were up-state on farms, unless the farms had broken down and the animals were just wandering about loose up there, who could he get to bring him where he needed to be, Asia had a car, she probably even knew where to get gas, gorgeous Ah-see-ah not Ay-sha, Italian signorina, not a brown girl, a dancer, no, bitch, not a stripper, she was pure class, *ballet;* probably had a line of men a mile long waiting for her with full gas cans in each hand. Now if he only had the really useful superpower of talking slick to girls.

Turned out he had the chops after all. He made the call, found a few words and told ballet girl what had happened to him, all of it, the hot granny, the whispering, *bam,* Stanley Kubrick space-odyssey FX, the works, and she didn't believe-believe him but believed him enough to go to the graveyard with him and, man, he showed her. Having her to perform for, he was, truth, *amazing.* The sound trans-formations the color changes the lightning.

And right there in St. Michael's after he performed for her she danced for him. Oh yes. So *guess what.* He didn't just have a driver to go up the Hudson in search of sheep. He had a *girlfriend,* girlfriend. *Oh* yes.

And so it went on for maybe a year and a half. During the long months of self-rediscovery, of learning to walk as a jinni before he could run as a jinni and then fly, during the time of accelerated second childhood which Geronimo Manezes had also experienced, Jimmy Kapoor realized that some part of him had been waiting for this, that there were people, of whom he was one, who yearned for the world of dreams and imagination to become a part of their wak-ing lives, who hoped for themselves and believed of themselves that they were capable of becoming a part of the wonderful, of kicking away the dust of banality and rising, reborn, into their true miracu-lous natures. Secretly he had always known that his creation, Natraj Hero, wasn't up to the mark, wouldn't lift him out of the rut of noth-ingness, which increased his delight at discovering that he could step into the light not through the medium of a fiction but as himself;

himself made fictional, he thought, or better than fictional—actual, but finally, against all hope, extraordinary. Maybe this was why he took so easily, so naturally, to his newly revealed jinn self. Its existence in him was a thing he had always known, but he had not trusted the knowledge; not until Dunia *whispered* to his heart.

He was waiting for the word from the Lightning Princess. Sometimes for a change he headed south to Calvary or Mount Zion cemeteries and blew the heads off stone lions in those locations also, and performed new changes, he could turn solid objects into *smells* now, one minute it was a bench, the next it was a fart, it was the accumulation of all the farts farted by old farts male and female sitting on that bench thinking about other old farts, now deceased, Macfart shall fart no more.

He thought about his collection of vintage comic books, gone now in the fireball of his old home, and remembered in those old DC issues the real-life Superman, Mr. Charles Atlas in his leopard-skin briefs with his Dynamic Tension technique that transformed him into The World's Most Perfectly Developed Man. Weren't no girls snickering behind his back now. This wasn't Old Jimmy anymore, meaning ninety-seven-pound-weakling Young Jimmy. This was a real He-Man, as Mr. Atlas would say. He-Me, with long tall Ahsee-ah on his arm. Nobody was kicking sand in his face now.

Here, finally, came Dunia, between the headstones of St. Michael's, looking for him: not the princess anymore but the queen. In the graveyard at midnight she commiserated with him for the loss of his mother. She lost a father too. Are you ready, she asked. Oh, was he ready.

She murmured in his ear, giving him some bad guys to kill.

The parasite-jinn, as they manifested themselves here on earth during the War of the Worlds, were unimpressive creatures, their capacity for thought extremely limited. When pointed by their jinn overlords they went in the direction indicated to wreak stipulated havoc, as in the attack on the mayor's residence. Afterwards, they spent their time seeking bodies to inhabit, for without human hosts they could not survive in the lower world. Once they latched on to a man or woman they sucked the body dry of life until it was an empty husk, and then they had only a short time in which to find a new host. Some now say that these creatures should not be numbered among the true jinn because they were barely sentient, a slave class, or a lower form of life. That argument has much merit, but still our tradition accords them a place in the taxonomy of the jinn, if only because, as the story has come down to us, they were the first of the jinn ever to be slain by a human being: or, to be precise, by a hybrid being—mostly human, with a strong dash of jinni in him, which had been set free by the fairy queen.

Certain images that have reached us from the conflicts of the past, both still and moving, now seem pornographic. We keep these images in sealed containers in restricted rooms for the consideration of genuine scholars: historians, students of defunct technologies (photography, film), psychologists. We see no need to distress ourselves unduly by putting such objects on public display.

We have not in these pages lingered unduly, and we will continue not to dwell, on the details of killings. We pride ourselves that we have evolved since those distant times; and that violence, which for so long lay upon humanity like a jinni's curse, has become a thing of the past. Sometimes, like any addict, we still feel it in our blood, we become aware of its scent in our nostrils; some of us go so far as to clench our fists, curl our upper lips into aggressive sneers, and even, for a brief instant, raise our voices. But we resist, we uncurl, lower our lips, lower our voices. We do not succumb. We are aware, however, that any account of our past, and in particular the time of the strangenesses and the Two Worlds' War, would be sorely lacking if it turned its face entirely away from unappetizing matters of injury and death.

The parasite-jinn came and went from city to city, country to country, continent to continent. They had more than one place, one people to scare, and utilized the high-speed jinn transportation systems—the wormholes, the slow-them-down-speed-me-up time-shifts, even, at times, the flying urns—to move hither and yon. In the sealed containers in our restricted rooms we have preserved disturbing images of cannibal jinn parasites eating people's faces in Miami, Florida; and executioner jinn parasites stoning women to death in desert places; and suicide bomber jinn parasites allowing their host bodies to explode on army bases and then immediately possessing the nearest soldier and murdering more of his fellows in what was called an insider attack, which it was, but not in the conventional sense of the term; and crazed paramilitary jinn parasites in charge of tanks in eastern Europe, shooting passenger aircraft out of the sky—but let these few images suffice. There is no need to make a comprehensive catalogue of horrors. Let us say: they hunted in packs, like feral dogs, and were wilder than anything on four legs. And it was Jimmy Kapoor's appointed task, given him by the newly crowned Lightning Queen, to hunt down the hunters.

The men and women occupied by the parasite-jinn were beyond saving, dead the moment the parasites entered their bodies. But how to attack the parasites, who were disembodied until they seized (which is to say, killed) a living person, in such a way that they ceased to be able to do it? It was Jimmy Kapoor who solved the riddle: if solid objects could be turned into colors or smells or sounds, then perhaps, by reversing the technique, vaporous entities could be solidified. Thus began the Medusa operation, so called because the cloudy parasites, when Jimmy made them visible permanences, looked like stone monsters that people inaccurately called *gorgons,* even though of course, according to the ancient Greeks, Medusa the Gorgon was the petrifier, not the petrified—it was her gaze that turned living men to stone. (So it was also with Dr. Frankenstein and his monster. It is the nameless golem, the artificial man, that has come to be known by its creator's name.)

It is also perhaps inaccurate to call these petrified things "monsters." They were non-anthropomorphic, sinuous, complex shapes, twisting in and out of themselves, sometimes forming thickets of spikes, at other times extruding hinged "arms" that ended in blades. They could be many faceted, like crystals, or as fluid as fountains. Jimmy fought them wherever he found them, wherever his newly accessible jinn information system sent him in pursuit of these lesser demons, on the banks of the Tiber in Rome or on the shining metal heights of a Manhattan skyscraper, and he left them where he changed them, their dead bodies decorating the world's cities like new works of art, sculptural and, yes, it has to be said, beautiful. This was a thing men and women discussed even then, at the height of the war. The beauty of the gorgons gave pause, even in those distracted times, and the link between art and death, the fact that by dying the parasite-jinn had metamorphosed from lethal adversaries into aesthetically pleasing objects of contemplation, gave rise to a kind of relieved surprise. The making of solidity out of evanescence: that was one of the newest arts of war, and one that had the greatest claim, of all such arts, to be included in the catalogue of Art itself, high art, in which beauty and meaning combined in revelatory forms.

Their pursuer and nemesis did not see himself as an artist. He was Jimmy Natraj, god of destruction, dancing his destruction dance.

Zumurrud the Great declared that his Foundation was only the first step towards the creation of the global jinn sultanate, whose worldwide authority he now proclaimed, and also his own anointment, by his own hand, as the first sultan. At once, however, the other three Grand Ifrits expressed their displeasure at his self-declared primacy, and he was obliged to backtrack a little. Because he could not vent his annoyance on the other three members of the ruling quadrumvirate, Zumurrud embarked on a wild international spree of decapitations, crucifixions and stonings that created, in the very first days of the sultanate, a groundswell of hatred that would, in short order, fuel the counterrevolution. His alliance with the vicious and illiterate Swots of A. gave him what passed for a program of governance, and he set about enthusiastically proscribing things just the way they did, poetry, bicycles, toilet paper, fireworks, love stories, political parties, French fries, eyeglasses, root canal dentistry, encyclopedias, condoms, and chocolate, and burning anyone who raised an objection at the stake, or chopping them in half, or, as he gained enthusiasm for the work, hanging, drawing and quartering them, the traditional and excellent English penalty for high treason ever since the thirteenth century. He was willing (he told the other Grand Ifrits) to learn the best lessons of the former imperial powers, and announced the inclusion of these medieval penalties in the legal code of the new sultanate, with immediate and devastating effect.

Most idiosyncratically of all, he declared his implacable enmity towards all forms of sealable containers, all jars with lids that could be screwed down or bottles that could be corked, all trunks with locks, all pressure cookers, all safety-deposit boxes, coffins and tea chests. His fellow Grand Ifrits Shining Ruby and Ra'im Blood-Drinker had no memories of incarceration, and reacted to these declarations with dismissive shrugs. But, he told them, once you've spent an eternity trapped in glass you develop a hatred of your jail cell. "As you wish," Shining Ruby said, "but wasting one's time on little things is not the hallmark of greatness." Zumurrud ignored this slight. Men had imprisoned him. Now he would have his turn. That was a hatred in him born of those prison years that could not be assuaged, not by all the proscriptions and executions in the world. Sometimes he thought he did not so much wish to rule over the human race as to preside over its brutal extinction.

In this matter at least, Zabardast, who had also known imprisonment, was in full agreement with Zumurrud: it was time for vengeance.

The revenge of the jinn burns with unquenchable fire.

It wasn't long before Zumurrud's bloodthirstiness began to worry what remained of Ghazali. The philosopher's dust, when informed by the great jinni of the thoroughness with which he was fulfilling the dead man's demand that the human race be made afraid so that their fear might drive them to the divine, was obliged to consider the difference between scholarly theory and bloody practice, and concluded that Zumurrud, while undeniably assiduous, might have, in a certain sense, *gone too far.* When Zumurrud heard this he understood that the philosopher was no longer useful to him. He had gone beyond anything that could be taught by this old dead fool. "My duty to you is done," he told Ghazali. "I return you to the silence of the grave."

Zabardast, always the more controlled of the two senior dark jinn, always the more inward and soft-spoken (though in reality no less ruthless, perhaps even more so, because of his greater intelligence), proposed that the new sultanate be quartered, like the bodies Zumurrud was hacking to bits. It was too large to be centrally governed and Zumurrud's "Foundation" in the remote land of A. was scarcely a grand metropolis, fit to be a capital city. It was already the case, he pointed out, that most of Zumurrud's activity was in what might loosely be called the "East," whereas he himself has done his best work, made the most mischief and created the most fear, in the powerful "West." That left Africa and South America for Ra'im Blood-Drinker and Shining Ruby. The rest of the world—Australasia, Polynesia, and the territories of penguins and polar bears—could probably be ignored for the moment.

This was a dispensation that pleased nobody, not even its proposer (for Zabardast secretly planned to take over the whole world), but which all four Grand Ifrits briefly accepted—*briefly,* until the quarrels began. Shining Ruby was particularly displeased with his lot. The jinn are happiest in those lands in which their stories are best known, more or less at home in lands to which their stories traveled in the baggage of migrant peoples, and ill at ease in zones less known to them, in which they too are less known. "South America?" complained Shining Ruby. "What do they know about magic there?"

Their wars of conquest sprang up like black flowers all over the globe, and many of these were small proxy wars, waged by men controlled by the jinn in every way a man can be controlled, by possession, enchantment, bribery, fear, or faith. The dark jinn sat indolent on their clouds wrapped in fogs of invisibility so thick that for a long time even Dunia couldn't make out where her mightiest enemies were. They sat up there watching their puppets kill and die and sometimes they sent the lesser jinn down to join in the destruction. Within a very short time, however, the old failings of the jinn—their disloyalty, their lack of application, their whimsicality, their selfishness, their egotism—rose to the surface. Each of the four quickly came to believe that he and he alone was, and should be recognized as, the grandest of the grand, and what began as squabbling escalated at speed and changed the nature of the conflict in the lower world. This was when the human race became the canvas upon which the dark jinn painted their mutual hatred, the raw material from which each of the quartet sought to forge the saga of his own absolute supremacy.

Looking back, we tell ourselves this: the craziness unleashed upon our ancestors by the jinn was the craziness that also waited inside every human heart. We can blame the jinn, and we do, we do. But if we are honest we must blame human failings too.

It is painful to record that the dark jinn took particular pleasure in watching assaults on women. In the age before the separation of the Two Worlds women in most parts of the world had been considered to be secondary, lesser entities, chattels, homemakers, to be respected as mothers but otherwise disdained, and though these attitudes had changed for the better in some parts of the planet at least, the dark jinn's belief that women were provided for men's use and support were still those of the dark ages. In addition the frustrations caused by the sexual boycott imposed by the jinnia population of the upper world had made them angry, and so they watched without criticism as their proxies turned violent, as women were not only violated but killed thereafter, these new women, many of whom rejected the idea of their inferiority, and needed to be put back in their place. Into this war against the female gender Queen Dunia sent a soldier of her own, and the tide of battle began to turn.

Teresa Saca had her superhero name now. Not Madame Magneto or any of that tabloid nonsense, that was comic book stuff. Dunia's voice in her head saying *I'm your mother.* I too will be something's mother, she told herself, I will be Mother, the fiery mama of death itself. That other, more saintly Mother Teresa, she had been in the death business too, but Teresa Saca was more interested in the sudden-death variety than in hospices, no easing of the living into soft oblivion for her, just a hammer blow of voltage to bring life to a hard full stop. She was Dunia's avenging angel, the avenger, or so she told herself, of every spurned, wronged, abused woman who had ever lived.

Moral exemption was an unfamiliar state to be in, the condition of having permission to kill, to destroy without feeling guilt at the destruction, there was something here that went against the human grain. When she killed Seth Oldville she had been full of rage but that didn't make it right, she understood that, rage was a reason but it was not an excuse. He might have been an asshole, but she was still a murderer. The criminal was guilty of the crime, and that criminal would be her, and maybe justice had to be done, but, whatever, she added silently, they need to catch me first. And now all of a sudden her jinnia ancestor *whispered* into her and set her inner warrior free and tasked her with helping to save the world. It was like those movies where they took guys off death row and gave them a shot at redemption, and if they died, hey, they were going to get fried anyway. Fair enough, she thought, but I'm going to take a lot of bastards down with me when I go.

Closing the eyes revealed the grid system of the jinn, and her mistress Dunia had sent her the coordinates she needed. Turning sideways and leaning just so slipped her through a crack in the air into the travel dimension and then she was going wherever the grid decreed. When she emerged from the tunnel between the dimensions, she barely knew which country she was in—yes, the information Dunia had planted in her mind told her its name, A. or P. or I., but that alphabet soup didn't help much; one of the characteristics of her new reality, of this new way of getting around and of the alternate reality that had created it, was this loss of connection to the material world—she could have been anywhere, any brown barren space, any lush green park, any mountain, any valley, any city, any street, any earth. Then after a time she understood that it didn't matter, whichever country she was in it was always the same country, the country of attacks on women, and she was the assassin who came to avenge them. Here was a "man" possessed by a jinni—possessed, enchanted, bribed by jewels, it didn't matter. What he had done condemned him, and here was the lightning in her fingertips that carried out the sentence. No, there was no need for moral introspection. She was neither judge nor jury. She was the executioner. *Call me Mother,* she told her targets. These were the last words they heard on earth.

Floating through the impossible corridors between time and space, the tunnels bored through the spiraling Magellanic clouds of nonexistence, possessed by the melancholy solitude of the wandering murderer, Teresa Saca contemplated her youth, its desperation, the nights when she floored the accelerator and drove her first car (her first actual car of her own, not the stolen red convertible of her first wild ride), a convertible, ancient, electric blue, as fast as she could go down country roads and through the swamps, really not caring if she lived or died. Always self-destructive then, there were drugs and unsuitable men, but she learned in school the only lesson worth learning, *beauty is currency,* and as soon as the breasts showed up she straightened her long black hair and headed for the big city to spend it, the only currency she had, and hey, she didn't do so badly, look at her now, she was a mass murderer with superpowers, that was quite a career path for a girl from nowhere.

That girl didn't matter anymore anyway. The past dropped away from her. She discovered she was good at this, the sudden appearance, the startled horror on the face of the target, the thunderbolt like a bright lance through his chest, or sometimes, just for fun, his genitalia, or his eye, they all worked. And then back into the nothingness towards the next rapist the next abuser the next subhuman creature the next piece of primordial slime the next thing that deserved to die, whom she was happy to kill, whom she killed without remorse. And with each act she became stronger, she felt strength filling her, she became, and this seemed to her a good thing, less human. More jinnia than flesh and blood. Soon she would be Dunia's equal. Soon she would be able to look the Queen of Qâf in the eye and stare her down. Soon she would be *invincible*.

It was a strange war, haphazard, wayward, as the jinn are. It was here today and gone tomorrow, then back again without warning. It was colossal, all-consuming, and then distant, absent. One day a monster rising from the sea, the next, nothing, and then, on the seventh day, acid rain from the skies. There was chaos and fear and attacks by supernatural giants from their cloud eyries and then lazy hiatuses during which the fear and chaos continued. There were parasites and explosions and possessions and everywhere there was rage. The rage of the jinn was part of what they were, amplified, in the case of Zumurrud and Zabardast, by their long captivity, and it found an answering rage in many human hearts, like a bell chiming in a Gothic tower and being answered by its echo from the bottom of a well, and maybe this was what war was now, maybe this was the last war, this descent into random raging chaos, a war in which the conquerors were as viciously at war with one another as with the wretched earth. Because this war was formless it was hard to fight, harder still to win. It felt like a war against an abstraction, a war against war itself. Did Dunia have the skill to win such a war? Or was some greater ruthlessness required, a ruthlessness which Dunia did not possess, but of which she, Teresa Saca, was becoming more capable with every

thunderbolt poured into the heart of a guilty man? At some point it
would not be enough to defend the earth. It would be necessary to
attack the upper world.

I'm too old to be in an army, thought Mr. Geronimo in the cloud tunnels. How many of us are there in Dunia's raggle-taggle brigade,
gardeners and accountants and murderesses, how many members of
her bloodline has the fairy queen *whispered* to and drafted to face the
most fearsome enemies in the known worlds, and what chance do
we really have against the unleashed savagery of the dark jinn. Can
even Dunia in her wrath bring all four of them down and their minions too. Or is the fate of the world to surrender to the darkness descending by finding the answering darkness within ourselves. *No,
not if I can help it,* an inner voice replied. So he was a soldier in this
war in spite of all his doubts. The aches and groans in his much-used
body. Never mind. It was hard to know what a just war looked like
anymore but this one, this oddest of conflicts, was one in which he
was prepared to play his part.

   "Anyway," he told himself, "it's not as if I've been given a frontline role. I'm more like the medical team than the vanguard. I'm the
MASH."

   To bring down those rising and to raise up those in the grip of the
crushing curse. This was his appointed task: the adjustment of faults
in gravity. In his mind's eye the global grid system located the victims, the ones most in need flashing brightest on his retina. What a
way to see the world, he thought. The plagues of rising and falling
were everywhere, sprinkled over the world by Zabardast the Sorcerer, the random terror of their arrival exceeding what would have
been caused by a "normal" plague; and so everywhere was where he
had to go. Here was a ferry approaching the gambling dens of Macao,
a crowd shrinking back from him in wondering fear as he appeared
from nowhere to save a traveler whose cries of pain they had all ignored, Mr. Geronimo bending over him whispering and the man

rising to his feet, raised from the dead, or near-dead, and Mr. Geronimo turning sideways and gone, leaving his Chinese Lazarus to his fate, the poor man's fellow travelers still eyeing him as if he bore an infectious disease, maybe he would go and gamble his savings away that night just to celebrate being alive, but that was someone else's story to tell, and here was Mr. Geronimo on a mountainside in the Pir Panjal fishing a railway tunnel worker out of the sky, and then here, and here, and here.

Sometimes he arrived too late and a riser, already too far gone, was dying of hypothermia or breathing difficulties in the thin cold air of an Andean sky, or a crushee had been crushed in a Mayfair art gallery, his bones broken and compacted, his body a burst concertina leaking blood through flattened clothes, his hat atop the whole sorry mess, looking like an installation. But often, accelerating down the wormholes, he showed up in time, he raised the fallen, lowered the risen. In some places the disease had spread rapidly, there were great crowds of the terrified floating above the lampposts, and he brought them all softly down with a wave of his hand; and then, oh!, the gratitude, bordering on adoration. He understood. He had been there himself. Proximity to calamity released the human capacity for love. The expression on the face of Alexandra Bliss Fariña after he restored the glory of La Incoerenza and brought her and Oliver Oldcastle back down to earth: every man alive would wish to be looked at in that way by a beautiful woman.

Even if standing next to that woman was her hairy estate manager, wearing exactly the same adoring look.

The lifelong pessimism of the Lady Philosopher had been wholly dissipated by Mr. Geronimo's small miracle, burned off by his local magic like clouds by the heat of the sun. This new Alexandra looked at Geronimo Manezes as a sort of savior, capable of rescuing not only herself and her estate but the whole incoherent earth as well. It was to her bed that he retired at the end of these long strange days— What was a "day" anymore? he asked himself; the wormhole journeys across space and time zones, the staccato arrivals and departures a hundred and more times a day, disconnected him from any real sense of the continuity of life, and when exhaustion claimed him, the bone-weariness of the rootless, he came to her. These were stolen moments, oases in the desert of the war, and each of them made promises to the other of longer moments in the future, dream-moments in dream-places which were their dreams of peace. Will we win? she asked him, curled into his arm, his hand cradling her head. We will win, won't we?

Yes, he told her. We will win, because the alternative is to lose, and that is unthinkable. We will win.

He slept poorly now, overtired, feeling his years, and in the half-sleeping nights he wondered about that promise. Dunia was gone, he didn't know where, but he knew why: she was hunting the biggest game of all, the four great enemies she had made it her business to destroy. Messages and instructions from her poured daily and nightly into the newly opened jinn area of his brain. She was still running the operation, no question about that, but she was a hidden general, moving too far and too fast to be seen personally by her troops. And could "we" really win, he wondered, were there enough of us, or were there in reality more people seduced by the darkness of the jinn, was "victory" what people actually wanted, or did the word seem triumphalist and wrong, did people prefer the idea of making an accommodation with the new masters, and would the dark jinn's overthrow feel like freedom or just the ascent of a new superpower, the Lightning Queen come to rule them instead of the Giant and the Sorcerer. These bubbling thoughts sapped his strength but the woman lying beside him gave it back. Yes, "we" would win. "We" owed it to our loved ones not to lose. We owed it to the idea of love itself which might die if the dark jinn ruled the world.

Love, for so long dammed up inside Mr. Geronimo, was flooding through him now. His powerful intoxication with Dunia herself had started it, probably doomed from the start, being a thing of echoes, each seeing in the other their true love's avatar . . . but that already seemed a long time ago, she had retreated from him into queenliness and war. Love itself had remained in him, he felt it splashing around in his insides, a great tidal sea of it ebbing and flowing through his heart, and here was Alexandra Bliss Fariña ready to dive into those waters, *let us drown in love together, my love,* and yes, he thought, maybe one last great love was permitted him, and here she was, ready for him, and yes, why not, he would take the plunge as well. He was so tired in her bed that there was little in the way of love-making, one night in four or five was about his speed these days anyway, but she was full of understanding. He was her warrior to be loved and waited for and she would take what little of him she could get and wait for the rest.

And outside her bedroom door when he set off again on his travels stood Oliver Oldcastle, not angry Oliver of old but new, grateful, obsequious Oldcastle, as dewy-eyed as any spaniel, cap in hand, a sickly yellow-toothed smile affixed to his usually lugubrious face as if tied on with a piece of string. Is there anything I can do for you sir, anything you need, just say the word. I'm not much of a fighter but if it comes down to it I'm your man.

These fawning obeisances got Mr. Geronimo's goat. I think I liked it better in the old days, he told the estate manager, when you were threatening to kill me.

The
Faerie Queene

In the cradle of life, between the Tigris and Euphrates, where once the land of Nod, which is to say Wandering, stood to the east of Eden, it was Omar the Ayyar who showed Dunia, his queen, the first signs of the rifts appearing in the body of the four-headed monster which had set out to rule the earth. In those days she was moving around the world like a bright shadow resembling a blurred light in the corner of the eye, and with her, inseparably, was her favorite spy, both of them searching high and low for the four Grand Ifrits. Those boys have got better at hiding out than when we were fooling around in the old days, she told Omar. Back then I could see through their cloaking devices without even trying. But maybe in those days they secretly wanted to be found.

If relatively little has come down to us about the master spy of Qâf, Omar the Ayyar, it is very probably because of the residual prejudice among the jinn towards male homosexuality, cross-dressing, and suchlike practices. The jinnias, or jiniri, of Peristan evidently had no objection to lesbian activity, and indeed during the period of the sex strike there was a dramatic spike in such behavior, but among the male jinn the old bigotries were widespread. Omar's well-known professional exploits, his intelligence-gathering in the guise of a harem eunuch or in women's clothing, had won him a great reputation as a spy, but they also made him an outsider among his own kind. He himself would say that he had always been an outsider anyway. His dress was deliberately flamboyant, with brocade shawls flung over his shoulders with meticulous abandon, and many outrageous hats; his manner was decadent and brittle, and he set himself up as an aesthete and dandy and affected not to give a damn what any of his peers thought. He gathered kindred spirits around him in the intelligence service of Qâf, which had the unintended consequence of making many people in Fairyland profoundly distrust this team of brilliant butterflies who were also the most effective snoops in the upper world. However, Dunia had always trusted him totally. In the final conflict against the Grand Ifrits she came to feel like an outsider too, setting out to avenge the father whom she had never managed to please by murdering members of her own race. Omar the Ayyar accompanied her every day as she hunted down the dark quartet, and she came to feel that they were kindred spirits in many ways. Her fondness for the human race, her love of one man and their descendants, set her apart from her people too. She was aware that she did not possess the personal characteristics which had made her father so widely loved and admired. She was direct, truthful and forceful, whereas her father had been oblique, distracted and charming. Her insistence on the sex strike made things worse. She could foresee a moment in the not-too-distant future at which the ladies of Peristan would lose sympathy for her, and shrug their collective shoulders at her war against the Grand Ifrits. What was the lower world to them anyway? And why was she so hot and bothered about it? This was a war she could lose if it went on much longer. It was essential to find the four dark jinn before very long. She was running out of time.

Why was she so bothered about it indeed? There was an answer to that question, a reply she carried with her everywhere, and which she had never given, not even to Omar the Ayyar, the supreme gatherer and keeper of secrets, and it was this: *she knew she was partly responsible for what was happening.* In the long centuries of calm during which the slits between the world had silted up and the upper and lower worlds lost contact with each other and went about their separate business, there were many in the valleys and lakes of Fairyland who thought that was just fine, the lower world was messy and full of argument, while in their fragrant gardens they knew something very like eternal bliss. In the mountain kingdom of Qâf things looked a little different. For one thing, the Grand Ifrits had their eyes on the kingdom, and it was necessary to remain vigilant and keep defenses high. And for another, the (then) Lightning Princess missed the earth, and her many widely dispersed heirs upon it. During the time of separation she often dreamed about reuniting the Duniazát, releasing their powers and building a better world with their help. So she had searched the worlds between the worlds, the layers between the layers, looking for the ruined gateways, trying to reopen them. She had been an archaeologist of the buried past, excavating the lost, broken, clogged pathways, always hoping to find a way through. And yes, she knew that other, darker forces in Fairyland were engaged in the same work, and she could not deny that she was aware of the risks to the lower world if the roads were reopened, but still she tried, as any mother would, to be reunited with her scattered brood, which was all she had left of the man she once loved. In the world below, the searches of the jinn for the way through to their lost playground manifested themselves, or so we now believe, as storms. The heavens themselves cracked under the jinn's yearning fists. And yes, in the end they opened and what followed, followed.

Well, so it was. Unlike most of her kind Dunia was capable of human responses: responsibility, guilt, remorse. Like all of her kind she was able to fold unwanted thoughts into deep cloudy places within herself where, most of the time, they lay forgotten, like fogged images, like vague curls of smoke. She had tried to hide Ibn Rushd in that way and failed. And then he came back to her in the form of Geronimo Manezes and for a moment she felt again that old lost human emotion: love. Oh, how like her beloved he was! The face, that adored face. The genes descending the centuries to burst out of his skin. She could have loved him if she had allowed herself to do so, and yes, there was a soft spot in her for him even now, she could not deny it, even as he was in the arms of his Lady Philosopher whom she could cheerfully have fried alive with one flick of her lethal wrist.

But she would not. Because Mr. Geronimo was only an illusion of the past after all, and now that illusory love had been replaced in her breast by genuine hatred.

It was time to find her erstwhile playmates and destroy them. Where were they? How were they to be found?

Look on the ground, not in the skies, Omar the Ayyar told her. They will be perceived by their effects.

And there in the cradle of life, poised at the summit of the ruin of the Great Ziggurat of Ur, the "house whose foundation created terror," they saw the enchanted armies turning upon each other as if the Sumerians and Akkadians of old, so long symbiotically integrated into a single plural culture, had lost their minds and begun to slaughter their neighbors in the streets. Black flags were borne into battle against other black flags. There was much shouting down there about religion, about unbelievers or heretics or unclean godless ones, and it did seem as if the religious shouting enabled the warriors to put extra venom into the downswings of their swords, but Omar saw what was really happening, he understood that the Grand Ifrit Shining Ruby had left his unwanted South American redoubt and come to confront Zumurrud the Great on territory earmarked for Zumurrud's desert Foundation. Shining Ruby, the Possessor of Souls: his bewitched army marched in lockstep against the mercenary regiments Zumurrud had bought with jewels, drugs and whores. And it was Shining Ruby's possessed men who prevailed. The sheer savagery of their assault terrified the Zumurrud mercenaries, who had not been given nearly enough jewels to make these crazy white-eyed trance-killers from hell worth standing up to. The mercenaries dropped their weapons and ran away, leaving the field of battle to Shining Ruby's men. Where is Zumurrud? Dunia asked Omar. Is he even here? That lazy bastard is probably asleep on a mountain somewhere while his creatures take a beating. Overconfidence always was his problem.

Then a wormhole appeared in the sky, boiling with smoke at its edges, and out came Shining Ruby in triumph riding a flying urn. To hell with those Latino latitudes, he cried. The cradle of civilization is mine. I will plant my standard in the Garden of Eden itself and all men will fear my name.

Stay out of this, Dunia told Omar the Ayyar. You're not the fighting type.

Here once again we must overcome our long-standing cultural distaste for acts of extreme violence and set down an account of one of the very rare murders within the tribe of the jinn, and, to our knowledge, the first ever carried out by a jinnia queen. Rising in wrath from the ziggurat and ascending into the sky on a carpet of sheet lightning, fully revealed in all her terrible majesty, Dunia certainly took Shining Ruby by surprise, shattering his urn with a thunderbolt and sending him tumbling to earth. But it takes more than a bad fall to kill a Grand Ifrit and he rose, puffing a little but otherwise unharmed, to face her. She flew at him releasing spears of lightning and forced him to shed his human form and stand on the earth as a pillar of fire and then she wrapped him in herself, becoming thick, choking, airless smoke, denying the fire the air it needed, strangling him in great nooses of smoke, suffocating him in smoke, pitting the essence of her femaleness against his deepest male nature, squeezing him in smoke, and letting him flail and thrash and sputter and flicker; and so die. When he was gone and she took human form again nothing remained of him, not even a little pile of ash. Until that fight to the death she had not been sure of her strength, but after it she knew. There were three remaining Grand Ifrits and now they had more reason than she to be afraid of the coming fight.

After the death of Shining Ruby his army was released from his spells of possession and the soldiers stood in confusion, blinking and scratching their heads, not knowing where they were or why. The mercenaries had dispersed and not even those who witnessed the sudden perplexity of their foes retained any appetite for the fray and so the battle ended in comic absurdity. The jinn world, however, was

not amused, and Dunia's deed was greeted with outrage. News of
the event spread almost instantaneously via the jinn's internal communications network and horror spread through Fairyland. For
several days Dunia didn't care. It was often true in wartime that the
civilians at home were faint of heart and images of death and destruction made them long for peace. News and gossip focused on
such images and undermined the necessary work being done by
those on the front lines. She scorned to face her critics. She had a war
to fight.

She sent Omar the Ayyar back to Peristan to find out what he
could, and when he returned he said, I think you had better come. So
in a bother of frustration she left the lower world and returned to the
peaceful gardens on the other side. When she arrived she understood
that by killing a Grand Ifrit she had exhausted the sympathy of her
people, and not even the memory of her lost father was enough to
win it back. Shining Ruby, long, slender, prancing, a harlequin playboy of a jinni, a fair-faced fellow with a wealth of personal charm,
had been well liked by the ladies of Peristan, and his murder snapped
their antiwar solidarity and brought the sex boycott to an end. Most
of the male jinn were at war, of course, which did nothing to improve the love-hungry ladies' mood. But one of the great ones had
returned and there was a great commotion at the palace of the baths
because he had come there to disport himself with whichever and
however many of the ladies of Fairyland were of a mind to join him
at play. The cries of delight emanating from the great bathhouse told
Dunia what she needed to know. A metamorph was present, and
pleasing the ladies in many different guises, a dragon, a unicorn,
even a big cat. The sexual organ of the lion—and of many other
large cats—is bedecked with spines that face backwards, so when it
is withdrawn it rakes the walls of the lioness's vagina in a way that
may or not be pleasurable. In the palace of the baths there were sex-
starved jinnia ladies who were ready to try anything, even that. It
was hard to know if the screams that ensued expressed pain or pleasure or some interesting combination of the two. Dunia didn't care.

The size of the crowd and the excitement of the women told her that the metamorphic entity inside must be a major talent. One of the Grand Ifrits had come home to visit. Ra'im Blood-Drinker, she said to herself, saggy-ass Ra'im who is so difficult to kiss on account of that serrated tongue, your lustful appetite has brought you within my grasp.

The fictional Greek god Proteus was a powerful metamorphic deity of the sea, as fluid in his transformations as water itself. Blood-Drinker was fond of transforming himself into sea-monsters and it is possible that he and Proteus were one and the same, that Proteus was the name the ancient Greeks gave him during their time. Dunia slipped into the grand bath hall of Peristan and there in the enormous bottomless saltwater pool was the Ifrit prince, now a long slippery eel, now a nameless spiky bug-eyed monster of the deep ocean trenches, and around him were the ladies of Fairyland squealing with anticipatory joy. Dunia had to move swiftly. As she plunged below the surface of the water to grab Ra'im Blood-Drinker by his sex—because whatever fantastic sea-beast he was impersonating at that moment, he would make sure he retained the equipment he needed to make love to the ladies of Fairyland—she *spoke* to him in the unvoiced private language of the jinn. I never did like fucking fish, she said, but fish-man, your time has come.

This was what she knew about male metamorphs: they would elude you, they would turn themselves into water and slip through your fingers, unless you were quick enough to grab them by the balls and hold on tightly. Then you had to cling on until they had tried everything they could think of; and if you were still there at the end, with their balls in your fist, then they were yours.

Easier said than done.

This was no ordinary metamorph, but Ra'im Blood-Drinker, the Grand Ifrit. He was a shark gaping at her with his great jagged teeth and a serpent winding around her to crush her in his coils. He was seaweed binding her and a whale trying to swallow her and a great stingray that could mortally damage her with his tail. She clung to

him and avoided his traps. She was a black cloud with a hand emerging from it clutching his manhood. She was dazzling in her speed,
her twists, her feints. She matched his moves and surpassed them.
She was invincible. His transformations multiplied and accelerated.
She was equal to them all. And finally he was spent, gasping his last
breaths as she rose above the water and burned it with her electric
hands and he was caught: tossed, fried and done. His body lay upon
the water like a shipwreck.

Fish supper tonight, she said, and left him to sink beneath the
surface.

She came out of the palace of the baths to face a hostile crowd.
There were boos and cries of *Shame on you*. Ah, the confusion and
fear of the jinnias of Peristan faced with one of their own, the Queen
of Qâf Mountain, no less, become a murderer, killer of dark princes.
They had all fled the baths when the fight began, and now they saw
the palace broken and damaged, its golden arches fallen, its vaulted
glass roof smashed, the palace turned into a mirror of so many war-
smashed structures in the lower world; and yes, they knew the ruins
could be rebuilt in a trice, a magic spell would give them back the
palace immaculate and unspoilt, that was not the issue. No magic
could raise Ra'im Blood-Drinker from the dead. And Shining Ruby
was gone as well. Those truths were irreversible. The ladies of Fairyland turned their backs to Queen Dunia and she understood that she
had lost her place in their ranks. No matter. It was time to return to
the lower world and bring the war to an end.

In the midst of the battle there had been time to do one small good
deed. The foolish Signor Giacomo Donizetti of New York, former
seducer of unhappily married women, afterwards victim of a wicked,
though not undeserved, tit-for-tat hex that obliged him to adore all
women unreservedly, and presently wretched and rudderless, was of
no use to her as a fighter; but maybe she could heal him. She was the
mother of all her flock, the useless ones as well as the worthwhile,

and she saw the good in this stray sheep of the Duniazát, hiding beneath the lechery and cynicism, and she pitied him for the spell cast
on him by this or that small-fry bad jinni. Breaking the enchantment
was easy and then Giacomo was once more immune to doctors' re-
ceptionists and bag ladies, but he remained a lost soul until she *listened* to his heart and *whispered* to him what he must do, and wherein
his salvation lay. Soon after that he opened a new restaurant.

It was an insane time to open an upscale eatery, even for somebody
who had once been among the princes of the city's nightlife. Those
days were long gone and now, in wartime, people rarely ventured
out to dinner, and when they did it was to grab something easy,
something that required no investment of time or money on the part
of either the vendor or the purchaser. Into that devastation of what
had formerly been the gastronomic capital of the world came Giacomo Donizetti restored to his peacock finery with an establishment
of polished wood and even more highly polished metal and glass. It
shone like a new sun, and even though almost nobody went to eat
there Donizetti's extraordinary kitchen staff, pulled together from
all the newly unemployed master chefs, pâtissiers and sommeliers in
America, daily produced a menu as dazzling as the furnishings, so
that the empty restaurant with its perfect table settings and even
more immaculate waitstaff became a beacon of hope, a Statue of Liberty made not of copper but rather of food and wine. Afterwards,
when peace returned to the world, it made Giacomo Donizetti's fortune, becoming something like a symbol of the resistance, an em-
blem of the city's old characteristics of defiance and optimism; but in
those days people marveled at the epic folly of opening such a place:
a brilliantly illuminated and opulent saloon containing the best of
everything, except customers.

He had named the restaurant in the Venetian manner, Ca' Giacomo, and its cuisine was Venetian too, featuring such delicacies as
baccalà Mantecato, or creamed cod, *bisato su l'ara,* which was eel
roasted with bay leaves, and *caparossoli in cassopipa,* or clams with
parsley. There was rice and peas, *risi e bisi,* and stuffed duck, *anatra*

ripiena, and for dessert there was a trolley bearing fried cream and *torta Nicolotta* and *torta sabbiosa* as well. How did Donizetti do it? people wondered. Where did he find the produce, and where did he get the cash? He answered all such questions with a Venetian mask of indifference, and a shrug. *You want to eat? Don't ask. You don't like it? Eat someplace else.*

His patrons' pockets were deep. Zumurrud the Great was not the only one with caves full of precious stones larger than dragons' eggs. And a jinnia queen can put meat and fish in your freezer with just a flick of her hand.

He tried repeatedly to thank her but she waved him away. It's good for me too, she said. Wherever I've been, whoever I had to kill, I can come here every night and eat with the kitchen brigade. If I am your only customer, so what? It's my money I'm losing. *Fegato, seppie,* Venetian *baicoli* biscuits. A glass of good Amarone wine. Yes. This heals me too.

In the unexpected lull that followed the deaths of Shining Ruby and Ra'im Blood-Drinker, things began to feel different in the city, though everyone was hesitant to use the word *better.* However, as the resistance grew; and as the mobs of the parasite-jinn disappeared from the city's streets, many of their number standing petrified here and there as signs of a shift in the conflict; and as the strangenesses diminished in number, frequency and ferocity; so people began to venture out into the streets and parks again. Like the first crocus of spring, a runner was sighted on the promenade along the banks of the Hudson, not running away from a monster, just running *for fun.* The rebirth of the idea of pleasure was itself like the arrival of a new season, even though everyone knew that as long as the malevolent Zabardast and Zumurrud were out there—these names had become familiar to everyone on the planet—the danger remained. Liberation radio stations began intermittently to broadcast and all of them asked the same question: *Where are ZZ Top?*

As the calendar marched towards the thousandth day of the time of the strangenesses, Mayor Rosa Fast took a bold decision and returned to her office with little Storm by her side. Also by her side was her newly appointed security chief, Jinendra Kapoor, conqueror and petrifier of the parasite-jinn.

Judging by what you did here, Mayor Fast told Jimmy, you're at least partly made of the same stuff as them. But when you're fighting monsters it's good to have a few monsters on your side too.

I'm not coming into the office, he told her. I've been in enough offices in my life and I'm not coming into any more.

I'll call you when I need you, she said, and pressed a small device into his hand. This works on a maximum-security frequency, she said. They haven't penetrated it yet. It will ring, and vibrate, and these lights around the edge here will flash red.

When Commissioner Gordon wanted Batman, said Jimmy Kapoor, he sent up the Bat-Signal. This is like waiting for your burger order to be ready in Madison Square.

It's what you're getting, she said.

Why is the kid looking at me like that?

She wants to see if I can trust you.

And can you?

If I couldn't, Mayor Fast said, your face would right now be covered in the sores of your treachery. So, I guess you're okay. Let's go to work.

The kidnapping of Hugo Casterbridge from the Heath near his Hampstead home was a new twist in the dark spiral of the war. The composer set off for his usual early morning walk accompanied by his Tibetan terrier Wolfgango (on the original score of *The Marriage of Figaro* Mozart's name had been absurdly Italianized, to Casterbridge's great and often-stated amusement). Afterwards members of the public remembered seeing Casterbridge waving his stick at the traffic on East Heath Road as he crossed over onto the Heath. He was last observed walking northeast along Lime Avenue towards the Bird Sanctuary Pond. Later that morning Wolfgango was found barking unstoppably at the sky and guarding the abandoned knob-kerry as if it were a fallen warrior's sword. Of Hugo Casterbridge, however, there was—briefly—no sign.

It is at this point, near the end of our account of the conflict, that we are obliged to leave London as abruptly as Casterbridge had left it, and return to Lucena, in Spain, where everything began, where the jinnia Dunia had once presented herself at the door of the Anda-lusian philosopher with whose mind she had fallen in love, and where she bore Ibn Rushd the children in whose descendants she had now awakened their sleeping jinn natures, to help her in her fight. Lucena at this time retained much of its old-world charm, though in the old Jewish quarter of Santiago no trace remained of Ibn Rushd's residence. The Jewish necropolis had survived, as had the castle and the old Medinaceli palace, but it is to a less folkloristic part of town that we must turn our gaze. In the centuries that had passed since the time of Ibn Rushd the entrepreneurs of Lucena had gone into the furniture business with considerable enthusiasm, so that it sometimes seemed that the town was entirely composed of factories making things to sit on, lie on, or put your clothes away in, and outside one such factory its owners, a pair of brothers named Huertas, had built the biggest chair in the world, some eighty-five feet tall; and it was on this chair that the Grand Ifrit Zabardast seated himself calmly, cold as a reptile, a giant not quite as big as his erstwhile friend Zumurrud the Great, with the helpless figure of Hugo Casterbridge held in one hand, irresistibly reminding the older cinemagoers in the gathering crowd of Fay Wray wriggling in the mighty grasp of Kong.

And it was from this chair that he issued the following challenge to his female adversary: *Aasmaan Peri, Queen Skyfairy of Mount Qâf, or whatever you call yourself now, you, Dunia of this debased lower world, you who show yourself to be more in love with this pathetic globe, and your own half-breed rodents within it, than with your own kind, O*

*trivial daughter of a far greater father, watch me now. I killed your father.
Now I will eat your children.*

He asked Hugo Casterbridge if he had any last words. The composer replied, It's a terrible thing when one speaks metaphorically
and the metaphor turns into a literal truth. When I said that the gods
men invented had arisen to destroy them, I was being largely figura-
tive. It is unexpected, and almost gratifying, to discover I was being
more accurate than I thought.

I am not a god, said Zabardast the Sorcerer. You can't imagine
God. You can barely imagine me, but I am the one who is going to
eat you alive.

Certainly I could not have imagined a cannibal god, said Casterbridge. That is . . . disappointing.

Enough, said Zabardast, opening his great mouth wide, and swallowing Casterbridge's head in a single gulp. And after that the arms,
the legs, the torso. The crowd that had gathered screamed and ran
away.

Now Zabardast for once raised his voice and roared. *Where are
you?* he bellowed though his mouth was full, and bits of Casterbridge
fell from his lips as he spoke. *Dunia, where are you hiding? Don't you
care that I just ate your son?*

She was silent, and nowhere to be found.

Then something very unexpected happened. Zabardast the Sorcerer put his hands to his ears and began to shriek uncontrollably.
The fleeing crowd stopped and turned to look. Nobody could hear
anything, though the dogs of Lucena began to bark agitatedly. On
the giant chair the Grand Ifrit writhed in agony and cried out as if a
hot arrow were piercing his eardrums and scalding through his
brain, and all of a sudden he lost control of his human shape, exploded into a fireball, burned the great chair of Lucena to the ground,
and then his fire went out, and he was gone.

Now there was a boiling in the heavens and a wormhole opened
and Dunia and Omar the Ayyar descended from the skies.

When I worked out how the poison spell worked, how to use the dark arts and compress the murderous occult formulae, how to sharpen its barbs and spear it to its goal, Dunia murmured to Omar, it was too late to save my father. But it was in time to kill his murderer and avenge his death.

It was one thing to seize tracts of the earth and declare a kingdom. It was another thing entirely to rule it. The dark jinn, fractious, inattentive, vain and cruel as they were, feared but also hated, found in a short time—even before the thousandth day arrived—that their vision of colonizing the earth and enslaving its peoples was a half-baked loaf, which they possessed neither the efficiency nor the culinary skill to cook properly. The only gift of power they possessed was the gift of force. It wasn't enough.

Even in those violent and amoral times, no tyranny was ever absolute; no resistance was ever absolutely crushed. And now that three of the four Grand Ifrits were gone, the grand project began to come apart at speed.

We say again: more than one thousand years have passed since these events occurred, so many of the details of the collapse of the imperial project of the dark jinn are lost, or so inexact that it would be inappropriate to include them here. We can assert with some degree of confidence that the recovery was swift, indicating both the resilience of human society and the shallowness of the control of the jinn over their "conquests." Some scholars compare this period to the later stages of the rule of the Mughal emperor Aurangzeb in India. The last of the six Grand Mughals did indeed extend the empire's rule all the way to the southernmost tip of India, but the conquest was a sort of illusion, because as his armies returned to his northern capital, so the "conquered" lands of the south reasserted their independence. Whether or not this analogy is accepted by all, it is certainly the case that after the fall of Shining Ruby, Ra'im Blood-Drinker and Zabardast the Sorcerer, their enchantments failed all over the world, men and women returned to their senses, order and civility were everywhere restored, economies began to function, crops to be harvested, factory wheels to turn. There were jobs again and money regained its value.

Many, including the present authors, trace the beginnings of the so-called "death of the gods" back to this period, ten centuries ago. Others prefer other, later origin points. It seems to us self-evident, however, that the use of religion as a justification for repression, horror, tyranny, and even barbarism, a phenomenon which undoubtedly predated the War of the Worlds but was certainly a significant aspect of that conflict, led in the end to the terminal disillusion of the human race with the idea of faith. It has now been so long since anyone was gulled by the fantasies of those antique, defunct belief systems that the point may seem academic; after all, for at least five hundred years, such places of worship as survived the Dissolution have taken on new functions, as hotels, casinos, apartment blocks, transportation termini, exhibition halls, and shopping malls. We hold, however, that it remains a point worth making.

We return to our narrative to consider the behavior of the figure who was ostensibly and certainly in his own estimation the most powerful of all the jinn: the single surviving Grand Ifrit, the highest prince of the dark jinn, Zumurrud the Great.

Of all his jewel caves this was the best, the one he came to when he wanted comfort. To wash away his pain and grief and lift his spirits he needed to be alone with what gave him the greatest joy, and that was emeralds. Deep below the sharp harsh mountains of A. it lay, a city of emerald whose only citizen he was: Sesame the Green, more beautiful to him than any woman. Open, he commanded her, and she opened for him. Close, and she closed around him. There he rested, wrapped in a coverlet of green stone in the heart of a mountain, mourning his lost brethren, whom he had both hated and loved. That all three of them had been bested and destroyed by a jinnia was hard to credit. Yet it was true, just as it was also true that one of the

most fearsome of the earthly warriors the Lightning Queen had unleashed against his own cohorts was a female, one Teresa Saca, whose
thunderbolts at times rivaled those of the Queen of Qâf herself.
There were times when life seemed incomprehensible. At such times
the green jewels spoke to him of love, and cleared his thoughts of
confusion. Come to me, my precious ones, he cried, and gathering up
armfuls of the magic stones, he pressed them against his heart.

How could it be that things were suddenly going so badly? For
more than nine hundred days there had been no real obstacles in the
way of his grand design, and now, calamity upon calamity. He
blamed his fellow dark jinn for much of the growing débâcle. They
had shown themselves to be untrustworthy, even traitorous, and
they had paid the price. Even the manner of Zabardast's end had
been a kind of treason, for the sorcerer jinni had known that he,
Zumurrud, had planned to make an example of one of the Lightning Queen's creatures, a certain Airagaira, who had been subdued
and captured with great difficulty after his attack on the Glory Machine which Zumurrud had ordered to be built outside the city of B.
Zumurrud had neutralized the thunderbolt abilities of this earlobe-
less Airagaira by fastening him to a strike termination device that
automatically sucked the fellow's lightning harmlessly down into the
ground. Thus fastened to a stake beside the machine he had vandal-
ized, he was to be an example to all of the failure of resistance. Then
Zabardast had upstaged the plan with his self-indulgently exhibitionist piece of saturnine cannibalism, and look how that had ended.
It was impossible to trust anyone, even one's oldest allies.

In a kind of angry stupor Zumurrud the Great tossed and turned
on his emerald bed, the stones pouring over his body as he moved
this way and that. Then at a certain point his foot touched something
that was not stone and he reached down for it. It was a small bottle,
not a fancy artifact of precious metals studded with gemstones such
as might be expected to lie hidden in a jinni's treasure cave, but a
cheap affair, plain, rectangular, made of thick blue glass, and missing
its cork. He picked it up and regarded it with disgust. It was his old

prison. Once he had been lured inside by a mere mortal and re-mained captive within those blue walls for centuries until Ghazali the sage of Tus set him free. He had kept the bottle here in the heart of his treasure, buried under precious stones, as a reminder of his caged history and his humiliation, which was the cause of his rage. But as he held it in his hand he understood why it had come back to visit him at that moment.

Prison, he addressed the bottle, you emerge from the shadows like the answer to my unasked question. Curse of my past, now you will be the curse of another's future.

He snapped his fingers. The bottle was corked again: stoppered tightly and ready for use.

La Incoerenza is still standing after a thousand years, a well-looked-after place of secular pilgrimage and reverence, the house restored and maintained, the gardens carefully tended in memory of the great gardener who created them long ago; it is a sight to see, like all the great battlefields of the world, Marathon, Kurukshetra, Gettysburg, the Somme. Yet the battle fought here, the terminal conflict of the War of the Worlds, was like no other ever fought on earth. It in-volved no armies; it was, instead, a fight to the finish between super-natural entities, so potent that it has been said of them that they contained armies within themselves. On each side stood a single ti-tanic figure, superhuman, implacable, one male, one female, one fire, the other smoke. There were others present. The greatest of the dark jinn had brought half a dozen of his cohorts as seconds, and Dunia the Lightning Queen had summoned her most reliable soldiers too: Omar the spy, and the earthlings Teresa Saca, Jimmy Kapoor and Geronimo Manezes. Observing from the sidelines, knowing that their fate, and the fate of the earth, depended on the outcome, were the owner of the estate, the Lady Philosopher Alexandra Bliss Fariña, whose lifelong pessimism was about to be permanently validated or overthrown, depending on the outcome of the fray; her hirsute estate

manager Oliver Oldcastle; and the mayor, Rosa Fast, who had been
alerted by her security chief, Jimmy, a.k.a. Natraj Hero. (Little Storm
was not present, it being rightly deemed too dangerous for her to be
there.) Everyone who was at La Incoerenza on that night, the so-
called Thousandth Night, has gone into the history books, and when
their names are spoken nowadays it is with the hushed tones reserved
for participants in the greatest episodes of the human story. Yet the
primary combatants were inhuman.

It was arranged as once, in ancient times, duels were arranged. A
challenge was issued, by Zumurrud the Great, sent at speed down
the jinn communications networks, and accepted. The location was
specified by Zumurrud with undisguised scorn. *That place where
your fancy boy who reminds you of your dead lover now disports himself
with the woman he prefers to you. I'll crush you while he watches and
decide what to do with him afterwards, when all the world is mine.* The
offering and return of insults was a part of the convention of the
challenge to single combat, but Dunia maintained her dignity, and
the time and place were set. He's giving you home advantage, Omar
the Ayyar told her. That's his overconfidence talking. It makes him
vulnerable. I know, she said. Then it was time.

At La Incoerenza, a place of immense beauty dedicated by its creator Sanford Bliss to the idea that the world did not make sense,
Dunia and Zumurrud finally came face to face to decide what kind
of sense the world would make from then on. It was after sunset and
moonlight lay uneasy on the great river at the foot of the estate. The
flying urns on which Zumurrud and his party had arrived hovered
by the sundial on the lawn like giant fretful bees. The wormhole
through which they came boiled in the sky above them. Mr. Geronimo, Jimmy Kapoor and Teresa Saca moved around the edges of the
great lawn, on the lookout for any dishonorable attack by the seconds of the Grand Ifrit. The two principals circled each other on the
lawn, considering their first moves. Clouds ran across the sky and
when the moonlight was lost and an unearthly darkness enclosed the
fighters, filling their nostrils with the smell of death, Zumurrud the

Great attacked. It was he who had summoned the wind and now its ferocity increased. The figures on the periphery had to take shelter for fear of being blown away, for this was a wind from hell, its purpose the annihilation of Dunia's human form so that her smoky essence could be blown away to the four corners of the earth. But she was not so easily vanquished and held firm. Then rain joined the wind and that was her magic, a rain so heavy that it seemed as if the river itself had risen from its bed and was falling upon them, a rain whose purpose was to extinguish the fire of which the Ifrit was made. But that failed too. Neither of these warriors would be so easily broken. Their shields were more than equal to the task of deflecting these assaults.

Through the howling of the wind and the pounding of the rain Mr. Geronimo heard a woman's voice shrieking abuse at the jinni entourage, *How would you like it if your world was devastated the way you have ruined ours?*—that was the question this voice asked over and over again, punctuated by much bad language. Mr. Geronimo realized that the screaming woman was Teresa Saca, whom Dunia had summoned to fight at their side. She seemed more than a little deranged to Geronimo Manezes. It was also unclear if her wrath was aimed only at the Grand Ifrit and his followers. It was an anger that seemed to spread like a plague, infecting everything it touched, and maybe, Mr. Geronimo thought, a part of this anger was directed at Dunia as well. It was a hate-filled shriek that if aimed at any human group of people, tarring them all with the same brush, would have been called—yes—racially prejudiced. Teresa Saca, it seemed to him, listening to her shriek into the raging elements, matching their fury with her own, crackling with electricity around the edges of her body, was bigoted against all the descended creatures of the upper world, and therefore, of course, against the jinnia within herself as well. Her hatred of the other was also a hatred of the self. She was a dangerous ally.

Meanwhile, like a cornerman at a title bout, Mr. Geronimo was becoming worried about Dunia's approach to the fight. She seemed content to react rather than take the initiative, which felt like a mistake to him. He tried to tell her, wordlessly, but she was *listening* to nobody now, all her effort bent on the battle. Zumurrud was changing form, unleashing the worst of all the monsters within him: the creature with iron teeth and a thousand heads with a thousand tongues, once known as the Blatant Beast. With the thousand tongues he could not only bark like a dog, snarl like a tiger, growl like a bear, yowl like a dragon, and seek to bite his adversary with many three-pronged serpent stings; he could also hurl literally hundreds of hexes, spells and enchantments at Dunia simultaneously, paralyzing spells, weakening spells, killing spells. And there were many tongues to spare for abuse, abuse in many languages, the languages of men and jinn, which revealed in Zumurrud a level of moral degradation that shocked all who heard it.

And as he watched Zumurrud in the form of the Blatant Beast assault Dunia in many hundreds of different ways, and saw her whirl and spin and deflect and defend like a great Valkyrie, or a goddess of Olympus or Kailash, and as he wondered how long even she could withstand so ferocious an assault, and as he listened to Teresa Saca's screams, *How would you feel if it happened to you,* Mr. Geronimo experienced a sort of inner vision or epiphany. The doors of perception opened and he saw that what was evil and monstrous about the jinn was a mirror of the monstrous and evil part of human beings, that human nature too contained the same irrationality, wanton, willful, malevolent, and cruel, and that the battle against the jinn was a portrait of the battle within the human heart, which meant that the jinn were somehow abstractions as well as realities, and that their descent to the lower world served to show that world what had to be eradicated within itself, which was unreason itself, unreason which was the name of the dark jinn within people, and as he understood this, he also understood Teresa Saca's self-hatred, and knew, as she knew, that the jinn self within them both needed to be expunged, the irrational in man as well as jinn had to be defeated, so that an age of reason could begin.

We listened to what he told us. We are still listening, after a thousand years. This is Mr. Geronimo the Gardener, after all. We all know what he understood that night, the Thousandth Night, when Dunia, the Lightning Queen Aasmaan Peri, which is to say Skyfairy, fought against Zumurrud the Great.

She was tiring. Zumurrud could see that. This was the moment he had waited for, as a matador waits to see the acceptance of defeat in the eyes of the bull. This was the moment when he abandoned the persona of the Beast, resumed his own form, produced the blue bottle from a fold in his red shirt, removed the cork, and cried out with all his force:

> *Jinnia foolish, jinnia blind,*
> *Now I hold you in my mind!*
> *In this place confinèd be,*
> *Ever more belong to me.*

This was said in the Secret Language of the jinn, in which the most potent of spells are written, and which demands an immense expenditure of power on the part of the speaker. The humans watching the scene did not understand the words but they saw their effect, saw Dunia stagger and fall, saw her being dragged feet first along the grass towards the little bottle which gaped at her like the devil's mouth.

What did he say? the Lady Philosopher screamed at Omar the Ayyar, but Omar was watching wide-eyed as Dunia was pulled towards the bottle. Tell me, Alexandra cried, and so Omar absently did, repeating the words of power in a whisper and offering a rough translation. Then Zumurrud in triumph spoke again.

> *Jinnia fierce and jinnia grand,*
> *Now I hold you in my hand.*

In this place confinèd be,
Ever more belong to me.

What? Alexandra demanded, and Omar told her. It's over, he said. She has lost.

Then Dunia screamed. It was the scream of power Mr. Geronimo had heard when her father died. It knocked humans and jinn flat on their backs and it broke Zumurrud's hold over the spell. He staggered backwards clutching at his ears and the little blue bottle spiraled through the air and landed in Dunia's right hand, and the cork in her left. Now she drew herself to her feet and reversed the spell.

Mighty, proud and strong Ifrit,
Come and sit thou at my feet.
In this place confinèd be,
Ever more belong to me.

What did she say? cried Alexandra, and Omar told her. Now it was Zumurrud being pulled towards the bottle, headfirst, his beard stretched out before him as if an invisible hand had grabbed it and was pulling it, and its owner, into the prison of the blue bottle. And Dunia cried out once again, with her last strength:

Feared and powerful Ifrit,
Today your mistress you must meet.
In this place confinèd be,
Ever more belong to me.

She knew at once, everyone knew, that she had overdone it. Her strength failed her. She fell into a deep swoon. The spell broke. Zumurrud began to rise in all his gigantic puissance. And the bottle,
to everyone's surprise,
chose to spiral almost lazily through the air,

and came to rest in the outstretched right hand of Alexandra Bliss Fariña the Lady Philosopher,

and the cork in her left hand,

and to the consternation of all, and the joy of her allies, she repeated, word perfect, the first entrapment spell cast by the Lightning Queen, and Zumurrud crashed again to the ground, exhausted as he had exhausted Dunia, and was drawn relentlessly forward, until his whole huge spent body had squeezed into the tiny blue bottle, whereupon Alexandra pushed the cork into the neck, and he was caught, and it was over, and his flunkeys fled. They would be found afterwards and dealt with, but let that pass.

Mr. Geronimo and Omar the Ayyar and Jimmy Kapoor crowded around Alexandra and asked, *How? How on earth? How in the name of? How by all that's? How, how, how?*

I was always quick with languages, she said deliriously, giggling lightly, as if she were flirting with young bucks at a summer garden party. Ask anyone at Harvard, she tittered. I picked them up in no time, like shiny pebbles on a beach.

Then she fainted away entirely, and Mr. Geronimo caught her, and Jimmy Kapoor snatched up the bottle before it hit the ground.

And that might have been an end to it all, except that Geronimo Manezes noticed that one of them was missing, and *Where's Teresa Saca?* he cried out, and then they saw that she had taken the last of the flying urns, Zumurrud's own urn, and was riding it up into the sky, into the wormhole that joined the upper world to the lower, and if they had been able to look upon her face they would have seen that in her eyes there rose an awful tide of blood.

If your world was devastated the way you have ruined ours, Mr. Geronimo remembered.

She has gone to attack Fairyland, he said aloud, and to destroy it if she can.

There are many kinds of casualty in battle, the invisible ones, the injuries to the mind, rivaling in number the fatalities and the physi-

cal wounds. As we look back at these events we remember Teresa
Saca Cuartos as one of the heroes of that war, the electricity in her
fingers responsible for many successes against the jinn armies; but
also as a tragic victim of the conflict, her mind broken not only by the
calamity she saw around her but also by the violence with which she
had been bidden by the Lightning Queen to respond to the disaster
of war. In the end, rage, no matter how profoundly justified, de-
stroys the enraged. Just as we are created anew by what we love, so
we are reduced and unmade by what we hate. At the end of the cli-
mactic battle of the War of the Worlds, with Zumurrud the Great in
his bottle prison, held tightly in Jimmy Kapoor's fist, and Dunia
slowly emerging from unconsciousness, it was Teresa who cracked
and headed for the hole in the sky.

She must have known it was a suicide mission. What did she expect? That she would pass unchallenged into the upper world and
that those perfumed gardens, those towers and palaces, would dis-
solve before her wrath and leave not a rack behind? That all that was
solid there would melt into air, into thin air, before her avenging
fury? And then what? That she would return to earth an even
greater hero for having brought about the ruin of the fairy world?

We don't know, and perhaps should not speculate. Let us simply
remember with grief the madness of Teresa Saca, and the inevitability of her last moment. For of course she did not make it into Peristan. The giant urn was not an easy vehicle, as hard to ride as an
untamed stallion, obedient only to its fallen jinn master. As Mr.
Geronimo and the others watched her rocket into the air—the wind
had died down, and the rain also, and a full moon brightly lit her
ascent, or so the story goes—they saw that she was having trouble
keeping her seat. And as she approached the stormy edges of the
wormhole, the slit between the worlds, the air became more turbulent, and then even more turbulent, and she lost her grip on her enchanted steed, and those below watched in horror and she slid first
this way and then that; and fell. To land like a broken wing on La
Incoerenza's sodden lawn.

Epilogue

We worry, sometimes, about the idea of heroism, especially after the passage of such a long time. If the protagonists of this account had been asked who they considered to be heroes from a thousand years earlier, who would they have chosen? Charlemagne? The unknown author or authors of the *Arabian Nights*? The Lady Murasaki? A millennium is a long time for a reputation to survive. Writing this chronicle (we repeat) we are keenly aware that much of it has degenerated from the status of a factual account towards the condition of legend, speculation or fiction. Yet we have persisted, because the figures in our story are among the very few to whom the idea of heroism still attaches itself, a millennium after they lived and died, even though we know that the gaps in the record are immense, that there were undoubtedly others who resisted the attack of the dark jinn as worthily as those we have named: that the names we hold in such reverence have been randomly selected by the broken record, and that maybe others unknown to us would have more richly deserved our awe had history troubled to remember them.

Yet we have to say it: these are our heroes, for by winning the War of the Worlds they set in motion the process by which our new and, we believe, better time came into being. That was the hinge moment, when the door from the past, where lay what we used to be, swung shut once and for all, and the door to the present, leading to what we have become, opened like the stone gateway to a treasure cave, perhaps even Sesame itself.

So we mourn Teresa Saca Cuartos, in spite of all her faults, for she had what it took when it was needed, she was as flamboyantly tough and brave as she had to be, and a breeze of fearless glamour wafts around her memory. And we celebrate Storm Fast, the baby of truth, who grew up to be the most feared and fair of judges, in whose court no falsehood could be uttered, no matter how minor. And Jimmy Kapoor—well, everyone knows *his* name, it's one of the few whose popularity has survived an entire millennium, because not only did he get his Bat-Signal after all, the image of the dancing multi-limbed god projected on the sky stabbing the hearts of evildoers with fear, but long after he grew old and gray and then departed this life he was the hero of a myriad entertainments, a multi-platform star of screen and game, of song and dance, and even of that ancient and stubbornly persistent form, hard-copy books. The failed graphic novelist became the hero of one of the longest-running series of graphic novels, and novels made of words as well, a corpus which we now number among the great classics, the mythos from which our present pleasures derive, our *Iliad,* let us say, using an antique comparison, or our *Odyssey.* Present-day visitors to the Library look wide-eyed at these relics as once their ancestors would have gawped at a Gutenberg Bible or First Folio. "Natraj Hero," a.k.a. Jimmy Kapoor, is one of our true legends, and only one man from the time of the strangenesses is held in higher regard than he.

The figure of Geronimo Manezes, Mr. Geronimo the Gardener, has come to mean most of all to us—the man who came unstuck from the world, then returned to it to rescue so many of his contemporaries suffering from the dual curses of the rising and the crushing, of frightening and potentially fatal detachment from, or oppressively excessive attachment to, our enigmatic earth. We are pleased that he and his Lady Philosopher, Alexandra Bliss Fariña, found a happy ending in each other's arms, watched over by the protective eye of Oliver Oldcastle; we walk with them in the grounds of La Incoerenza, sit silently with them as they hold hands in the sunset and watch the great river flow forward and back beneath a gibbous moon, bow our heads as they do when they stand on the estate's hill by the grave of Mr. Geronimo's lost wife, silently asking her permission for their love, silently receiving it; and we hover above the partners' desk at which, seated on opposite sides, they wrote the book—in their own language, in spite of Alexandra's suggestion that it might sound better in Esperanto—which has become our most admired text from antiquity, *In Coherence,* a plea for a world ruled by reason, tolerance, magnanimity, knowledge, and restraint.

That is the world in which we now live, in which we have disproved the assertion made by Ghazali to Zumurrud the Great. Fear did not, finally, drive people into the arms of God. Instead, fear was overcome, and with its defeat men and women were able to set God aside, as boys and girls put down their childhood toys, or as young men and women leave their parents' home to make new homes for themselves, elsewhere, in the sun. For hundreds of years now, this has been our good fortune, to inhabit the possibility for which Mr. Geronimo and Miss Alexandra yearned: a peaceful, civilized world, of hard work and respect for the land. A gardener's world, in which we all must cultivate our garden, understanding that to do so is not a defeat, as it was for Voltaire's poor Candide, but the victory of our better natures over the darkness within.

We know—or we "know," because we cannot be certain if the story is true—that this happy state of affairs could not have come to pass were it not for the great sacrifice of Dunia the Lightning Queen, at the very end of the story here retold. When she came to her senses after her duel with Zumurrud she knew that there were two things she must do. She took the blue bottle from Jimmy Kapoor. Such bottles have a magic of their own, she said. You can hide them, but they choose when to reappear. This time, this bottle must not appear again anywhere on earth, so I will hide it in an impossible place. And she went away for what remained of the night and when she returned she said only, It is done. Since that day a thousand years have passed and the bottle has not come to light. It may lie beneath the roots of Mount Everest or under the bed of the Mariana Trench or deep within the core of the moon. But Zumurrud the Great has troubled us no more.

When she returned, that last morning, after concealing the blue bottle in the heart of darkness or the fire of the sun, she told her allies gathered at La Incoerenza, It is clear that the two worlds must be separated again. When one drips into the other, chaos ensues. And there is only one way to close the slits so tightly that they will remain closed, if not forever, then for some approximation of eternity.

A jinnia, remember, is made of fireless smoke. If she chooses to shed her female form she can move through the two worlds like smoke, pass through any door into any chamber, through any aperture into any crevice, filling the spaces she enters as thoroughly as smoke fills a room; and then, if she so chooses, she can solidify again, taking on the character of the spaces she has entered, becoming brick among bricks, or stone amongst stones, and those spaces will be spaces no more, it will be as if they never existed, or never will exist again. But the jinnia, when she is so dispersed, so scattered, so multiply mutated and transformed . . . even a jinnia queen . . . loses the strength, or, even worse than the strength, the will, the *consciousness,* that would enable her to gather herself once more and resume her unitary form.

So you would die, Geronimo Manezes said. That's what you're telling us. To save us from the jinn, you would sacrifice your life.

Not exactly, she said.

You mean you would continue to be alive? he asked.

Not exactly that, either, she replied. But reason demands it, so it must be done.

Then, without a word of farewell, without sentimentality or discussion, she left them. She was there, and then she was not there. They never saw her again.

As to what she did, what became of her, whether or not she did indeed use herself to close the passages between the worlds, we can only speculate. But from that day to this, no member of the upper world, Peristan, Fairyland, has ever been seen on this lower soil, the earth, our home.

That was the thousand and first day. And that evening Mr. Geronimo and his Alexandra were alone in her bedchamber, and, making love, both of them felt as though they were floating on air. But they weren't.

So ended the time of the strangenesses, which was two years, eight months and twenty-eight nights long.

We take pride in saying that we have become reasonable people. We are aware that conflict was for a long time the defining narrative of our species, but we have shown that the narrative can be changed. The differences between us, of race, place, tongue, and custom, these differences no longer divide us. They interest and engage us. We are one. And for the most part we are content with what we have become. We might even say that we are happy. We—we speak briefly of ourselves, and not the greater "we"—we live here in the great city and sing its praise. Flow on, rivers, as we flow on between you, mingle, currents of water, as we mingle with human currents from elsewhere and from near at hand! We stand by your waters amid the sea gulls and the crowds, and are glad. Men and women of our city, your costumes please us, close-fitting, colorless, fine; great city, your foods, your odors, your speedy sensuality, casual encounters begun, fiercely consummated, discontinued, we accept you all; and meanings jostling in the street, rubbing shoulders with other meanings, the friction birthing new meanings unmeant by the meaners who parented them; and factories, schools, places of entertainment and ill repute, our metropolis, thrive, thrive! You are our joy and we are yours and so we go together, between the rivers, towards an end beyond which there is no beginning, and beyond that, none, and the dawn city glistening in the sun.

But something befell us when the worlds were sealed off from each other. As the days lengthened into weeks, months, years, as the decades passed, and the centuries, something that once happened to us all every night, every one of us, every member of the greater "we" which we have all become, stopped happening. We no longer dreamt. It may be that this time those slits and holes were closed so tightly that nothing at all could leak through, not even the drips of fairy magic, the heaven-dew, which according to legend fell into our sleeping eyes and allowed us our nocturnal fantasies. Now in sleep there was only darkness. The mind fell dark, so that the great theater of the night might begin its unforeseeable performances, but nothing came. Fewer and fewer of us, in each successive generation, retained the ability to dream, until now we find ourselves in a time when dreams are things we would dream of, if we could only dream. We read of you in ancient books, O dreams, but the dream factories are closed. This is the price we pay for peace, prosperity, understanding, wisdom, goodness, and truth: that the wildness in us, which sleep unleashed, has been tamed, and the darkness in us, which drove the theater of the night, is soothed.

We are happy. We find joy in all things. Motorcars, electronics, dances, mountains, all of you bring us great joy. We walk hand in hand towards the reservoir and the birds make circles in the sky above us and all of it, the birds, the reservoir, the walking, the hand held by the hand, all brings us joy.

But the nights pass dumbly. One thousand and one nights may pass, but they pass in silence, like an army of ghosts, their footfalls noiseless, marching invisibly through the darkness, unheard, unseen, as we live and grow older and die.

Mostly we are glad. Our lives are good. But sometimes we wish for the dreams to return. Sometimes, for we have not wholly rid ourselves of perversity, we long for nightmares.

About the Author

SALMAN RUSHDIE is the author of eleven previous novels: *Grimus, Midnight's Children, Shame, The Satanic Verses, Haroun and the Sea of Stories, The Moor's Last Sigh, The Ground Beneath Her Feet, Fury, Shalimar the Clown, The Enchantress of Florence,* and *Luka and the Fire of Life.* Published in 1981, *Midnight's Children* is the only book to have ever won more than one Booker: It was awarded the Booker Prize in 1981 and the Booker of Bookers Prize in 1993 by two separate panels of judges, and it won the Best of the Booker Prize by a public vote in 2008. Rushdie is also the author of *East, West,* a collection of short stories, and three works of nonfiction, *The Jaguar Smile, Imaginary Homelands: Essays and Criticism 1981– 1991,* and *Step Across This Line,* as well as the co-editor of two anthologies, *Mirrorwork* and *Best American Short Stories 2008.* Rushdie's memoir, *Joseph Anton,* was published in 2012 and became an internationally acclaimed bestseller. It was called "the finest new memoir to cross my desk in many a year" by Jonathan Yardley and praised as "a harrowing, deeply felt and revealing document" by Michiko Kakutani. His books have been translated into over forty languages.

Knighted in 2007 for his services to literature, he has received, among many distinctions, the Whitbread Award for Best Novel (twice), Germany's Author of the Year Award, the Budapest Grand Prize, the Commandeur des Arts et des Lettres (France's highest artistic honor), the Austrian State Prize for European Literature, and the European Union's Aristeion Prize. He is a Library Lion of the New York Public Library and the most recent winner (in 2014) of the Hans Christian Andersen Literature Award in Denmark. He is a member of the American Academy of Arts and Letters and currently serves as a Distinguished Writer in Residence at New York University. He holds honorary doctorates and fellowships at six European and seven American universities, is an honorary professor in the humanities at MIT, and is a former University Distinguished Professor at Emory University.

salmanrushdie.com

About the Type

This book was set in Granjon, a modern recutting of a typeface produced under the direction of George W. Jones (1860–1942), who based Granjon's design upon the letterforms of Claude Garamond (1480–1561). The name was given to the typeface as a tribute to the typographic designer Robert Granjon (1513–89).